praise for
RESCUED HEART

"Loved it! Kept me guessing clear to the end as Eddie and Bianca navigated one harrowing event after another. Not to mention the family drama they have to figure out. It's a beautiful story of learning to forgive and remembering that we are enough in God's eyes."

—Kate, GOODREADS

"Brimming with nonstop action, danger, and suspense, *Rescued Heart* was a fast-paced read. I enjoyed Eddie and Bianca's story, Eddie's heart for the inner-city youths, and the chemistry between the two. Besing weaves spiritual elements throughout, including forgiveness and that true worth rests in the Lord."

—Allyson, GOODREADS

"Love this story. An actress and a Last Chance County firefighter scramble to survive as love starts to bloom. Heart touching love and heart racing adventure will keep you glued from the front cover to the back cover."

—Jesus Beach Girl Read, GOODREADS

"Rescued Heart is a captivating story with a light faith thread, a journey from brokenness to healing and forgiveness, and just enough of a mystery to keep the reader guessing!"

—Jeanne, GOODREADS

RESCUED HEART

LAST CHANCE
· FIRE AND RESCUE ·

RESCUED HEART

MEGAN BESING

LISA PHILLIPS

sunrise
PUBLISHING

Rescued Heart: A Last Chance County Novel
Published by Sunrise Media Group LLC
Copyright © 2025 Sunrise Media Group LLC
Print ISBN: 978-1-963372-35-9

This book is a work of fiction. Names, characters, places, and incidents are either products of the author's imagination or used fictitiously. Any similarity to actual people, organizations, and/or events is purely coincidental.

Scriptures taken from the Holy Bible, New International Version®, NIV®. Copyright © 1973, 1978, 1984, 2011 by Biblica, Inc.™ Used by permission of Zondervan. All rights reserved worldwide. www.zondervan.com The "NIV" and "New International Version" are trademarks registered in the United States Patent and Trademark Office by Biblica, Inc.™

For more information about Lisa Phillips and Megan Besing please access the authors' websites at the following addresses: https://www.authorlisaphillips.com https://www.meganbesing.com..

Published in the United States of America.
Cover Design: Ana Grigoriu-Voicu, Books-Design

LAST CHANCE
· FIRE AND RESCUE ·

Expired Return

Expired Hope

Expired Promise

Expired Vows

Rescued Duty

Rescued Faith

Rescued Heart

Rescued Dreams

To my favorite son, I love you.
It's a true blessing to be your mother.
(Even if you no longer hug me in public.)
I pray you cling to the One who rescues our hearts.
Always.

"Search me, God, and know my heart; test me and know my anxious thoughts. See if there is any offensive way in me, and lead me in the way everlasting."

PSALM 139:23-24 NIV

ONE

THIS MIGHT BE A PARTY, BUT BIA PEARL WAS here to play her part—just like any other scene. All that mattered was the chance to smile for the cameras. If only the dress code allowed sweatpants and flip-flops.

At the opened double front door stood a woman wearing an expression darker than her charcoal knee-length dress. Her peppered hair was slicked back in a bun so tight it seemed to lift her thin brows while her frown deepened. Not exactly the expected welcome at a fundraiser event.

Bianca picked up the front of her dress and pressed on a smile. Her heels clicked on the gold-and-black swirled marble just off-beat to the jazz music playing somewhere beyond the narrow hall.

The woman adjusted her grip on the leather folder pressed against her chest. "Invitation?"

Bianca opened her clutch and produced the shiny golden ticket. Invitation, phone, and black-tie-appropriate attire. Check. See? She didn't need Hollywood's top-tier agent. But someone on her side would be a plus for a change. "I'm so glad the rain held off. Knowing my luck, I probably would've broken a heel in a puddle."

The woman raised one of her penciled brows. "Yes, well, most of tonight's invitees arrived by chauffer."

Bianca secured her clutch under her arm. Everything accounted for minus the whole tardy thing and chauffer. Still a win. As long as she found her costar, Carter Cane.

The woman placed Bianca's offered golden ticket inside a folder on the table. "Enjoy the evening, Ms. Pearl."

Bianca stepped around the woman. "Please tell me I haven't missed the mayor's welcome speech."

Even if she had, there would be time for someone to take pictures of her and Carter. Her contract and movie depended on it. So did her wallet and promises.

The woman slid in front of Bianca. "I'm afraid I can't let you in."

Bianca glanced behind her. But no one else was there. "You can't let *me* into the auction?"

Was this some kind of hidden test? The tabloids had been labeling her with all kinds of lies for years. However, a hot-tempered actress she was not. At least, not normally. "Is there another volunteer I could speak with? I think there's some confusion."

The woman bristled. "I'm Janice Nelson, the mayor's new assistant. There is no confusion. You will not be entering on my watch."

Bianca pushed back her should-have-been-more-curled hair. "What exactly did that ticket I gave you do? If it's because I'm late, I promise you, none of the people on flight 412 enjoyed the unexpected seven-hour layover. And having to change into this dress at a gas station down the road wasn't exactly on my itinerary; however, I would recommend their homemade peach turnovers."

Plus, she may or may not have gotten lost trying to find a town she'd never heard of. Last Chance County wasn't exactly LA.

Janice lifted her chin. "Tardiness, though frowned upon, is not the reason. I'm afraid you are not dressed for this event."

Bianca ran her hand down the front of her dress. Velvet may not yet be back in style, but when fashioned into a flowing floor-length, off-the-shoulder dress stained the color of rubies, it was very much appropriate for a formal evening. Even if her outfit cost less than the dinner plate during tonight's fundraiser auction. "I guess I missed the memo about wearing our cat pajamas. Or were we supposed to wear our puppy ones? And I'm really bummed about missing out on wearing my flip-flops."

Not even a twitch of a smile. Apparently, it was a good thing Bianca's current movie wasn't a comedy.

Janice checked her watch. "You're missing your mystery mask."

Bianca rubbed the spot between her temples. If she grimaced any longer, there would be talk about her worry lines over her ex instead of what kind of budding relationship she and Carter might be forming on set. "I'm sorry. I don't know what a mystery mask is."

Janice drew in a long inhale through her pointed nose. "Your event mask for the masquerade auction. Part of the mayor's requirement for the evening's event."

Bianca swatted her forehead. "Oh, *masquerade*. Somehow, I heard *mystery*." Only Bianca found this laughable. The red-eye flight here was supposed to have created more time to rest. Not what the day had become.

Janice heaved a sigh and threw open her folder. "Here." She handed over a white domino mask with a single row of tiny pearls that ran parallel with the rounded edges. "Don't take this off until the grand live reveal."

Now, the grand live reveal Bianca *did* know about, and she wasn't looking forward to kissing Carter—pretend or not. But the movie's success depended on a social-media takeover, which would ignite tonight with one perfectly timed photo op.

Lord, please let me not have made a mistake by accepting this role.

Bianca slipped the mask on over her eyes. Just another season of pretending. Then the world would see who she really was, and she'd have the money needed to prove to her family that she kept her promises. That she had changed for the good.

Janice scrutinized her for two more of Bianca's heartbeats before finally stepping aside and opening the doors behind her. "The mayor thanks you for your support for his reelection campaign, and remember, half of tonight's proceeds go to a worthy cause."

Supporting a campaign? "Actually, I'm only here because the director arranged—"

"Step inside, Ms. Pearl."

Right. Bianca picked up the front of her dress. It was probably wise she hadn't joked about where the other half of the money went tonight.

Dimmed chandeliers hung from beamed rafters. Tables dressed with black tablecloths and white flower arrangements made an S shape in the rectangular room. It seemed black tie applied to all, decorations included. The stage was in the center, surrounded by a tile dance floor over the carpet. Music drifted from the band, and Bianca tapped her finger on her purse to the beat.

A windowed wall led out to a patio larger than Bianca's current apartment. That was now the only thing she missed about her ex—his house. But looking back, she should have known Nathan hadn't been truthful about who even owned his house. Right now, she'd settle for the court to find the money that had disappeared when they had frozen her account. And for Nathan to stop trying to contact her.

The judge may have exonerated him, but Bianca knew the truth. Too bad no one believed her.

The women at the table nearest to the door had enough feathers on their masks to stuff at least three pillows. Servers in all white carried trays of drinks or food that didn't look big enough to even be one bite. The air smelled like sweet citrus, either from the appetizers or the combination of perfumes swirling about.

Security guarded each of the exits, and they were the only ones whose identities weren't hidden by masquerade masks. Flowers and feathers and decorations made it difficult to find which tables had open seats.

Good thing she and Carter had exchanged numbers at the cast reading. Bianca sent off a text.

Bianca

Where are you seated?

She checked the tables in the first two rows. No open seats. No lone, tall, broad-shouldered men.

Wait. The far corner table contained an open seat. And a masked man in a navy suit with his arm around an empty chair. With the right styled hair and a magazine-worthy jawline.

Had to be Carter.

Bianca wound her way past the other tables and nodded at those already seated. As she slipped into the open chair, she placed her hand on Carter's shoulder. "So sorry I'm late. You will never guess what happened. The—"

"Did it have to do with the sunshiny doorkeeper? Because Janice made me park in the back parking lot. If I had to guess, she's allergic to vehicles not made in this decade. Either that or maybe people in general. And I'd bet she's probably related to the puppet who lives in the trashcan." The man's deep voice had Bianca locking gazes with a dark-eyed stranger.

A quick intake of breath, and then Bianca slid her hand away. "You're not Carter."

The man placed his palm over his heart while a toothpaste-ad-worthy smile stole all of her focus. "Somehow, I'm disappointed now too. I'm only Eddie."

"Shh!" The older woman to his right leaned into Bianca's space and sent them both a glare. "We're not supposed to use our names until the reveal."

Yes. That was the biggest problem here.

Bianca's cheeks heated under her mask. Could this day get any worse? First the layover. Then Nathan had tried to call her. The media had posted again how she'd been a liar at his trial. Plus, being late to meet Carter for their orchestrated kiss and photo. And now . . .

Lord, when are things ever going to be easier?

Eddie touched her elbow. "Do you need help finding this guy?"

What she really needed was about seven more hours of sleep and for God to answer a few more of her prayers. "I—"

The room erupted into applause. Bianca faced the stage, where the man she assumed was the mayor of Last Chance County stood. A mustache framed his wide smile as he waved in his black pants and charcoal suit jacket, complete with a red bow tie.

He was handed a microphone. "Thank you, everyone, for coming. I appreciate your support for my reelection and the youth of our great city in this masquerade auction."

He pointed to his face. "As you've noticed, I'm not wearing a costume mask. But you are, and boy will the social feeds go crazy when we go live and announce all of my wonderful guests. I bet I'll even be surprising some of my dear friends here tonight. With Last Chance County hosting a movie crew, you never know who might be in the chair beside you."

The mayor took a red piece of paper from the grouchy door lady, who now stood beside him. He held up the paper. "You will find one of these tucked inside your napkin. If you can guess everyone who is sitting at your table tonight, there will be a special prize for you after the close of the auction." His grin grew. "Trust me, you want to win it. For now, let's open the night up with some dancing. Take the nearest hand and come join me on the dance floor to celebrate a night of priceless art."

The band on the stage took the cue, and the drummer joined in with the rest of the piano and jazz sounds. The mayor kept his steps to the beat as he exited the stage, heading to the center of the dance floor.

Bianca stood with the crowd. Eighty percent of the men wore black suits, while the others wore gray. Stupid masks.

She checked her phone. Still no reply from Carter. In its place was a picture text from her sister, Madeline. She was surrounded by their mom and grandma and her bridal party while Madeline held a sign that read: *Found my dress at Crystal's Bridal.*

Bianca gripped her phone. She kept missing so much. Things had to be resolved with her family before her sister's wedding.

Her mother's voice popped into her head. *Honey, if you came to your sister's wedding . . . people would look at you, not Madeline. You wouldn't want to steal her day, would you?*

No, she didn't want to steal the spotlight. But feeling a part of the family again would be a nice change.

Eddie cleared his throat. He squinted at her under his mask that barely covered the space around his eyes. The chandelier hanging above their table highlighted the sparkle in his gaze. He had a clean-shaven jawline and wide shoulders. He could star in a movie. Maybe he was one of the extras? Or one of the financial backers for a luxurious resort rumored to be coming to the town.

He slipped his hands into his pants pockets. "Might I suggest a deal? I help you find this Carter guy while you help me dance close enough to the mayor to ask him a question."

Bianca straightened her back. "What kind of question?"

She wouldn't lead an undercover tabloid reporter to swoop in on anyone. No, she was here for a restart. Not to repeat the past.

Eddie tilted his head toward the swarmed dance floor. "I need to make sure he's still going to sign off on an important grant for some inner-city youth."

"Oh." Not connected to the media, the movie, or even the resort. She glanced at her phone. Still no reply from Carter.

Eddie held out his palm. "What do you say? Teammates for the night?"

Carter lived for the spotlight and would not miss an opportunity to be among those dancing.

Bianca slipped her hand into Eddie's. "One song."

His grip sent a warmth through her. "I'll take what I can get."

She could offer him nothing more than teammates, each needing something from the other. A simple exchange.

So why did her heart flutter as if this was a start to something more? Love had left her misguided and at rock bottom. She could not let it happen again. This time, she would seek the qualities God wanted for her future relationship.

Eddie stepped forward. "I'm assuming we're looking for a man in a mask."

She laughed as she followed his lead to the dance floor. Finally, someone with a sense of humor. "However did you guess that?"

Her teammate for the song pulled up beside a woman in a purple dress and a white sequined mask and her dancing partner. The man's lack of enthusiasm did not remain hidden behind his pointy-beaked mask.

Eddie clasped Bianca's hand in his and held it out in a waltz form. He rested his other hand on the middle of her back. His attention scanned the crowd, but his whisper tickled her neck. "And I suppose this Carter also looks sharp in a suit? Since you assumed I was him and all. A fellow strapping lad in his prime."

Bianca rolled her eyes. "He's also as humble as you as well."

Eddie's chuckle harmonized with the melody of the keyboard. "I feel like you have the advantage since I already gave you my name."

Bianca took in the movements of those dancing around her. No one seemed as practiced as Carter would be with his ballroom training. No one except the man she'd mistaken for her costar. "My friends call me Bianca."

Not that she had many of those lately. Except Frances, the waitress who had not only listened to Bianca's woes caused by the situation with her ex but shared the true Hope with her. However,

Frances was currently thousands of miles away in California and thirty-plus years Bianca's senior.

"Well, Ms. Bianca, it's good to know that we've gone from teammates to friends."

Bianca lifted on her toes to gain a better view over the sea of feathers before her. "We can be best friends if you spot Carter."

He spun her in a counterclockwise rotation. "Is that him? Beyond the woman with the red glitter mask?"

Bianca squinted. "I don't see . . ."

A camera light flashed to the side of her, and the mayor walked in front of the man in question.

Bianca tilted her chin. "I spot the mayor, though. He's heading across the dance floor toward my right."

Eddie whipped his head around. "You up for some more spin moves?"

She tightened her hold on his hand. It was a better plan than tramping through all the dancing pairs. He sent her twirling across the dance floor to the thump of the drum. On her fourth spin, nearing the edge of the dance floor, he caught her against his chest and glanced around. "I've lost him."

Just over Eddie's shoulder, a security guard held a door open for the mayor.

She pointed her finger. "There."

The mayor disappeared behind the door just as Eddie turned. A man with a dimpled chin, dressed in a black suit and corresponding mask, jogged over in front of the same security guard that had opened the door for the mayor. Both the guard and the man glanced at the nearest security guard stationed at another door. Then the suited man pulled out what looked like a roll of bills from his pants pocket and held it out to the guard.

Bianca gasped. *Not this again.*

Nathan had taken a handoff the day before the police had stormed their home.

The guard tucked the bills into his palm and opened the door enough for the man and himself to slip through with no one else the wiser.

Bianca squeezed her fingers around Eddie's. "Did you see . . ."

Another bribe. No one had believed her last time.

Last Chance County was supposed to steer her to her happily ever after. A renewed career. Restored family. The actual truth about her character. Looked like this party had just become her most challenging scene yet.

TWO

JUST WHEN EDDIE RICE HAD BEGUN TO THINK that being voluntold to attend the auction as the Last Chance County Fire Department representative might not have been the worst thing ever, he had to witness a kind of potential bribe.

He released Bianca's hands. It was probably for the best not to spend any more time with the beautiful and funny woman. He had to stay focused on the kids who depended on him.

"Where are you going?" Her voice pitched high.

The security guard who had taken what appeared to be a bribe followed behind the man in the black suit, leaving the door unwatched. "It looks like now would be a great time to go talk to the mayor. Good luck finding your Carter."

"But . . ."

Eddie jogged to the door. He twisted the handle, and it opened to a hallway with sconces along the wall and more wood paneling than would fill the entire decade of the eighties. The edge of the man's suit jacket zipped around the corner at the end.

This very well could be a misunderstanding. Or very much not. The latter kept Eddie moving forward.

At the curve of the hall, the smell of something burning hit his nose. Eddie fisted his fingers. Perhaps the mayor's rushing away could be kitchen or food related?

Eddie rested his hand on the first door. It wasn't warm. No signs of smoke billowed from under any doorway or in the hall. The fire alarm on the ceiling remained silent. All appeared normal—except the handoff he'd witnessed.

He had to find the mayor.

A thud sounded from the other side of the wall. Eddie tried the handle and the door opened. Inside, he nearly ran into a tower of crates that had *fragile* stamped on the sides.

He backtracked and flipped on all three light switches, which were next to a keypad on the wall. Only a light aimed at the far wall actually kicked on and shined onto a floor-to-ceiling portrait of some medieval-looking knight.

Either someone had lied about their organizational skills, or what was more than likely the storage for tonight's auction had been blessed more than expected.

Along the other wall was a line of filing cabinets. A variety of vases rested on the cabinets. A glass piano was in the corner, surrounded by a stack of paintings, and when he spotted what looked like an abstract metal peacock, the smoke smell hit him once more.

Eddie slipped farther inside. Signed football helmets and basketballs in clear cases. Boxes each labeled for the night's auction. But no fire.

Eddie sniffed. Something still smelled like smoke. An item in here could have survived a fire elsewhere and simply have smoke damage.

He stepped around another stack of memorabilia. Based on the sheer number of items, there would be more than enough funds brought in tonight. Maybe he didn't need to fear why the mayor was taking so long about signing the grant needed for the rec center.

A flash of light in the shadowed corner to the left of the exit made Eddie do a double take. Between a stack of boxes, another flicker of light revealed the man in the black suit, who stood beside a set of mannequins wearing dresses. He flicked on a lighter and moved the flame straight for one of the dresses.

Eddie shoved his shoulders between two towers of boxes. "Hey!"

The man twisted around. He had a dimpled chin and a spotty five-o'clock shadow. His eyes behind his domino mask widened, and he froze. Except behind him, a piece of fiery sleeve fabric fell onto the dress's skirt. Flames shot up the entire dress.

Eddie hurdled over a set of cases. There'd be no arsonist on his watch. "Stop!"

The man smirked and tossed the lighter at the flaming dress. He ducked behind a barrier of boxes that zigzagged to the exit as the greedy fire engulfed the carpet around the mannequins.

Eddie's gaze swung back from the fleeing arsonist and onto the fire roaring up the sleeve of the other dress. Eddie sprinted for the door. There would be no stopping those flames without a fire extinguisher.

The man stood from his hunched position. Eddie leaped over a section of the clear cases only to land on a box, his foot trapped inside.

Eddie kicked the broken box off his shoe, but the man reached the door first. He swung it open only to stop.

A feminine voice that sounded like Bianca said, "Goodness, you scared me. You haven't by chance seen—"

The arsonist grabbed hold of Bianca and shoved her.

Her heel snapped, which sent her straight into an arched pane of painted glass propped up against a box.

The shattering glass wasn't as loud as Bianca's whimper as it crashed into Eddie's heart.

The man raced out, and the door banged shut.

Eddie raced to Bianca. Blood and glass sprinkled the carpet. A gash ran along her hairline.

Bianca pushed herself up. "This was so not a part of tonight's deal."

Eddie steadied her. "You can turn in your complaint after we get out of here. You sure you can walk?"

The glow of the fire blossomed from the dress and a tapestry hanging from the ceiling. The fire roared up the tapestry and hopped over to the nearest stack of wooden crates.

Bianca gasped. "Is that . . ."

"A fire? Unfortunately, yes." Eddie pulled out the handkerchief from his suit jacket. "Does anything else hurt besides your head?"

She stumbled on her uneven heels and pointed a shaky finger at the fire. "We've got to call a firefighter."

The masquerade mask had disappeared, no longer shielding her full beauty. Nor was it hiding the paleness of her skin or the gash the length of his finger on her forehead. She wasn't simply Bianca who had mistaken him for someone else. She was the Bia Pearl—movie star.

How he wished he could be in two places at once.

He shifted the handkerchief against her wound and tucked her against his side. "Honey, I am a firefighter, and first, we're getting you out of here."

She leaned against him, and he yanked on the door handle.

Except the door didn't budge. Locked.

He tried again. The keypad on the wall flashed red.

"Are we locked in?" Bianca whispered.

"We can't be locked in from the inside. That wouldn't meet fire codes." He used both hands and tugged on the handle again. Even rammed his shoulder into the door.

Still nothing.

Bianca coughed, and Eddie whipped his gaze back to the fire.

Flames rolled up the wall. A ceiling that wasn't tiled, so they couldn't escape through the crawl space.

Zero windows. Only one door. No easily accessible vent system. Trapped.

The fire popped and hissed, pillaging closer. This room would be gone in a matter of minutes. So would they. Unless he got them out of here.

Think.

Eddie ripped off his mask from around his eyes and turned in a circle. Lieutenant Crawford had applauded him on his quick and creative decisions in the smoke house training, however, this was a real-life scenario. God's mercies were new every day. Just like the fresh chance to prove himself, especially when it actually counted.

Lord, we really need You.

He pulled out his phone, unlocked it, and handed it to her. "Call 911."

As Bianca dialed on speaker, Eddie rummaged in the first crate. There had to be something in here that he could use to break open the door.

A female voice answered the call. "Nine-one-one, what's your emergency?"

"Yes, I . . ." A cough stole Bianca's voice.

"This is Eddie Rice, firefighter with Eastside." He yelled over his shoulder as he dug into the next crate. "I've got a fire inside the mayor's event. We're trapped in what looks to be the auction storage room. Flames escalating fast with no accessible exit. We're locked in with some kind of electric keypad."

"Did you say the mayor's—"

"Yes!" Bianca added in, with blood now trickling down her face.

"A fire truck's five minutes out," the dispatcher said.

"That's too long." Bianca banged on the door and used the handle to stand. "Help! Someone help us—"

Another cough thundered through her.

Eddie's chest squeezed. He slipped off his suit jacket. "Hold this over your mouth. Stay low to the ground and remain on the line with dispatch."

Smoke embraced his lungs like a thief. He bent over and squinted at the door handle. There was a spot for a key. His foster brother's lock-picking skills would have actually come in handy. Too bad Eddie had never paid attention.

Eddie pushed the numbers one through four on the keypad, but it only beeped angrily.

"Four minutes out," came the dispatcher's reply over the phone's speaker, which remained in Bianca's grip.

Eddie winced.

Bianca was right. That wouldn't be quick enough.

Sweat dripped down his forehead. This was his job. Firefighters rescued people. But there was no way to save Bianca on his own strength.

Lord, help.

Smoke burned his eyes. The heat prickled the back of his neck as sweat dripped into his vision. He shoved over the first stack of disheveled crates. The crash was dwarfed by the crackle of the roaring fire. A diamond necklace, a piece of broken pottery, and a box of chocolates tumbled onto the floor. None of which was going to save them.

The ting of metal hitting the ground sounded—an axe that looked like it belonged in that medieval painting. He gripped it and took a running step, forcing all his strength through his swing. The axe struck the door handle and vibrated through Eddie's body. A ting and a thump ricocheted through the air as the axe head flew off the handle and sailed somewhere behind him.

But what mattered most was that the door handle dropped to the ground.

Eddie spun around. "Bianca!"

Where was she? Please, let the axe head not have struck her.

She popped up from behind a piano.

Eddie reached out his hand to her. "Our eviction notice is overdue."

Her gaze flicked to the opened door but snagged on the bright flames engulfing what was more than likely an antique harp. "Wait! This stuff is priceless. We need to put out the fire before it's too late."

"That's another firefighter's job." He pressed the handkerchief up to her head and placed her hand over the top of it. "You're far more priceless than any material stuff. If only more people realized their true worth."

Eddie put his arm under her elbow and did a quick sweep of the smoky hallway, but there was no fire extinguisher hanging anywhere. He didn't remember seeing one in his quest here either, but he'd been focused on finding the mayor.

Where had he gone?

The dispatcher's voice vibrated over his phone's speaker. "Your fire crew is pulling up the drive."

Out in the hall, Bianca stared at the phone in her hand as if she'd never seen it before. "We could have—"

Eddie pulled the door shut to keep the fire from escaping faster. The how and why of the arson would have to wait.

With a glare at her broken heel, Bianca kicked off her shoes. "This is why I shouldn't ever wear heels." She glared at the smoke detector up ahead on the ceiling. "Shouldn't that be going off?"

"A great question." Things were adding up, and not in a good way.

Eddie clenched his jaw and examined the woman as he took her hand in his, setting off in a run. Her dress had ripped up her leg on one side, and a portion of her sleeve was stained with blood. "You should have stayed in the ballroom. This isn't a movie stunt."

She exhaled. "I'll keep that in mind the next time I think someone might need my help. I'll let them know I can only pretend."

Eddie shook his head. "That's not what I meant."

While keeping up with his pace, she pulled his blood-soaked handkerchief away from the wound on the side of her head, and the broken skin glared at him. "Pretty sure you needed me in there. I helped get the other firefighters here. But more importantly, how did the fire start? Who was that man? And what was that exchange we saw between those two men?"

"Right now, I've got to get you and everyone else out of here. And you need to put pressure back on your head. Use my jacket now." Eddie's dress shoes slid on the floor as he rounded the corner. What he wouldn't do to have his boots on.

At the start of the paneled hall, a light-blue-suited man, not a black-suited one, strolled toward them, still wearing his masquerade mask, a cigar in his mouth.

He frowned. "Bia? We're about to miss our opportunity to . . . is that blood?"

Bianca released Eddie's hand. "Carter, there's a fire! We have to get everyone out."

No wonder Bianca had thought Eddie had been Carter, with their similar build and hairstyle.

Eddie ran around Carter and through the same doorway that returned him to the ballroom only for Janice to block his path.

Not the grouchy lady. Again.

Eddie put his hands up around his mouth. "Excuse me, ladies and gentlemen."

The music stopped. People lifted their glasses at him as if awaiting him to raise a toast.

The angry woman huffed beside him. "What do you think you're doing? I knew you were trouble with that truck of yours. I never should have allowed you to enter. Invitation or not."

Eddie motioned for the main doors. "There is a fire in the building. Please proceed to the exit in an orderly fashion."

A collective wail erupted, and then the door to the ballroom flew open. A wave of suits and dresses thundered through the exit.

Janice took off for the door.

Eddie checked over his shoulder. Where was Bianca? Carter?

Carter sprinted past him as Bianca jogged toward Eddie with her dress tangling around her bare feet.

She blinked at him. "Don't you need to get a fire extinguisher?"

"Lives are more important than buildings." He reached down and grabbed the section of her dress off the ground. "I can't let you be trampled by the stampede of frightened people leaving the mansion. Especially not after you helped rescue them by calling the fire department."

That and the fire was past the point of a typical extinguisher.

She sent him a faint smile as they trailed the others.

As they broke the threshold of the house, the siren of a fire truck overtook the disorder roaring a few steps ahead of them.

Rescue Squad 5's fire truck pulled up to the curb, Ridge Foster, back from the accident that had injured his leg, in the driver's seat. Chief Macon James hopped out of his chief's truck. The masquerade attendees swarmed down the steps, but they weren't the only civilians the crew needed to deal with.

Ambulance 21 had made it to the security gate, except the picketers and nosy bystanders at the end of the drive, waiting to steal a peek at the famous guests, were now slipping past security and running up the drive, blocking the route for the ambulance.

A woman with hips wider than the feathered hat on her head bumped into Bianca, who stumbled on her bare feet. Eddie steadied her and spotted Macon heading for the stairs.

"Chief!" Eddie yelled, and Macon jogged up to them. "Sir, the fire is in the east wing. It's taken over a section of an inner room's wall. A man deliberately set a dress on fire."

Bianca removed the jacket from her wound, and her arm brushed against Eddie's side. "He locked us inside that room."

Macon eyed Bianca. "Thanks, Rice. Now, better get her to Bently and Russell."

Eddie placed his arm around Bianca. "Yes, sir."

Bianca put her hand on his chest. "Wait, the mayor!"

Eddie tensed. How could he have forgotten? "We witnessed something that makes me fearful for the mayor's well-being."

Macon nodded and hollered instructions to the crew as Eddie tucked Bianca against himself and headed down the driveway.

A cameraman joined them. "Ms. Pearl? What's happening inside?"

Bianca curled further into Eddie's side.

"Let us through." Eddie dodged the man with the camera.

Another person with some sort of microphone connected to a phone stuck it close to her mouth. "Bia, has there been an explosion? Has anyone else been injured?"

Bianca covered her face with his jacket.

Eddie jerked away from the paparazzi, but that only seemed to alert the crowd to their direction.

"Bia!"

"Bia Pearl!"

"Give us a quick look."

The incomers swarmed around them.

"What happened to your dress, Bia?"

"Who are you wearing tonight?"

"Is it true that you're dating your costar, Carter Cane?"

"Ms. Pearl, how is tonight going to affect the film's timeline?"

"What do you think about your ex's not-guilty plea?"

Bianca fisted Eddie's shirt beneath the covering of his jacket.

Eddie tugged her closer. "No comment."

He hadn't paid attention to the trial of Nathan Kensington. But no one's past needed to define someone else's.

Trace Bently, who was driving Ambo 21, laid on the horn. The paparazzi made a path. Kianna Russell, in the passenger seat, pointed to the rear of the ambulance, and then she disappeared to the back.

"Hang on tight," Eddie whispered in Bianca's ear. "Almost there."

A muffled "thank you" came from under his jacket.

Eddie shouldered his way through the crowd and made it to the back of the ambulance.

Kianna opened the door, and Eddie helped Bianca climb in. "I assume she'll need stitches. She's lost a fair amount of blood and—"

"Blood." A gulp came from a girl with a beanie on and two braids resting on her shoulders who had snuck up behind him.

The man with the microphone returned. "Will Bia Pearl be disfigured?"

Someone wearing a ball cap shoved his phone in through the open crack in the ambulance's rear door.

Kianna snatched the phone and tossed it out, then pulled Eddie inside.

Eddie shut the door. As he turned, he expected to see Bianca curled into a ball on the stretcher, but her eyes locked onto his.

She swallowed. "How bad is it?"

There was little good from the evening so far.

Eddie rubbed his hand through his smoke-scented hair. "Our crew will get the fire out. No one else should get hurt."

Her eyes slipped closed. "Good. That's really good."

Kianna leaned in and inspected Bianca's incision.

But Bianca didn't lift her attention to Kianna. Her gaze remained on Eddie. "And my face?"

Eddie inhaled. He was afraid that's what she'd really meant.

Kianna grimaced.

Bianca pulled the slit in her dress closed over her leg. "Give me the truth. Is this an end-of-my-career type of scar we're looking at?"

Kianna wiped Bianca's cheek with a cloth. "Several stitches. Not as many as I first expected with the amount of blood. The actual wound is near your hairline, which will be helpful to hide the scar. Bangs might help some."

Bianca pressed her lips together.

Eddie cleared his throat. "My grand-ma'am used to say that scars give character."

Fear filled her eyes. "Unfortunately, the entertainment industry believes differently. The world wants what it wants. Perfection."

Eddie shook his head. There was only One who was perfect. He could still hear his foster mother's voice in his head. "Doesn't mean—"

Out through the front window, a couple of guys rocked the front of the ambulance. "Let us see Bia!"

"We've got to get out of here," Kianna said to Trace, who sent a look to Eddie.

Eddie nodded. "I'll clear them away."

He jumped out and did as promised. Cleared a path for Bianca to leave. The ambulance's flashing lights reversed back down the drive, and Bianca's fearful words rang in his memory.

The world wants what it wants.

Eddie raced toward the mansion to help his crew. Raised his eyes to the sky.

He hadn't gotten what he wanted in too long, but now, it looked like even the kids wouldn't get the rest of the needed funds for their youth center.

THREE

THE TUNGSTEN LAMP POINTED AT BIANCA MADE her eyes water. She rested her hand on Carter's chest. "You saved me. I never could have done it without you."

She held on to her smile. Right words. Wrong man. Or at least, not the firefighter that had taken over her dreams again last night.

An extra moved off-screen over her costar's shoulder, and Bianca zeroed in on her mark—the point of Carter's chin. She couldn't glance over. Couldn't spike the camera—look directly at it—and ruin the shot. She needed everything real to fade away. To be and to feel as her character.

Except all Bianca currently felt was her pain meds wearing off. She fisted the fabric under her fingertips.

Though a hoodie shadowed Carter's face, her costar's gaze locked onto hers. "I think you have it backward. You rescued me."

His words brought to mind when the firefighter had steadied her. Made her feel safe despite the chaos.

Fingers traced her cheek, and Carter's pinkie hit her stitches. Bianca flinched.

"Cut!" The director hooked his hands onto his hips. His gray shirt would have blended him into the array of crew members behind the lighting and cameras, but Leo's glare couldn't be ignored. "Bia, what was that?"

Bianca wiped her sweaty palm down her face, and the fresh makeup smudged onto her fingers. Great. "Sorry, I . . ."

Hesitated. Daydreamed. Panicked.

Beside her, Carter sighed. "You've really got to remain in character, Bia."

Bianca winced again. If only she could redo the previous week. If she'd missed the entirety of the mayor's event, yesterday's headlines wouldn't have read: *Are Both Acting and Carter Old News for Bia Pearl?*

The complete opposite of what her contract said must happen concerning the hype around her and Carter's relationship on and off the set. Worse may have been the pictures of her injured face.

Leo stormed toward the camera. "Roll it back. I need to see if her stitches are visible. Bia, go see Tiff. Make sure she works her magic."

Bianca ducked out of the crowd and sat in her chair. She grabbed her phone and a water bottle. Usually, the best makeup artist in the business would have beaten Bianca to her seat. Except Tiff wasn't waiting behind the cameras. Maybe she had taken the day off, since one of the makeup assistants had done Bianca's makeup earlier?

An assistant walked by, and Bianca waved her over. "Have you seen Tiff?"

The girl pushed up her glasses.

Bianca stopped. She knew the woman. "Hey, Grace. Your new hair color looks great." Grace pulled her honey-chestnut hair over one shoulder. "I've had this color for almost two years."

"Guess it has been that long since we've worked on a set together."

Grace pushed her hair back. "Tiff had a family emergency. Her actual replacement just arrived." She checked her phone. "Name's Riley."

"Bia!" Leo shouted.

"Yes, sir." Bianca rushed to the camera the director glared at.

"See that." Leo shook his finger at the screen. "I count two stitches."

Grace wrinkled her nose. "That one's only a hair stuck in—"

"It will be fixed in fifteen minutes. If the press doesn't die down about you and that firefighter . . . The point of your contract was to create hype about the movie. Not self-promotion. I took a chance on you despite your relationship and tabloids history. Don't make me regret my choice."

Bianca locked her jaw. "I'll fix it."

She marched for the makeup trailer and pulled out her phone. One text message from Frances.

<u>Frances</u>

Good morning, sweetheart.
Accountability check to see if you've
done your devotion this morning? Keep
yourself in the Word and don't listen
to what people say online. They don't
know the truth. Keep shining for Him.
Hope you're feeling okay. **Praying**.

Bianca hugged her phone to her chest. She could use all the prayers. First, get her makeup touched up. No stitches. Easy enough. Next, she had to do damage control on her and Carter's supposed relationship, spreading news about the movie. Then she'd squeeze in some Bible reading . . .

Her phone buzzed with another text. But it wasn't from Frances.

<u>Unknown</u>

Lady B, **call me**.

She blocked the sender's number and shoved her phone into her pocket. Third, get Nathan to stop trying to contact her. He knew the truth about her, but he allowed his lawyer's lies to save him.

Eddie's face from when he'd told her the truth about her injury popped into her head.

She exhaled.

Lastly, she'd figure out how to stop that firefighter from sneaking into her mind.

She pushed out the doors of the warehouse they had been filming in, and the afternoon light made her squint.

Heels click-clacked on the concrete behind her. "Bianca, wait."

Bianca turned to find Grace jogging toward her.

Grace heaved in a breath. "Sorry about Leo in there. He's a little stressed over some behind-the-scenes details about the movie's finances." Grace pushed up her glasses. "Never take his mood personally. He can't *truly* be upset with you for having to get stitches after someone attacked you."

"Doesn't help when the media missed the memo about me being attacked. Apparently, I slipped off my heels that night because I'd had too much to drink and rammed into a window. Not exactly good publicity for a family film." Bianca held on to her smile as she passed some extras, who waved at her. "Unfortunately, there are a few details that didn't get accomplished at the masquerade auction."

Grace juggled her phone and notebook in her hand as they took the steps to the makeup trailer. "Yes, the staged photos of you and Carter. I have a suggestion about that. I would have run it by your agent, but she hasn't returned my calls."

Bianca's smile slipped. "She's probably busy with her other clients." Her *current* clients. Alexis had forbidden Bianca from signing this movie contract. No, it wasn't a great upfront contract. More hoops than benefits. But it wasn't like Bianca had any other options.

Before Grace could reply, a tall woman in ripped jeans and a navy tank top, her brown hair pulled back into two messy buns, stepped out of the trailer.

Grace cleared her throat. "This is Riley. Your replacement makeup artist."

The woman stiffened. "You're Bia Pearl."

Bianca clasped her hands together. "And you're exactly who I need."

Grace pointed at Bianca's hairline. "The director's hypersensitive about her stitches. I suggested giving her character a haircut, but that was also ignored."

Riley frowned. "Stitches? They happened on set?"

"No, thank goodness. That might shut production down for hours." Grace took the door handle from Riley and motioned for her and Bianca to enter. "Bianca had to be rescued by a firefighter at the local mayor's campaign auction. Surprised you haven't heard. It's all over the news."

Bianca failed to hold the sigh in as she eased into the chair that she had previously sat in this morning.

Riley shrugged one shoulder. "Been a little busy getting here."

Grace spun the chair Bianca sat in to face her. "You're probably wishing Carter could've been the one to rescue you. But the reason I wanted to talk with you . . ." She sent a side glance to Riley, who had moved over by her makeup table. "What if you don't suddenly try to plaster Carter as your fake boyfriend on your social media?"

Bianca gripped the armrest of the chair. Pretending on- and off-screen was the package deal. "No choice in that, I'm afraid."

Grace pressed her lips together. "Because your contract says that you and Carter must jointly promote the movie. However, it doesn't give a timeline, and after your apparently ex-agent texted me to stop calling her about you . . ."

Bianca's gaze snapped up to Grace, who winced.

Grace held out her palms. "I probably should've led with how I already knew she'd dropped you, but I read everyone's contracts. I found wiggle room. Especially for you to not have to fake date Carter . . . just yet."

Riley walked over and rotated Bianca's chair to face the mirror. Grace stayed next to Riley as if they were in a three-legged race.

Riley swirled a sponge into a shade of foundation.

Grace made a strangled noise and grabbed another color of foundation off the counter. "Tiff likes to use this to blend. Bianca's skin has a redder undertone." She handed it over to a scowling Riley and then squatted until she was level with Bianca. "I know it's good to have a hero on your social media. It's good for you as an actress, and it's good for your viewership. That's probably why your contract is worded for the costars to jointly promote. But what if we ditch Carter for the time being? We use the hero who actually saved you instead. Let's milk that a little while. We're just going to take what the media gave us and see what we can do with it. My guess is your followers will rise, which means more people will hear about the movie because they're following you. Plus, it'll help your reputation to be seen with a real hero too. This film's supposed to be a romantic mystery adventure for the entire family. So its genuine audience will latch on to an everyday, hardworking hero they relate to. Not Carter, who was photographed last night doing shots and kissing three different women."

Bianca shook her head. "Those photos could've been photoshopped."

Grace twisted her lips to the side. "Could have. But that doesn't stop people from believing what they want to believe. What if you ride this firefighter-hero wave that the media has hand delivered? Gain more followers. Both you and Carter improve your online characters. Finish filming and then . . . bam. You and Carter are seen together. Plant the rumors about dating then. Contract still validated. Which conveniently will be right before the movie goes live. And in my opinion, will be better timing for promoting the movie. Perfect plan, right? When it works, I was hoping . . . you'd let me be your official media assistant or personal assistant. We could argue over titles later."

Bianca blinked at Grace. "My assistant? But you're . . ."

"An assistant to an assistant." Grace licked her lips. "I'm way overdue for a promotion around here, and I'm so tired of getting coffee . . . I mean, I'd love to get you coffee—"

"You could get me an espresso." Riley dabbed the mixed foundation on Bianca's hairline.

Grace rolled her eyes. "Being a set assistant and your assistant might come in handy. I mean, yeah, you need one, especially since you currently don't have an agent. And I think I'd be a great one if people would give me a chance."

"Amateur." Riley grunted. "One huge pothole in your perfect plan."

Both Bianca and Grace stared at Riley.

Riley handed Bianca a handheld mirror. "You assume the firefighter will drop everything and be at her beck and call. Not everyone in the world jumps at the command of the Bia Pearl."

Bianca inspected Riley's touch-up on her stitches in the mirror. "She's right. Carter's job depended on rumors of us together. But not Eddie's."

Grace held up a finger as she moved to the corner where some dresses hung on a rack.

Grace grabbed the third hanger of what was probably supposed to be a dress but looked more like a long tube top. "Except this green dress will make your eyes pop. Just go over to the firehouse. See if he's willing to step in and play the role of a hero on your social media for a couple weeks. Boost your targeted audience. You and Carter can still promote the movie together—later. Wear this. How could your hero say no?"

Bianca wrinkled her nose. Two fake relationships instead of just one she'd never wanted in the first place. Not the direction of her restarted career she'd prayed for. "I prefer it when my portrayed character wears more fabric."

Riley raised a brow.

Grace shook the dress on the hanger. "It covers all your important parts. At least try it on." She pulled Bianca from the chair. "Your contract works on back-end residuals. The more the movie makes, the more you will too. People love firefighters. The hero works at Eastside. Your hair and makeup's already done."

Riley wiped down an eyebrow brush. "Isn't she supposed to be filming?"

Grace lifted her chin and sent her hoop earrings swinging. "We have a little lag time in the filming schedule today. I'll talk to Leo."

Riley cocked her hip. "And ask him what? His coffee order? You can't request a director to stop filming."

Grace's shoulders sank. She didn't meet Bianca's eyes.

Both Grace and Riley had a point, but Bianca did need a way to check off all the boxes on her contract—like getting people to the theater, growing the movie's social-media sites, and creating a must-see atmosphere about the film—or she wouldn't get paid enough to have agreed to the indie-produced film. They hadn't offered her a typical union contract with plenty of guaranteed cash. Instead, she'd agreed to a small weekly contract with a much heavier royalty percentage. "First off, thanks, Riley." She gestured to her forehead. "This looks spot on."

Bianca touched Grace's arm. "Second, we can try out you being my assistant, especially for my media stuff, because honestly, I hate it."

Grace pressed the dress to her chest. "You'll give me a chance?"

She didn't exactly have anyone else lining up to support her.

Bianca held up her finger. "Let me finish this scene, and then we'll both talk to Leo. He'll have an idea of whether or not the producers will agree to your revised plan."

Grace bobbed her head. "Then you'll go get your firefighter?"

Bianca laced her fingers together. The exact person she was trying to get out of her mind.

Would he really agree to a plan that would save her career?

Maybe if she could figure out a deal. One he couldn't resist. "Okay. Give me the dress."

FOUR

SOMETIMES QUIET DIDN'T HUSH THE THOUGHTS in Eddie's head. He hopped out of his truck and glared at the spot in the mayor's drive where he'd last seen Bianca almost forty-eight hours ago. No, that wasn't true. She'd been in his dreams last night. Except, opposite of reality, he hadn't rescued her from the masked arsonist.

"Rice." His chief waved him over to where he stood behind two wooden barricades in front of the steps leading up to the mayor's house. This time, they weren't covered in a carpet overlay.

When Eddie swung his leg over the caution tape, Macon tilted his chin toward where Mayor Gregory Harrelson and Police Chief Conroy Barnes stood outside the entrance. "Thanks for coming. Once the police chief is done speaking with the mayor, I want us to meet with him. We need more of the story. Things aren't meshing together perfectly yet."

Eddie pointed to the front door of the mansion. "What does the arson investigator think?"

Macon inhaled. His broad shoulders rose and then fell. "Your statement was enough to rule it deliberate, yet we have no further clues on who or why, unless you can give additional ones."

The wind blew, and the scent of smoke hit Eddie's nose, even though the fire had been put out nearly two days ago. "What did the security cameras reveal?"

Macon squinted at one of the cameras placed above the front door. "There's no actual footage of the guests arriving at all. If you hadn't been there, I'm not sure we would have gotten the exact location of the fire inside so quickly."

Eddie swallowed. Would Bianca have still seen the supposed bribe and followed the arsonist? She would have been trapped and hurt without him to help her.

Macon's gaze swept over the property. "That night, the police took names and questioned everyone, but no leads."

The mayor and the police chief stepped down toward them.

Gregory was dressed in a silver button-down shirt complete with black suspenders. He stuck out his hand to Eddie. "Thank you, young man. I heard you were the first on the scene."

"It's Eddie Rice, sir."

Gregory kept shaking his hand.

Eddie's phone buzzed in his pocket, but he ignored it. "I'm the one wanting the grant for the rec center."

Gregory squinted. "Ah, yes, I see that now."

Eddie stiffened. The mayor hadn't even recognized him. Not a great sign for the youth center.

Conroy, the tallest of the men, eyed the uninvited crowd that hovered behind the gated driveway. "Can you recap that night for us, Rice?"

Eddie crossed his arms. This was not at all what he'd hoped he and the mayor would be discussing the next time they spoke. "After the speech, you and one of your guards left the ballroom. Once you exited, I saw a handoff of some sort between a security guard stationed at the door and a man. When the pair followed you through the doorway, I worried you might be in danger. In precaution, I trailed behind."

Gregory frowned.

"When I got to an empty hallway, I smelled smoke. I opened the first unlocked door to check to see if they or you had entered."

The mayor trailed his fingers along his mustache. "You need to be awarded for your keen eyes. I thank you for your dedication to my well-being. Not everyone is on my side about Last Chance County's future."

Conroy shifted and sent Macon a look Eddie couldn't quite read.

Eddie smiled. "Well, sir, my good deed could be awarded to the kids of this city." When the mayor didn't grin, Eddie cleared his throat. "As I peered inside what I assumed to be a storage room, other than the smoke smell, nothing seemed out of the ordinary until I spotted a man with a lighter."

"You saw him?" Gregory pulled out his phone and checked his screen.

Eddie heaved out a breath. If only it were that simple. "He wore a masquerade mask, so we never saw his entire face. Only that he wore a black suit."

Gregory sighed. "The masquerade masks sounded like a grand addition to the night when Janice brought the idea to me." He turned to the police chief. "It's obvious who's behind this. My campaign funds are nowhere near where they were projected to be. Roger Pointe is responsible. He tried stealing my supporters, however my team found a way to outsmart him with the auction. But now he's broken the law to try to stop me again. And the voters think that he's the right man for our town? If only the news would report the entire truth."

Conroy held up his palm. "There's currently no *usable* evidence that Mr. Pointe has done anything wrong."

Gregory ran his thumbs underneath the front side of his suspenders and then gripped the elastic fabric. "He never should have run against me. He's not even been here long enough to know what Last Chance County needs. Obviously, I must weed through my security guards. Can we do anything else to find the arsonist? What was the man lighting on fire?"

Eddie's phone vibrated again in his pocket. "A dress a mannequin wore."

Gregory's brows pinched together. "Was it the red or black dress?"

Bianca's dress had been a deep red. And for some reason, that was the only color that popped into his mind. "Uh . . . I'm not sure which he lit first . . ." Eddie's phone buzzed another time, and he slid his hand into his pocket and rejected the call. "How much of the auction donations were damaged?"

Gregory's face went slack. "Nearly half. The rest, we're waiting to see if they have smoke or water damage."

Which meant less additional money for the children of the town. The grant would cover the remaining down payment, but they'd need more.

Someone hollered from the driveway, and Conroy's radio crackled on his belt.

Conroy lifted his chin. "My team has been dealing with the movie protesters, and we're seeing if this has anything to do with the Jane Doe body your team found earlier in the week. But I promise, Mayor, that we'll get to the bottom of the fire and—"

"Still no information on the Jane Doe?" Gregory shifted his feet. "A murder really doesn't help my reelection campaign."

Pulling up the woman's body flashed in Eddie's memory. Rescue squad had been called out to where a couple of hikers had found a dead body in a ravine. The forest surrounding Last Chance County had not appeared postcard worthy on that morning.

Conroy gave Eddie a look. "Like I said, anything else about the arsonist could help give closure to the woman's family if they're connected."

Eddie slid his hands into his pockets. "Square and dimpled jaw.

Probably around five ten. Masked. Black suit. Walked with a bit of an uneven gait. But I stopped focusing on him when Ms. Pearl got hurt by the suspect."

Gregory shook his head. "The poor dear. The news didn't get her story right either. I never should have okayed that film. I thought I was doing the town good. Hoped to lower the townspeople's taxes. But now I'm not sure the added revenue is worth it if it brought in criminals. The sooner they wrap up the filming, the better."

Conroy stepped closer inside of their formed semicircle. "Sir, so far none of the protesters have done anything except picket. We have no evidence this was about the movie."

"Then you haven't seen all the litter that had the environmentalists knocking on my front door," Gregory mumbled.

Macon motioned for Eddie to continue.

Eddie's phone vibrated in his pocket for the millionth time. Probably the kids on his baseball team. They were going to have to discuss what waiting patiently meant again. "The smoke got thick fast. That's when I made the decision to get Ms. Pearl out and worry about the fire later. I hit the door handle with some kind of axe that had been in a crate."

A gasp flew from Gregory. "Not the hammer replica signed by Chris himself? It could have brought in close to a million."

Macon placed his hand on Eddie's shoulder. "Famous signature or not, it seems to have saved Eddie's and Ms. Pearl's lives."

Gregory paled but had the decency to paste on a smile. "Which I'm entirely grateful for. Things would have been far worse if Bia Pearl had died on my watch."

Only the movie star mattered, it seemed.

"Thankfully, nobody died." Conroy gave the mayor's bodyguard, waiting a few paces away, a chin nod. "Sir, the sun is hot. Would you like a drink?"

"Excellent idea."

After Gregory was escorted inside, Eddie followed both chiefs into the house.

Eddie pulled out his phone. Twenty-two messages and five missed calls. A few from rescue squad members, but most, like he'd thought, from his youth baseball kids. One from his mother—

He stopped. What in the world?

He swiped past her message and opened the one from Zack Stephens, his closest firefighter friend, who had sent him a news link. It was a picture of Eddie and Bianca. The two of them staring into each other's eyes. It had been cropped in a way that hid her wound and their location. And reality.

With the mayor's fountain spraying behind them, it almost looked like a romantic getaway postcard picture with her hand in his. All the blood and smoky ash had been photoshopped off her face.

Another message popped up on his phone from Scout, one of the boys on his ball team.

Scout
Scarlette says you've got some
explaining to do at **practice**.

Eddie groaned as he scrolled through the next texts.

Scout
Practice is at five p.m. **Right?**

You're late!

Are **you** coming?

Scarlette says you're a chicken
for **not coming.**

Then he opened the one from his mother.

Mary
When did you move to Last
Chance County?

Eddie gripped the phone in his palm. So much for staying below her radar. He wished his mentor had been a garbage truck driver or a dentist. Someone less likely than a firefighter to hit the news. Maybe then Eddie would have had a job where his mother couldn't locate him after ten years.

Ten years after she had given him up. Freely.

Macon pivoted back to Eddie. "Everything all right?"

Eddie shoved his phone in his pocket. "Nothing to worry about right now."

Macon narrowed his gaze and then glanced at his own phone.

Great. The last thing Eddie wanted was for his chief to see the news. The article he'd seen yesterday had only focused on Eddie's heroic actions. It didn't exactly say "team" for the fire station, which was the award the station had received. Or was supposed to have received at the auction before the chaos.

But instead, Macon's arms went slack at his sides. "It's Tuesday, right? What time is ball practice?"

Eddie ran his hand over his hair. "Uh, now, sir. But I got someone to cover for me before . . ."

Macon waved him off. "You can't be late for your first official head-coach practice."

Eddie shrugged. "If I show up with you, sir, then it will more than make up for it."

Macon smiled and crinkles appeared around his eyes. "I have to let go of the reins on coaching."

He had been the ideal coach. But Macon and his wife Natalie were expecting their first child soon. Plus, Eddie had promised to watch over one of the players, Will, while Will's father couldn't, so it had seemed like the logical step to move Eddie from assistant coach to head coach—until one factored in his lack of experience.

Macon raised his hand to Conroy. "You good without Rice for tonight?"

Conroy lifted the notebook in his hand. "If you think of anything else, just call."

Macon hooked his thumb over his shoulder. "Get out of here, Rice. Those kids need you. Who else is helping you out this year?"

Eddie winced. "Zack, when he can. Eli is trying it out tonight." The man who, in a roundabout way, had gotten Macon's brother Houston's old job as youth pastor—before Houston had left to be a hotshot firefighter in Montana.

Macon only nodded. Apparently, no hard feelings over the past. Must be nice. "No matter who's your assistant, you're going to be great for those kids."

Eddie hoped so. Had promised his old foster brother he'd be there for his son. To give the kids hope—something Eddie and Joe hadn't had when they'd been his players' ages.

Once Eddie hopped into his truck, he drove toward the ballpark on the south side of town—the park that needed everything from a paint job to reliable bathrooms. At least they had willing kids who wanted to play—or wanted someone to show them some attention.

Eddie tightened his grip on the steering wheel. How he wished someone had rounded him up to play ball when he was younger. Instead, he'd found unworthy activities on the street.

He pulled into the parking lot, right next to Eli's SUV. A group of boys sat on the bleachers outside of the field, around Trenton, one of the boys with a cell phone, who the kids called Tank even though he looked more like a stork with his thin arms and legs.

Eli wore a striped polo and khaki shorts. Every strand of his hair seemed gelled into full obedience as he stood on the pitcher's mound, being coached how to throw the ball by Scarlette, the team's youngest and its only girl. And whose brother, Scout—one of the few who truly loved the game—was digging his worn tennis shoes into the batter's box dirt.

Scout shifted his stance and dropped his bat onto little shoulders that resembled his grandmother's more than the boy cared to acknowledge. But size didn't disprove the ability to endure hard things. "Come on, Scar, let Preacher-man pitch. Eli knows how."

Debatable. Eli knew less than Eddie about baseball, and Eddie hadn't ever touched a ball until Houston had organized the team and gotten Macon involved last year.

Eddie shouldered the extra equipment bag from the bed of his truck. "Why aren't you guys all warming up?"

None of the boys on the bleachers looked up from Tank's phone. But Will, the freckle-faced boy with more shadowed circles under his eyes than bases on the field, said, "Hold on, Tank's got a new girl, and he says she's hot."

Will looked nothing like his dark-complected father, Joe. Nearly blond, and blue eyes to match.

The only boy on the team who claimed to like books—Jacob, on Tank's right—twisted his baseball hat around. "Except he magically can't find her picture anymore."

Ned, the wannabe comedian, leaned down by Tank's ear. "Probably 'cause he made her up. No hot girls go to Southview Middle School."

Tank rammed his elbow into Ned. "She's real. And way hotter than your butt-ugly g—"

"Hey now." Eddie dropped the bag on the ground in front of the boys. Dust floated up, covering Eddie's tennis shoes. "Is our appearance the most important thing?"

Will rolled his eyes. "Gotta be to you. Your new girlfriend's hotter than a Carolina Reaper pepper."

Hotter than . . . Eddie rubbed his forehead. This practice was going horribly wrong, but what came out of Eddie's mouth wasn't quite the top priority. "I don't have a new girlfriend."

Didn't have time to even try to locate the right kind of girlfriend. One he might have an actual future with, who believed in what he did. His last girlfriend had claimed he was only the fun kind of man. Not the forever kind.

That wasn't him anymore, though. Thankfully, God had straightened out his priorities.

"Sure you do." Will reached for Tank's phone. "Tank can find one of *her* pictures online. She's everywhere."

Eddie opened his mouth at the exact moment Scout, over in the batter's box, hit a ball that thumped against his bat.

A second after, Eli groaned, grabbed his shin, and fell onto the ground.

Scarlette's eyes bugged. "Uh, Coach?"

Eddie sprinted for Eli.

Eli held up a shaky palm. "I'm okay . . . I think." He reached his hand out, and Eddie pulled him up to his feet.

Eddie steadied him. "Want to go sit in the dugout?"

As Eli nodded, Eddie helped him to the home team side dugout, where the other equipment bag sat, still zipped up. "Boys, the last one on the field runs laps after practice."

"You can't make us . . ." Jacob closed his mouth as the others ran to the gear bags and grabbed out baseball mitts.

Tank pulled out a ball. "I'm throwing with Will."

Will shrugged. "As long as I'm not with Scarlette."

Scarlette stuck out her tongue. "At least I can catch—"

"Everyone, three laps around the bases. And if I hear whining, it will be seven." Eddie eased Eli onto the bench. "Then make two lines at second. Scout, you get a ball and cover first and throw grounders to one line while . . ."

Another car pulled into the parking lot. A black car that looked like it belonged to Zack.

Finally, more help.

Scarlette waved her hand in the air as she ran past third base. "I'll go to third."

Eddie shook his head. "You'll take some grounders. Tank, you'll take third."

Zack climbed out of his car and threw a baseball hat over hair that had already been lightened by the sun during their outdoor fire training.

Eddie whirled back toward some whispers on the field among the running foot stomps. "No more unkind words about our teammates or anyone else. And if I hear one more word about how hot someone is—"

"Then it's a good thing you weren't at the fire station earlier." Zack opened the gate and murmured to Eddie.

As the kids began their second lap, Zack put his keys and wallet on the bench and frowned at Eli. "What happened to you?"

Eli rubbed his shin. "Scarlette's a good pitching coach." His tired gaze found Eddie's. "How did you get the kids to listen to you? It was chaos before you arrived."

This wasn't still chaos?

Eddie shoved his hands into his uniform pockets. He needed to change into his shorts. "I'm not really sure. I think they just know that I've been where they have."

Eli hung his head. "Since Zack's here now, I think I'm going to head home and ice my leg."

Please don't quit. "I'll check up on you later."

Zack grimaced. "Maybe elevate your leg too? Do you need help out of here?"

Eli waved him off. "Nah, I'll get there."

Eddie patted Eli on his back. "Thanks for covering for me."

"I would say anytime, but I might think twice beforehand."

Eli hobbled to his vehicle, and Eddie whispered to Zack, "You sure you can't help out more?"

He was going to need all hands on deck with this team.

Zack tossed a ball in the air. "Wish I could, but volunteering with the foster kids and time with Naya—"

"I get it." He now had a girlfriend. The forever kind of girl. "Thanks for when you can come."

Eddie checked on the kids' progress doing their warm-ups. Then on Eli, who had opened his driver's-side door.

"Sorry, Eli," Scout yelled from first base.

Eli waved and crawled into his vehicle.

At least one of the boys seemed to have had an attitude adjustment since he'd joined the team. Now for the rest of them not to base a girl's worth on their "hotness."

Speaking of . . .

Eddie grabbed a mitt. "Do I want to know why the squad called someone hot? Especially since most of the men are either married or in a relationship. Did someone actually catch fire?"

Zack pulled his hand back and rotated his arm over his shoulder. "Move your arm straight over your shoulder, Will." Then to Eddie, he said, "No flames. It was mainly Izan and Ridge. Well, Ridge was mostly making fun of Izan, who dropped a sponge when a certain woman showed up in heels and a dress to the firehouse."

Another car pulled into the parking lot. A small white one. Had Scarlette and Scout's grandmother gotten a new one? She was one of the only family members who picked up their kids from practice. And she happened to have been friends with his grand-ma'am, a.k.a., his old foster mother.

How he missed that woman. Without her, he may never have been introduced to the Lord.

A ball went right underneath Tank's mitt and between his legs.

"Get your mitt in the dirt, Tank." Eddie leaned into the dugout fence that separated him and Zack from the fielders. "Who in the world came and spooked Izan? Please don't tell me it was that girl he dated last month."

Zack chuckled. "I guess her gum smacking and loud talking about how she needed Izan to take her out for lobster didn't only bother me."

A ball zipped under Will's legs.

"Gum popping aside, she didn't have the right priorities going on in life for him." Eddie grabbed his own mitt and jogged out onto the field. "Jacob, you go to second. Will you're at center."

However, Jacob didn't move. He only pointed, open-mouthed, at a woman wearing sunglasses and a strapless green dress, walking toward the dugout or bleachers—he couldn't tell which exactly— in heels taller than their catcher's helmet.

That was not Scout's grandmother, Naomi.

"Whoa," came Trenton's breathy voice. "Now that's one hot—"

"Tank! Don't you dare finish that statement, and run to left field." Eddie lifted his sunglasses.

It was her. The woman he'd prayed for God to heal.

Scarlette came and tugged on Eddie's elbow. "Coach, I thought you said you didn't have a new girlfriend."

"I don't." Answering was quicker than saying it wasn't any of her business.

Scarlette sank her hand onto her hip. "Then how come Bia Pearl was in your arms on the internet and now she's at our practice?"

Eddie swallowed.

Bianca slid her sunglasses on top of her head. Her hair shined under the sunlight like it was in a shampoo commercial. Her dress fit a little too perfectly, and her legs seemed a mile long in those heels that managed to walk over the gravel parking lot.

And somehow, he'd liked the floor-length red dress from the other night better. But that was hardly important.

He checked over his shoulder at his boys in the outfield. All gaped at Bianca.

Forget chaos. Practice had just gotten a lot more hazardous.

FIVE

SOMETIMES, AS AN ACTRESS, BIANCA WISHED the spotlight could be turned off. Instead, she put a smile on her face and flipped her hair over her shoulder. All eyes on the field were fixed on her, except those of the man who had saved her life. The man she needed to help her again.

After the last take, Leo had rubbed his chin, considering Grace's idea. "I like it. I believe the producers will too. Make this happen between you and the firefighter hero, and your contract is still safe. Once the media grows tired of you two, you'll move on to Carter before the movie hits."

Move on. As if a fake relationship right after another fake relationship could be considered normal. It really shouldn't be. Not that she'd had better luck with her actual relationships.

She put more swing into her hips, just as she would do when playing her current lead character on-screen.

This was a performance. Like too many things in her life. The more that people saw them together, the quicker the media would catch wind of their supposedly blossoming relationship, and the more the movie's future audience would grow.

Her left heel wedged in the gravel, and her ankle twisted. She caught herself on the side of the dugout.

A snicker came from two of the boys on the field, and Eddie sent them a glare. Then he turned to Bianca. "You okay?"

Bianca pressed her lips together and said the first thing that popped into her mind. "You're around. Of course I'll be fine."

The cheesy compliment tasted like vinegar on her tongue, but she kept her smile.

Eddie tilted his head at her as another man walked out of the dugout and cleared his throat.

The man with his young-looking face half hidden with a baseball cap, dressed in shorts and a T-shirt with a faded emblem, seemed vaguely familiar, but outside of the movie crew, she hadn't met many people in Last Chance County.

He stepped closer to Eddie. "She's the one who arrived at the station earlier."

That's where she'd met him. He must be one of Eddie's firefighter friends.

Bianca opened the gate and entered the field near the dugout. "Eddie Rice, you're one tough firefighter to find. And apparently, besides being a hero, you're also a baseball coach." Wait. Her stomach flipped. "Which one is your kid? Or is your wife bringing him or her to practice?"

Why had she and Grace assumed he was single?

The other firefighter failed to mask his smirk behind his hand. "Coach here isn't married, or dating anyone, and although he'd claim all the kids here, they're not actually his."

Eddie sent his friend a scowl and then stepped closer to Bianca, lowering his voice. "How's your head feel?"

Feel? She almost stumbled again. No one had asked her that the entire day. Besides Frances. The only concern had been about her stitches showing.

"I've been worse." She angled her face toward him, ignoring the pain. "Do you think they did a good job fixing me up?"

He inspected the left side of her face. "Glad you're healing well."

She put her hand on his arm. "I have you to thank for rescuing me."

"Healing is God's department." He stepped back, and her hand was left stretched out in the space between them. "And I believe you said *you* helped rescue *me*?"

"Want me to finish practice, while you two"—his friend flicked his finger back and forth between Eddie and Bianca—"catch up?"

Eddie handed his friend a glove. "How about you take the pitchers on the practice mound?" He grabbed a bat. "Thanks for stopping by, Bianca. It's good to know you're doing well. We don't always get to follow up with those we help. Unfortunately, we've got to get back to practice."

Not where she'd thought their conversation would go, but improv twist accepted. "Could I help field?"

Eddie finally looked her up and down. "This isn't a pretend practice for any cameras. You won't want to get your outfit dirty."

Bianca grabbed a mitt from the equipment bag. "I know all about real practices. I played softball in high school."

She kicked off her heels and marched to the outfield. The grass wedged between her toes like a welcome-back hug. She glanced over her shoulder. "You want me in right field?"

A tall, skinny kid shoved past another shorter boy. "You can stand beside me any day."

"Enough, Tank," Eddie growled and then shook his head at Bianca. "The last thing we need is for you to get hurt on my watch again."

Bianca stopped in the middle of left field. Was that what he thought? That it was somehow his fault that she'd gotten injured. "Eddie, if you hadn't been on watch, I would've gotten even more hurt."

Or worse.

"Coach." The only other girl on the field crossed her arms. "Just let her play. Girls don't get hurt *that* easy."

"Yeah, if Scarlette can do it, then any girl can."

The girl—apparently Scarlette—sent a glare toward the boy in center beside Bianca.

Eddie headed toward the pitcher's mound. "Fine. Bianca, take left field. Tank, come back to third. But everyone needs to pay attention to where the ball is at all times."

Bianca thumped her fist into her stiff mitt. This was going to be just like riding a bike.

The boy beside her in center field stage-whispered to the shortstop, "See, I told you she was hotter than—"

"Will, you go with Zack and practice pitching." Eddie kept his gaze off Bianca and on his players. "Scout and Scarlette, get your bats and helmets. We're running out of practice time."

Scarlette sent a thumbs-up to Bianca, then grabbed her gear and stepped up to the batter's box first. Her braided ponytail stuck out of the helmet, just how Bianca used to wear her hair to play.

Eddie stepped up onto the pitcher's mound. "Remember, watch the ball hit your bat. If you're bunting, don't run until you—"

"Make contact, and keep my bat at an angle." Scarlette wound up as if she were going to swing away, but when Eddie pitched, Scarlette tilted her bat out. The ball hit the barrel and rolled on the line to third. The catcher popped up, grabbed the ball, and threw it to first. But not nearly fast enough.

"Nice bunt, Scarlette." Eddie grabbed another ball from the bucket beside the mound. "Good throw, Lincoln. Just a little quicker on the fielding."

Praise and correction. Of course he'd be as excellent a coach as he was a firefighter.

Eddie held up another ball. "All right, Scarlette, swing away."

Bianca tucked her hair behind her ears and tugged up the front of her dress. She totally should have worn something with straps.

Scarlette choked up on the bat, moving her fingers toward the barrel.

Eddie pitched, and Scarlette swung, sending the ball in the air right to left field. Bianca sprinted forward. The shortstop jumped, but the ball cleared his mitt and bounced on the edge of the infield. Bianca bent over and grabbed it with her bare hand. Scarlette had rounded first, heading toward second. There was still time to make the throw.

Bianca wound her arm back. Except the second baseman wasn't near the bag. He gawked at her.

So did the shortstop. The third baseman had his phone out, aimed at her.

Eddie raced over, and in one quick motion of his hand, swiped something off the side of her dress along her leg.

Bianca turned in a circle. "Was it a bug?"

"No." Eddie's cheeks darkened. Was he ... blushing? "Your dress had sort of flipped up on the hem, and your leg ..."

Scarlette took her helmet off and adjusted her ponytail from second base. "Don't worry. It was only the top of your leg. We couldn't see your underwear."

It was Bianca's turn to blush. "Th-that's good."

Not exactly.

She dropped her gaze away from Eddie's stormy expression.

He sighed. "Scout, it's your turn up to bat. Tank, hand over your phone."

Tank groaned. "But ..."

Eddie shook his head. "Make sure it's unlocked. Ms. Pearl doesn't need anyone to see that video."

No longer Bianca. Only Ms. Pearl. Sometimes she got tired of her middle name. Maybe joining practice to win over Eddie wasn't part of the perfect plan.

Once Tank surrendered the phone, Eddie made a few swipes on the screen.

Bianca pushed back her shoulders and held out the borrowed mitt. "Thanks for protecting me again. You're right. I don't need any more poor press."

She yanked at the hem of her dress along her legs and dropped her voice lower. "I really don't mean to cause a distraction."

Eddie lifted the bill of his baseball cap. "Was there something you needed?"

Finally, her cue. "Actually, I was wondering if we could spend some time together and maybe talk."

Eddie's gaze shifted to hers. "About the fire?"

Something seemed to burn in his eyes, and Bianca hesitated. "Um, that wasn't exactly on my agenda."

A laugh echoed from behind Bianca's shoulder, and Eddie pointed his mitt right at Tank, who was on third base. "Don't you dare throw another dirt clod."

This was never going to work. She needed to suggest a different scene location. "What time is practice over? We can meet at, say, eight?" Practice wouldn't be longer than three hours, would it?

Eddie rubbed his fingers along the seams of the baseball in his hand. "I have to run a lot of these boys home. It will be too late. But I'm glad you stopped by. It's good to know that you're... doing well. If you ever need to talk about the fire, or if you remember anything about the arsonist, I know the police chief or my crew would be ready to hear your report."

His crew. Not him. He was declining her.

Rejection never got easier.

She handed over the mitt. "If I think of anything new about the fire, I'll let your department know. Good luck with the team, and thanks again for everything the other night."

She grabbed her heels, slipped them on, and filed out the gate to her rented car.

"But, Coach . . ." one of the boys whined, but Bianca didn't hear Eddie's reply.

She hopped inside and pulled out of the parking lot.

So much for the new plan.

She turned on her favorite song. A call buzzed over the car's speakers. She clicked the accept button and cleared her throat. "Hello?"

"So, when should I schedule your first outing together?" Grace's cheerful tone hummed through the car speakers.

Bianca pulled the visor down. Too bad it only blocked the lowering sun, not reality. "He was busy. He's a youth baseball coach, and my dress was the opposite of helpful during practice when I tried to field the ball."

"Why would you try to field a ball? But a baseball coach too—that's even more perfect. How old is his kid?" Grace sucked in a breath. "Wait . . . is he married?"

"We should have thought of that before now. His friend said he wasn't married. Or dating. Not that it matters. Things did not go well." At a cross street, Bianca checked both ways. Was this where she had turned earlier?

"Nope." Grace popped the ending *p*. "You're right. Not married. Based on his social media. Doesn't look like he actually has a kid either. That's a shame. The media eats up a single parent, underdog story."

Rows of white chipped houses filed past on the left-hand side of the road. This did not look familiar. But what really did lately?

She pulled into the next parking lot. "Single or not, I don't think he's interested in me. Which is fine. I'll go back and have Carter and I take pictures. I'll start posting the original plan. The media will change."

Hopefully.

"Except you can't." Grace's strangled tone paused. "I may have already leaked stuff about you and Eddie. The good news is you two are already trending. If you want to raise your social numbers and eventually movie attendees, then the rescue firefighter has got to agree to fake date you. It's what the media obviously craves. You have to give the people what they want. Plus, you're Bia Pearl! The man has got to be crazy if he doesn't want to be seen with you. It's not like he's got to marry you."

"Assistant improvement suggestion—maybe make it sound a little less horrible the next time you talk about me and marriage in the same sentence."

"Oh, there's a red jumper here in wardrobe. Now, this outfit says 'date me' for sure."

Bianca shook her head even though Grace couldn't see her. The color red also represented the word *stop*.

She put her car in Park and gripped the steering wheel.

Was it wrong to ask Eddie to do this favor? To her, it wasn't lying about a relationship; it was part of her job—to pretend. But he wasn't an actor. He was a real-life firefighter hero who had a heart for children. Nothing fake about him.

Her gaze landed on the color red on a storefront diagonal from her parking spot.

Kitty's Family Clothing Outlet, *where we dress you for less.*

The store was sandwiched between a pizza shop and some kind of birthday party store. On the corner, a teal fabric awning fluttered in the breeze over the bakery. Painted on the window was a heart-shaped chocolate chip cookie and the words: *You won't just like our cookies, you'll love them.*

She could really use some comfort sugar right about now. Bianca brushed a piece of dirt off her dress. Her outfit and flirty ways had not been helpful for baseball practice. It was like he'd known that wasn't the real her. Though her softball skills were rusty, that didn't mean she couldn't help. If she were actually dressed for the role of baseball assistant, she could help show Lincoln how to jump quicker to field the ball from his catcher's position.

Her attention locked onto an exercise outfit on a display mannequin in the store's window. "Hey, Grace, I've got an idea."

"Come back and I'll meet you at wardrobe and—"

"I've got my wardrobe covered." She turned off her car. "I'll let you know how it goes."

They wouldn't have to lie. She and Eddie could make another deal.

"Bianca, I totally believe in you. But Leo talked to me again after you left. Just remember, there's a lot resting on this film doing well. And don't tell anyone, but one of the producers is talking about pulling out. So there might be even less for marketing than planned. So we need all the creative ways to draw people to both you and the film. Please get your hero to say yes to a real or fake date. I'm not picky."

That was not the encouraging speech Bianca needed.

Lord, please let this work.

After going inside Kitty's store and purchasing a T-shirt, tennis shoes, and shorts and changing into more appropriate baseball practice gear, she stopped by the bakery. She grabbed a couple packages of cookies in case things didn't go well and headed back to the field.

Eddie had looked like he could use some help with his baseball team, and at the auction, he'd needed to talk with the mayor. Surely she could get that arranged.

But would that be enough for a deal?

She turned back into the baseball parking lot and hopped out. She jogged to the dugout. Her tennis shoes hit the gravel far better than her heels.

Tank spotted her first as she reached the gate. "Hey, Bia's back." The kid squinted. "I think it's her?"

Eddie frowned, shouting at her from the pitcher's mound. "Did you get lost?"

Bianca waited at the dugout. "Depends. I was wondering if you and the team needed another helper for tonight." She pulled on her shirt's baggy hem. "One more suitably dressed."

Eddie pointed to home plate. "If you can hit. We're having a hard time remembering to get our gloves on the ground."

Bianca lifted the latch and grabbed a bat and helmet from the dugout. "What if I promise to give the team cookies if they don't allow any passed balls?"

The boy on first thumped his fist into his mitt. "I could go for some cookies."

The catcher stood and lifted his catcher's mask. It wasn't Lincoln this time. Scarlette's dirty face lit with a smile. "They chocolate chip?"

Bianca rested the bat on her shoulder and walked toward home plate. "You better believe it."

"Then you got yourself a deal." Scarlette lowered her mask again. "Get down and dirty, guys."

Eddie stepped onto the pitching rubber. "Hope you're not expecting me to lob it in to you."

She held up her bat, bent her knees, and shifted her weight to her back leg. "Wouldn't dream of it."

He threw it, and Bianca swung. Hard.

And missed.

Scout snickered.

Scarlette raised her catcher's mask. "If she strikes out, it still counts for us not missing a ball, right?"

Bianca sent Scarlette a scowl. "It was one strike. Let a girl get warmed up."

Scarlette shrugged. "No offense. I like cookies."

Bianca choked up on the bat. "A girl after my own heart."

Eddie lined the seams of the baseball up in his palm. "I'll slow it down—"

"Don't you dare." Bianca pointed the end of her bat at Eddie. "Same heat."

"Bet you two cookies she can't even hit it to the pitcher's mound," Tank muttered behind his mitt toward the shortstop.

Bianca dug her foot into the batter's box and widened her stance, pulling her bat farther back. One deep exhale.

Eddie wound up the next pitch, and when it crossed the plate, Bianca whacked it over the center fielder's head.

Scarlette jumped to her feet. "Wow, I think you've just become Coach B."

"Coach B?" Bianca smiled and hit the bat against the bottom of her tennis shoes. "That has a nice ring to it."

For the first time since she'd seen him today, Eddie smiled. A deep one, revealing two dimples. No wonder she'd thought he was a movie star the other evening.

Tank bent his knees and put his mitt between his legs. "Everyone gets lucky once. Double or nothing."

Eddie raised his brow, and Bianca smirked. She hit each pitch, and the boys fielded perfectly.

Soon Bianca's arms and sides ached, and thankfully, Eddie put his mitt down inside the bucket. "All right, everyone, a much better second half of practice. I need the field raked and the gear returned to my truck. After everything's picked up, if you need a ride, have a seat on the bleachers."

Zack jogged over from where he and two other boys had been inside a batting cage, throwing pitches. "If I'd known my position on the team was up for grabs, I would have brought my batting glove."

Zack and Eddie each picked up a bucket, while Bianca scooped up a ball that dumped out. "I'm not trying to take anyone's spot. It's been a while since I practiced."

"How long has it been since you played?" asked Eddie.

She shrugged. "My senior year of high school."

Zack ran his knuckles along the scruff on his chin. "That makes one of us."

Bianca stopped. "You guys didn't play ball?"

"The opportunity didn't exactly come up when I was their age." Eddie reached out his hand toward Zack. "I'll load everything. I know you want to meet up with Naya."

Zack sent a grin first to Eddie and then to Bianca. "Good to meet you, Bianca. Don't be a stranger, on or off the field." He waved, and the gate swung closed just as Eddie stepped through. He put up his arm, but when he did, the second bucket of balls tipped.

Bianca grabbed the handle. Her fingers brushed against Eddie's. His gaze snapped to hers, and a rush of warmth spread through her skin.

He cleared his throat. "Thanks for helping."

Bianca moved her hand away and opened the gate fully. "It was . . ." A little embarrassing. "Fun."

She followed him, and he put the equipment in the back of the truck.

"Sorry about earlier." She crossed her arms over her chest. How did one go about asking someone outside of the entertainment industry to fake date them? "I, ah . . . would like to help out more with the team. If you wouldn't mind."

He lowered his brows. "You have time for that?"

"I'd make time." She inhaled long and slow, but it didn't loosen the tightness in her lungs. This was just another part. "I was thinking we could help each other out—again."

He rested his arm on the tailgate of his truck.

Bianca twisted the hem of her T-shirt. "Have you seen that we're trending online?"

Eddie sent his fingers through his hair. "I've seen a picture or two of us. I should have suggested you completely cover your face with my suit jacket quicker. I'm sorry. I've never had to deal with paparazzi before."

The man was apologizing to her for something out of his control.

She touched his arm, and he stared at her fingers. "It's totally not your fault at all." She dropped her hand against her side. "But because of that, I sort of need a favor. Another deal, perhaps? What if I assist you with the kids and also coordinate that meeting you were hoping to have with the mayor?"

Eddie narrowed his eyes. "And in return?"

She barely refrained from wiping her sweating palms on her shorts. "You and I could have a cup of coffee while I'm here filming in Last Chance County. Or eat at a restaurant or two. I'll pay for dinner, of course. Perhaps have a picnic here at the field with the kids. Even at the park, walking—"

"You're asking me out?" His tone didn't seem all that welcoming.

Bianca wanted to cover her face now. An actress really should be better at this. "Here's the thing. I was supposed to be sort of fake dating . . . someone else to help promote the film. Not that anyone was supposed to know that. But after you rescued me . . . well, once the media gets ahold of something . . ." She blew out a breath. "Now it kind of needs to be you."

She squeezed her eyes shut, but at his silence, she peeked through her lashes.

His brows lifted. "You want us to . . . fake date? That's really a thing?" He glanced at her and then back at the field. Then he frowned.

Not a good sign. "Only a couple of outings. It's asking a lot, I know, but I really could use a teammate's help, please." Why did her voice sound so unsteady?

Eddie shook his head. "I don't think faking a relationship would be a good idea. Those kids . . . it's important that they see me as reliable, trustworthy, and a truth speaker."

Reliable. The word that Nathan's lawyer had claimed she wasn't when she'd testified about Nathan's second phone that she'd found in her purse the day the police had shown up. The one that had gone missing after she'd surrendered it to a different officer days later.

She backed up. "I understand." Her career was sinking faster than the tabloids had predicted the day Nathan had first been indicted.

Eddie's fingers landed on her elbow. "I don't think you do. Most of these kids don't have ideal family situations. Most of the time, I'm the only one who keeps their word in their life. I can't have a relationship that's a lie. Kids are smart. They'd know it, and it would prove to them again that adults let them down."

"I understand about adults letting people down," she half mumbled as she took a step toward her car.

Scarlette popped up from behind the other side of the truck, and Bianca put her hand to her thumping chest.

A smirk covered the girl's face. "Or, Coach, you could make us all pinkie swear to the fake-dating deal, and then Coach B could pay to have our indoor rec center built." Her pigtails swung behind her as she marched around the truck bed. She put her fists on her hips. "The grant money to cover the down payment still hasn't come in yet, right? This would be like double-stamping it to make sure we get enough funds."

Eddie aimed his finger at Scarlette. "Eavesdropping is not cool."

"Neither is the word *cool* anymore, but Coach B needs help, and she can help us right back. Can't you? You're a movie star. And movie stars got money."

Bianca held on to her practiced smile. One would assume actors had money.

Eddie sighed. "It's *have* money, not *got* money, and it's rude to talk about someone's income or force them to do something for money."

Bianca rested her right elbow on the back of the truck bed.

"Extortion is totally not cool." She'd had enough money issues from Nathan to last a lifetime. "I don't know what kind of center you're wanting to build, but you're probably talking millions and millions of dollars, which, movie star or not, I don't have. But I can offer my endorsement for the center, do some fundraising, and give a donation *if* the movie is successful."

The word *if* couldn't be avoided.

Scarlette winced. "Thought it was a good plan, but that long word sounds like jail time."

Eddie crossed his arms. "Extortion sort of means blackmail."

Scarlette hung her head. "Oh."

The end of practice was quickly resembling the botched beginning. "But I'm all for helping. A teammate helping another teammate."

Scarlette pushed out her bottom lip. "Could you still make a promise to help each other? Do a handshake-friend-deal thing. No need to spit. That's too messy. I'll be your witness."

Eddie pinched the bridge of his nose. "Scarlette, you're going to make an incredible lawyer one day, but Scar, I can't let money trump what I know is right."

His words hit Bianca hard. Was what she was asking him to do wrong? "You're right, money and fame don't come before truth. Just please take the time to reconsider the deal. My job kind of depends on it."

Scarlette pressed her palms together under her chin. "Counteroffer her, Coach. Ask to be in her movie along with funds for the rec center. No, wait!" She snapped her fingers. "Ask that both you and *me* be in the movie, and then Will's gonna wish he'd chosen me to partner—"

Eddie held up his palm to Scarlette. His deep-brown gaze shined not with hope but pity. "Sorry. It's a no." He met Bianca's gaze. "I'm sure you'll be able to find another man to take my place easily enough."

Strike two. If he didn't reconsider, Bianca would lose everything she'd worked for.

Bianca's fingers trembled as she pulled her keys out of her pocket. "Thank you for letting me practice with the team. Playing ball was more fun than I remembered."

With a nod, he headed to the field with Scarlette chasing him.

Bianca tugged out her ponytail holder and rewrapped her hair in a bun. There couldn't be a strike three. She'd have to come up with a new plan. One that didn't include fake dating anyone.

SIX

THE FIRE STATION'S WORKOUT ROOM LIGHTS seemed to scowl down at Eddie. If only the music thumping in his earbuds would drown out Bianca's plea from the other night.

Just please take the time to reconsider the deal. My job kind of depends on it.

He'd thought his first practice as head coach had been destined for destruction when she'd tried to field in that dress. He never should have allowed her and the kids to talk him into letting her practice.

No, she hadn't gotten hurt on his watch, but it hadn't been beneficial to the team for him to falter in leadership. However, then she'd returned, dressed to practice, and her fakeness had disappeared too. More like someone the kids could look up to.

Like the woman who had mistaken him for someone else at the auction. The one he'd accidentally flirted with. He'd been the one to offer her a mutual deal the night of the fire. But a dance differed from a fake date. Or two.

And the email he'd received this morning proved that he couldn't lose his team's trust. Now he only needed to figure out a way to tell the kids the bad news.

He adjusted his shoulders on the bench beneath his back as Zack moved into position to be Eddie's spotter. "Can you hit me with another ten pounds?"

With the bench press bar separating the two of them, Zack turned for the weight rack. "Two fives coming up."

Eddie positioned his hands on the bar above his chest. "Make it tens for each side."

Zack's hands remained empty of the requested extra weights. "Is there a reason why you're trying to outdo your max weight during today's shift?"

Eddie kept his focus on the ceiling tile with a faint dark stain. "No better time to get stronger than the present."

Zack simply crossed his arms. "What's in the present that you need to get stronger for?"

Sometimes it wasn't wise to spend so much time with the crew. They learned too much. Which reason did Zack want? The one where Bianca had yet again been in his dreams last night, and he'd only got a handful of hours of rest. Or that an even bigger nightmare had landed in his inbox this morning. One from the mayor's assistant.

Eddie huffed. "The grant money's not happening for the youth center."

Zack relaxed his stance and then picked an additional ten-pound weight off the rack. "Sorry, man. I thought you were only moody because you somehow botched things with Bianca the other night."

"There was nothing to botch. She's a movie star."

Zack secured one of the clips on the bar to keep the weights from sliding. "Pretty sure movie stars are still people. You might have more in common than you think. Naya showed me an interview where Bianca talks about her faith."

Eddie loosened his grip on the bar. Did they share more than he realized?

He shook his head. Not what mattered at the moment. "The mayor didn't even have the decency to tell me himself. Not that he even remembered me when I returned to his house after the fire."

Zack slid the weight onto the left side of the bar. "Have you prayed for another way to raise the funds?"

Eddie froze. Not exactly.

Bianca's beautiful face popped up in Eddie's mind, followed by Scarlette's pouty one.

Had God provided another way?

He rolled his shoulders, but the pressure remained, just like the truth. Fake dating a movie star was not an option. No matter if she'd looked like the perfect coaching assistant, with dirt on her cheek and her shirt half untucked from her oversized shorts when she'd returned.

If the woman under the facade had asked him to go have coffee with him, and if she served the Lord too, that might have been a different story.

But he'd finished being the casual dating guy.

Zack grabbed the second ten-pound weight and added it to the opposite side. Eddie inhaled slowly and then exhaled as he pushed the weight bar up.

"Come on, Rice." Zack spotted his hands under the quaking bar. "A little more."

Eddie gritted his teeth and willed his arms to give more. The bar lifted higher. Then another inch. At that exact moment, Bianca's voice reentered his mind.

There's no one else it can be except you.

The look in her gaze had been defeat. She hadn't been pretending when she'd said that.

Sometimes his compassion felt like a weakness, allowing others to manipulate him. Yet it could be a strength . . . where he saw the true heart of the situation—the person.

The weights clanked against the safety bar, and Zack helped center the bar into its resting position.

Eddie wiped his palms on his shorts. Did her job really depend on him being in some pictures with her? "Give me a second. I want one more try."

He needed something to go right today.

Zack stepped to the end of the weights. "Let me exchange the tens for fives. You'll nail that and still get a new max-out number."

Except at that moment, the fire alarm blared.

"Rescue Squad 5. Building collapse. Person trapped." The dispatcher gave the address.

Zack barely beat Eddie out the door. They raced down the station's hallway and into the open bay area where the fire truck awaited them. Ridge and Bryce sprinted right behind.

Eddie jumped into his turnout pants and then boots. He had his jacket on before any of his other crew members. He grabbed his helmet and gloves and hopped into his seat.

Once Bryce slammed his door shut, Ridge pulled the fire truck out of the station and flipped on the lights and sirens.

Zack bumped his fist against Eddie's arm. "You ever gonna tell me what happened between you and Bianca at your truck?"

"Wait." Ridge honked the horn and eased them through a crowded intersection. "Rice wasn't here yesterday when she showed up. How'd he see her?"

Zack leaned closer to Ridge. "After the secretary gushed over how much she loved one of Bia Pearl's movies, she mentioned that Eddie coached a youth baseball league on the south side of town. Bia Pearl showed up there. Twice."

Ridge weaved the truck through a two-lane road lined with parked cars on each side. "Twice?"

Eddie watched as they zoomed through a stop sign. That was kind of how he felt about the current conversation—a little out of control. "Shouldn't we focus on the rescue we're heading into and not Bianca?"

It was Bryce's turn to smirk. "*Bianca*, not Bia Pearl, is it? No wonder you were trying to raise your max lift today."

Eddie eyed his lieutenant, who shrugged and then added, "I overheard as I walked by the weight room."

Eddie pulled his jacket away from his chest. "Do you use everyone's first and last name when you talk about them now?"

Bryce widened his grin. "Don't know. I haven't known any movie stars."

Ridge slowed the truck when he got to a gate across the road. "This says it's our location."

A boundary fence stretched on both sides of the gate. A row of picketers marched on the grassy sidewalk, sandwiched between the road and fence.

The gate arm lifted, and a man in a security uniform with a walkie-talkie pressed up near his mustached mouth ran out to them and pointed ahead. "Straight back toward the city scene."

"The city scene?" Eddie stuck his head out the window. A parking lot stretched before them. Trees bordered a sidewalk, and through the branches there was a row of trailers. One of the doors had the word *wardrobe* on it.

Eddie swallowed. "Where are we exactly?"

Zack grimaced. "Pretty sure it's Last Chance County's new movie set."

Eddie's stomach ached like someone had punched him in the gut. Was Bianca hurt?

Another security guard held up his hands, and Ridge parked. Everyone jumped out of the truck.

"They're this way." The security guard heaved out a breath as he stood beside Bryce, wiping sweat off his brow. "But your truck's not going to fit."

"What do we have?" Bryce asked.

"Somehow a set building collapsed, and a woman's leg is pinned."

A woman. Like Bianca?

Eddie ran to the side of the truck and opened the correct compartment for the stored jack.

As Eddie followed the others down a sidewalk path skirted with trees, he came around the corner of four two-story buildings. A crowd stood around a heaping mess of downed wood and pieces of drywall. The dark-headed woman was half covered with a stack of broken boards. She had the same slender frame as Bianca. With all the dust covering her face, he couldn't quite tell who lay trapped.

Eddie's chest tightened. But then the woman squatting next to Bryce looked at him.

"Bianca." Her name flew from his mouth.

She wasn't trapped, but another woman was. One of the closest boards near the trapped woman's thigh seemed to be connected by a cable or a thick wire.

"Lieutenant! We might have a live wire." The last thing they needed was for anyone to get shocked on top of the already dangerous situation.

One end of the cable disappeared into the pile of wood above his head, and the other reached up to a telephone pole. He spun around. Zack and Ridge headed toward Bryce. A security officer in front of the formed crowd stepped forward.

Eddie pointed to the cable. "Can you find someone to make sure all the electricity is shut off?"

The security officer opened his mouth but then snapped it shut. "On it."

Eddie carried the jack to Bryce, who knelt next to the pile of wood and debris that lay on top of the woman's legs.

Bianca held the trapped woman's hand. Her fearful gaze sank into his heart.

He set the jack into position under the leaning debris. "You've got to get out of here."

Bianca squeezed the woman's hand, resting in her palm. "I'm not leaving Heidi."

The woman lying on the ground released a scream—one that Eddie would hear in his dreams for nights—but she didn't move her legs.

Bryce met his gaze. "I noticed it." He grabbed his radio. "I need a stretcher and a neck brace." Then to Eddie, "First, let's get the boards off her."

"Want me to finish placing the jack or start throwing off the boards?" Eddie stepped over a section of wood with three nails sticking upward and broken glass covering the concrete to get to the other side of Heidi.

Bryce came directly over the trapped woman's face. "Ma'am, we're with Last Chance County Fire Department. I'm Lieutenant Crawford, and we're going to get you out of here."

Bianca patted the woman's hand. "Her name's Heidi."

Bryce narrowed his gaze at Bianca. "And you need to—"

"P-please don't leave me, Bia." Tears leaked out of Heidi's eyes, and blood coated her hair.

Bianca wrapped her other hand around the woman's elbow. "We won't, Heidi. I'm so sorry."

"I've got the stretcher and brace." Ridge's voice rattled back on the radio.

Then came Zack's voice. "Trace and Kianna pulled in."

Eddie eyed the pile of leaning wooden beams. "I need confirmation on that wire."

Bryce pointed to the people crowding in. "Make sure *everyone* stands back."

Eddie understood Bryce's tone. *Everyone* included Bianca.

The security guard pushed through the crowd and stopped before the debris. "Wire is a prop."

A prop? He'd take it. Eddie slid in the jack and pumped it upward. The pile of broken wood and drywall groaned, but not as much as Heidi.

Bryce dropped to his knees. "We've got a piece of wood refusing to lift off her shins."

Eddie cranked the jack higher. A top piece of board slid off and angled straight for where Bianca knelt.

Eddie leaped in the direction of the falling board. "Bianca! Get out of here."

The board stopped on an extended nail poking through a broken two-by-four.

Bianca clung to the woman's hand. "I promised her I wouldn't leave."

Eddie shoved the piece of board to the ground. "And I promise you'll make it harder for us if you're in the way."

Bianca's eyes speared him, but then she released her grip and climbed through the jagged debris.

Eddie took the vacant spot beside Heidi, who breathed quick, shallow breaths. Her eyes closed and her fingers fisted the sides of her pants.

Bryce moved a splintered section of a two-by-four and wedged it under the gap beside the woman. But the heap didn't move. "We need the other jack."

Both Zack and Ridge raced toward them, the jack in hand along with the brace and stretcher.

Eddie placed his face in front of Heidi's. Her coloring had paled even more.

Ridge adjusted a yellow backboard beside the woman. "What's the plan?"

Zack set the other jack down.

Eddie took out his flashlight and shined it into the space the previous jack had lifted. "Her leg's pinned farther back."

Eddie took the other jack. "I'll go in deeper and set the jack."

Bryce shook his head. "The heap might cave in. It will be safer to do it from the outside."

Bianca stepped into the debris, closer to the woman again. No. He had to get that woman out of here before she did something crazy, like go in the hole herself.

Eddie gritted his teeth. "Safer for me, but would it be quicker for her?"

Bryce held his gaze. Then nodded. "Get it done."

Eddie shifted over the piece of wood that held the first jack. He pushed in the second jack, then quickly pumped it. Once. Twice. His heartbeat thumped at twice the rhythm.

Ridge readied the fasteners on the brace and lowered beside Heidi. "I'm going to place this around your neck."

"Rice, I think we're clear enough," said Zack.

Eddie paused and glanced at the team.

Bryce leaned over the woman's face. "Ma'am, we're going to get you out of here on the count of three."

Zack and Ridge took over the positions around Heidi as Eddie held the jack level.

"One. Two. Three!" Bryce yelled as they transferred Heidi over to the board.

Eddie eased down the second jack, but a section of wood on the ground made him stop. Deep V cuts had been sawn into the board.

"Foster and Stephens, get her to the ambulance," Bryce commanded.

Eddie picked up the sawed board. "Lieutenant."

Bryce turned.

Eddie shoved aside a section of smashed ceiling tile and grabbed another piece of wood that had identical cuts. "Please tell me I'm seeing things and these aren't cuts to weaken the structure."

Bryce's shoulders sank as if he'd sighed internally. "We are on a movie set. Maybe, like the wire, those boards are props." He lifted his gaze. Another security guard stood behind a woman wearing glasses next to Bianca.

As Bryce waved him over, the balding guard first pointed to his chest and then jogged over.

"Yes, sir?" He looked at Bryce and then flicked his gaze to Eddie. Did the man know something?

"Who is in charge on the set?" Bryce asked.

The security guard wiped sweat off his forehead. "The director, Leo. Or actually, the producer, though he only calls. Leo is…" He pointed at the alley that led toward the parking lot. "He's there with the police."

Officer Olivia Tazwell, a toned blonde, stood beside Leo. She nodded as the director put his hands on his hips.

Bryce and Eddie neared the alley, and Olivia spoke first. "Leo's the movie director, and he's—"

"Thankful that you rescued one of our stunt doubles, but…" His lips formed a tight line, and wrinkles morphed around his pointed nose. "Heidi's now safe in the ambulance. I don't want to sound uncaring, but how long will it take to get your crew out? If I don't get this shot in tonight, it's going to cost production another ten grand at least to reshoot."

Eddie squeezed his fingers around the cut board in his grip. Was this guy serious?

Bryce stiffened next to Eddie. "Sir, was the collapse of the building part of the script?"

Leo's phone buzzed in his palm. "It's going to have to be now. There's no way we have the time to rebuild this set."

"Lieutenant," came Ridge's voice over the walkie. "We've got a situation here at the truck."

Bryce eyed Olivia before responding to Ridge. "I'll be right there." He lowered his voice to Eddie. "I'm leaving you in charge."

Once Bryce took off in a jog, Eddie moved one of the two-by-fours toward Olivia, who frowned. "Is this cut board a movie prop?"

Leo took the board. "If it is, it's nothing that I've ordered within the last day or two."

That wasn't exactly conclusive. "Sir, I'm afraid the building may have been tampered with."

Leo closed his eyes. "Thought we'd have one good day."

Olivia pulled out a notebook. "What kinds of problems have you been running into?"

Leo typed on his phone. "Some props have gone missing. A fence lock was destroyed, and protesters have ruined more than one of our takes. Don't get me started on the drainage issue on the honeywagon. It's as if Last Chance County isn't the perfect spot for my movie as promised." The man dug his fingers into his hair. "How long are we shut down for?"

Olivia wrote something on her notepad. "I'm going to need any security footage and names of everyone that was here. I'll need to interview all the witnesses."

"That's practically the entire crew," Leo spat, and then closed his eyes again. "Sorry. We'll help in any way we can." He snapped his fingers, and the woman who had been standing beside Bianca jogged over. "Grace can print off a list of everyone who was on set."

Grace unlocked her phone. "Do you need a hard copy, or will an emailed spreadsheet work?"

"Email will work," Olivia replied, and then to Leo said, "Why don't you head over to my car. I'll take your formal statement first. We'll let the fire department get a jump on their work so the movie won't be held up longer than necessary."

Eddie took a step back. "I've got to get everything taped off."

Leo held up his hand. "If we're at least fifty feet away from the roped-off area, could we resume filming?"

Before Eddie could give words that probably matched Olivia's scowling facial expression, the balding security guard returned. He blew out a breath and extended a thumb drive. "My boss has all the footage of the week put on the zip drive. However, the camera—" He tilted his chin back behind Eddie.

Everyone turned to where a telephone pole stood between a tree planted in a huge pot and a building with a purple awning.

"—had been looped. Didn't even capture the collapse."

"I got the collapse from the backside, at least." Leo shook his head. "I really am cursed. Or this film. Maybe both. I never should have agreed to a movie about the Valencia gem."

Olivia took the thumb drive. "Thank you . . ."

"Thad. Thad Walker, ma'am," the security guard stammered.

Another police officer, Junior Ramble, came up beside Olivia. "Ramble, could you take Leo to my car, and Mr. Walker, could you round up those who want to give their statements next?"

"Of course. Right away." Thad answered with far more warmth than Leo, whose once-reddened face had become an ashen color.

But Grace didn't move. She shifted on her feet until the men had walked in the direction of the cop car. Once they were out of earshot, she stole a glance at Eddie before squaring her shoulders up to Olivia.

"Leo's worried about the timeline and the financial backing." Grace nibbled on her bottom lip before checking over her shoulder to where Bianca listened to a woman who had tears streaming down her face.

"But without cameras to prove what happened . . ." There was another glance toward Eddie. Who was this woman exactly? "What if someone could be here on set undercover? Looking for clues."

Olivia shook her head. "I don't have that kind of authority to assign. With being short-staffed as is, an undercover stint would probably be difficult to arrange."

Grace faced Eddie. "What about you, Eddie Rice?"

Him?

Eddie ran his finger along the collar of his turnout jacket. "I don't think my crew offers that kind of help. But there are great private security options in town."

"I think you're exactly the man for this particular job. Especially after your daring rescue of Bia Pearl."

Somehow, this wasn't going to go well. "I believe the woman rescued is named Heidi."

Grace lowered her voice. "It was supposed to be Bianca in that building, not Heidi."

Olivia scowled. "You think someone's after Ms. Pearl?"

"No one is after me." Bianca stepped up beside Grace and whispered something. All Eddie caught was, "He said no, we need to leave it alone."

She didn't bat her lashes or twist her fingers through her hair. Maybe he'd misjudged her when she'd first arrived at the field yesterday.

Bryce jogged up behind them. "Sorry about that."

Eddie widened his stance. "Everything good?"

Bryce sighed. "Nothing an accident report shouldn't take care of. Now, what did I miss here? Need anything else from us, Officer? One of my guys is already taping off the area."

Olivia tilted her head in Bianca's direction. "It seems Bia Pearl was originally supposed to have been in the building."

Bryce's eyebrows lifted.

Grace spun toward Bryce. "Since the police are overloaded with cases, I've suggested Eddie Rice hang around the set."

Eddie crossed his arms. That wasn't how it'd gone down.

Bianca slid her arm around Grace's. "Eddie's got enough on his plate. I'm sure the police will find all the clues they need. Thank you so much for saving Heidi. We'd better go check on her."

Grace did not budge. "The crews here will probably remember little details about the moments leading up to the collapse and are probably less likely to call the police to give an update; however, they might mention it in conversation to someone they view as a buddy."

This needed to stop. He was all for solving this case, but this was a rehash of Bianca's suggested deal at the baseball field.

Eddie squared his shoulders. "Lieutenant, they want me to pretend to be Bianca's . . . date. This is a horrible idea. Rescue doesn't need me out of rotation. If I'm gone from the station, then they'll be a man down. Plus, I'm a youth mentor. The kids can't catch me in a lie."

Or he'd be a hypocrite.

Olivia's phone dinged. Her expression puckered. She turned her screen toward Bryce and Eddie.

Eddie caught the mayor's name and the words *The movie must be able to keep filming.*

Bryce dipped his chin. "Gotta love election year."

Apparently, they were being strong-armed by Gregory.

Instead of supporting the movie, the mayor should support the kids of Last Chance County.

Eddie eyed Bianca, and Scarlette's words popped into his head.

Could you still make a promise to help each other?

Zack might have been right. Maybe God had provided another way, and Eddie had dismissed it too quickly. What if Eddie, Bianca, and the mayor could all work together?

If Eddie was seen with Bianca, he could help protect her. *If* someone was actually after her. Assumptions and gossip over their relationship wouldn't exactly be him lying.

Nothing like the empty promises his own mother had fed him growing up. The ones he refused to allow the kids he mentored to endure.

However, one thing was certain: he needed another way to raise money for the youth center. A movie star's assistance with fundraising would provide more than he could do on his own.

Lord, is this Your plan? Or am I trying to make it the plan?

Bryce gave Eddie a look as if he could read his thoughts, but Eddie couldn't decipher which way his lieutenant leaned.

Finally, Bryce said, "It's up to you first. Then double-check it with the chief."

Eddie glanced at Bianca before focusing on Grace. "Before I make a decision, I'd like to talk to the mayor."

Grace's thumbs flew against her phone's screen. "No problem. Here." She held out her phone to Eddie. "It's calling his direct number. Leo practically has him on speed dial, which means I do too." She shimmied the screen.

He took Grace's phone and placed it to his ear just as Gregory's voice said, "Is there still a problem with the police restrictions?"

Eddie stepped a few feet away from the others. "Sir, this is Eddie Rice. The firefighter—"

"Yes, yes. Sounds like you've been a hero once again for our town."

Eddie shifted the phone to his other ear. "Sir, just doing my job. Speaking of . . . Grace, the director's assistant, wants me to hang around the film set as an extra set of eyes and ears."

"That sounds fabulous. Yes. I'll talk to your chief and make sure—"

"Actually, sir, before you finalize anything, since surveillance isn't part of my firefighter job, I thought we could discuss something."

The mayor lowered his voice. "I'm listening."

Olivia and Bryce spoke to one another, but both Grace and Bianca watched Eddie. By agreeing to hang around Bianca, he'd help make sure everyone on set was safe, and the youth might benefit too. Wouldn't it be a win-win? "I'll stay on the set and make sure the movie goes forward, and you—"

"Son, you might need a reminder that I can't be bought."

Maybe Eddie needed a lesson on extortion like Scarlette. "Of course, sir. I . . . could you just take another look at the grant? A youth center would help give the kids of this town a safe place to play in the winter."

"Listen, I can't say yes to this for political reasons, but I promise the grant will be awarded fairly to a nonprofit in our town."

Bianca ran the tip of her finger along one of the stitches at her hairline. The injury she'd gotten in the fire.

And that's when Eddie knew his answer. Grant or not, wasn't it his job to help the people of their community? No matter how long they resided in it. "Then, sir, I'll do my best to keep Last Chance County safe."

He only hoped this decision wouldn't be one more thing in his life to regret.

SEVEN

BIANCA'S FLIP-FLOP-COVERED FEET FROZE ON the top step of her set trailer. "Oh!"

Eddie had one foot on her bottom step, and was dressed in dark-washed jeans and a fitted burgundy shirt that made his brown eyes pop with a whole new meaning to the word *brooding*.

Words. It was past the time for actual words out of her mouth. She licked her lips. "You're . . . here."

Early. She was supposed to have said *You're early*. No wonder she spoke better with a memorized script. On second thought, maybe tonight's "outing" was not the best idea. He'd been at the set for half the day. He had to be tired, no matter what the fresh set of clothes showed.

His expression proved that yes, indeed, she'd made things even more awkward. "Do you not need me anymore?"

Bianca juggled her lipstick, a clutch, earrings, and two different pairs of shoes in her arms. "I still need you . . . That doesn't mean what it sounds like." Except maybe it did.

Guess she didn't have time to shoot over to wardrobe and inspect what felt like the fiftieth outfit-and-shoes option she'd tried on in the full-length mirror.

She plopped her black heels that crisscrossed up her ankles down on the top step and tossed her red wedges and beloved flip-flops back into the trailer. "One second. Let me finish getting ready real quick."

Eddie cleared his throat. "I can go wait in my truck until—"

"It's my fault." Grace raced over. "Sorry. Apparently, I told you both two different times. I promise I won't make that mistake ever again."

Bianca secured the last strap on her heels and then slipped in her earrings. "Appreciate your help, Grace." As Bianca straightened, her nose twitched. "Care to be my mirror? Is this outfit first-date worthy? Sorry. Not *date*. I mean . . . whatever we're officially or unofficially calling this between us."

Grace tilted her head.

Eddie's Adam's apple bobbed.

In the silence, Bianca's nose twitched once. Then again.

Oh no. She spun around and sneezed into her elbow.

"God bless you," Eddie's baritone murmured.

Bianca blinked her watery eyes. "Thanks."

She brushed her fingers along the imaginary wrinkles on her black halter jumpsuit. At least there were no paparazzi to repeat the horrid picture of her last public sneeze. Which had been on the stands in court. Bad press really was a thing—especially if it produced horrid memes.

Bianca's gaze lifted, and this time, her attention landed on Grace. Her grin proved how pleased she was with this fake-dating deal.

Please, God, let this not be another mistake.

She, the movie, and even Grace had a lot riding on this outing.

Once her shoes hit the ground, she found the reason for her sneeze. "You brought me flowers."

Eddie released what might have been a grunt and shifted the bouquet of roses into an upright position from against his thigh. How had she missed those? Red blooms tipped with glitter while their ends were wrapped in gold-and-white chevron tissue paper and completed by a gold ribbon. Ritzy and bright and not at all what she'd picture Eddie might pick out for his date.

Not that she really knew him. But they did look like a bouquet Nathan would have brought home, despite her explaining her allergies countless times.

"Aren't they gorgeous?" Grace pushed up her glasses. "They barely arrived in time. That's why I was late. Well, that and Riley stopped me on my way. Perfect with your outfit, right? Though I think they may clash with Eddie's shirt. Maybe we should go to wardrobe and find him something else—"

"No," Eddie answered at the same time Bianca said, "I like his shirt."

Grace's gaze bounced between them. "Fine. No wardrobe changes. But at least one of you needs to smile." She held up her phone. "He can do the whole Heathcliff thing, but, Bianca, you have to be the smitten movie star."

Right. Always in some kind of role.

Grace waved her hand. "Get closer together for some pictures."

Bianca's nose itched, but she reached for the flowers. Except, when she took a step closer, one of her heels sank into the soft dirt, and she wobbled. Then pitched sideways.

Before Bianca could get her hands out to brace herself against a fall, arms wrapped around her and anchored her against a solid body.

Eddie's concerned gaze zeroed in. "You okay?"

The smell of cedarwood, mint, and a slight citrus scent trumped the flowers and enfolded her as she pressed her hand against his chest. "Apparently, I have a bad habit of picking the wrong outfits."

Eddie raised his right brow. "I see that."

But there was nothing wrong with his outfit. If Eddie in a suit made him worthy of a movie contract, the sight of him in a pair of jeans was somehow even better. More like this was the real him—a guy who saved lives. Cared about local kids. The kind of man she could fall for. Which would, of course, be a terrible idea.

"Don't move." Grace instructed. "That's a perfect pose."

Eddie tensed beneath Bianca's touch.

"Now…" Grace inspected her phone screen. "Eddie, could you move your lips up on the ends?"

Eddie's glower deepened. "Whatever happened to allowing me not to smile?"

Which resulted in Bianca's real smile. The one that ticked up higher on the left.

Grace moaned and stomped behind Bianca. She scooped up something—the forgotten bouquet. "They got trampled."

She pointed them right under Bianca's nose, and Bianca released another sneeze.

Eddie stepped between them. "The flowers might do better in some water."

Grace's face lit up. "True. We could take some more photos later after they perk back up. Do you have a vase inside, Bianca?"

"Does a coffee mug count?"

Grace stroked the wilting petals. "These guys need more than an old mug." Her watch buzzed on her wrist, and Grace gasped. "I'll find us a vase. You better get going. I don't want you guys to be late."

As they walked toward the parking lot, Grace headed in the direction of the props trailer, probably in search of a vase.

Eddie slid his hands into his pockets. "If you tell her you're allergic to those flowers, then both of us will be saved from taking more photos later."

Bianca's shoulder brushed against his, and a shiver coursed through her body. "She's been so awesome, helping me with things. And she looked so excited. I didn't want to hurt her feelings."

Eddie huffed. "Good to know. You care about her feelings but not mine."

"That's not—" Then she noticed his smirk. She purposely knocked her shoulder into his. "I think you can survive a few more pictures."

"That's yet to be decided."

They passed the staged ambulance that would be the scene location for tomorrow afternoon's filming, and Bianca clenched her purse in her hand. The flowers did remind her that she needed to send Heidi another bouquet. Grace could probably find Heidi's home address, since she'd been released after the successful surgery to set her broken leg.

The trees outlining the start of the parking lot swayed in the breeze. "Thanks for all you guys did for Heidi yesterday. She's been promised a full recovery."

However, the road there wouldn't be an easy trip. And if Bianca hadn't requested a stunt double last minute, then Heidi never would have been injured.

"It wasn't your fault." The softness to his voice brought tears to her eyes.

"If I was the supposed target, then it is my fault."

Eddie's shoe hit the top of a persistent dandelion that grew through the sidewalk crack. "So far, I personally haven't found anything on set that would point to you being targeted."

Bianca shifted her purse to her other hand. "Except the cut boards."

He pulled out his keys. "Even those don't prove that *you're* the target. The movie in general could be the target."

She ducked under a low-hanging branch. "Grace must have forgotten to mention that the limo is going to drive us. Perks of dating—I mean having an outing with a movie star."

Eddie fisted his keys. "Right."

The limousine idled beside the first row of parking spaces. It wasn't like the limo driver, Justin, would mind staying in tonight.

"If you want to drive, I'll go tell Justin. I'm sure he'd be glad to have a night off."

Eddie spun his keyring around his middle finger. "Might want to see my truck before you make your decision. Grouchy lady sure didn't appreciate it the other night." A sigh seemed to rumble across his shoulders. "Maybe that's where I went wrong," he mumbled.

"Wrong with what?"

He shrugged. "Nothing. I got an email from Janice this week. It didn't improve my assumptions about her."

Bianca wrinkled her nose. "I understand now. You're saying I'm as grouchy as her. Well, that's not true at all. If you're more comfortable driving your truck, it's what I want too."

He actually smiled. Or at least, it was a half grin that pulled out one dimple. "I'll go pull it around."

She had been right. Justin loved the idea of a free night. Eddie brought over his black truck—it was a couple of decades old, but the paint had been buffed into a shiny display.

She opened the passenger-side door and climbed into the seat.

Eddie had his hand relaxed on top of the steering wheel. "Last chance to change your mind."

Her stomach chose that moment to grumble.

Eddie put his truck into gear. "The mighty actress has spoken."

She buckled in and pressed her lips together to hide her smile. And remembered that she'd never put on her red lipstick.

She pulled down the visor, but there was no mirror.

At a stop sign, Eddie asked, "What's wrong?"

She opened her clutch. "Looking for a mirror to put on my lipstick." She drew out her phone, set it on selfie mode, and then applied her lipstick.

She pursed her lips together and caught Eddie's lowered brows.

"Did I get some on my face or on my teeth?" She checked her phone again, but the red hue was only on her lips.

He shrugged and turned the truck toward the left. "Thought you looked fine before."

Fine? "Is that your way of saying the lipstick looks bad?"

His focus remained on the road. "Never said that."

"You didn't *not* say that either. I don't know you well enough yet to be able to read you."

He grunted and then slowed down the truck.

Bianca glanced out the window. "The buildings are really tall, pressed up together here."

Eddie laughed. "Says the girl who lives in LA."

"Lived." She adjusted her seat belt across her chest. "I don't anymore." She didn't know where she wanted her new home to be. "I mean, this downtown looks different from the one I grew up in. The tallest building there was the church. Its steeple used to be taller than the courthouse until someone supposedly climbed it and sawed it off."

Eddie tapped his thumb along the steering wheel. "I think that's why I like Last Chance County so much."

Bianca leaned her shoulders back and glanced at Eddie. "It reminds you of your hometown?"

Eddie wrinkled his nose. "No."

"Where did you grow up—"

"We're almost there." Eddie flipped down his sun visor.

Only a country music song filled the truck cab.

Back to business, apparently.

Pops of color on the store signs filled the street in front of them. None of them gave Bianca the right words to ask more about Eddie's hometown.

Perhaps, like her, his past wasn't filled with only happy memories but also mistakes that still affected him.

He turned down a one-way street and stopped for a row of people on the crosswalk. He released a low whistle. "Main is packed. Guess the picketers have to eat sometime too."

Bianca secured her purse against her lap. "Better here than breaking into the studio again."

That stunt had cost them two hours of filming. Longer production time meant she went longer without her much-needed bigger paycheck.

Eddie put on his turn signal. "We're going to have to walk. Those heels may not have been a good idea. If you want me to swing back by your trailer to get you another pair of shoes, I can. Or I can drop you off at the door and then park."

In the movies, this moment would be when the audience murmured an "aww." Instead, Bianca simply smiled. Was it really him thinking of her needs, or was he postponing going out with her?

The money for the kids' rec center was probably the only reason he hadn't already made a U-turn. "As much as I want to be in a pair of flip-flops, I've got to play the part. We both need to walk."

Eddie put on his turn signal. "More pretending it is."

Silence fell until he finished parallel parking.

She went to open her door, but a car zipped past her window.

He opened his driver's-side door and paused. "Want me to come around and open your door, or do you want to slide across and climb out my door? Though the second option won't exactly be movie-star worthy."

She slid right over the truck's bench and then realized her mistake. He hadn't exited fully, and she was pressed right against his side.

He swallowed. Then hopped out. But instead of leaving her to catch her breath, he extended his hand to her.

She took his offer, his grip strong and warm, and the urge to lace her fingers through his shot through her.

She dropped his hand and locked all her fingers around her purse.

Boundaries, like in acting with any attractive costar, needed to be set. Didn't matter that the butterflies in her stomach were confused.

People flowed down the sidewalk ahead, some looking at their phones, others carrying shopping bags. One woman struggled with the wheels of her baby stroller.

Someone here would recognize her, and the plan would run smoothly.

Bianca slipped her hand onto his elbow.

Eddie tensed and stopped walking.

She removed her hand. "Sorry. I'm so used to—"

"Pretending." His voice was flat.

She shifted on her heels. "Are you changing your mind about tonight?"

About our deal.

He extended his elbow. "No, we both still need each other. I'm not used to . . ."

Dating. Actresses. Me.

He slid his keys into his pocket. "To the spotlight."

She rested her hand on his elbow, and they strolled past a store that had teddy bears in the windows. "You picked up on my flower allergies, offered to take me back to get more comfortable shoes, and you helped me from your truck." She tapped her finger on his arm. "I have a feeling you know exactly how to make this a memorable evening. Remembering to smile once or twice wouldn't hurt."

"No promises."

As the people on the sidewalk stared, he drew closer to her. "We may have a bit of a wait at the restaurant. I know it's a weeknight, but you'd be surprised how many hit up Rachael's."

Bianca put on her smile. "I read the reviews. But Grace called and made a reservation."

He stepped past an elderly couple shuffling into a card store. Then he dipped his head closer to her. "Rachael's only makes reservations for parties of ten or more."

She had not read that online. "I guess they made an exception for us."

Eddie put space between them. "You mean for *you*. I think I'm starting to understand."

"Understand what?"

"Did Grace call the restaurant and then hope gossip would take over? Or has she planted specific people to take pictures this evening? Like that woman with the stroller."

Bianca held her smile as they passed a blonde teen, who did a double take. "Sometimes paparazzi are called directly," Bianca whispered. "But I don't think anyone was tipped off tonight. I thought organic and low-key would be better. Someone will take a photo of us somewhere and tag me, and then the rumor mill will start, and if not, Grace will—"

"She is here!" the blonde teen screeched.

A group of teen girls each waved a phone and a notebook in their hands. However, it was actually the mom pushing the jogging stroller that beat the others to Bianca.

The mother positioned the stroller horizontally on the sidewalk, slowing the teens, and pulled out her phone. "Selfie! My followers are going to love this."

The teen with a skirt and tank top held out her notebook. "Can I get your autograph, Bia?"

"Wait!" Her shorter friend shimmied her legs and shoved over her notebook. "Can we get a picture first? I can't believe you get to be in a movie with Carter Cane."

The girl wearing her hair in a bun grinned. "How many times do you get to kiss him?"

Eddie stepped away from Bianca.

She tightened her hold, but he still slipped from her. He leaned against the nearest shop window and crossed his arms.

Hard to get pictures together when they were so far apart.

Notebook girl's arm dropped against her thigh. "Hold up, is this your boyfriend?"

Bianca's gaze locked on Eddie's.

Bun girl gasped. "He's the firefighter who saved her life. Oh my goodness, you guys are totally together. I need his autograph too."

A storm of emotions settled in Eddie's eyes. The man's one condition was that they didn't lie. How was she supposed to accomplish that?

Eddie hooked his thumb down the sidewalk. "I'm going to make sure our table's ready."

Bianca blew him a kiss. "You're the best."

See, that wasn't a lie. They could do this.

But Eddie clenched his jaw before marching away.

Bun girl let out another squeal. "Him or Carter? How did you even choose?"

The shorter girl held out her camera. It was streaming live. "You saw it here, guys. Bia and her new beau."

Bianca's smile curved down a bit before she caught herself. This was exactly what she wanted to happen. People believing that she and Eddie, the hero, were dating.

She placed her purse underneath her elbow. Except they weren't.

Instead of frowning, she sent a wink to the camera and then put her finger over her lips as if she was keeping a secret.

The girls around her giggled, and then Bianca sent them a wave. "I better go catch up to my hero."

Another truth.

A round of *aww*s hurried Bianca's steps. Eddie had been right. Heels had not been a good idea. "Eddie."

He picked up his pace and crossed the street.

Her heels clicked against the concrete, and the cute but evil black fabric pinched her pinky toes. "Eddie!"

This time, he stopped.

She hated that she had to choose between him and her fans.

When she reached the crosswalk, it flashed the okay to go. Except halfway across the street, a horn blasted back at the light, and Bianca whipped her head in that direction.

Only to find a car barreling straight for her.

EIGHT

SOMETIMES LIFE REQUIRED NO THINKING.

Eddie took two running strides and dove toward Bianca. He never should have left her. It shouldn't have mattered what gossip those girls gathered. He should have been there to protect her. That was his job.

His arms hooked around her waist and pulled her to his chest. He twisted his body. His back thumped against the road. Hard. But he was alive.

What about Bianca?

The car never pumped its brakes.

Please, Lord. Let her be okay.

She grunted in his arms.

His lungs squeezed tight as he held her.

Bianca was alive.

The spot below his shoulder blades throbbed. He more than likely had road rash, but had he turned his body enough to save Bianca from any pain?

Or had the edge of the car clipped her?

But no words escaped his mouth to ask. All he could do was suck in another breath and hold her.

Bianca pushed against his chest, and he released her.

Her eyes flashed wide as she rested on her knees. Frozen—all besides her shaking hands. But nothing looked broken. "You . . . it . . ."

At least, not on the outside.

Footsteps thundered toward them.

"Her firefighter!" one of the girls that stood on the sidewalk yelled. "He saved her again."

The girls remained on the corner of the sidewalk, gawking down at the girl's phone. "Please tell me you got it on camera."

Bianca's head dropped into her palms, and Eddie wrapped his arm around her shoulders. Where was his jacket when they needed it?

Her body trembled beneath his arm. Shock. Must have been the reason she hadn't moved out of the way of the car.

The truck driver who had slammed on his brakes and honked at the car that had actually run the red light jogged over to them. "Do I need to call the police? Ambulance?"

Bianca placed her hand on Eddie's arm. "You saved me. Again."

Eddie held out his other hand. "Can you stand?"

He'd had to ask her that question two too many times.

When she tightened her hold on him, he moved his hip, and he bit down on a gasp.

Bianca turned to the driver. "Please call 9-1-1. He's hurt."

Eddie's back cramped, but he had to walk or his muscles would tighten up. "I'm not." Not enough for an ambulance. "Though it would be wise to have Trace and Kianna check you out to make sure you're good."

Bianca shook her head. "I've had enough of ambulances for one week."

"Bia Pearl, are you okay?" It wasn't one of the three girls who held up their phones. At least fifteen people now gathered on the sidewalks, holding their phones. All pointed at Bianca.

Eddie stepped in front of Bianca. "This is not the time to record anything."

Her trembling fingers landed on his chest.

He willed his heart to slow and placed his hand over hers. "Can you take a deep breath for me?"

He inhaled, puffing out his chest, and ignored the ache in his back on his loud exhale through his mouth.

She blinked up at him and drew a breath. "I . . . I . . ."

"That's it." He spoke so only she could hear. "One more—"

"You guys won't believe it." The stroller lady's voice drifted to them. "Bia Pearl has been in an accident."

Bianca sucked in a breath and closed her eyes. After three short heartbeats, she opened her eyes and put on a smile. It was unsteady, but only he seemed to notice fakeness from his position.

She lifted her left hand at the crowded sidewalk. "We're okay, everyone. Thanks for your sweet concern."

We're, not *I'm.*

"How long have you and the firefighter been dating?"

He didn't know who'd asked the question, but he and Bianca needed to get out of there.

He tucked her against his side.

She leaned into him and held on to her smile. But to him she whispered, "Is there a way we could go back for my flip-flops?"

Flip-flops? Eddie frowned at the road and then at her feet. She still wore her heels. Had she hit her head?

Then he noticed the glassiness in her eyes was no longer from shock but a wall of restrained tears.

Oh. Flip-flops must be code for *home.*

He ran his thumb over her smooth skin. "Whatever you need. I've got you."

They hobbled past the girls with their phones, recording every step to Eddie's truck. A police car's whirling lights and siren came down the road. Finally. Not just bystanders wanting a show.

But of course, the car stopped back at the intersection they had already walked past.

Eddie turned both of them around by their linked hands. "We'd better go give our statements."

Bianca stopped walking. "I'm really starting to hate that word. I think"—she heaved a pant—"I'd better sit for a minute. Pretty sure my feet are numb. I could go for *actual* flip-flops right about now."

Her watery eyes pierced him. Eddie clenched his teeth against his screaming, bruised body. He went straight to the passenger-side door of his truck and helped her in. "I'll go talk to the officer."

She scowled down at her lap. "Oh no."

"What?" She could have internal bleeding. He should have thought to check. He was failing her as a trained emergency personnel.

"Bianca, tell me if you're really hurt. I can even carry you to the officer's car. He can get us to the hospital quicker than my truck—"

Her fingers touched his lips, and he stilled.

She dropped her hand. "I lost my purse. I must have left it on the road."

His lips tingled from her touch. "I'll find it."

As he jogged away, his shirt rubbed against his scrapes, but he kept his pace. Her purse wasn't on the ground. Wasn't pushed up against the curb. Or thrown somehow to the sidewalk.

He walked in a circle. She'd been in the middle of the road when the car had turned down the street. There's no way it would be on the opposite side. Unless she'd thrown it.

He lifted his gaze and spotted something black. No wonder he hadn't found the purse on the ground. The shortest teen hugged it while taking a selfie.

He stepped in her direction. "Her purse, please."

She paled and extended it to Eddie. "Th-thanks for rescuing Bia Pearl. She's like, one of my favorite celebrities. Aren't you the luckiest guy that you get to date her? That ex of hers didn't know how wonderful she is. None of them did. But you do, and it shows in how you hold her."

Eddie clutched the purse. How had he held her? No wonder people said "no comment" so much to fans. Bianca's exes were none of this girl's business. Or his. "Her safety is very important."

"Rice!"

Eddie spun to find Officer Ramble. The purse girl slinked away, and as Junior neared, Eddie lowered his voice. "Have you heard the story yet?"

Ramble's gaze darted around the lingering crowd. "Bia Pearl would have gotten hit by a car if you hadn't saved her. You're her hero. Once again. I've received those exact words from multiple accounts so far."

Eddie shrugged but stopped. His shoulder stung, but his road rash would get checked—eventually. "Something like that. Except leave out the hero part. She's in my truck. A little shaken. I need to do a more thorough check, but with the crowd . . ."

Junior nodded. "The firehouse is closer than the precinct. It would be fine to go over anything there without listening ears."

"That works." Eddie stared back at the road he'd dove across to reach Bianca. The pavement didn't have any brake marks. "Does anything about this incident seem suspicious?"

Junior tilted his chin and then inspected the ground. "Currently, it looks like a traffic disobedience and wrong-place-at-the-wrong-time thing."

Eddie used the purse to shield his mouth from the crowd. "Even with yesterday's building issue on set?"

Junior rested his palm on his gun belt. "We'll comb through the traffic-cam footage. And any bystanders' videos. We'll know more later."

That would have to be good enough. For now. The media didn't need to catch wind of rumors.

As soon as Eddie eased into his truck, he extended the purse, and Bianca took it. Then he inched the seat belt across his body. He could have received an Oscar for not releasing a groan when his back brushed against the seat.

Bianca's hands sagged into her lap. "You're hurt."

Apparently, he'd forgotten not to flinch. "Been through worse."

She turned her big eyes at him. "I'm so sorry, Eddie. I never should have made you go with me tonight. Twice now I've caused people to get hurt."

He reached for her but instead fisted his fingers. "You couldn't make me do anything." If he hadn't gone with her tonight, would she have been targeted by that car?

He shook that image away. "This wasn't your fault. Neither was yesterday's event."

She squeezed the purse to her chest. "I should have moved. But the last car scene I was in, that's what I had to do. Stand there." She extended her arms. "I had to stiffen and wait for the special-effects people to lift my harness up. I went into acting mode." She leaned her head back. "I should have been the one to hit the ground, and instead I landed on top. How did that even happen? For real. Are you hurt? Remember, you're against lying."

Eddie put his key into the ignition. He'd never thought sticking to the truth would come back to bite him. "I'm going to be sore, but I'll be fine. Ice should probably be in both of our futures."

She shrank closer to the passenger-side door. Something else was bothering her.

"Bianca?" He hadn't meant to whisper her name.

Her gaze flashed back to him.

He pulled his eyes away and watched Junior speak to the three girls. "You can tell me if you're hurt or whatever. I promise I'm not going to run to the press or whatever social media is all the hype . . ."

A half-laugh, half-hiccup cry blurted from her mouth. "All

the hype? Sounds like you're about to star in a seventies-themed movie."

Eddie smirked. "Only if I get to drive a fast car."

Probably not the wisest thing to say at the moment.

Her face sobered. "Do you think tonight is related to yesterday's sabotage?"

There it was. Except he didn't know if it was a good thing or bad that he could read this woman. She was smart. And possibly rightfully worried.

Eddie buckled his own seat belt. He shouldn't lie. "Officer Ramble doesn't seem to think so currently."

Bianca paused. "You don't agree?"

Eddie started the truck. "We don't need to borrow any trouble. Officer Ramble suggested we meet him at the firehouse to go over things without the world watching."

"Thanks, Eddie. I'm afraid I've been nothing but a giant burden to you."

He slanted his head. "Not sure *giant* would be the word I'd use."

Her face flushed to its original color. Exactly what he'd hoped for. Redirection tactic.

Eddie pulled away from the curb. "Maybe I'd use the word *gigantic*. Even *massive*. Or *humongous*."

She shook her finger at him. "Edward . . . James Rice. That's mean."

He slowed at a red light. "Truth sometimes hurts."

She huffed, and a curl danced in the air by her face. "Especially when it isn't said in love."

He sobered. She had a point. "You aren't a burden, Bianca, big or little. A little more accident-prone than most."

Her mouth popped open. "Says the rescue firefighter who has been through more situations than I have."

Another point for her.

He stole a glance in her direction. "Did I really hurt your feelings?"

Her fingers traced along a section of her curls over her shoulder. "Did I really guess your middle name right?"

She could have misdirected *his* question because he really had hurt her.

The light turned green, but there was no one behind him. His foot hovered over the pedal. "Not even close."

She lifted her chin. "Is it Kenneth?"

"No."

"Michael?"

The light turned yellow, and he finally hit the gas. "Nope."

"Edward . . . Alexander?"

He rolled his eyes. "How did we even get on my middle name?"

She sat up straight. "You asked to know if you hurt my feelings, and I want to know your middle name. Thought we were making another deal. Seems to be the way we spend our time together."

Eddie still hadn't decided whether that was a good or a bad thing. "You haven't guessed it. However, I won't be telling you my middle name."

A frown pulled her brows low. Somehow, she looked cuter irritated than with her perfected fake smile.

He refocused on the road where he was supposed to be looking.

She shifted closer to him. "You're stuck with me for a while. We might as well get to know each other. I'll even throw in my actual middle name."

The next stop sign seemed to come out of nowhere, and he slammed on the brakes. "I don't like my middle name."

She threw up her hands. "Who really does? Here, I'll go first. Mine's Bianca P—"

"Bianca, stop." His fingers squeezed the steering wheel. "No one needs to know my middle name because I'm named after someone who doesn't deserve to be talked about."

She slid back toward the passenger-side door. "Sorry I asked, and no, you didn't hurt my feelings earlier." Bianca rushed out the words in one breath.

Earlier, perhaps not, but he sure had now.

He opened his mouth to apologize, but her growling stomach interrupted their silence.

She crossed her arms over her body. "Ignore that."

He knew exactly what would fix his mistake. He made a U-turn. "That's too bad. There's a burger place on the way that may very well hold the world's fastest drive-thru record."

Bianca drummed her fingernails on the passenger-side door. "Do they have milkshakes?"

Eddie made a left at the junction that would take them by the mom-and-pop restaurant called Tator Lane. "Had a marshmallow one from there last week."

She wrinkled her nose. "Marshmallow?"

Eddie turned up the radio. "Sometimes the least expected things make the best surprises."

Only the music in the cab hummed above the engine. Eddie glanced over at her to see her blinking at him.

"You're right." Bianca held his gaze. "Not all unexpected things are bad."

Kind of like the actress beside him.

She was strong. Filled with humor, and surprisingly good with kids.

But she couldn't be the girl for him.

As if she knew, she cleared her throat. "My friend Frances, she makes the best apple-pie shakes. Though I'd never eat another one if I could have her with me in Last Chance County. But she loves her job as much as I loved mine."

Eddie flipped down his visor. "Loved? As in you don't any-more?"

She slipped her feet out of her shoes. "Is that what I said? I still love it. It's just . . . sometimes it feels more like a job and less like a dream that I always wanted. Do you ever feel like that with being a firefighter?"

He placed his left hand up on top of the wheel. "My job allows me to help people. There's a brotherhood among our squad. Plus, I wanted to follow in my mentor's steps." The neighbor his foster mom had connected Eddie with when he had gotten in trouble.

Bianca picked at a stain on the fabric that covered her thigh. "Hadn't thought about firefighters being like brothers. Sometimes a movie cast gets close."

Eddie heard what she hadn't said. Sometimes they didn't. Sounded like she could be a little lonely. Guess he'd never really thought about the logistics of acting. Being away from friends and family. Another plus for being a firefighter.

Officer Ramble was already at the firehouse when they arrived with three marshmallow shakes and two to-go orders of double cheeseburgers and tots. Junior took the offered milkshake and had finished their statements when a limo pulled into the parking lot.

Grace hopped out of the passenger side. She wrapped her arms around Bianca, who flinched. "You should have called me. Do we need to take you to the doctor? Hospital? Do you need more stitches?"

Bianca patted Grace's back as if she'd been the one almost hit by a car. "How did you know where we . . . I was?"

Eddie narrowed his attention on Junior. "Did you?"

Junior matched Eddie's expression. "Course not."

Grace pulled out her phone. "That tracker app I mentioned. Your phone and mine are connected. Remember, I said it would make handling your social accounts easier." She tapped on her phone screen and twirled it around. "Once I saw you'd started trending online, I had to make sure you—"

Bianca grabbed Grace's phone. "That app tracks me? Like my location? I didn't know it did that."

Grace's shoulders sagged. "I . . . I, but you said . . . I thought it would be a good idea, especially with the building accident. I was worried and wanted to be able to help if anything else ever happened. Sorry. I was only trying to be the best assistant and friend."

Bianca swiped a few things on Grace's phone and handed it back. "You've been a great assistant-in-training and . . . friend." Bianca peeked over at Eddie. "I already have a hero."

Grace's smile returned. "Yes, you played your part so well, Eddie."

Eddie squeezed his empty milkshake cup. He hadn't played anything. Had the battle wounds to prove it. "Let's not downgrade what happened by pretending it was a scene in a movie."

Real life wasn't a make-believe story. Acting allowed someone to shield emotions, which wasn't always healthy.

Officer Ramble cleared his throat. "If I think of any more questions, the chief or I will reach out."

Eddie and Bianca both together said, "Thank you."

Grace hooked her arm around Bianca. "We should go. Leo's made call time an hour earlier tomorrow." She spun Bianca in the direction of the limo. "You probably should do a live tonight. Talk about the close call. You'll be trending for a week."

Worrying about social-media stats wasn't what Bianca needed in order to heal from tonight's shock.

At the limo's door, Bianca mouthed toward Eddie, *Thank you*.

He dipped his head and watched them leave.

Junior let his notebook drop to his side. "The town may be split between the movie filming and that new resort coming, but all I know is that the precinct was busy enough before Hollywood and the protesters arrived."

Eddie extended his hand to Junior. "Thanks for suggesting the firehouse for our statements."

Junior shook Eddie's hand. "It's much easier to get the entire story without eavesdroppers throwing in opinions and twisting the facts. Since you're here, have Bently or Russell check out your shoulder and whatever injuries you have half hidden. If your shirt has road rash, I can't imagine what's underneath."

Based on the sting driving along his side, Eddie could imagine it all. But he wouldn't need Trace or Kianna. However, a full-length mirror in the locker room might come in handy.

Before he even made it to the bay area, someone called his name.

"Hey, Rice." It sounded like Zack. "Can you take a minute in the conference room?"

Eddie passed his lieutenant's office and slipped into the conference room opposite the chief's office. And then noticed what was written on the whiteboard.

Dating a movie star . . . for beginners.

Eddie spun around.

Ridge blocked the exit. "Where do you think you're going?"

Zack rose from a chair and closed the door. "Class is about to start. We believe it's exactly what you need."

Izan twisted his chair to face Eddie. "Can't let you blow your big break."

Eddie rolled his eyes. "Funny. What I need is some pain meds. Bianca isn't only a movie star, she's a woman. Not some silly joke."

Her words echoed in his mind. *Not all unexpected things are bad.*

Eddie blinked but still couldn't clear the look she'd given him after she'd taken a sip from her marshmallow milkshake.

Her real smile. The one she hid from the world.

But not from him.

He raked his fingers through his hair, and dust floated into the air. Maybe the crew was right. Perhaps a class was needed. One that showed him how *not* to fall for a movie star—someone who made a living of telling tall tales. Something he had to avoid.

NINE

BIANCA BLEW OUT A BREATH, AND A SECTION of her hair fell over her brow. Her curls required more hair spray. But what Bianca really wanted was time to process her real life. Yet, as the saying went, the show must go on.

If only Grace hadn't arrived so early to the fire station last night. She'd meant well by coming. But Eddie had seemed to understand what Bianca needed even before she herself had. Probably because of his firefighter training.

Last night had gotten better until she'd ruined it all with the push for his middle name. Their time together had gone downhill from there.

Bianca lifted on her toes. A cameraman moved a camera in her view. Leo pointed at a playback screen while another assistant nodded. Still no Riley.

She looked over Carter's shoulder. "Have you seen Riley? I really could use a hair touch-up."

Her attention snagged on Eddie, who was speaking with one of the special-effects guys.

Since Eddie's arrival this afternoon, he had been close enough to wave at, but with blockages of cameras, directors, and windjammers, which helped pick up her and Carter's voices, it had been impossible to speak to him about how he felt after their fall.

Ice really had been a friend to her foot last night, which was the only thing that had struck the ground.

Carter ran his palm over his own hair. "Hopefully she, or anyone"—he lifted his voice—"has already left to get me a coffee."

"Quiet on the set," Leo yelled behind a megaphone as someone opened the back of the ambulance and scooted the gurney farther into the scene.

Carter paced to his mark. "How many more times do we have to do this scene?" He huffed the very thought that also ran through Bianca's brain.

From her position by the set ambulance, Annette, one of the minor characters in the scene, winced. So far, it seemed the barely-nineteen-year-old couldn't actually say her lines *and* move the props at the same time.

Bianca offered her a thumbs-up. She'd been in the girl's shoes not too long ago.

Out of the corner of her eye, Bianca saw Grace arrive beside Eddie. He leaned closer to her and whispered something. A smiled popped on Grace's face.

What had he said?

The director shouted, "Action."

Bianca swung her attention to Carter. "I can't believe he's gone."

Carter marched over and wrapped his arms around her. He tugged her against him. Not anywhere close to how Eddie had protected her.

Carter rested the point of his chin on top of Bianca's head. Right near her stitches. "He was like a brother to me too."

Bianca smelled onion bagel on his breath. Not exactly comforting.

Stop thinking and remain in character. "What are we going to do without him?"

Carter blocked her face from the camera, and his foot landed on her toe. The bandaged one that had scraped against the pavement. She bit on her bottom lip, strangling her moan. They needed one good take to get a break.

He finally moved his foot and put his hands on her cheeks. "What are we going to do without the clues?"

Annette tapped Bianca on the shoulder. "I'm so sorry for your loss." She lifted up a notebook. "Before . . ." She pinched her lips together.

Oh, the poor girl. Please let her remember the line.

Annette jiggled the notebook. "Before your brother passed . . . he said I needed to give this to you."

Carter grabbed the notebook and flipped through the pages. He shook his head and pointed to the third page. "This is it. He had all the clues for the jewel the entire time." He looked straight at the camera. "He lied to us."

"Cut!" Leo glared at the playback scene and then spoke to one of his other assistants who stood under the shaded tent over the main camera.

The assistant nodded. "We should have enough for that scene. Everyone, take five."

The wayward curl drooped into Bianca's vision. She really needed that hair spray. Grace should be able to find Riley.

But before she could move toward Grace, Annette stepped in front of Bianca with tears in her eyes. "I'm so sorry. I don't even know why I kept messing up. They weren't even hard lines. It's like my brain forgot what a notebook was."

Bianca put her hand on the girl's arm and offered the encouragement she wished she'd gotten once. "You nailed that last take, and that's all that matters. We all have our off days."

Bianca kept her grin instead of massaging her temples.

Annette smiled and headed to the water table.

One of them should be happy. All Bianca wanted to do was

take a hot shower and climb into bed. Her legs ached. Probably from a lack of water, which she hadn't drunk much of today, but it could have also been left over from last night. Her slight headache was from lack of sleep. Every time she'd closed her eyes, she'd seen the car again. However, instead of coming after her, it had headed for Eddie.

And in her dreams, she hadn't been able to save him.

Just like she'd been unable to completely restore her relationship with her family.

Lord, You haven't forgotten about that, right?

Her gaze sought Eddie. Grace remained at her location in the corner, but Eddie was gone.

When Bianca reached Grace, her step-in assistant handed over Bianca's phone while tapping away at something on her own. "Finally. I've been needing to send these out."

Bianca glanced at her screen. One missed call and two messages from the same unknown number.

Unknown

I've got good news, Lady B.
Answer your phone!

Only one person called her Lady Bianca. And Nathan should not be contacting her. Unless he had news about her money. But if that was the case, then he'd lied to her about not knowing what'd happened to it.

She slipped her phone into her pocket. "Did you see where Eddie went?"

Grace didn't look up from her screen. "Had to leave."

Bianca deflated. "Was he in pain?"

She should have tried harder to check on him. He had been slipping out during the takes and probably talking to different extras and crew members. The real reason he was actually here.

Bianca pulled out her phone. "Maybe I should send him a text and see if he's okay."

Except she didn't have his number.

Grace paused her fingers and tilted her head. "He said something about a baseball game tonight."

Bianca ran her finger along her relaxed curl. "He probably needs a break from all of this film chaos he's not used to. Speaking of chaos . . ." She lifted a flattened section of hair. "Have you seen Riley? Or better yet, have you heard how Tiff and her family are doing?"

Grace's fingers clicked away on her phone. "Speaking of Tiff, she never allowed your hair to look like that."

Bianca tucked the flattened section of hair behind her ears. "Tell me how you really feel."

Grace winced. "Sorry. I didn't mean it like that. But I'm right. Tiff would have already doused you with three different hair spray sessions. But no, she still hasn't answered my text about how her family's doing. She must be pretty busy, because she usually answers me pretty quickly. Wow. Last night has been great for your ratings. You've gotten five thousand new followers in the last hour alone." Her phone vibrated and her eyes widened. "Oh, that's perfect."

She turned her phone around. "They're changing up the filming schedule. Only Carter and your stand-in are required tonight. Speaking of stand-ins, I wonder if any of them would like to also do your last stunt. You can't get a redo of last night's outing, but you could go watch Eddie's game. Do a live feed from the hometown ball field. That's got 'boy next door meets tough firefighter hero' written all over it. The perfect combo."

Bianca picked at a chip in her pinky nail. "He hit that road hard last night. But I should be able to talk to him between innings. Plus, I'd love to see the team play." And maybe get Eddie's number. In case she ever needed to check on him.

Grace eyed her as if she'd read Bianca's thoughts, but then finally nodded. "Maybe get a picture of Eddie in a baseball hat, and you kiss his cheek while holding a ball in the frame or something. Definitely a live for sure."

At the thought of kissing, Bianca licked her lips. She hooked her thumb over her shoulder. "I should get out of these film clothes."

Grace shooed her. "Hurry. The game starts in an hour."

Back at her trailer, Bianca pulled on her favorite pair of jeans plus a T-shirt and headed to her car. The drive toward the south side didn't have much traffic, but the parking lot at the game resembled a Black Friday sale.

Eddie's truck sat at the end of the parking lot, right in front of the setting sun that hid behind a forgotten warehouse building. The coach wouldn't be leaving anytime soon. She parked behind his vehicle and tossed her ruined hair in a ponytail.

She should have brought a baseball cap, and she really wished she had her old softball mitt. It was still in a tub in the back of her parents' house. Unless they had thrown it away without telling her. Which was possible.

The crowd packed the bleachers, and lawn chairs were lined up along the right field fence. But it was the news camera that made Bianca slow her steps. How had the paparazzi known she'd be here?

Channel 10 News was printed on the side, and the cameraman filmed a man in a brown suit. Not her.

The man turned and Bianca kept walking. It was the mayor. So, not paparazzi bothering Eddie or the team.

Finally, something going right.

Scout leaned over on the pitcher's mound with his team in the field, playing defense. The scoreboard in center field announced that the game was tied at the top of the third inning.

A girl in a side braid had her fingers resting on the fence by the dugout. She turned around and squealed. "Bia Pearl!"

Bianca smiled. She really could have used a hat. "Hey, so nice to meet you."

The girl snapped a picture of Bianca and then started texting. "I'm going to have my cousin print your picture, and then you can sign it. I bet she'll want one signed for my aunt, one for me, my cousin, and then my brother's girlfriend too. Oh, I think Mrs. Williams, she's not *that* old, will want one. She lives in the apartment across from ours. Probably Sally and . . ."

The girl took an actual breath, and Bianca managed to get out the bad news. "I'm not sure how long I'll be here tonight."

A piece of wrapped bubblegum hit Bianca's shoulder. "Coach B." Scarlette waved at her from inside the dugout fence. "Better get in here quick. We need you."

Bianca didn't wait for another invitation. She picked up the piece of bubble gum.

Once she was inside the gate, Scarlette crumpled her nose at the girl with the one braid. "Sorry, Jazzy, you and your cousin will have to wait. Coach B doesn't do autographs until *after* the game."

Jazzy huffed and stomped away.

Bianca hugged Scarlette. "Thanks. I didn't want to hurt her feelings, but I didn't want to sign a million things either."

"Don't sign them. They'll sell them at her aunt's store." Scarlette shrugged. "Good thing Coach saw you. It was his idea for me to save you."

Make that three times that he'd rescued her.

Bianca offered a half smile. "Sorry I'm late."

Eddie stood in the middle of the dugout and kept his attention on the boys in the field. Then he swiped something down under the bench. A matching team hat. "Here. You're right on time. Neither of my other coaches are here tonight."

Bianca pulled on the hat and straightened one of the magnetic batting names on the lineup hooked to the dugouts inside the protective fence. "Where do you need me?"

"Tank! Pay attention to the ball, not the cameras." Eddie sighed. "If you're willing"—he sent a glare toward the cameraman and the mayor—"you have more experience with all that nonsense."

Bianca lowered her baseball cap. "Cameras aren't nonsense. They help people smile." She sent a wink to Scarlette. "Or that's what I told my father when I explained to him why I wanted to be an actress."

Of course, her words hadn't helped her case that night.

Scarlette tilted her head. "Guess they kind of do make people smile, don't they?"

Bianca took a seat beside her on the bench. "Sometimes. Though I guess some movies are made to make you think or—"

"Cry." Scarlette shook her head. "I don't like sad movies."

"Me neither. But sometimes they help you process things. Life isn't always happy. My dad wasn't happy when he learned I didn't want to go to college. That I wanted to act instead."

Scarlette scooted closer, and the dimming sunlight highlighted her widened eyes. "But you're a good actress, right?"

Bianca pressed her hand to her chest. "You mean you haven't watched me?"

Scarlette hung her head. "Grandma said that I can only watch those movies when I'm older."

Eddie glanced over his shoulder at Bianca before turning away.

Heat ran up her cheeks. Had Eddie watched her movies? "That's a good idea. Most of my movies have been for adults. Not all of them have been very God-honoring. But this next movie, you can watch."

She pointed at the cameraman. "He's part of a news crew, not paparazzi. They shouldn't bother the team." Though tonight might be the perfect time to arrange Eddie's talk with the mayor.

Bianca pushed back her shoulders. "Where do you want me to coach?"

Eddie pulled out a piece of gum from his pocket and unwrapped it. "You want first or third?"

He was letting her pick? "I'd rather have first base this game."

"This game. You hear that, Coach E?" Scarlette beamed her grin at Bianca, her left front tooth wiggling as she pressed her smile wider. "Sounds like Coach B means to be coming to all of our games. About time. I could really use another girl—"

"One day at a time, Scarlette." Eddie put his fingers through the chain fence and leaned up against it. "Will, slide over to the left. A little more. One more . . . whoa."

One day at a time. She was a short-term coach. Temporarily in their lives. She knew that.

Bianca crossed her arms over her chest. Then why did it sting?

Scarlette stepped closer. "He's only grouchy because the mayor's here and he said no to our grant."

Eddie whipped around. "How do you know that?"

Scarlette popped her hands on her hips. "Why else would you have given him the glare that I give Scout when he won't share his candy?"

This girl was smart.

Eddie gave Bianca a look that proved he thought the same thing. He stuck out his finger toward Scarlette. "He had said no, but he's going to take another look at our paperwork. I'll break all that information to the boys *after* the game. Not a word before."

Scarlette made a zipping motion with her fingers.

Bianca pressed her lips together. No wonder he'd changed his mind about helping her.

"And . . ." Eddie cocked his head. "You better listen to my signs this time at bat, or you'll sit out the entire next game."

Scarlette's hand flew back to her hip. "But—"

Eddie folded his arms. "No buts, unless you want to become best buds with the bench."

Scarlette picked up her helmet and slammed it on her head. "Yes, sir." Then to Bianca she murmured, "See? Grouchy."

Scarlette gave her a wink before a ping echoed from home plate. As the batter raced toward first, Tank backpedaled. He waved his right arm while his left tracked the ball. "I've got it."

And he did, making the pop fly their third out.

Eddie clapped his hands as the boys ran into the dugout. "Let's get those bats ringing."

The boys got to their bench and stopped.

Will elbowed Tank. "Told you she'd be back."

Tank grinned at Bianca. "Did you see my catch?"

Scout whipped off his hat. "You missed mine last inning."

Bianca stepped closer to the fence. "I guess you'll just have to catch another one."

Being cramped in the dugout felt more like home than being in front of the camera lately. Why was that?

Will dropped his mitt on the bench. "Do you have any bruises like Coach? I watched you hit the ground online like a million times."

Bianca sought Eddie, who seemed to be staring at his feet. How bad were his bruises? "I think someone may have lied last night when they claimed they were fine."

Eddie clenched his jaw. "Never lied. Bruises don't change my answer."

Scarlette placed her hand on Bianca's arm. "Glad Coach saved you, Coach B."

"Me too." Bianca's voice quivered before she could help it.

Eddie clapped again. "All right, team. Coach B will be on first base. Listen to her as if she were me." He waved his hands in front of his chest. "Scratch that. Listen to her *better* than you listen to me."

Bianca shrugged. "I mean, of course they will. They all voted that they liked me better."

Tank raised his hand. "I'd totally vote for that. She looks better in our hat."

Scout pointed to Eddie. "I bet even Coach would agree. His ears stick out—"

"Get out there." Eddie took off his hat and swatted at the boys.

Scarlette squeezed by the boys. "Your ears are just right, Coach."

Eddie crammed his hat back on his head, and maybe a bit more over his ears than before.

Bianca followed him onto the field.

Eddie stopped at third base. "Thanks for coming."

"Scarlette's right." Bianca reached and adjusted his hat, lifting it to show his face more. "Your ears are just right."

He bumped into her shoulder. "Yeah, but Tank's right too. You look better in our hat than I do." He smiled. A real one. The kind she'd been frozen by when they'd first met. Double dimples.

He stepped away and into his position in the coach's box, while Bianca's legs moved slower than jelly to her spot at first.

Scout hit the second pitch and made it to first base, but then when Jacob hit, the visitors pulled a double play. Now they had two outs.

Scarlette smacked a floater over the first basemen's head, and it bounced. The girl may be short, but she sprinted as if on fire. The right fielder hadn't arrived at the ball yet.

Bianca hesitated. Should she play it safe?

The right fielder scooped up the ball with his mitt instead of with his palm, and the ball fell back onto the ground.

Bianca pointed toward second and circled her other arm like a windmill. "Go, Scarlette, go!"

Scarlette hit her foot on the inside corner of first base and curved for second right when the fielder picked up the ball.

Bianca cupped her hands over her mouth. "Get down!"

The outfielder threw the ball. Bianca's hands went to her cheeks.

What had she done? She should have played it safe and kept her on first base.

Scarlette took two more steps and then slid. Sort of. The ball sank, and Scarlette ducked under the second basemen's mitt. Dust sailed through the air.

The umpire stood staring at the play. Finally, he swung his arms out in front of him. "Safe!"

Scarlette sent her a wink.

Bianca laughed. Yeah, she missed this game. But more than that, she missed being a part of a team. A family.

She'd given up so much to reach her dream of being an actress. She needed to figure out who she really was. Not the person whose life was dictated by climbing the fame ladder.

God might have brought her to Last Chance County for more than a film.

Scarlette's double started the team off on a rally, and soon they scored five more runs. But their team spirit came to a halt when Will spun around toward Eddie as he and Bianca walked into the dugout.

Will flung out his hands. "You should have told us about the money. It's not fair."

Bianca stopped. Eddie had told the team about their deal? "Umm . . ."

It wasn't fair because she was making their coach pretend? Or because he wanted the donated money she'd promised now?

Eddie stepped around Bianca. "Scarlette." He said her name low and slow.

Scarlette's baseball bill swung faster than her head. "Wasn't me. I didn't tell. Honest."

Bianca shook her head. "Wasn't me either." Though she and Eddie should probably talk more about who knew exactly what about their business arrangement.

"Mr. Pointe told me." Will gestured to a man wearing a suit at the opposite end of the fenced dugout, who smirked and slipped out of view.

Oh, this had nothing to do with Bianca. At least, not directly.

"Coach, you said you would tell us if we did or didn't get the grant for the youth center. You lied."

Bianca placed her hand over her beating heart, which seemed to thunder in the silent dugout.

With his jaw clenched, Eddie inhaled. "I didn't lie. Yes, I got an email saying the grant money wasn't happening, but the mayor is going to take another look at our proposal."

Tank threw his helmet. "If he said no once, he'll just say it again. Who cares about the stupid game now? Their catcher was right. We're rejects. That's why their team has new uniforms and we're stuck with these old—"

"No." Every one of them gaped at Eddie. "Your worth is not in anything we have or don't have. Not in any abilities, either. I'm sorry I didn't update you on the grant. But you know how much I want the youth center for you. One way or another, things will work out."

Scarlette peeked out from behind her brother. "Because you have hope for more money besides the grant, right, Coach?" The girl said Eddie's name, but her eyes locked on Bianca.

Bianca fidgeted with the extra hair tie around her wrist.

Eddie's nose flared with his deep breath. "Right now, we must focus on our attitudes. And this game."

Scout whispered to Jacob, "When my grandma changes the subject, that means she doesn't think something's gonna happen but doesn't want to tell us."

Scarlette shot her brother a glare. "Except this time's different."

Tank swiped his glove off the bench and headed out of the dugout. "The only reason we're winning is because the other team's starting pitcher went to Hawaii on vacation."

Will pulled on his baseball hat. "Wish I could go to stupid Hawaii."

Scarlette pushed on the snap of her catcher's shin guards. "I wish this stupid gear worked."

Bianca bent down and straightened the connecters on the catcher's shin guards. "Sometimes, the snaps only need a little lovin'."

The snaps clicked together at the same time Will's stomach growled.

Bianca smiled. "Someone's worked up an appetite."

Will's face went white. He grabbed his mitt and ran out onto the field.

Eddie came over beside Bianca. "Was that Will's stomach or yours again?"

"I could go for another one of those shakes, but it was his." She'd even texted Frances about her restaurant needing to add marshmallow shakes to their summer menu.

Eddie closed his eyes.

She frowned. "What's wrong?"

Eddie put his hand into his back pocket and pulled out a five-dollar bill. "Lincoln, run to the concessions and buy all the popcorn this will get you. Some of you might have to share."

A grin broke out over the skinny boy's face. "Yes, sir."

Bianca grabbed her keys off the bench. "I might have some cash." Maybe.

Eddie placed his hand on her arm. "That will get them through the game, at least. I forgot their warm-up snacks. No wonder Will's on edge. He may not have eaten lunch."

She squeezed her keys. No lunch? "Does that happen a lot?"

Eddie rubbed at the crease on his forehead. "Once is too much."

Bianca pressed her palm over her chest. He was right. These boys needed more than a simple youth center. "I'll keep my end of our deal," she whispered. "About helping fundraise and collect donations."

Eddie's lips pressed into a line. "Not sure you and me"—he glanced behind him and cleared his throat—"is such a good idea. I'm still worried about the kids finding out and thinking I'm lying to them. Then who are they going to trust and depend on? You saw what happened with Will and the grant. Lying. It breaks trust. I can't afford—"

The metallic clunk of ball meeting bat had both of them whirling around in time to see the other team's batter send the pitch soaring over the fence.

More than Scout's shoulders sank as the batter jogged around the bases. The whole team's hope sank.

Bianca may not be able to win the game for them or buy them a youth center—yet. But maybe she could do something. No kid deserved to go hungry.

Frances's voice came into her head.

Don't envy someone else's gift. Use what the Lord has blessed you with. If it's giving, do it with the right heart.

Bianca grabbed her phone. Hopefully, the pizza shop beside Kitty's Family Clothing Outlet could deliver on such short notice. She might not be able to solve all their problems at the moment, but she could feed a bunch of hungry kids.

As her phone rang, Eddie's words circled back to her.

You saw what happened with Will. Lying. It breaks trust.

He'd been talking about their fake dating and agreement. But her heart seemed to whisper that it wouldn't be lying if their time together wasn't really fake.

TEN

SUITS AND BASEBALL DID NOT MIX. AT LEAST, not in Last Chance County.

Eddie marched toward one of the suited men in question. He shoved his hands into his pockets. He would not, could not, hit this man. Some of his players saw enough violence at home and in the streets. But Roger Pointe could have only one reason to tell Eddie's team about the previously failed grant money—to get more votes for his own election campaign.

Eddie cleared his throat. "Mr. Pointe, a word."

Beside Roger Pointe, a stocky man with dark hair that drifted down over his even darker brows turned toward Eddie first but then slinked behind the mayor's opposing candidate, who finally turned.

An innocent expression brightened Roger's face as he extended his palm. "Well done, Coach. I hear it's not every day this team pulls off a victory."

Eddie stared down at the offered welcome. "The season has only just begun."

Roger tsked and reached into his pocket and pulled out a golden container with a crown engraved into the metal. He opened it and picked out a pearl-shaped mint. "Based on the frowns on your team's faces, it sure doesn't look like a win. I wonder why that is. Though it could be that you're struggling to fill your chief's role as head coach. Leadership doesn't come naturally for everyone."

The old Eddie would have taken the bait, comparing himself to Macon. Instead, he took in a slow, deep breath. "I believe you had something to do with the frowns tonight."

Roger popped in two mints and wrinkled his nose. "Those frowns will turn right side up as soon as the election is over and I'm declared the winner."

Eddie crossed his arms. "You're a smart man, Roger. You know that's not what I'm talking about."

The other man behind Roger shifted his gaze between Eddie and the mayoral candidate almost like a pinball. He edged closer to Roger's ear. "I'll go bring the car around, sir."

Roger patted him on the back. "Thanks, Kelson." He pulled out a pocket watch. "What can I help you with, Coach? My door will always be open to all fine taxpayers of this soon-to-be-great town."

Eddie squeezed his hands around his arms. "Why did you tell one of my kids about the failed grant? How did you even hear about that information?"

The pocket watch shut with a click. "The better question would be why you hadn't told them something that greatly affects their lives."

Eddie rolled a pebble in the dirt with the tip of his shoe. Would he have told the team about the grant before tonight if the mayor hadn't decided to take another look?

"There's a right time to discuss hard things, and during the middle of a ball game—"

"Interesting. You, as these kids' mentor, practically a hero these days . . ." He angled his chin at the dugout, where Bianca had been standing when Eddie had seen Roger. "I would have assumed the truth would always be welcome. That's what I promise once I'm elected as mayor. Leading in truth. Here I thought you were always a man of your word."

Eddie refused to allow the growl that caught in his throat. "Truth offered in love." Exactly what Bianca had said yesterday. Something he often failed at himself. He took in a deep breath. "Roger, can you see that with you telling them, with cameras around, it looks like it's some kind of hidden plot to promote your name over Gregory's?"

Roger fisted his hand and plunged it against his chest. "You wound me. I think Gregory has blinded you. It's time for you to stop hanging all your hopes on a mayor who has obviously let you and these kids down. Then you would see how you and I could be on the same team."

Eddie wasn't sure if he'd get a truth or a lie. It was like he was a little kid and listening to his mother's fabrications. But he still had to ask. "What kind of team would that be?"

Roger raised his brows. "One that wants the best for Last Chance County. After all, it was your beloved mayor who denied the grant money for the youth center. Was it not?"

How had he even gathered that information? "He's reconsidering things currently."

Roger tapped his finger against his chest. "Well, currently, I can guarantee those kids a future youth center."

It was Eddie's turn to raise his brow. "How would you plan on doing that?"

Roger winked. "You let your new future mayor worry about the details. Just *full* support from our local hero will be enough."

There it was. Nothing was ever free.

"Eddie." The current mayor, Gregory Harrelson, and a cameraman stepped up to Eddie.

Roger offered his hand to Gregory. "Surprised to see you here. Thought you golfed on weeknights."

Gregory wagged his finger at Roger's chest. "I'm going to figure out how you're doing it."

Roger looked around him. "How I make time for the youth of this town? Easy. I'm a better mayor."

Gregory's face bloomed red. "You set that fire at my auction."

Roger lifted his chin. "I was nowhere near your house that night."

Gregory fisted his hand. "You won't steal any more of my backers from me. I'm going to figure out how you got into my house, and when I do . . ."

Rap music blared from the road, gaining Eddie's attention. A car with a Fella's Pizza sign whipped into the parking lot. Two teens hopped from the car. Each pulled out two huge pizza carriers.

Roger spoke Eddie's thoughts out loud. "What's all of this?"

The taller teen shrugged as he shifted the carriers. "Probably dinner."

Bianca waved the teens into the dugout. "Perfect timing. I think inside here would be good."

What in the world?

Eddie held up his finger to Roger and Gregory. "Excuse me a moment." He ran into the dugout just as the teen deliverers brushed past his shoulders.

Will bit into what looked like a slice of bacon ranch pizza. "This is on point!" Then, with his mouth still full, he wiped the edge of his mouth with his arm. "Coach, you should have started dating Coach B way sooner. I vote we do pizza for every win. This is way better than the peanut butter sandwiches you bring."

Eddie scowled. An actress swoops in, throws money around, and she's the good guy. "Will, first of all . . ." Eddie's gaze stuck on something colorful and huge out in the left side of the field. The hum of fans kicked on, and the thing started to blow up. He'd been distracted for longer than he thought. "What is that? Did you throw more money at them?"

Bianca pulled the end of her ponytail over her shoulder and picked at the ends. "Not exactly. It came free with the pizza order."

Eddie narrowed his eyes. "Blow-up slides don't come free with pizza. Not in the real world."

Scout swallowed down his own gulp of pizza. "They do when you're dating Bia Pearl."

Eddie crossed his arms. "We're not—"

"Scout!" Scarlette motioned from beside the slide. "It's almost blown up, and we have to race Tank and Will first." Scarlette put her hands up around her mouth. "Coach B, will you time us?"

Bianca jiggled her phone. "Sure will. Why don't you get a couple of practice rounds in first?"

"Sweet." Jacob fist-pumped at the same time that Tank yelled, "This is the best day ever!"

Apparently, the grant issues were all forgotten with some pizza and a slide. Things that were very temporary.

Once all his players ran to left field, Eddie shook his head. "You can't bribe them too."

Bianca's smile fell. "You said the boys were hungry. I got pizza—"

"One, two, three . . . twelve boxes?" He threw up his hands. "You think I can't pay for pizza because I'm just a firefighter and you're a famous actress? If you're not bribing, then you're spoiling them. And a free slide? Really? I told you. I'm not okay with lying."

"It's fifteen boxes." Her eyes almost sparkled in the baseball field lights as she met his glare. "Enough for each of them to take some home for tomorrow's lunch. I think the words you are looking for in this situation are *Thank you, Bianca*. Just because you're angry with those suits over there doesn't mean you can take it out on me."

Bianca opened a box of pizza. "And yes, hangry is a thing, but your attitude's still not okay."

His stomach chose that moment to incriminate him and growl. Oh, she was right again. His anger was misdirected. But still, she wasn't perfect. "You should have asked. This isn't your team. You can't always get what you want."

The box lowered against her stomach. "Trust me, I don't get what I want a lot. Can we at least agree that the kids needed food?"

A bug flew past his ear, and he swatted at it. "Will you agree that you overstepped in how you handled it?"

She eyed the kids out by the blow-up slide. "The slide really was free as long as I agreed to stop by later and sign an autograph. Or ten. I can't remember how many they asked for. And I think you should know that they also asked how they should deliver it, and I told them they could go through the gate by right field. But I shouldn't have assumed that would be fine. I overstepped."

Eddie reached into one of the pizza boxes and pulled off a pepperoni. She had done a kind thing, and that had gotten lost in his anger. "Thanks, Bianca."

She bobbed her head. "You're welcome. Now, if you want to tell me what all that was all about"—she lifted a pepperoncini out and pointed to where Roger and Gregory remained, red faced and muttering to one another—"you might feel better. I mean, I'm pretty sure listening comes free with your pizza order."

"You must have used some special coupon. Or is it only because you're the Bia Pearl?"

She picked up two boxes of pizza and then stacked them on top of a third. "Definitely option one."

She patted the bench beside her.

Eddie found himself sitting and leaning his elbows onto his thighs. "Maybe Roger was right. I should have already told the kids that the grant had been previously denied."

She pulled apart two slices and put them into two empty boxes. "Does that man spend much time with these kids?"

Eddie took another bite of pizza. "Hardly. Both he and the mayor are here for themselves."

Her knee bumped against his leg. "Then why are you letting

him get inside your head? It's not like you aren't currently working on another path that can help get the kids more funds for their youth center, right?"

Roger had also guaranteed Eddie not just money but an entire youth center. "Maybe you're right."

Could he trust Roger? For that matter, could he trust Bianca or Gregory? What Eddie really needed was to trust God's timing. However, that was easier said than done.

Bianca put her fingers around her ear and leaned toward him. "I'm sorry, did you say I was right?"

Of course the woman was cute when she smirked.

Eddie swiped his finger in some pizza sauce and dotted it on her cheek.

Her eyes bugged. "You dirty dog."

Eddie chuckled. "I was afraid your head was getting too big. It was about to float away. Had to hurry and weigh it down."

Bianca reached for a napkin. "Bet you did."

He stretched around her and swiped all the napkins.

She grabbed for them, but Eddie jerked them above his head.

She gave him a saucy look. "I think pizza makes you feisty."

"No one has ever called me feisty. But you"—he handed her the napkins—"were gutsy when you sent Scarlette to second."

She wiped the sauce off her cheek and balled up the napkin. "That gutsy decision started the rally that saved us the game."

Eddie leaned closer, not wanting any of his players to hear. "You had our worst slider going in for a squeeze play and one of my strongest hitters on deck."

Bianca dropped her forehead into her palm. "These are things I would have known if I'd been to more than one practice."

"Next one's Tuesday. I mean, you don't have to. You're busy and . . ."

And the truth was, she wasn't actually a part of his or the kids' lives. He wasn't sure what made her prettier—the smirk earlier or her genuine smile now.

"It's a team date. Speaking of . . ." She pulled out her phone. "Mind taking a picture?"

Reality sank in his stomach. This was not a potential assistant coach before him. Not a real friend, or anything more, no matter what his heart had done earlier when she'd smirked. All he could do was nod his head once.

She scooted over and rested her shoulder against his. Her cheek next to his.

Eddie swallowed.

She held up the phone. "Say 'baseball.'"

A bee buzzed by and hovered by her face for a minute.

"Eddie. Let's get one where you're looking too."

He took his eye off the bee and smiled. After she'd taken the pictures, she swiped through them. She paused on the one when the bee must have flown close. In the photo, Eddie didn't appear to be watching a bee but rather Bianca.

He looked like a man who wasn't faking anything.

A call popped up on her phone with an unknown number.

Bianca hit ignore.

"Spam callers even have famous actresses' numbers too?"

She dropped her phone into her lap. "I'm not *that* famous. And they do when they're my ex who can't take a hint."

Foot, meet mouth. Eddie wiped a napkin over his lips. Her ex had been tried in a big jury case, but Eddie hadn't followed it. Something possibly about fraud?

She stood and pocketed her phone. "One of the things I hate about acting is how my life is picked apart. From my past relationships to how I supposedly lied on the stand. But trust me, you can't believe everything you read on the internet."

He rose to his feet. "It's none of my business, but he shouldn't be bothering you . . . Hold on, is he angry with you? Could he be behind the car accident yesterday? Even the building? Or he saw you and me and assumed . . . got jealous?"

Bianca stared at her phone. "There's no way he'd jeopardize . . ." She shook her head. "No. He's already moved on to another woman. Some heiress to her father's company. I should have known he'd only been after my money, but I haven't always made wise decisions when it comes to men."

Eddie fisted the napkin in his palm. "You're definitely more than money."

She gave him a closed-mouth smile. "Says the man who made a deal with me."

It was more with the mayor than her, but she wasn't exactly wrong. Her donations and help fundraising remained a huge bonus in his decision. "That's not fa—"

"Fair?" She raised her brow. "What's not fair is that my accounts were frozen along with Nathan's when he was indicted. I spoke the truth under oath and was labeled a liar. When I told everyone in an interview that I'd decided to follow Jesus, they said I was only doing it to clear my name and conscience for lying. When Nathan was found not guilty, all his accounts were released. Yet mine are strangely almost empty. And no one seems to believe me. So I'm stuck trying to regain my finances through a horrible movie contract."

Eddie blinked. People had called her a liar just because she'd said she followed the Lord? He needed to say something. Encourage her. "Then you probably shouldn't be wasting money on overpriced pizza."

Based on her scowl, that wasn't the best thing to have said.

"Coach B, come and time us," Scarlette called from the bottom of the blow-up slide.

Bianca walked around him.

Eddie grabbed her hand, and she stilled.

He released his touch. "That didn't come out right." He met her gaze. "I'm sorry your interview didn't go well, but I'm impressed by your boldness for the truth, and if Nathan ever comes around, call the police. Or me."

She simply nodded.

What would it be like if those he rescued called him a liar for following Christ?

He fell in step behind her, and when they neared the team, Bianca held out her phone. "Who am I timing first?"

Scarlette grabbed her phone. "It's the coaches' turn to race."

Bianca waved her hand in front of her. "No, I don't think we should . . ."

Eddie lifted the bill of his baseball cap. "She's right. I'd probably win anyway."

Both Bianca's and Lincoln's mouths popped open.

But it was Scarlette who set her fist on her hip. "You gonna let him get away with that?"

Scout took Eddie's phone. "On your mark, get set, g—"

Bianca dashed up the steps.

Eddie pulled her back.

"Hey!" Bianca pushed on his chest, but instead of going down, they both managed to make it to the top of the blow-up slide while only slipping twice.

Bianca laughed and panted until her attention locked on something below. "Oh." She scooted back. "It's higher than I thought it would be."

She was scared of heights? "I thought I read that you do your own stunts."

He refrained from rolling his eyes. Now she'd know he'd researched her a little after the night of the masquerade. And after Zack had mentioned her interview about Christianity. But she only stared at the ground.

She curled her knees up toward her chest. "Sometimes I do. But it doesn't mean I don't freak out right before those high stunts. I know the Lord is always with me, but that doesn't mean I won't ever get hurt."

Wasn't that the truth. Eddie laced his fingers around hers. "Come on. Together. One, two, three."

Bianca didn't move but released her grip. "You go ahead."

Eddie scooted over closer to her. "And hear how you let me win? Never."

He got a side smile out of her then. He offered his hand, and she put hers into his. "I won't let you fall."

She laughed then. "I'm so silly. It's a slide and an irrational fear."

Eddie shrugged. "But God's here for it. So am I."

Instead of smiling brighter, her face went slack. "Thanks, Eddie, for being such a good guy."

A good guy. That should've been a compliment. Except he couldn't help but hear one of his old foster brother's words when they were younger: *Good guys have no fun. No life.*

That comment had come right before Eddie had found his teen self behind bars.

Bianca smiled over at him. But it looked . . . fake. Shouldn't be surprising. She was an actress. "Okay. I'm ready."

An actress who acted out their relationship for not only the kids but also the world.

"One, two, three." Bianca shoved off, and Eddie trailed behind.

"Coach B won!"

"I'm next."

"No, I am."

Both Scout and Tank raced up the steps and tumbled down the slide together. Tank landed on top of Scout before leaping off the slide. But Scout didn't get up. He lay there, holding his hand.

"Ah, Coach." Will frowned. "I think Scout's hurt."

Tank shook his head. "He's faking because I beat him."

Scarlette raced over and pried her brother's hand off the top of his other one. She gasped. "His pinkie's bent weird."

Eddie's knee landed in the grass in front of Scout, and he inspected the pinkie. It was as he'd feared. "I'm so stupid."

Bianca squatted beside Scout. "Accidents happen."

"Not if I'd put a stop to all this extravagance when it got here. This never would have happened."

Bianca jerked back as if she'd been struck.

Great. Both hangry and whatever word meant upset and angry together.

He'd probably been too harsh, but right now he had to get all the boys safely home and Scout to the hospital.

He pointed to the team. "Get everything loaded up. Tank, help Scout to my truck."

Scout grimaced. "My legs still work, Coa—"

"Scarlette, get in the truck too. All the rest of you wait in the dugout. I'll call Zack. He'll make sure you all get taken home."

Of course tonight would be one of the only nights Scout and Scarlette's grandmother had volunteered at the women's shelter and missed a game.

Bianca stood. "I'll wait with them."

Pain etched across Scout's face as he took another step, Tank and Scarlette beside him.

Eddie grabbed his phone back from Jacob. "Scratch that. I'm calling the crew. The ambo team will be quicker."

Bianca stepped in front of Eddie. "It will be quicker if you take Scout. The ambulance may be clear across town. I can help watch the team. I'm right here."

"You're right. You are." And he wasn't sure if that was turning out to be a bigger problem. He needed to fix this situation before his team—and possibly his heart—got hurt too.

ELEVEN

BIANCA STRAIGHTENED THE RED BOW TIED around the store-bought package of cookies.

Cookies make everything better. Bring some with you. Forgiveness is way easier to swallow when it's surrounded by sugar, Grace had said once Bianca told her the plan of visiting Scout.

Bianca had thrown her post-filming hair into a ponytail and grabbed her keys. *Pretty sure that's not how forgiveness works.*

Yet, with the afternoon sun on her back and her shifting feet on Scout and Scarlette's front porch, she hoped the cookies wouldn't make things worse. Not like the time she'd sent her mother cookies for the first Mother's Day she wasn't home for.

Bianca knocked her knuckles against the doorframe. No footsteps pounded from behind the white front door with black shutters, a window on the right-hand side big enough for two kids to crawl through at the same time. The homey bungalow was exactly how Will had described Scout and Scarlette's house on Oak Street when she'd managed to talk some sense into Eddie about her taking the rest of the team home after the broken finger accident.

Maybe they weren't home. She glanced to the driveway, where

Bianca had parked beside another car. That could be the neighbors instead of Scout and Scarlette's family.

The sound of tires hitting the speed bump a few houses down made Bianca turn. It looked like the blue car that had followed her from the set. It slowed in front of the house, but the driver didn't pull out his phone or camera.

She knocked again. Finally, the door creaked open.

A smiling woman with almost as many wrinkles as gray hairs, dressed in an apron, blinked up at her. "Sorry, sweetheart, but I don't want to buy any cookies."

She'd started to close the door when Bianca finally got out some words. "Is this Scout and Scarlette's house?"

The grin slid from the woman's face. "May I ask who wants to know?"

Thankfully, Scarlette's curly locks poked around the door, and her eyes dropped to the cookies. She grabbed them quicker than she had stolen any base. "Total yum. These are—"

"Scarlette Joy Smith." The woman Bianca assumed to be the girl's grandmother sank her fist onto her hip. Almost an identical pose to Scarlette's last night. "You do not grab cookies from strangers."

Scarlette rolled her eyes. "Grandma, that's Coach B."

Her grandma narrowed her eyes first at Scarlette, then at Bianca.

Bianca laced her empty hands in front of her. Perhaps cookies hadn't been a good idea. Flip-flops might have also been a miscalculation if she needed to make a run for it. "I think I've made a mistake. Please tell Scout that I'm sorry for the slide accident and for his—"

"Ah, you're the pizza lady. You can call me Naomi or Grandma. Or both." Naomi opened the door wider as she shot Scarlette a glare. "Well, young lady, you shouldn't assume the cookies were for you. If they're not, you're going to find yourself embarrassed."

A shudder ran down Bianca's back, and she squeezed her fingers together. The last thing she'd meant was for the cookies to bring embarrassment. "They're for both Scarlette and Scout. I only wanted to come by and check on him to see how he was doing."

"Momma!" another woman's voice called out from somewhere inside. "Where's my black pants with the double buttons? I'm going to be late for work."

"Hanging by the washer on the blue hanger," Naomi hollered over her shoulder and stepped aside. Then to Bianca she said, "Come on back and see Scout for yourself."

A slender woman wearing a robe dashed down the hall, carrying a pair of black pants. "Found 'em. Thanks, Momma."

"I don't want to intrude." Bianca lifted her gaze off Scarlette, who had her bottom lip pushed out. "Looks like a bad time. If you will, please let Scout know that I stopped by and . . ."

Naomi opened the door wider. "Nonsense. It's never a bad time for company. Plus, Scout needs rests from his screen. Between you and me, he's milking this broken bone thing for all it's worth."

Bianca put her hand to her stomach. He'd for sure broken his pinkie. She'd prayed it was only a sprain.

Scarlette pulled out two cookies without even taking the bow off and stuffed one completely in her mouth. She mumbled something that sounded like, "Yeah, if I could play games all day, I might wish my pinkie was—"

Naomi dropped her hand on the girl's shoulder. "Don't think we best wish for painful things. They come in life as it is."

The entry wall opened into a quaint yet clean living room. A loveseat hugged the focal wall with framed family pictures. Two rocking chairs beside the window faced the television.

The rocker on the left tilted forward, and the top of Scout's head moved into view. "Why is this level so hard?"

Naomi motioned for Bianca to go to Scout. "Perfect time to rest from the screen."

"But Grandma, my pinkie . . ." Scout turned around. When his gaze landed on Bianca, his scowl vanished. "Hey, Coach B."

Scarlette plodded around Bianca and shoved another cookie in her mouth. "She brought cookies."

Scout hopped up and snagged the package. The bandage made his pinkie about three times its normal size. "These are the best."

Bianca nodded at his hand. "How's your finger?"

He scooped out two more cookies. "The doctor said I don't need surgery, and I can go back to baseball in 'bout four weeks."

Naomi tsked. "We'll see about those four weeks. Don't forget that little *about* word."

Scout stopped the next cookie from entering his mouth. "But the tourney is in four weeks and three days."

"A tourney isn't more important than you being healthy." This came from the younger woman, now dressed in black pants and a white-collared, button-down shirt. She had the same big brown eyes as both Scout and Scarlette. The woman was probably around Bianca's age, but she only came up to Bianca's chin.

The woman cocked her head to the side. "And you are?"

"Coach B, Momma," Scarlette said at the same time the woman mumbled, "Bia Pearl."

Naomi hummed. "Thought you looked familiar."

Scout clutched another four cookies out of the package. "Mom, Coach B bought us pizza and the blow-up slide last night."

An awkward laugh bubbled out of Bianca. She swallowed down what felt like dry, crumbled cookie pieces. "I'm so sorry about the slide and Scout's pinkie."

Scarlette sent Bianca a smirk. "Coach B is with Coach E."

Their mom put both her fists on her hips. "She's *with* Eddie?"

How was Bianca supposed to answer that without lying? "I mean, he's not with me right now in your house . . ."

Scarlette rolled her eyes.

Apparently, that wasn't the right response.

Their mother blinked at Bianca, just like their grandmother had only moments ago. This time, Naomi slapped her leg, and a cackle as booming as a diesel engine filled the room. "Oh, you must be with Eddie all right. He always liked a girl who could make him laugh."

For some reason, that info didn't lessen the tightness in Bianca's stomach.

She curled her toes on her flip-flops. "Yes, well, I wanted to see if I could pay for Scout's hospital bills since you never agreed for him to go down the slide."

Their mother's laughter stopped, and she adjusted the collar on her button-down shirt. "I don't need charity. I can handle my family's bills." She pressed a peck on Naomi's cheek. "I'll be home late. Don't wait up. I'll bring home some leftovers from catering for tomorrow. Love you, kids. Behave."

After a few pounding footsteps, the slamming of the front door rattled the windows in the living room.

Bianca tightened her grip on her wallet. Well, that hadn't gone as planned.

Naomi smiled at Bianca. "Coffee?"

Bianca adjusted her purse strap. "I best be going. Thank you, though. Glad you're feeling okay, Scout. I'll see you later, kids."

Would she still be welcome at their next practice?

Before Bianca could trace her steps back to the entryway, Naomi hooked her hand onto Bianca's elbow. "My legs aren't as young as they once were. Help me walk you to the door."

Ten silent shuffles later, they arrived not only to the front door but to a framed painting on the wall, which she'd missed beside the door. A painting of a rocky beach shore during twilight. A boat floated in the waves, while a lighthouse stood bright and tall.

Then, along the bottom of the framed piece, was a quote.

Let your light so shine before men, that they may see your good works, and glorify your Father which is in heaven.

Frances had sent her that verse the day Bianca had to testify. Wasn't that what Bianca had tried to do with Scout's mom? Provide a good deed in place of a bad one? Except it'd gone horribly.

Naomi straightened the frame that was already lined up horizontally. "Was a wedding gift from my momma. Wish I had more of her paintings. Her words of wisdom. Though these weren't her words but God's."

Bianca backed up and bumped into a short bookcase. She caught a picture of Scout and Scarlette before it fell. "I'm sorry. I should have just left the cookies and money on the doorstep. I didn't mean to make your daughter upset."

She should have called Frances and asked for advice instead of listening to Grace. But then Frances would have asked if she'd been in the Word, and she hadn't. For two straight days.

Naomi placed her hands on Bianca's shoulders as if to straighten her posture. But instead, she lifted a sad smile. "My Jade has her own issues of the heart, I'm afraid. Her ex did a number on her worth, and sometimes accepting help is the first step in surrendering her worries, and sometimes it's the last."

Bianca placed her hand over the woman's. "I understand about exes. Which you may or may not have heard about in the news. Please tell Jade I didn't mean to offend. But also, if she changes her mind . . ."

She'd figure out a way to pay for it if it was before the completed contract timeline.

Naomi's glance returned to the painting. "Sometimes our good works are overlooked. But they're never about us anyway but the One who created all things. As long as we're shining brightly for Him, that matters more."

Bianca stared at the lighthouse. Why did people refuse gifts? Was it because of pride or something else? Or did she not have the right heart about giving this time?

The lighthouse's beam shined along the jagged rocks as if announcing where the boat's troubles rested ahead. Was she shining brightly enough for God? Could others in her life see Him through her? Once she'd announced in an interview that she followed Christ, the media had twisted her words. Said she was only trying to make her image better after she'd supposedly lied under oath.

Frances had reminded Bianca that she only had to fear the Lord, not man. However, some days it was hard to block out the world's voices.

Naomi touched Bianca's fingers. "An accidental broken pinkie isn't the fault of the one who bought the gift to begin with. So you come back and check up on us anytime. I may not have the gift of painting like Momma did, but I'm not shy around a piece of pork steak."

Naomi reminded her of an older Frances. "I'll keep that in mind. Thank you for your kindness." Bianca said goodbye and headed down the porch steps, but before she reached the sidewalk, a familiar black truck pulled up behind her car.

Eddie.

He shut his truck door harder than seemed necessary. Eddie, dressed in jeans and T-shirt, walked up the sidewalk. Purpose laced his expression, but his mouth remained in a tight line. "Didn't expect to see you here."

Bianca pulled her purse strap higher on her shoulder and walked down the steps. "Whatever you do, don't ask to cover Scout's medical bills."

Eddie's shoulders hunched. "Tell me you didn't."

Bianca shook her head. "I'm afraid Jade went to work in a bad mood because of my offer."

"You and your deals." He stopped right in front of her and clutched the keys in his fist. "How did you even find their house?"

Was he really that against her coming to see Scout?

Jade's words came back to mind. *She's with Eddie?*

Oh. "You and Jade dated?"

His face lurched into a frown. "What would make you think that?"

Bianca put her palm to her forehead. Maybe it was best if she stopped thinking altogether. "I don't know exactly. You seemed extra close to Scout and Scarlette, and you knew so much about Jade. Plus she had said that—"

"That she was like a sister to me. That's how we typically explain it when that topic comes up."

"How often has the topic come up?" Bianca pressed her lips closed and headed toward the end of the driveway. She really should have hit snooze this morning. But there was no ignoring a four a.m. call time.

Some things didn't need to be asked when one was tired. Side note: cookies did not always make a day go better.

Eddie grunted. "Probably too many times. Her mother was friends with my grand-ma'am. The previous women I dated always had questions about Jade and the kids."

Was sinking into the ground a current option?

"I'm glad they have you to count on, then. Despite what my actions may or may not show, I know money doesn't fix everything. I only wanted to help."

Like all those who'd helped her.

Eddie leaned his hip against her car. "Sometimes helping means being there right beside the person. I know I had someone in my life who offered big promises, but all I really wanted was for them to show up."

Bianca stepped beside her car. "Couldn't it be both?" She hugged her arms around herself and stared at the road. "When I started getting into youth theater, my teacher helped me apply to this prestigious acting camp, but when I actually was chosen, my parents realized they couldn't pay for it. I don't know who was more crushed, my teacher or me, but my teacher told me to write a letter about why I wanted to go to camp. Somehow, a stranger ended up covering my fees."

She shrugged. "I had the best time at camp. Learned so much. It's when I realized I could actually maybe make my dream come true to become an actress. I promised myself if I did, I wanted to become like that woman who gave me a chance to build my dream because of her giving heart."

Eddie dipped his head. "I wish more people in Last Chance County would notice the needs of the kids here."

Wasn't that what she had been trying to do? Except she was making Eddie give something to her in return. Not exactly like the generous woman of Bianca's childhood.

The blue car that had followed her had returned. The driver drove in the opposite direction, his window rolled down and his phone aimed at Bianca and Eddie. One day she'd get to live her everyday moments without being watched and talked about.

However, this had been her dream. She fisted her fingers and leaned against the hood of her car with a smile directed at Eddie.

Eddie squinted at her. "What are you doing?"

She held on to her smile. "There's someone taking our picture from the road."

Eddie stiffened. "Of course there is. How could I have forgotten?"

The problem was, she had forgotten. And she wasn't sure that was a good thing.

TWELVE

EDDIE JUGGLED THE TWO BOWLS OF OATMEAL in his hands, knocked on Macon's half-open door, and peeked inside. "You wanted to see me, sir? I went ahead and grabbed you some breakfast…"

It wasn't only Macon. The police chief twisted toward Eddie from the corner behind the door where a floor-to-ceiling bookshelf sat. Apparently, the morning would be full of surprises too. But hopefully nothing like the other night's visit to the ER with Scout.

Or yesterday's conversation about Bianca and the giving woman of her youth.

Eddie failed to completely cover his yawn with his elbow. "There's plenty of breakfast left. Want me to go grab another bowl?"

Macon waved him forward. "That's okay, you can give mine to the chief. Natalie cooked me biscuits and gravy before work. I can't say that I'm hating this nesting period she's in."

Eddie handed Conroy one of the bowls.

Conroy sat. "Thanks. I actually haven't eaten yet."

Eddie took his seat, and the sunlight beaming in through the window wasn't the only thing that made him feel like he was in the spotlight. There was only one reason why both chiefs would need to talk to him. Well actually, two. "Have you made any connections to the set collapse or the fire?"

The news had been strangely quiet about the events.

Conroy rested his ankle on top of his knee and scooped another spoonful of oats. "I hoped you were the one with some more news."

Eddie set his bowl on the edge of Macon's desk in front of his framed photos. "I sent you everything I've gathered. Besides Thad, the security officer who likes to talk to me about his grandkids, there hasn't been anything that seemed promising. Other than a few of the crew members asking me to meet up for some wings. I can use that invite to ask more questions if you think it would help."

Conroy took a deep breath. "The mayor's not going to like it, but I'm going to have to put even more cops all over that set."

Eddie shrugged. He had warned Bryce and Olivia and Grace that he was no undercover officer. "I'm no cop. I talked to those who had been around the set during the day of the collapse and before. Theories and speculations. Gossip. But nothing seemed to be worth repeating."

Macon leaned his elbows on his desk. "Surely someone on that set didn't have an alibi for the days leading up to the collapse of the set build."

Conroy steepled his fingers. "There's someone without an alibi all right. Far too many of them. There are ten separate contracted-out businesses, including food, beverages, cleaning, construction, and massage personnel with multiple employees each that arrived on set just within a two-hour window. Not counting the rest of the days. So far, we've got no motive unless the protesters have stepped up their game. Nothing connecting to the Jane Doe or the hit-and-run car incident either."

Eddie tightened his grip on the chair. "Thankfully Bianca didn't actually get *hit* in that incident. Though she did mention her ex has been texting her, and she didn't seemed thrilled. Not sure if there's anything more there." Eddie folded his arms over his chest. "What about the fire at the mayor's event? Any ID on the arsonist? Maybe I could sit with a sketch artist again."

Not that it had led to a very clear resemblance the first time. Eddie could remember exact conversations from when he was a teen, but he couldn't remember what color eyes the arsonist had from only a little more than a week ago.

He had to be missing something. Something simple. But he hadn't even heard anyone yelling.

Eddie sat up straight. But he had observed whispers. "This might not help, but I overheard two people in construction uniforms. They had been whispering. One was short, and the other had narrow shoulders from behind. The taller one had shoved the shorter one, who said it hadn't been his fault. I asked them if everything was okay. They tipped their hard hats and got into a truck with a construction label on its side."

Conroy set his bowl next to Eddie's. He pulled out his phone and typed out a note. "At this point, we're looking into everything." He rested his phone on his thigh. "We may have a small lead. We're bringing a suspect in for questioning who'd been seen with a lighter at the event. However, my crew has to locate him first."

That wasn't exactly comforting.

They were really pinning too much hope on Eddie's investigative abilities. "All the props and storage areas are locked every time I check them. The security guys make their rounds. There's an unofficial smoke break area by the tree beside the parking lot. Leo survives on coffee and jellybeans. There never seems to be enough assistants when one is yelled for. The only people who usually raise their voices are Leo and Carter. But nothing points to why a set could have been sabotaged. I'm sure I could ask more questions and run by the debris again, but there are only so many hours in the day that I can be there."

Macon's chair squeaked. Then the two chiefs shared a look. One Eddie had a feeling he wasn't going to like.

"What are you not telling me?"

Conroy thumped his knuckles against the armrests. "Every time my men show up, it's like the entire crew turns the other way. The mayor gets phone calls. Which means I get phone calls."

Eddie leaned forward in his seat. "They're probably worried you're going to shut down filming. I've heard grumbles of production money issues."

Conroy nodded. "I read that in your notes. And I've also heard that from other sources."

"So what I'm hearing is you don't need me there anymore." Why did his chest suddenly feel tighter? He should be happy to be done at the set.

Except, done at the set meant he'd see Bianca less. Which shouldn't be a big deal. *Shouldn't* being the key word.

Macon picked up a pen. "Perhaps when you're on call, you should stay on set instead of waiting here."

Eddie's back straightened and his healing road rash clung to his shirt. "You want me to go to a film set and not do my job?"

He understood they needed to find answers, but it didn't make sense for him not to go on fire runs. "No disrespect, but I'm a firefighter. Chief, if I'm not on a run, I leave rescue squad a man down. That's too dangerous."

Macon glanced to Conroy. "The mayor requested it, and unfortunately, he holds the funds for all of our paychecks. You're still going out on calls. You'd meet up with the crew. You'll just be waiting for any calls while at the set instead. That will give you more time there to find anything that might help Barnes find a lead. This town seems to be getting hit from all sides, and we're going to have to think outside the box to get everything accomplished."

A wrinkle creased across Conroy's forehead. "Sorry to put this on you, Rice. We're being pressured by the mayor to find answers yesterday. And quietly. Currently, you have a special position beside Bia that helps greatly, and apparently Gregory likes you."

Eddie's mouth hung open. "He sure has a funny way of showing it."

Conroy rested both of his feet back on the ground. "I understand. Trust me. Between the movie and protests over that and the resort, my guys are stretched. I appreciate your sacrifice on this."

Not that hanging out with Bianca had been too much of a hardship.

Macon clicked the pen in his hand. "If for some reason something comes up where you can't make it to a run, then I'll take your place. The last thing I want is to jeopardize Rescue. But I also need to offer what's best for our town too. And if that means one of my firefighters has to pretend to be an undercover officer, so to speak, I think you're a great man for the job."

Eddie pulled his collar away from his neck. There seemed to be far too much pretending in Last Chance County.

Conroy's phone vibrated. "What about with Bia? Anything out of the ordinary since the car incident?"

Eddie picked a piece of lint off his pants. "Other than me being stupid and practically blaming her for Scout breaking his pinkie?"

Macon set down his pen. "Scout broke his finger? How did that happen?"

"A minor hairline fracture. He and Tank slid down a blow-up slide Bianca sort of arranged to cheer up the kids after Roger Pointe let slip that the mayor originally denied the grant for their youth center."

Conroy released a heavy breath. "I'm ready for this election to be over."

Macon did not have the same sympathetic expression on his

face as Conroy. He frowned. "Why didn't you tell me about the grant's denial?"

Before Eddie could come up with an answer that didn't sound like he was failing Macon's team, Conroy's cell phone buzzed again. He narrowed his gaze at the screen, and then his brows rose. "Looks like a deceased male has been found on the set." He looked over the screen at Eddie. "Either of you wouldn't currently be free now, would you? Take another look around the collapsed site while I tag along with my officers?"

Eddie rose to his feet. "Was it an accident or . . ."

"All I know is he was found in the trees between the parking lot and the sidewalk beside the smoking area."

Macon stood as well. "Rice, take a radio and your gear with you in your truck. I'll have another with me packed in the chief's truck too, in case a call goes out. I'll be praying things start getting back to boring around this town."

After Conroy left, Eddie grabbed his turnout gear. As he headed for his truck, his phone rang. He shuffled his gear to read his screen. The name "Mary" made him hit the ignore button. It was never good when his mother tried to call.

He really wished his grand-ma'am hadn't given Mary his number before she passed.

Eddie turned onto the road with the security gate to the film set. Normally there were tourists or fans standing around trying to get a peek at the actors, and a few protesters planted at random corners around the set. But today the entire sidewalk overflowed with angry faces.

Rows of people holding signs with the word *movie* with a red line crossing it out raised their posters and shouted, "Stop the show! Protect our home!"

Thad came out of the security booth and waved Eddie forward.

Finally, the line of protesters snaked to the other side of the road, and Eddie rolled down his window. "You all right?"

Thad wiped the sweat off his brow. "I think my mom was right. I should have been a doctor. At least then I wouldn't have to listen to them holler the same six words."

Eddie turned down his radio. "It isn't even that catchy a tune. When did the protesters arrive?"

Thad's focus remained through Eddie's window and on the protesters. "I haven't been on the clock long. Can you believe it about that body? Riley found him. Poor new girl. About fainted away."

Eddie nodded toward the set beyond the gate. "Glad you guys are getting some more security help. Sounds like you might need it."

"She's not with us." He pointed to his chest where his badge sat. "She's the newest makeup person. I forget her actual title. They all have one, these fancy movie people. I'm only the security guy. Pretty sure Riley replaced Tiff, who had a family emergency. Tiff is a real sweetheart. Brought me a soda once. Gave me glitter makeup for my granddaughter too."

The protesters pivoted and turned back toward Eddie's truck.

Thad groaned. "Better lift the bar for you to enter before the protesters circle around and try to get in again." He deadpanned, "It's sure fun having them around."

"Thanks, Thad, for your hard work. Just think of the stories you'll have to tell the grandkids."

Thad chuckled and opened the gate.

Eddie parked behind the coroner's vehicle. As he hopped out of his truck, one of the cameramen, who seemed to know all the gossip, set one of the two hard-shell suitcases down on the sidewalk, right in front of the yellow caution tape that wound around the trees.

This could be Eddie's chance to learn something that he'd been overlooking. "Need any help?"

The cameraman set the other container down. "If you help, I'll owe you a coffee plus an order of wings."

Perfect. Eddie picked up the container on the right. Good thing he'd been doing his arm workouts. "This thing's heavier than it looks."

The cameraman hugged the other container to his chest. "Tell me about it."

Eddie followed him on the sidewalk. "Where we heading?"

"All the way to the river. I would never have loaded up the gear for the next location if I'd thought they were still going ahead with the shoot."

Eddie's boot kicked a pebble as they took a gravel path between the ambulance set and a building that was painted to resemble an old shack. "Who's in the scene?"

"Only your girl. But we can't afford to let the police shut us down because of the body."

Eddie adjusted his grip. *Your girl.* Not exactly. "Do you know who died?"

"I think one of the construction workers."

The suitcase slipped in Eddie's grip, but he caught it against his leg and hoisted it back into position. "Construction?"

"Easy." The cameraman flinched. "That stuff you're carrying costs more than my monthly paycheck."

"I got it. Sorry, man. What's your name again?" What Eddie was really sorry about was that he couldn't just hand the suitcase back and say he needed to go tell the police about the construction worker. But Conroy probably already knew by now.

"Everyone calls me Chip." He shuffled the suitcase against his chest. "First the building and now this. I think that's why Bia said she would do the scene. Because I know plenty of other stars who would refuse based on the temperature of the water alone."

Eddie slowed his stride to match Chip's reduced speed. "Was Heidi supposed to do the stunt, then?"

Sweat lined the creases on Chip's forehead. "Exactly, and Bia's new stunt replacement hasn't shown yet. Which to me means she could argue against the scene if it's not in her contract. But she hasn't. Probably because Bia Pearl's the ideal cast member. Minus the bad press she usually gets about her personal life. No offense."

Eddie griped the suitcase tighter. "The media isn't always right." Bianca probably felt guilty about Heidi and had taken the spot. Too worried about what others thought. Plus, based on their conversation yesterday and his own deal with her—money mattered.

The sun chose that moment to dip behind a cloud. On the sloping bank down to the river, Bianca stood with her arms wrapped around herself. She faced the water as a car was being raised up by a cable reaching to a platform above the river.

"Where do you need the suitcase?"

Chip tilted his head. "I'll take it from here. Thanks, Eddie."

Eddie waved and came up beside Bianca. "Going for a swim?"

A soft chuckle. "A simple swim sounds perfect." But when she turned toward Eddie, her face was pale. That laugh and the smile she still wore both were fake. She was in pretend mode. "I have to go up there."

Eddie inspected the towering platform. It was about double the height of the slide, and she'd frozen at the lower level.

Eddie put his hand on her elbow. Was he steadying her or himself? He wasn't sure. He leaned beside her ear. "You don't have to do this stunt. I heard it wasn't even supposed to be you."

She adjusted the safety straps around her waist. "We don't have a lot of options right now."

"If it's not in your contract, then you really don't—"

"You sound like Grace. The bottom line is, if the movie doesn't get made, I don't get paid. Not really. And neither do some of the crew." She lifted her chin, and her beautiful eyes flashed a rush of emotions. "Which means *you* don't get your donation either."

One of the other camera crew members down closer to the water paused. An assistant by the lights blinked over at them. Why were they always being watched and possibly listened to?

Eddie hooked his arm around her shoulder. The last thing either of them needed was for the paper to hear about their deal. He steered her closer to the tower, away from listening ears. Her body shook beneath his hands, and he rubbed his palms up and down her goose-bumped skin. "Don't do this for me. Or the team. There are other ways of raising money for the youth center."

She leaned into his touch until she seemed to think better of it and stepped away. "If there was another way, you wouldn't have agreed to . . ." she motioned between them. "Us."

Eddie clenched his jaw and still hated the fear in her eyes. There potentially was another way, or at least that's what Roger had said. However . . . "You're still my choice."

Her sigh made him want to wrap her up and protect her.

She ran her hands along her arms. "I used to love doing my own stunts. Loved seeing the final edited movie, knowing I'd done that. Listening to the crowd as they laughed and cried." She shook her head. "Leo said that if we don't get this critical shot before the police shut us down, then the movie may be postponed. If that happens, we may not have enough funds to keep going. There was a lot of red tape to get this stunt approved, and time is money in the film world. More than just me and you are depending on me not screaming for dear life when that car drops."

She was doing this in part for him. He couldn't let her do it alone. "Then I'll be in the car with you. Not for the directors or for the movie. For you. Because you hate heights."

A half laugh, half cry bubbled out of her. "I really do."

He opened his mouth but was cut off by someone who hollered from the bottom of the platform. "We're ready for you, Bia."

She exhaled slowly. "Well, here goes. Pray for me."

He could do more than pray. He matched each step with hers.

They reached the ladder to climb up. Two guys that Eddie had met a couple days ago, Jeff and Aaron, hooked Bianca's harness to the safety line that went up the ladder and onto the platform.

She climbed four ladder rungs and then stopped. He could see her knuckles go white, even from his position on the ground.

Eddie pointed to the harness around Jeff, who remained on the ground. "Got another one of those? I want to go up with my girl."

"Uh . . ." Both of the guys glanced at each other.

"You know I'm a firefighter. I know all about OSHA standards."

Which probably wouldn't exactly okay him going up there.

Jeff slipped out of his harness and handed it over. "I need to get to my son's birthday party by seven. Anything that can speed this up, I'm all for."

Eddie stepped one foot into the harness. "As soon as I get this on, Bianca, I'm racing you to the top." Eddie hooked onto the safety line faster than it usually took him to get in his turnout gear.

He scrambled up to the same rung of the ladder, placing his feet on the outside of Bianca's. She hadn't moved. Her head remained pressed to a higher rung. Her legs shook the ladder.

He placed his cheek against hers. "I see you squandered your early lead to the top."

Finally she whispered, "Is it squandering when I knew I didn't need it to beat you?"

There was his snarky girl. Well, not his. Couldn't be.

A shaky inhale and then, "Thanks, Eddie."

"We got this. Reach up with your right hand first, and I'll keep you steady. Then bring up your right foot."

She shook her head. "Maybe I'll go back to the ground and help the writers rewrite this scene. My character can be thrown out on the ground and watch her car with the secret codes about the jewels in it disappear. Add in a few explosions. That would totally be better."

He had another idea. "On your mark, get set . . ."

Bianca let out a groan. "Not this again." But she moved upward before he got to the "go" part. "If I win, I'm going to need another milkshake. Or five."

A grin burst onto his face, and he tried to focus on her hands and feet on the ladder. "Told you marshmallow would grow on you."

Or perhaps she was the one growing on him.

Bianca climbed onto the platform, and for a second was out of sight until he joined her and two other guys already on the platform.

The man with a beard, who Eddie didn't remember, frowned. "Who are you?"

The other guy checking Bianca's safety connection bumped the bearded man's arm. His name was Ted or Ed or Jed or something. "That's her—"

"Hero," Bianca answered for him. "Do you guys mind if Eddie helps me into the car?"

Bearded guy hesitated. "We'll have to double-check your harness afterward."

Bianca threw on one of her smiles she used for fans. The one that made her dimple shine almost as bright as her eyes. "Of course. And remind me again what the car is going to do in the scene?"

Bearded guy tapped his fingers on the car being held beside the platform. His focus remained on the crane and pulley overhead, completely missing Bianca's trembling hands. "You're going to climb into the driver's window. Then we'll change out safety connections from here"—he touched the cord that linked to the platform—"to the system that's in the car. Once you're all strapped in and we've given the signal, the car will tilt until its nose faces downward, and when it's exactly where we want it, it'll drop. As soon as it hits the water, the car will level out. You unstrap your safety cords and climb out, swim toward the cameras, and bam. We get it all in one take."

Eddie shifted his feet. Sounded like an awful lot of things would have to go right to get it in one take.

Bearded guy pointed below to the river's edge. "Camera one is at surface level. Then two right there on the dash, which will get your facial expressions on the way down."

Bianca fisted her hands and nodded. "Is there any way I can be teleported into the swaying car?"

Bearded man laughed. He really was missing her cues.

Eddie scooped Bianca up and cradled her against his chest.

Her eyes flung open as she squeaked, "What are you doing?"

Her nails dug into the back of his neck.

"Teleporting."

At that, she smiled her soft grin and loosened her grip. "Can you tell me when I'm inside the car? I'm not sure if I can look down at the ground and still be able to finish the scene."

"Just look at me instead." Eddie paused in front of the car's open window. "Or I can fireman-carry you back down the ladder."

She laid her head against his chest. "As excited as Grace would be to put that on my social-media page, you better only place me in that car."

Once she was in the car, Eddie triple-checked her connection and only then allowed the safety guys to do their job.

The younger one gestured toward the ladder. "We'll need you to, at minimum, be at the back of the platform."

"Eddie." Bianca's call had Eddie rushing over to the car that was now being tilted downward toward the water.

"Stop." Bearded man thrust his arm out in front of Eddie. "We gotta get this in one take."

But with the way Bianca's eyes locked onto his, Eddie was about to demand someone rewrite the scene. "Do I need to get you out? Just say the word, Bianca, and I'll make it happen."

Her fingers squeezed around the steering wheel. Her hair swung down in front of her face. "Will you think less of me if I ask you a favor?"

He squatted, inching closer. "Anything."

And he meant it.

She blew out two quick puffs of air that made her cheeks chipmunk out. "I don't want to be a drama queen, but I really think I'm going to need another marshmallow shake as a reward if I survive this. If I don't, drink one in my honor."

He reached through the open window and tucked a piece of hair behind her ear. "You'll not only survive, but I'll order you two shakes that will probably be here before you get dried off."

She licked her lips. "I don't want to think about what I'd do without you."

Eddie swallowed. "Well, right now, you don't have to."

"Right," she murmured, but her expression did not bear the grin he'd expected.

"Quiet on set!" a megaphoned voice bellowed from below.

Bearded man tugged Eddie back toward the ladder.

Five thundering heartbeats later, Leo hollered, "Action!"

The car tilted forward until it was nearly vertical. Then the crane released the chains, and the car plummeted for the river.

Even though it was scripted, Bianca's scream hit him right in the gut.

The car struck the water with a splash and rippled the river. But instead of the car's back end splashing down into the water too, only the hood remained submerged.

"Isn't the car supposed to lean back into its normal position?" Eddie asked.

Bearded guy put his arm back in front of Eddie. "It will level. Give it time."

Except both time and water poured into Bianca's open window. She moved her hands, but what was she doing?

Eddie shoved the bearded guy's arm away from him. "She's supposed to be out by now."

"We wait until—"

"Eddie!" Bianca shrieked his name a second before the driver's-side door of the car plunged farther into the water.

"Bianca!" Eddie pushed the bearded guy out of the way. "Pull up the car. Get her out of there!"

The younger guy headed down the ladder. "The car can't sink. It had rubber added . . ."

There wouldn't be time to go down the ladder. Eddie unhooked his harness.

"Wait, what are you—"

"Saving her." Eddie sprinted toward the edge of the platform.

And jumped over the edge.

THIRTEEN

BIANCA YANKED ON HER SEAT BELT, BUT IT ONLY tightened against her chest. "Help!"

She kicked her feet through the river water pouring in the opened windows and swelling around her legs. Another shiver jetted through her body as darkness invaded the first seat of the car.

"Eddie!"

This was so not the scene plan. The scariest thing was supposed to have been the heights, not drowning.

She arched her back against the car seat and tilted her head toward the ceiling. The water rose to her shoulders. Fast. She never should have done the scene. She should have listened to Eddie.

The car was supposed to level out. Float, not sink. Why wasn't her safety harness releasing her?

God, I want to see You, but not today. Not like this.

She pulled her numbing legs up through the water and pushed her feet against the dash. Nothing loosened. Still stuck.

God, please help!

She gathered one last gulp of air and then open her eyes under the water. She could barely see the steering wheel in the murky water.

Her ears popped, whether from the pressure of sinking deeper into the river or from not being able to get more air.

She wasn't going to be able to prove to her parents that she'd changed. Save their house before the foreclosure was finalized. No youth center either. Wouldn't see her sister get married. And she'd never see Eddie again.

Her fingers tugged on the left-hand side of the seat belt and shoved it back in, hoping it would give her enough slack to slip out. Her pinkie hit something—the seat recliner.

Her chest burned. She tugged on the lever and rammed her back against the seat. She only needed a little more room. Except the chair didn't move.

Stars filled her vision.

She swallowed and cleared her ears, but she needed air. Now.

God, I'm sorry for everything. I should have worked harder. Been better.

She willed her lungs to loosen, but her heart thumped oddly in her chest. Pain threaded into her sides.

This was it.

Eddie's face burst into her mind. She would never get to help him. Never get to tell him that she wished things could be different between them. He was the best man she'd known. She blinked slowly at the memory of Eddie coming toward her and all the times he'd rescued her.

Something touched her shoulder.

She jerked. This wasn't a memory. Eddie was there to save her?

Even in the shadowed water, panic showed on his face. He wrapped his arms around her sides and pulled, but her body remained rooted.

She took his hand and ran it along the seat belt.

His fingers left hers. Darkness filled her vision.

Hurry. Bubbles escaped her lips.

He pulled something out of his pocket. A knife.

Her lungs screamed. She released more air bubbles, and water slipped into her mouth. It tasted like dirt and death. She couldn't let Eddie die trying to save her.

She pushed at his chest, but he batted her away and reached farther down beside her seat. One heartbeat. Two. And then suddenly the seat belt and safety cords floated in front of her.

Eddie yanked her out of the window and thrust her up, toward the light.

She kicked, freedom in sight. Her lungs were on fire. Burning. Finally, light filled her vision. She crested the water and gulped for the glorious, chilled air.

She kicked, but her legs felt like they were tied down. Water filled around her face again.

Arms circled around her—strong yet gentle. Eddie.

She wrapped her sluggish arms around his neck, breathing hard. His chest vibrated. He said something. Her ears rang. She shook her head.

People swam toward them. Their mouths moved, but all she could do was cling to Eddie.

He spun to his back in the water and pulled her on top of his chest.

She willed her legs to kick but wasn't sure her body listened. The thump of Eddie's heartbeat echoed not only in her ear but under her fingertips. He'd jumped in after her. He'd saved her.

Thank You, Lord. Thank You for this man in my life.

She closed her eyes. She had more time.

The water disappeared around her shoulders, and she opened her eyes.

The river rippled around Eddie's knees.

Voices shouted from the shore. The river's current lapped against the bank. But all she could see was her hero.

He stared down at her, and his chest heaved. "Thought I lost you."

She heard his words above any of the other muffled shouts. His mouth remained right by hers. She cupped his chin. Her fingers danced along his five-o'clock shadow. In his arms, she was more than simply safe. It was like coming home.

She lifted her lips toward her hero. Eddie's eyes remained locked on hers. His heartbeat jumped under her palm. She closed her eyes, and hands pulled at her sides.

Her eyes flew open. No longer as close to him as she wanted to be.

Eddie shifted her tighter against him. "I've got her." His voice sounded like gravel.

Chip held out his palms, soaked up to his chest, and pointed behind Eddie. "The ambulance has arrived. I just wanted to help get you both to the shore."

Eddie glanced down at Bianca as if to ask if she wanted Chip to hold her. Bianca simply answered by lacing her fingers back around Eddie's neck.

A collection of safety and special-effects crew members circled around them with shock and fear in their expressions.

As Eddie reached the shore, his foot stumbled onto the bank.

"I can walk." Her throat, though raspy, finally released words.

Eddie's Adam's apple bobbed. "If I let you do that, you might beat me to the ambulance."

Two paramedics raced toward them from the ambulance on the hilltop.

Eddie set her feet on the ground, and Bianca lowered to sit on the grass, but he didn't let go of her hand.

She squeezed her fingers around his.

The first medic flashed a light in Bianca's eyes. "How long was she underwater?"

"Thankfully not any longer." Bianca coughed. "Thanks to Eddie."

Eddie tightened his hold on her fingers. "She never lost consciousness."

A brief nod from one of the paramedics and then, "Any pain? Symptoms? Head injuries?"

She shook her head, and then Eddie leaned closer to the medics. "Can we get her into the ambulance so she doesn't have an audience?"

Bianca squeezed his hand again.

His gaze lifted off her and moved to the fence on the other side of the river.

Oh.

Not only did it seem the entire film set had encircled them—watching, waiting, and who knew what kind of unauthorized pictures being taken—but there was also a line of heads peeking over the far wooden fence row. It could be fans, or more than likely protesters today. Either way, people ready to sell a story about her to the press. And those stories were never good.

But did it really matter what the world thought of her? Frances kept promising her it didn't.

Inside the ambulance, an EMT listened to her heart while the other spoke to Eddie.

Bianca's head throbbed, and she rubbed her thumb over Eddie's hand. What would she have done without him?

Eddie stopped talking and glanced at her.

She blinked away tears. "I think I like having you around."

A half smile showed a small dimple on the left side of his cheek. "If you want to keep me around, there are other ways besides getting into danger."

Bianca tightened her hold on his fingers. "Good to know. I think I want to totally be done with danger."

The ambulance doors burst open. Carter's eyes flashed with panic. "Bia!"

"Sir." The EMT at Bianca's side held out her gloved palm. "I need you to wait outside." Then to Bianca she said, "Does anything hurt?"

"Just my chest a little."

Carter squeezed inside and yanked on Bianca's arm that Eddie had been holding and pulled her to a sitting position. "They're talking about shutting us down."

Eddie grabbed Carter by the wrist. "Get out before I throw you out."

Carter blinked but didn't move. Eddie latched his grip on Carter's other arm, and they both exited.

A shiver ran through Bianca, and she tightened her hold on the blanket.

The EMT set down the blood pressure cuff. "I recommend you head to the hospital for a more thorough checkup for your lungs."

She took a deep breath. "My lungs feel sore, like I've been swimming all day, but I think I'm okay."

A knock sounded on the ambulance door. "Bianca?" Grace poked her head inside. Her gaze searched Bianca from her drenched jeans to the water dripping from her hair. "Hey, girl. So glad you're safe. Want me to ride with you to the hospital?"

Bianca shook her head. "I don't think I need to go." She balled a corner of the blanket into her fist. If she was going to the hospital, she'd rather it be Eddie with her.

Grace narrowed her eyes. "You sure you shouldn't go in?"

The EMT raised her brows. "My recommendation stands."

Grace tilted her head. "Bianca?"

Bianca pushed up to sit on the gurney. "I should give my statement before anything's decided. Carter said something about production being stopped."

Grace stared at her nails.

"Grace? Did they officially stop because of me?" Would it be safe if they did continue?

Grace sighed. "Nothing's official yet. If they did, it wouldn't be because of you. First the building. Now this, and the death. It's been madness from day one."

Bianca swung her legs over the side of the gurney. She had gotten far too caught up in herself. "Has the family been notified? Was it foul play?"

Grace's phone vibrated, and she swiped on the screen. "One of the construction workers appears to have had a heart attack. So horrible, but no foul play. But with everything, the police could delay the movie."

It also delayed Bianca fixing all the things. She scooted to the end of the gurney. "Let's go see if I need to make a statement." Bianca turned to the EMT. "Thank you for your help."

Had she actually thanked Eddie yet?

The EMT pulled out a clipboard. "Can you sign this release? It states you're aware of the recommendation and you refuse transportation. If you feel anything out of the ordinary . . ."

Bianca signed her given name, Bianca P. Lady. "I promise to get checked out."

Grace hopped out of the ambulance first. Bianca used the rear bumper step to get down.

She turned in a circle. Leo stood by the river with Carter, whose arms flailed as he spoke. Chip was packing up his gear.

Grace touched Bianca's elbow. "Do you need something? Water? Another blanket?"

Bianca peeked around the side of the ambulance. "Do you see Eddie?"

Grace frowned. "I heard his radio call him out on a fire run."

He left.

Bianca twisted her hair to one side and wrung it out. He'd left to do his actual job. Which wasn't to babysit her.

Water dripped down onto her soaked shoe. And that's when she realized she was missing her left tennis shoe.

Grace gasped. "You're missing a shoe. Let's get you back to your trailer. A good hot shower will get you feeling like normal again."

Bianca wiggled her shoeless toes in her sock. Without Eddie there beside her, it suddenly felt like she was missing more than a shoe.

FOURTEEN

EDDIE LIFTED THE TRAVEL MUG IN HIS HAND TO shield the sunrise climbing over the set's food tent. "I'll do it."

The director, Carter, and a blond, mustached assistant named Aiden stopped their not-too-quiet conversing. All three men whipped around from their huddle over a bucket filled with ice and water bottles.

Once yesterday's death of the construction worker and Bianca's stunt had both been ruled accidents, the mayor had pushed for the movie to forge ahead. Apparently, the best thing for his reelection campaign would be for the film crew to finish and leave. Which had put everything back on schedule, until Eddie had overheard the conversation before him.

Not that he blamed Carter's stunt double for quitting.

After a moment, Aiden nodded as if all had been decided. Leo tilted his head, but it was Carter's calculating grin that made Eddie square his shoulders and lower the travel mug in his hand. Earlier, he'd heard the word *police* from one of them, but once their words had turned to center around the film, Eddie had planned to head to the police station and show Conroy what he'd just found in the dirt by the debris.

Until he'd heard Bianca's name, which had led Eddie to opening his mouth.

Carter slipped his arm around Eddie's shoulders. "Excellent. See, problem solved."

Leo still had his face puckered in confusion. "What exactly are you willing to do?"

Eddie shrugged out of Carter's touch, a much looser hold than when Eddie had *helped* Carter out of the ambulance yesterday before a call had pulled him away. "Carter's stunt double refused to do the next scene, correct? I'll do it so the production can move forward."

Not for the film crew to leave town, but so Bianca could fulfill her contract.

Eddie ran his knuckles along his shaven cheeks. Somehow, he could still feel her tender touch from the river. The moment they would have kissed. It was probably a good thing Chip had offered his help when he had.

Leo narrowed his eyes and slid his hands into his jogger pockets. "You agree without even knowing the stunt?" Then he shook his head. "We'll need to go through the union and—"

"Whoa." Carter sidled up beside the director. "If the firefighter volunteers, let him. He's perfect for the fire scene anyway. Plus . . ." Carter stepped back over by Eddie and motioned between them. "He favors me. Sure, he's a little taller. He can hunch as he's rescuing Bia."

The memory of carrying Bianca out of the water made his knees lock. Perhaps he should offer to be in all her stunts. He still didn't see how the wrong harnesses and weights had been used. However, the special-effects guys' stories and alibis all checked out.

"I'll have no problem doing a fire scene, sir."

Carter whistled to another assistant that walked by and motioned for a drink. "Of course he's going to do it. He knows how important this is for his crew. Just think, the Last Chance County

Fire Department can get its name in the movie credits. You know that can be arranged."

Eddie should have rolled his eyes, but he refrained. The guy was trying to prove himself. He'd panicked after coming into the ambulance thinking the police were going to stop the filming.

This wasn't only about getting more money for the youth center. It was also about helping Bianca. A woman who was bound and determined to see the movie to the end to help others.

To help him.

Eddie checked his phone. "What time are the scenes?"

Leo rubbed his chin. "That's just it. The police still haven't given their official release to start filming near the collapsed building yet."

Carter crossed his arms. His white T-shirt stretched thin enough to see his collarbone. "We won't touch that mess. We only need the house across the path."

Eddie glanced over his shoulder to where there was empty roof-line. The cleanup crew had finished cleaning up the spot yesterday. But walking past the taped-off section five minutes ago, Eddie had found a truck key with a smashed plastic keychain where the rubble had been. It could be a clue or something the cleanup crew had accidentally left or lost.

Either way, he had to give it to Conroy as soon as possible.

The assistant typed away on his phone. "I'm trying to find another option. Can the scene be rewritten with a different kind of structure?"

Leo shook his head. "Got to be a house."

"Our smoke house might work." The words flew out of Eddie's mouth without any thought. "I mean, we'd need to get permission from my chief first."

Everyone turned to him, and Leo stretched out his palm toward Eddie. "Explain this smoke house."

"It's where our crews train in different smoke and fire simulations."

"With actual smoke?" This from Aiden. "How long does setup take?"

"If we get approval, not long."

Leo pulled out his phone and pointed it at Eddie. "You talk to your chief." Then at the assistant. "You figure out how we're going to get all the needed extras to the new location. And Carter, go make sure Bia is well enough to film this morning."

Eddie took a step backward and shifted the travel mug to his other hand. "I'll check on Bianca while I'm calling my chief." His fire callout yesterday had lasted until almost midnight, and he wanted to see how she was actually doing. Not hear an explanation about how Carter pretended she was.

Plus, Eddie had something she might want.

Footsteps crunched on the gravel walkway behind him. Eddie turned to find Bianca.

Her eyes landed on Eddie, but it was Carter who spoke next. "Look at her. Styled to perfection. She knows the show must go on."

Bianca produced a closed-mouth smile. "We don't get this far in our careers by giving up, do we?" Her lips may have been coated with picture-perfect lipstick, but she was hiding.

She adjusted the collar on her striped shirt, tucked into a pair of shorts that made her legs go on forever until they reached her boots. "I know we can't afford to lose anymore daylight."

Leo turned to his assistant beside him. "Make sure the wardrobe is ready to be mobile. Eddie will have to have a fire suit."

Aiden took off at a jog.

Carter raised his finger to the man's back. "Have them bring mine over too, and check on whoever was supposed to bring me my coffee."

The man could use a firefighter's training course. Then he might be a little less self-focused.

Bianca tilted her head, and her dangling earrings rested against her cheek. "Was your fire run okay last night?"

A fire was never okay. "Only a building lost. We got out all the family."

Leo covered the speaker on the phone call he was on. "You saved someone else from a fire?"

Carter grabbed an apple off a table and took a bite. "Did anyone capture the moment on film?"

Eddie clenched his jaw together. "Real life isn't like the movies."

"Right. Right. Of course . . ." Carter took another chunk out of the apple.

Leo moved his hand off the speaker. "Yes, Aiden's right. Eddie needs a fire suit. It should fit, right?"

Carter tossed his half-eaten apple toward the trash and missed. He elbowed Leo. "Have them bring me a mocha caramel latte, no foam, extra whip when they bring the fire suits."

Bianca leaned closer to Eddie. "Why are they bringing you a fire suit?"

Leo hung up his call and glanced between Eddie and Bianca. "Your boyfriend's volunteered to be your stunt double and possibly saved us time and money trying to find a replacement."

Apparently, selective hearing wasn't only a kid's ability. "I need to get permission—"

"Technically, he's my stunt double." Carter puffed out his chest. "But you get the idea." Carter gave a salute and headed toward a woman who'd just walked by carrying a drink tray.

Leo clapped. "I need this ball rolling. Where's Grace?" He followed behind Carter.

Bianca dipped her chin. "You don't have to do this."

He couldn't quite read the expression in her eyes. "Would you rather they find a union stunt double?"

She met his gaze then. "Seriously? You've saved me more times than I can ever repay you for. I want you to be the stunt guy. Always."

Eddie's own chest rose until she said, "Plus, it would take more time to find someone else. Do you know what happened to Hank?"

Eddie slid his hands into his pockets. "If that was the original stunt guy's name, he's refusing because of everything that's been going wrong. Supposedly, he thinks the set's cursed."

Bianca sighed. "Not cursed. But sometimes I wonder if someone doesn't want the movie to go ahead."

"Well, the mayor does. Which is probably one of the reasons you're still filming." He extended the travel mug. "This is for you."

She took it and moved the metal straw around, making it clink against the sides of the mug. "You made me an iced coffee? That's so sweet. Thank you."

Eddie pressed his lips together. Maybe this had been a stupid idea. "It probably would have made more sense to offer you caffeine in the morning, but no. I . . . it's actually a marshmallow shake."

Her eyes widened.

Was it a happy surprise or bad? Eddie put his hands in his pockets. "You mentioned wanting one yesterday, and with work and everything . . . I wasn't sure you'd gotten one. So I put one in the travel mug so it wouldn't melt."

She finally took a sip. "Oh my goodness. It's still frozen. How did you get this so early this morning?"

"It helps to be a regular customer."

She took another drink. "You're the best, Eddie. This is exactly what I needed." She tucked herself into his side for a hug. Her arm slipped around his back and squeezed, but she released him much too fast for Eddie's brain to respond.

She stepped away, and a strand of hair danced along her chin. The morning sunlight gave her face a soft glow.

He dropped his gaze to his shoes. He shouldn't be thinking about brushing her hair back behind her ear.

"Frances always says if one of her regulars wants pancakes but it's supper time, she personally goes into the kitchen and makes them." She held out her drink. "Do you want some?"

Eddie shook his head.

"This will help me get through today's filming."

Here was the truth she wasn't showing to Carter or Leo.

Eddie lowered his voice. "Finishing this movie, improving your career, the money, none of it is more important than you. Your safety."

The truth needed to be spoken, even if it might reveal a little too much of his rising feelings.

Bianca rubbed one of her palms up and down the goosebumps along her arm. "I'm struggling with not obsessing over that option, but I wasn't scheduled to do the river stunt. It's only the dangerous stunts that need special permission that have gone crazy. Have you heard anything more about the construction worker?"

Macon had updated him before he'd headed to the set this morning. "He had a pacemaker, and it looks like it's a heart-related death. Nothing to do with everything else."

And they were right back to where they'd started. "You don't have to do this next scene."

Bianca raised her brows, and the straw made a sucking sound. "I'm pretty sure you don't know how the movie business works. I have to do the work to get paid. Plus, if I can survive an almost drowning, doing a fire-and-rescue scene with a real firefighter should be easy. It's *you* who doesn't have to do this next stunt."

"*Should be* easy hasn't exactly . . ."

Loud breathing made Eddie glance over his shoulder. Grace jogged toward them.

She stopped in front of them. "There was a reason I didn't join the track team in high school." With another exhale, she extended the clothes in her arms to Eddie. "Here. It's time to go, Bianca. The limo is waiting. The mayor approved the smoke house, and some lieutenant is getting it set up for us."

Eddie's hands went through the right motions and took the firefighter outfit. The jacket resembled his turnout gear; however, the pants were too thin, and the helmet was lighter than standard issue. "The mayor?"

"What's wrong?" Bianca whispered. "Can he not do that?"

Eddie began to wonder what Gregory couldn't do. Besides approve the youth center for the grant on the first round.

He held out the uniform. "I suppose he can, though I hope my chief was warned. I still haven't called him."

He'd gotten sidetracked by a certain actress.

Eddie grimaced down at the pretend fire suit. "How about I wear my actual turnout gear? That way, if anything weird happens . . ."

Grace blew out another exhale and put her hands on top of her head, taking in another deep breath. "Can't. You have to match Carter." Her phone beeped from her pocket, and she dropped her arms. "Plus, there's not supposed to be fire. Only smoke. Hopefully, it fits." She inspected her phone. "Bianca, they need you in that limo, pronto."

Bianca eyed the fire suit in Eddie's hands. "I'll ride with Eddie so I can talk him through the scene."

Grace's phone beeped again. "I'll let them know." She reached toward the travel mug in Bianca's hand. "I can take that, if you're finished with it?"

Bianca tucked the mug against her side. "Thanks, but it's Eddie's."

Grace raised a brow. Her gaze pinballed between them. "O-kay. I'll see everyone at the fire station then."

After Grace left with a wide grin, Bianca bit the bottom of

her lip. "Thanks again for the milkshake. Morning or night, I'll always take one."

Eddie smirked. "I understand now. You're keeping me around for my rescue abilities and milkshake deliveries."

Except she didn't match his smile.

She shifted the travel mug to her other hand. "I'm pretty sure I never told you thanks for rescuing me for the millionth time last night. Thank you, Eddie. Grace said that you dove off that high …" She swallowed. "And I should have asked first if I could ride with you. If you don't want me—"

"There's no point in driving separately." Other than needing to keep his feelings securely off a future that wouldn't end well. Not when the life of the woman before him wasn't centered in Last Chance County.

He tucked the helmet and fire suit under his arm and walked beside Bianca. "Why isn't Carter doing this scene? Especially if it's only smoke."

Bianca shrugged. "I don't know what his contract says. All I know is that I do most of my stunts, but Carter rarely does any in this film."

She rubbed her hands against her arms as if she was cold. "The location's changed, but the scene setup should be the same. After you find me inside the house, I'll say my lines. I don't have very many. Then you carry me out. Once Leo says cut, you and Carter will switch places. Then the extras swarm around us."

Eddie brushed off a fly that landed on the helmet. Bianca actually did want to ride with him to explain the scene. That really shouldn't bother him.

She placed the travel mug and her hands back behind her, but not before he noticed that they were shaking.

He paused on the sidewalk, shifting the fire gear, and reached behind her and held one in his palm. "If you're this nervous, you can tell them no."

"Don't you ever get nervous before you go out on a call? Hard things sometimes bring nerves. Doesn't mean they're always wrong." She squeezed her fingers around his and then stepped into the parking lot. "This stunt is only going to be some smoke and nothing else, and it's at *your* smoke house. Super safe, right?"

Eddie locked his jaw to keep from flinching. There had been the one time when the doors had locked and Macon and the woman who was now his wife had been locked inside. But it'd ended up being an accident. "Even if things do go wrong, I promise I'll get you out."

She gave him a soft smile and opened the passenger-side door. "I know. I trust you."

Then why did she seem disappointed by that fact?

He also climbed into the truck, and once he was buckled, he started his vehicle.

She turned up the radio to an oldies song. "I was thinking . . . remember when I came to practice and first asked you for a favor, and Scarlette mentioned something about getting to be an extra? I would only need to text Grace, and we could probably make that happen."

Eddie pulled out onto the road and turned in the opposite direction from the picketers, who were back again today. "She'd love it, but she's in school."

Bianca leaned her head back. "That's right. Bummer. Okay, I'll see if there's another time she could come. And could you check with Jade before I bring it up with Scarlette?" She closed her eyes and massaged the space between her brows.

Eddie stopped at a red light. He should have brought her a coffee with her milkshake. Or maybe just a coffee milkshake. Did they make those? "You sure you're up for this?"

She rested her hands in her lap and kept her eyes closed. "Waiting on my pain meds to kick in. Just a headache. Probably from lack of sleep last night. But the good news is, at least my stitches are healing well."

She'd more than likely been up after his fire run. He should have called, since they'd exchanged numbers, and been there for her.

Eddie turned the radio to classical music and dialed down the volume. He figured that was more appropriate than offering for her to slide across the middle and use him as a pillow. His phone rang from its spot on the dash. Bianca stirred, and he hurried and silenced the ringer.

With a quick glance, he saw "Mary" as the caller.

His mother was as stubborn as he was.

He adjusted his grip on the steering wheel. It wasn't like her to call and text him so much in such a short time. But she knew the rules. She could text. Which she hadn't since the other day about his location change.

He flipped the phone over and put on his turn signal.

The street in front of the fire station was lined with cars, and the parking lot was near capacity. Once he parked his truck between two white passenger vans, he laid his hand on her arm. "Hey, we're here."

She released a little moan.

He traced his fingers up her arm. "Bianca . . ."

Her eyes fluttered opened, and a smile hit her lips until she sat up straight. "How long was I out?"

"Probably not long enough."

She stared at the fire station. "I can sleep once the movie's done filming. This place is bigger than I expected. Is the smoke house right there?"

He pointed to the back side of the truck bays. "No, that's for the fire trucks. You can't see the smoke house from the parking lot."

Eddie led her around the back of the building, and Zack met up with them.

Zack hooked his thumb over his shoulder. "Too bad we couldn't have charged for parking today. The youth center would finish out what you need in donations for the down payment in no time."

Eddie shifted the fire suit in his arms and peeked at Bianca. They hadn't exactly discussed who did or didn't know about their deal.

But Bianca simply nodded. "I think it's an excellent idea, Coach Zack."

"Coach Bianca, it seems you're wearing your acting hat today." Zack flicked the helmet in Eddie's hands. "What's this for?"

Her smile vanished. "Eddie's going to do a scene with me."

Even without her expression change, her tone let him know how she really felt about his volunteering for the job.

"Huh," was all that Zack said, but his gaze appeared to be calculating something.

Truck's Lieutenant Amelia Patterson and Izan were inside the smoke house control shed, while Bryce and Ridge spoke with Leo and the mayor.

Gregory really did want the movie to finish.

Grace appeared beside a camera set outside the entrance to the smoke house. She waved at Bianca. "Riley needs to check your makeup."

"Be right there." Then to Eddie she said, "I guess I'll see you in a few. Any other questions?"

Eddie took in the smoke house that now had a wreath on the door and a pair of old tennis shoes beside the entrance. "This is like one of my homes. I think I'm good."

As she walked away, she glanced over her shoulder. "After this, I'd like a tour of that home." She pointed to the fire station.

He gave her a thumbs-up. "That can be arranged."

Zack cleared his throat. "You've never brought a girl *home* to us before."

Eddie rolled his eyes. No, the one girl he'd planned to propose to had laughed in his face before she could meet his crewmates.

Then he'd gotten serious about Bible study and changing his flirty ways. "Don't start. This is work."

"Work, right." Zack chuckled. "That's how it sometimes starts."

"She can't be what I'm looking for. Despite what movies showcase, a famous actress doesn't fall for the boy next door."

"What about for the hometown hero?" Zack rubbed a spot above his brow. "Plus, I found giving God the job of looking for my future spouse works out best."

Eddie exhaled. Probably a bit too loudly. "God knows that because of my unstable past, I need a solid future. Not one built on half-truths, deals, and wishes." He'd had plenty of that as a child. He'd wished that his family would get back together. Wished his mom would stay out of jail. Wished for things that only prevented the truth from sinking into his young mind.

Eddie inspected the film crew setting up in front of the smoke house. "I'm afraid to ask, but do you know if the chief was even called about all this?"

Zack raised his brow at one of the sound guys unloading a light reflector. "He was called by the mayor himself. All our training needed to be postponed for the movie crew. We've never seen so many people running around. It's more chaotic than last Easter's egg hunt at the park. But the chief won't take it out on you. He wants Bianca safe almost as much as you do. We all are rooting for you two."

Eddie bristled. "You know it's only pretend." All of the rescue squad plus Macon knew the truth about why Eddie had been hanging out at the film set. "Her being with me. You guys wasted too much time and energy on that class you so helpfully provided me."

Zack laughed. "That class was entertaining once we got you bandaged up from your road rash." Then he sobered. "Bianca's a good actress, but I don't think she's always pretending with you. We know you're not an actor, so . . ."

Eddie put on the fake uniform helmet. "Yeah, well, it's not like she has a future in Last Chance County."

One of the reasons he needed to keep his head on his shoulders.

Zack patted Eddie's back. "Remember, don't limit God's plans. He has everything worked out. The future might surprise you. It sure did with me and Naya."

Zack may have gotten his happily ever after with his long-lost friend he'd made in foster care, but Eddie needed to focus on the kids he mentored. Their needs were more important than his dating life.

"A small town isn't the kind of place a movie star lives long-term." Eddie checked his phone. No new texts or calls. "Plus, I've got other stuff to worry about."

Zack faced him. "Like what?"

Eddie crossed his arms. "My mother called."

Zack narrowed his eyes. "What does Mary want?"

Eddie slipped his phone back into his pocket. "She hasn't left a message or text, other than the one from the other day that I told you about."

Zack frowned. "Next time she calls, I'll answer . . . if you want?"

A good friend. But not needed. "She knows the deal. She can text."

Leo put a megaphone up to his mouth. "Places, everyone."

Eddie pulled on the fire suit. "Guess this is it."

Zack winked. "Might be the beginning of your film career."

Eddie turned toward the cameras, but then over his shoulder said, "Maybe you should think about going into comedy."

Zack's laugh lasted until Eddie made it all the way over to Leo.

Leo gave him a once-over. "The suit fits. Good. So, you enter. Find Bia in the back room. Carry her out. Easy peasy. Let's get this in one take, everyone."

Carter came over and snapped on his own firefighter helmet that matched Eddie's. "Don't mess up by staring at the cameras."

Eddie clenched his jaw. "I'll just pretend I'm a real firefighter."

Carter whipped around. "Acting is harder than it looks."

Man, that guy. Eddie rolled his shoulders back. He needed to focus on his task and not worry about Carter. No wonder Bianca had said sometimes crews didn't bond.

Eddie took his mark on the front step.

At Leo's call to action, Eddie touched the door handle with the back of his hand like he would on a real fire call to feel if there was any heat on the door. It was cool. He opened the door and rushed in.

Smoke fogged his vision. Except this was nothing like a real-life fire or their practice simulations. Only in movies and on television did a fire scene still have enough visibility to actually see where he needed to go.

He moved through to the back room and turned to the right.

But instead of a dummy, like in their fire drills, Bianca lay on the ground in the corner. His boots thumped against the floor beneath him, but she didn't move when he entered.

His chest squeezed tight. Had something gone wrong?

He rushed to her and fell to his knees beside her. "Bianca!"

"Don't talk," she whispered. "Just scoop me up. And wait for my lines."

Carter had been right. Eddie was no actor.

He picked her up and easily cradled her to his chest.

She gasped and placed her hand on his cheek, stopping Eddie's legs from moving.

"You came. Why did you give up those clues? I can't believe you traded something that valuable for me."

His arms tightened around her body, hugging her against his chest. Somewhere in his brain, Eddie knew she was quoting her lines.

Except in reality, she was far more valuable than she realized. Not only to God as a person but who she was becoming to Eddie.

Even days ago, he'd hoped she'd come to their baseball game. Not that he'd shown it well after Scout got hurt. He'd gone out of his way for a stupid milkshake because he'd wanted her to share her genuine smile with him.

She was worth diving into the river. Braving a car. Now stunt doubling. He really would go to any length to save her. Because of his training and his job . . . or for something that wasn't feeling so fake between them?

Eddie stared at the woman looking back at him. She'd somehow seeped into his life, and he didn't hate it.

Lord, could this really be the woman for me? Because it doesn't make sense!

"Eddie?" she whispered.

Right. The movie. Their deal. All pretend. Or at least on her part.

He spun around and sprinted back out of the house.

"Cut!" Leo squinted at the playback camera. "We can use that. Thanks, Eddie and firefighters. Now, let's get the next scene with all the extras. Carter, jump in there."

Carter stopped in front of Eddie and held out his arms. "I'll take her off your hands. It'll give us extra time to practice our kiss."

Kiss. Eddie's eyes found Bianca's lips as if on their own.

Of course costars might kiss on film.

Bianca met Eddie's gaze. "It's only pretend."

Pretend. Just like she's doing with me. Here he'd been thinking how a future together may not be that crazy of an idea. But this was work to her. Only a deal to get what they both wanted.

She tapped her fingers on Eddie's shoulder. "You can put me down now."

Eddie set her feet on the ground as Carter stepped next to Bianca. Carter pulled from his pocket what looked like the scene's script. "Won't be too much longer until our big scene." He rolled up the script, and his grin slid from her to Eddie. "Then it will be my turn to have her all to myself. It's about time too. My views have been suffering." He sent Eddie a hooded glare.

With his arms now empty, Eddie needed something to hold on to. He folded his arms across his chest. What Carter said shouldn't matter. Bianca was an actress, and the most important thing Eddie needed to remember was that they weren't really dating. Didn't matter what false hope Zack had planted in his head.

However, that didn't exactly make the knot in Eddie's chest disappear.

"Hush, Carter." Bianca repositioned one of her curls. "Other people can hear you."

Carter's face erupted into a grin, and he gave her a wink. "Good. Maybe the timetable can get back to what it was supposed to be from the beginning, according to the movie promotion clauses in our contracts." Carter pointed the paper at Bianca. "Sweetheart, he may be helping *your* social standings, but . . ." He flapped the script at Eddie. "He's not doing a thing for my career."

Eddie locked his jaw. Perhaps the director would need him to do a stunt where he could tackle Carter and wipe the smugness off his face.

Bianca grabbed the script from Carter, unrolled the paper, and flipped to the third page. "Thanks so much for filling in, Eddie."

Eddie took off his helmet. Obviously, it was time for her to pretend with someone else. At least they were at the station. He had actual work that could be done, and he didn't need to watch Bianca kiss anyone. Real or not. "No problem. I'll see you around."

Or he'd finally run that found key to the police station.

Bianca looked up from the script and scowled. "Eddie, wait. What about the tour—"

"Clear the set," one of the assistants called.

Eddie obeyed the instruction and headed toward the firehouse.

Leo yelled behind him. "Extras, on my mark, run toward the happy couple."

Eddie's boots thumped against the sidewalk to the bays. All of that over Eddie's shoulder wasn't his world. It was all pretend, and he needed to remember that.

Before he made it to the truck bay, Grace jogged up to him. "Thanks for helping us out, Eddie."

"No problem," he grumbled.

"Umm . . . if you don't want to make the trip, I can take the fire suit back to the set for you. I know Bianca's done for a few hours after this, and it would be great to get a few shots of you guys together."

Eddie stopped, and a sigh escaped his mouth. He pulled off the uniform. "I think she's about done with my help."

Grace glanced over her shoulder. "For what it's worth, Carter's focused on his career, not Bianca."

He placed his helmet on top of the folded jacket and fire pants and handed them over. "It doesn't matter if Carter does have his eye on Bianca."

Grace tapped her finger on top of the helmet. For one, two of his heartbeats.

"Eddie!"

He turned toward Bianca's voice.

She raised her hand over the crowd. "Wait. We need you."

His heart beat oddly in his chest until Bianca pointed at a woman beside her. Apparently, his real career would have to wait again. The other woman wore a bright pink shirt and had slick straight hair that reflected the sunlight as she marched faster than Bianca toward him.

How many assistants did one movie need? He didn't recognize her. "Do I need to redo the fire scene?"

The woman lifted her chin, and her brown eyes locked onto Eddie's.

No. It couldn't be.

The woman waved, and her mouth popped open into a grin that he'd never seen on her before. "Eddington!"

Eddie stiffened. How he wished this were a movie scene instead of real life. Wished his legs would turn him around and sprint for the fire station.

Her black pearl necklace swayed across her chest as she snaked forward in heels he'd never once known her to have owned. The closer she got, the clearer the wrinkle lines around her eyes and mouth showed, despite her thick pink eyeshadow.

She stretched her arms out wide, and Eddie took a step back.

How was his mother in here? But more importantly, why had she hunted him down after ten long years?

FIFTEEN

BIANCA DIDN'T MISS EDDIE'S FLINCH WHEN THIS relative of his tried to hug him. She'd made a mistake.

She should have checked with Eddie before she'd agreed to this surprise reunion. Why hadn't she learned her lesson from the pizza incident?

After surviving the scene of kissing Carter's cheek, she'd been trying to process the frown Eddie had worn when he'd left for the fire station. That was when a woman who Bianca had assumed was a film extra had motioned her over. Usually, Bianca would have waved and gone on preparing for the next scene, but at their current last-minute location, there wasn't a specific section for the extras.

Something about the woman's fancier clothes and familiarity had made Bianca walk over. Now she realized it had been the woman's eyes. The rich mocha coloring matched Eddie's.

Bianca jogged the rest of the way toward the pair as Eddie glared at his relative. "What are you doing here?"

The woman extended her arms. "Can't your mother surprise you?"

Bianca gaped at the woman. "You're his mother?"

Eddie's frown and tightly crossed arms did not match his mother's expression. "I'm definitely surprised."

Bianca put out her shaking hand. "Why didn't you tell me who exactly you were?" Then again, would it have mattered? She would have assumed Eddie would have wanted to see her. Just as Bianca would have wanted to see her own family.

His mother's haughty snarl at Bianca flashed into a smile as she addressed Eddie. "I called you more than once. But you never answered, so I thought a surprise was in order. I arrived in time to see you holding your new girl." She put her hand on her chest, her eyes misting. "You've gotten so tall."

"Rice!" His lieutenant hollered from the bay area where Zack and Ridge jogged toward Eddie. "You're needed inside. Now."

Eddie shot Bianca a look. "Yes, sir."

She'd messed up even bigger this time. *So sorry*, she mouthed.

He avoided her gaze and marched away to the fire station.

Zack stopped beside Bianca while Ridge stepped in front of Eddie's mother. "Can I help you, Mary?"

Bianca squeezed her eyes shut. They knew this woman and were protecting Eddie. While she'd done the opposite.

Mary adjusted her leather purse on her shoulder. "I'd love a chair in the air-conditioning while I wait for Eddie to have his lunch break."

Zack shook his head. "If you want to see Eddie, you'll need to contact him."

She lifted her chin. "I've been calling him."

Ridge motioned toward the pathway to the parking lot. "Then he has his reasons for not replying."

Mary raised her brow and rested her hand on her thick pearls. "Doesn't that Bible he reads now say something about respecting his mother?"

Zack squared up to the lady. "Ma'am, according to the law, you're not his mother any longer."

Bianca pressed her fingers over her mouth. Oh, Eddie. She'd failed him.

Mary's eyes watered, and then she turned for the pathway.

Ridge hooked his thumb over his shoulder. "I'm going to go make sure . . ."

Zack nodded. "I'll catch Bianca up here."

Ridge gave a thumbs-up and trailed after Mary.

"I'm so sorry." Bianca sank her face into her palms. "She said she was a family member traveling through town and wanted to surprise Eddie. I guess I thought how I'd love it if my own family went out of their way to come see me . . . but I was too focused on my issues instead of thinking of Eddie. I didn't know he and her . . ." She lifted her face. "I really need to apologize."

Zack sighed. "Mary gave up her parental rights to Eddie when he was a teen. In my opinion, he hasn't forgiven her."

"Is Eddie actually busy in the firehouse, or can I go tell him I'm sorry?"

Zack slid his hands in his pockets. "Probably a good idea to give him some time first."

She sniffed. Time. She'd call Frances for prayers and wisdom. "Sure. Yeah. Obviously, you know him better than me. I understand. Thanks for explaining."

Zack paused. "I hope you'll get the entire story, but it's not mine to tell."

She glanced over her shoulder and spotted Grace waiting under a tree. "Thanks, Zack."

Zack nodded and headed inside the fire station.

Grace walked over and handed Bianca a cup filled with blueberries. "What was that all about?"

Bianca rolled the blueberries around in the cup. "I led Eddie's mother to him because she wanted to surprise him. But there are . . . issues."

Much worse than her own.

Grace grabbed three blueberries from Bianca's cup. "So head-lines aren't going to say 'Hero Brings Bia to Meet His Momma.'"

The cup dropped out of Bianca's grip, and blueberries bounced on the pavement.

Bianca's stomach tightened as she scooped up the blueberries.

Grace squatted along with her, grabbed a few berries, and put them into the cup. "You two still have a deal, right?"

Eddie's hurt expression as he'd stepped away from his mother made her heart ache all over again.

Bianca stood. Her legs shook, and she locked her knees. "Right now, I don't even know if he's okay."

That mattered more than any deal.

Grace grimaced. "If you hurry, you probably have a few minutes to run down there. Leo wants to move up the afternoon scene to the park. We need you to get back to wardrobe and to Riley." She put her hand on Bianca's arm. "But you can take the time—"

"Thanks, but he needs space." It wasn't about what she needed. "Can I get a ride back over in the limo?"

Grace checked her phone. "Perfect. I think Riley is going to ride over there with that group too, so it might be a tighter fit. We're hoping to get there and wrap it up quickly before the protesters catch wind of where we'll be next. I'll text Justin and let him know you're on your way to him."

"Okay, thanks." Bianca pulled off her heels. She didn't know who in real life would wear heels when they were searching for clues about a jewel.

The grass between the fire station's winding driveway and the sidewalk tickled against her bare feet. The limo was parked on the street. A group of boys was riding up the sidewalk in her direction. Three riders sat on the seats, and then two of the bicycles had a boy each behind the peddler, standing on the spokes.

The first set of boys sped past her. However, the second bike slammed on its brakes.

The teenager stared at her. "Are you Bia Pearl?"

She slipped her shoes back on. "Hi, boys. It's good to see you guys out riding bikes in the fresh air." The freckled-faced boy who had been standing on the spokes of the last bike hunched behind his driver. Wait. "Will, is that you?"

Will peeked out from behind the other boy. His freckles were on full display, but his gaze didn't meet hers. "Hey, Bia."

Bia, not Coach B or even Bianca?

The boy who had stopped first, who looked a few years older than Will, chuckled. "Who's Will?"

Will shrugged. "Jimmy's my nickname."

Bianca tilted her head. She'd heard of Will being short for William, but Jimmy? Wasn't that usually for James? "Why do they call you Jimmy?"

Will slinked down, almost completely out of view.

The first bicycle rolled back to them. "Hold on, who cares what Jimmy's name is? Can we get a picture with you, Bia Pearl?"

Her phone rang. Another unknown number filled her screen. *Please let it not be Nathan.*

She clicked ignore on her phone and took a picture with the boys.

After they'd taken a few group selfies, Bianca stepped closer to Will. "I'll see you in a few days?"

Will's driver whipped his head around. "You're hanging out with Bia Pearl, and you're not telling us? Dude, where at? What time's the party?"

"She's a movie star. If I spill, I don't get to go. Now let's get out of here or we're gonna be late."

The boys glanced at each other, then sped off.

Will went by Jimmy, and he didn't want the older boys to know he played baseball? That didn't make any sense. Her phone rang. The same unknown number from a second ago flashed on her screen.

This needed to stop. She hit the answer button. "Hello."

"Finally, babes."

"Don't even, Nathan," Bianca hissed. "The only reason you need to be calling me is to apologize and to tell me what happened to my money."

Nathan tsked. "I've missed you too. Listen, we need to meet up. I've got this new adventure I want to surprise you—"

"No." No more surprises. Bianca shook her head and headed to the limo. "The last adventure I heard you mention over the phone ended up with the police arriving and me looking like a liar. Tell me the truth, Nathan Kensington. What did you do with my money before the account was frozen?"

The pause let Bianca know her ex was more than likely rolling his stress ball in his hand. "Lady B, it's really not that simple."

Bianca leaned her hip against the back of the limo. "Then until you can give me a straight answer over the phone, stop contacting me." She hung up and blocked the number.

Lord, make him stop calling me.

With shaky hands, Bianca opened the rear door of the limo and slid inside. The middle partition window, as usual, was down between them.

Justin's brown bushy hair was in view. "Everything okay back there?"

"It will be." Bianca scooted to the middle seat. "Long time no see, Justin. How's your mom?"

He glanced back at her in the rearview mirror. "Much better. She only has a little cough. Thanks for asking. We're waiting for Carter and a few others, and then we'll get moving. As always, feel free to grab yourself a drink or snack."

She took a water bottle from the mini fridge and pressed the bottle against her heated neck. She really needed to think about something other than Nathan. Will's half-hidden face popped into her mind. "Hey, quick question. Do you know if it's somehow not cool to play baseball anymore?"

Justin adjusted the mirror. "I think it's cooler to play video games."

"I guess." At least the boys were outside. "And you wouldn't know why a boy would be called Jimmy, would you?"

Justin's brows rose over the top of his sunglasses. "If his name was James?"

She shook her head. "It's not."

Then Riley turned around from, apparently, her spot in the front passenger seat. "He could be good at picking locks. I once knew someone they called Little Jimmy because he was great at jimmying locks."

Bianca twisted open her water. She hoped that wasn't it. She waved at Riley and took a sip of her water. "Didn't know you were up there. You can come sit back here. Not that Justin isn't great company too."

Riley dropped out of view again. "I'm good. Justin's going to show me the ropes up here. My brother's . . . interested in being a limo driver. I'm seeing if he could handle it."

"Oh, I didn't know you have a brother."

Justin popped in a piece of gum. "Can't have too many limo drivers, you know."

Bianca smiled but dropped it when she glanced at the fire station.

Zack had said Eddie needed time, and she'd give him space. But she was pretty sure he'd want to know about Will.

She pulled out her phone and shot off a text to Eddie.

__________________ Bianca

I'm so sorry, Eddie. I really would like
to apologize in person when you'll let
me. But I ran into Will . . . Did you know
that he also goes by the name Jimmy?
He was hanging out with these maybe

fourteen-year-olds who didn't know he
played baseball. Is that weird, or am I
being a helicopter coach?

She pulled up Frances's name and sent her a text explaining about her mistake with Eddie and his mom and Nathan's request to meet. Her phone vibrated with a response from her friend.

Frances

Sorry, hun, I'll be praying
for wisdom.

That was it? Her phone buzzed again. But it wasn't Frances. Another unknown number.

Unknown

LB—really, we need to talk.
In person.

If only it were Eddie who was up for talking. Bianca deleted the message. Nathan had always called her LB for Lady Bianca. And he was wrong. They did not need to talk in person. He'd called her a liar under oath. Helped ruin her name and was the reason her accounts had been frozen and were now missing money.

Her phone vibrated again. Eddie's name finally crossed her screen. However, it was almost as disappointing as her ex's words.

Eddie

I'll check on him.

I'll. Not *we'll.* Just like Will, Eddie had dodged her questions. Maybe he'd also been busy, still upset, or worse, he was pulling away from her. Letting Eddie go was starting to feel like the biggest mistake of their entire deal.

SIXTEEN

EDDIE'S BOOT HIT THE NEXT RUNG DOWN ON the ladder, which rested against the side of the firehouse. A lunchtime rain shower had cleared out all of the movie crews. His mother had been spotted leaving too. And no further calls or texts. Except from Bianca.

It wasn't her fault that she didn't know his past with his mother. But maybe it was better to put some space between him and Bianca. Though, she'd been right to tell him about Will. Of course, the kid hadn't answered Eddie's call. He'd visit Will after work. Right now, Eddie had to focus on his job. Finally, back to doing what he loved.

A rescue dummy was draped over his right shoulder, and Amelia was hot on his tail. Only four more rungs until he could hit the ground and tag his fellow Rescue crew member's hand in the training relay race. Truck against Rescue.

"Come on, Rice," came Zack's shout. His friend had already completed the second leg of their relay.

Amelia grunted from above him. She must be lifting her rescue dummy on the roof.

Eddie exhaled and steadied his next step on the last rung. Victory was in sight. The sun dipped below the trees lining the street. His boots pounded the driveway, and his helmet hit against the mannequin's side. Eddie readjusted his grip and sprinted for the ambulance parked halfway down the driveway—the finish line.

"Put it in overdrive," Izan Collins yelled at his own lieutenant, but Eddie pretended the encouragement was for him, not Amelia.

Eddie tucked his chin and dashed forward.

On the sidelines of the first leg of their relay, Ridge cupped his hands over his mouth. "You got this, Rice. Hold on to the lead!"

Hold on.

Eddie's boots slapped against the wet asphalt as his mother's words from over ten years ago rang in his mind.

She'd tugged on the hem of the same navy shirt she'd been locked behind bars wearing almost twelve months before.

"I can't hold on to what's weighing me down. No more. I deserve happiness. It's right within my reach. I can feel it. I've got to make some hard decisions for both of us. That's what this book says. You'll understand one day."

"What book?" was all his young mind managed to ask.

With a glance over Eddie's shoulder, she lifted her hand to a taxi idling in the jail parking lot. "I have to get rid of everything I've been holding on to. It weighs me down, and it'll all send me right back in that jail. I can't keep surviving that. So I signed the paperwork."

She gave Eddie a pat on his shoulder. "You'll be okay without me. It's better this way."

She walked away from her son. No hug. No apology. Not even a backward glance over her shoulder.

Eddie rubbed at the spot on his shoulder where his mother's hand had rested. During the past twelve months in foster care, he'd grown taller than his mother. And apparently, she had grown out of being a mother to her only son.

Eddie blinked away that old jail parking lot in time to notice a puddle in the fire station driveway. He widened his stride, hurdling over the water. The heel of his boot slipped against the wet pavement. The next thing Eddie knew, his foot went out from under him. His left side hit the ground. Hard.

Amelia leaped over his rescue dummy, which now lay on the ground behind him.

Eddie rolled onto his back and groaned. He'd blown his lead. And worse, lost Rescue's victory.

Bianca's face popped into his mind. *So sorry.*

Bryce bent down over him, sending Bianca's memory away. "You hurt?"

"All my fingers and toes are movable." Eddie stared up at the purple-and-pink-painted clouds. "Sorry, Lieutenant. Not sure what happened."

Bryce squinted as if he knew exactly what had tripped his focus. "Give yourself a breather, and then I want to retime your leg in the relay."

Eddie sat and unsnapped his helmet. "Yes, sir."

Amelia strolled back over with her rescue dummy. "I'll race you again, Rice. I want to earn our victory fair and square."

Ridge came over next to Amelia and crossed his arms. "You only want a chance to rub it in our faces. Twice. It's not going to happen."

Amelia squared up to Ridge, practically nose to nose. "Bragging's not what a team player does. Why don't you and Collins go place the dummies on the roof for round two between Rice and me."

Ridge inhaled deeply but grabbed rescue squad's dummy.

Zack squatted beside Eddie on the ground. "I'm not sure you could duplicate those moves even if it meant you could win enough money for the youth center. You got some air, man."

"My body agrees with you." More bruises to go along with what he'd already earned. Eddie placed his helmet on his knee and raked his fingers through his hair. "But I think you need to work on your encouraging speeches."

Zack didn't crack a grin. "I think I need to work on my friend's-girlfriend-led-his-birthmother-right-to-him-and-we-need-to-talk-about-it speech."

"I'm certain that's not on today's training agenda." Eddie pushed himself to his feet.

Both Ridge and Bryce came and stood on the opposite side of Zack. Three against one.

Fine. Eddie popped his knuckles. "Just make it quick."

Ridge shook his head. "We're not going to make you do anything you don't want to."

Zack adjusted the hem of his turnout gear. "Since Mary showed up, it might be good to see . . ."

Eddie lifted his brow. "You think I should meet with Mary? You were supposed to understand the most why that wouldn't be a good idea."

Except Zack's foster-care placement hadn't been because his mother had stopped being a parent by her own selfish choice. Zack's parents had actually loved their son.

Zack tilted his head. "It could be exactly what you both need."

He didn't need that woman. "I've been more than fine without her." Eddie bent back down and retied his boot strings. "What I need is for her to leave me be like she did ten years ago."

Bryce widened his stance. "What if she's as stubborn as you are and keeps calling and texting and showing up?"

Eddie straightened. That was an unfortunate possibility.

Zack held up his palms. "Look. You keep saying you've put the past behind you. But burying something isn't the same as surrendering it over completely to the Lord."

Eddie flexed up the front of his boot and bent forward, stretching his calf muscle. He'd handed over his past when he'd surrendered his life to God. Hadn't he?

Ridge stepped forward. "Your feelings toward Mary aren't misplaced."

Eddie stood and rolled back his shoulders. There was a *but* coming. It was only a question of who'd actually say it. He eyed Zack.

Instead, Ridge said, "There's a chance she's changed from her old ways."

Eddie glanced heavenward. The Lord had changed *him*. Obviously, nothing was impossible with God. "Maybe," Eddie murmured as his chest tightened. "However, honestly, forgiving her in theory is much different from forgiving her when she's standing in front of me."

Ridge slid his hands into his uniform pockets. "Then it's a good thing that God shows us how to forgive. He won't leave you to do it alone. You could take one of us with you."

Zack cleared his throat. "Or you could take Bianca?"

Eddie snapped his attention to his closest friend. Had he been outside in the heat too long? "You want me to bring a movie star who not only led Mary to me but is also only *temporarily in my life?*"

"He's right." Ridge moved over to Eddie's side and faced Zack. "Unless it's to potentially shift some of Mary's focus off Eddie. But not sure if Mary's the kind to be starstruck."

Eddie curled his toes in his boots. "In jail she became obsessed with a Joel Gillian and that life-coach book of his." Had given her son away because of it.

"I think," Zack said, dropping his voice, "Bianca's been hurt by someone in her family too. It could be a bonding moment for everyone."

Eddie put his helmet back on. "There can't be any bonding moments between Bianca and me."

Because he wasn't supposed to have any feelings for her. They had a business deal. Teammates. Nothing more.

Zack narrowed his gaze at Eddie as if he'd located the target he'd been looking for. "Healing, then?"

Eddie snapped his chin strap closed. "Not in charge of her healing, either. I'm around her to keep her safe and to get her money." He grimaced.

Ridge shook his head. "Yeah, that sounded horrible to us too."

Eddie stepped out of the speech circle and spotted Amelia taking a drink from a water bottle. "Hey, Patterson. How about the rematch?" Then to Zack. "Bianca's not made to stick around Last Chance County, so stop making something out of nothing."

She'd leave him. Just like Mary.

Amelia came up behind Ridge. "Done pep talking yet? Let's get this rematch done." She repositioned her helmet. "What if we raise the stakes? If I win, the entire station goes on Truck's three-mile run."

Ridge rolled his eyes. "Nothing says *team* like three miles." He jogged past them with a stopwatch bouncing around his neck.

Zack thumped his hand against Eddie's back. "You got it, Rice. All of it."

Amelia walked to their starting position while Bryce matched Eddie's pace.

Bryce lowered his voice. "I know you've got a lot going on in your head. Just remember that, yes, God already knows it all, but He wants to hear about it from you."

Eddie swallowed. He hadn't prayed about Mary in a long time. *Sorry, Lord.*

Firefighting he could do. He wasn't sure about the Mary and Bianca thing.

Eddie stepped to the starting line beside Amelia.

Ridge held out the stopwatch. "You ready? On your mark . . ."

Amelia raised her arm. "The chief should count us down. It's only fair."

Ridge gave Amelia a glare. "Should he do the stopwatch too?"

Eddie gave Ridge a look. "Maybe you and Patterson should be racing instead."

Bryce smirked. "As much fun as that would be for the rest of us, Patterson, the chief is busy. Foster races into fires for a living. Surely he can handle the time."

Ridge raised his brows at Amelia and then to Eddie. "Ready? On your mark, get set, go!"

Eddie shot up the ladder.

On the roof, he was the first to his rescue dummy. Amelia only had hers hoisted onto her shoulder as Eddie had already started down the ladder. His boots hit the ground, and this time, as he neared the rain puddle, he went around it.

Amelia's boots thumped behind him, but he didn't turn, kept his sights on the goal—the ambulance ahead.

Zack waved him on from the sidelines. "She's coming! Go, Eddie, go!"

Eddie sprinted hard and rested his rescue dummy on the stretcher placed at the rear of the ambulance.

His fellow rescue squad members lifted their arms in victory. Eddie pumped his fist and smiled.

Until he spotted Bianca.

She waited farther down the drive, dressed in a T-shirt, jeans, and flip-flops. The wind blew her hair back, making her appear, even in her casual clothing, as if she were here for a photoshoot.

He unsnapped his helmet. After his short reply to her text, he was surprised to see her.

Zack jogged up behind him. "Why don't you go and straighten out a few things? I'll take care of the dummy and your helmet."

Eddie handed over his helmet. He walked down the drive and stopped in front of Bianca, only then noticing the two familiar cups in her hands.

"You brought me a milkshake?"

"I'm sorry." She set the milkshakes on the ground. "I don't want it to look like a bribe. I passed the restaurant on the way here and . . . Eddie, I never should have assumed that it was okay to bring someone to you without asking. I keep doing that. I don't mean to be self-focused, but I promise to try harder not to be. To think of your needs over mine."

The sincerity in her gaze made Eddie glance down. Which brought his attention to her mouth. Which was bad because he didn't need to be looking at her lips.

He stared at the grass to the left of the driveway and ran his fingers along his hair. "Before Mary left for jail that last time, she'd promised me that she'd become a better mother. Instead, when she was released, she stopped being my mother officially. Gave me up to follow her dreams of happiness."

Tears swam in Bianca's eyes. He didn't even have a second to open his arms out fully before she fell against his chest and wrapped him into a hug he hadn't even known he'd needed.

She tightened her arms around his back. "I'm afraid your milkshake is going to melt and be pointless."

He set his chin on top of her head. "It'll be all right."

It would. Because God had his future.

Milkshakes didn't exactly fix mistakes, but maybe it was time Eddie finally faced his past.

SEVENTEEN

ONE MORE DRESS FITTING AND THEN SHE COULD hide in her trailer. Maybe she'd go to bed early and dream of a way to fix her mistakes. Yesterday's milkshake hadn't exactly covered her actions with Mary. And with all the extra scenes and dress rehearsals, she hadn't seen Eddie at all today to judge how he was doing.

As Bianca reached the top steps to the wardrobe building, her phone vibrated in her pocket. Probably Grace telling her she was running late. Except her screen showed Frances's name.

Bianca swiped the Accept button and stepped under the shade of the building's roof. "Hey, Frances. Perfect timing."

"Oh, honey." The clank of dishes and mumbled conversation hummed in the background behind Frances's voice. "Based on your last text, it sounds like I should have called you last night, but three ball teams and a baby-reveal party showed up all at once and stayed all the way until closing. We ran out of pie and specials. Tips were a blessing, but my feet mooed until my head hit that silk pillowcase you bought me."

"I turned you into a silk fan, didn't I?" Bianca leaned against the siding. "Wish I could have helped fill in for you guys. I promise I would have only dumped one, maybe two drinks in someone's lap."

Frances's chuckle floated through the phone and felt like an embrace. Not as good as Eddie's hug—or rather, the one she'd given him—yesterday. "Doubt that. Weren't you a waitress in one of your movies?"

Bianca shifted the phone to her other ear. "Don't watch that movie. I never should have done that part either. The language alone did not glorify God—"

"We all have things we're sorry for doing. Stop rehashing what I know the Lord has forgiven you for. Tell me about your boy Eddie instead."

Where to start? "First, he's not actually mine. It's more like a partnership. Like the one you and your cook, Ace, have." Bianca pressed her lips together as if to remember her and Eddie's almost kiss from the river. "Though, he's better than any man I've ever dated." Bianca rubbed her palm across her forehead, and her fingers grazed her healing stitches.

"Don't look for a man that's better than the last. Look for one who points to the Lord. Now, I'm sorry to say, I only have four more minutes left on my break."

Bianca pressed her other shoulder against the building and spotted Grace coming down the sidewalk. "I don't have much time either." She explained the shortened version of Mary and what Zack had told her. "I thought if I couldn't fix the stuff in my family, I could at least get Eddie's family restored."

Frances hmm'd. "Unfortunately, some things aren't ours to fix. King David realized that the Lord's earthly dwelling place was lacking in comparison to the luxury he lived in. He wanted to build God a temple. Except God told him no. He wasn't the man for the job."

A gust of wind swept around Bianca. Dirt hit her face, and she tucked further against the trailer's siding. "Okay . . . how does that story apply to me?" It didn't exactly provide hope.

"For one, shouldn't it remind us of God's timing? David could have pouted, wallowed in pride about how it should have been him to build the temple because it'd been his idea, but instead, he kept following God and prepared his son for the task. Sometimes we can get too focused on the result and forget Who's actually in charge."

"I just wish I could do more. I did bring Eddie his favorite marshmallow milkshake. You really need to add it to your menu. It's almost as good as your apple-pie milkshake. And of course, I apologized. But I don't feel like it's enough."

"Forgiveness is more than feelings, honey. Emotions aren't always based on truth. But you know what is?"

Bianca inhaled. "God's forgiveness."

"If we try to earn it, we'll fall short every time. If this Eddie is a man after God's heart like you're painting him to be, it's not about striving to be perfect around him . . . Yeah . . . I see it, Ace, I'll take care of it. Give me one more minute . . . Sorry about that, honey."

Bianca smiled. "Maybe you should ask Ace out for coffee at someone else's restaurant sometime soon. He might quit barking at you."

Frances huffed into the phone. "I don't need you trying to set us up like the rest of the town. I stand by what I promised myself, that I wouldn't mix a personal relationship with Ace's and my business partnership."

Bianca stiffened. Wasn't that what she had secretly been hoping would happen between Eddie and her? If she could stop messing things up between them.

Grace walked up the steps as her thumbs flew across her phone.

"Hey, Frances, I gotta go. But next time, I need to talk to you about Nathan."

"What'd he do now?"

Bianca stood by the door with Grace, who was staring at her phone. "Hopefully nothing else."

Frances grunted. "I'm only a phone call away. Don't forget to read your—"

"I finished Romans this morning."

"Good girl. Keep reading. You won't regret it." Bianca heard Frances's smile in her tone.

Bianca hung up and slipped her phone into her pocket.

Grace opened the door for her with one hand while she typed with the other. "I'm almost done with this email. I think the outfits are on the third rack on the right wall."

Bianca zigzagged through the racks of clothes and made it to the far wall. Except there sat Riley on the floor, her phone in her lap. Two racks of ballgowns surrounded her. Apparently, everyone was longing for a break today.

Had she just wiped her eyes?

Grace leaned toward Bianca. "Is she . . . crying?" she whispered.

Bianca peeked around the rack. Riley hadn't struck her as an easy crier, but that could be why she was hiding. "We probably need to check."

Grace wrinkled her nose. "You can go first. She scares me a little." Then her eyes widened. "Wait . . ." she hissed as she scrolled through her emails. She stomped around the rack separating them. "Riley, please tell me they didn't fire you. I suggested for them to cut out the massages, but if they cut you instead . . ."

Bianca clenched her teeth together. That was not how she'd pictured asking if Riley was okay.

Riley scrambled to her feet.

Grace tapped again on her phone screen. "I knew production money was tight, but I never thought your job . . ."

Riley glanced at Bianca and then back to Grace. "No, not fired. You're stuck with me for a little longer."

Bianca reached her hand out, but when Riley recoiled, Bianca fisted her fingers against her sides. Riley probably wasn't a hugger either. "Is it something we can help you with?"

Riley crossed her arms. "I cry sometimes when I'm mad. Things will be taken care of soon. Then everything will be better."

Grace looked up from her phone. "Mad or sad. I'm great at being both too."

Bianca wanted to rub her temples. "I think what Grace means is, would you like to share what you're mad about?"

Riley popped the knuckles on each of her fingers before finally heaving out a breath hard enough to lift the two strands framing her face. "My brother . . . I'm not even the oldest, but I'm forever fixing his messes. First, he had money troubles, which eventually led to him having to get a new job. Now his work's having money troubles, and it's affecting everything that it shouldn't, including my life." She glanced up and narrowed her eyes. "It's not fair that some people never get what they deserve."

Bianca nodded. "Money problems affect so much." In her own life. Even with her family. And of course, Eddie would never have agreed to help if he hadn't had grant issues. Plus, the film's budget.

Riley blinked at her. "We've almost got things figured out. He says he's about to be promoted at his new job, which has actually been beneficial for the connections we need."

Something crashed outside, followed by what sounded like nails hitting the metal roof overhead.

Grace glanced up from her phone. "Is that rain? Was it even in the forecast?" She jogged to the only window in the room, on the other side of a mannequin wearing a teal evening gown. "Man, it's pouring." Grace's focus flew back to her vibrating phone. "A promotion rocks, Riley. That has to be good news. I was so pumped when Bianca let me be her assistant while I finish out this stupid assistant-to-an-assistant slash coffee-retriever gig."

Riley's gaze swung back to Bianca, and her eyes narrowed further. "What . . . ahh, happened to your neck?"

Grace frowned and inspected Bianca's face. A gasp flew from

her mouth. "Did you get hit in a scene? We really need to get a replacement stunt double set up."

"What?" Bianca marched to the standing mirror at the end of the racks. A dark shadow ran along her cheekbone, but there was also something gray on the sleeve of her shirt. She rubbed at her cheek. "I don't know what it is, but no one hurt me."

Riley brushed at the gray spot on Bianca's shirt, and Grace's laughter echoed louder than the thunder. "I'm sorry. I think I need more sleep." She wiped under her own eyes. "You were leaning up against the building when I got to the steps. That gray is the same coloring as the building's siding. No one's out to harm you. Thank goodness."

Riley chased Bianca's gaze in the mirror as if she, too, agreed that Grace really did need some more sleep with her laughter outburst.

"Well, good." Grace took in a deep breath. "Let's get you in that purple shirt and skirt."

Another clap of thunder rattled the window, and a flash of lightning reflected onto the tiled floor.

Grace grabbed the labeled clothes off the rack and handed them to Bianca. She shooed Bianca to go change behind the curtain.

Riley cleared her throat. "Do you guys have plans tonight?"

Bianca pulled on the purple shirt and the skirt. She tugged on the front of the shirt, which dipped almost to her bra. "This outfit's not going to work. What's the other option?"

"Show us," came Grace's hopeful tone.

Bianca's phone vibrated on the tile by her foot.

Please don't be Nathan.

She smiled at the screen.

Eddie.

She tucked the phone to her ear and came out from behind the curtain. "Hey."

Grace tilted her head at the purple shirt. "I don't think it's—" She pointed to Bianca's phone. "Sorry."

Bianca yanked on the hem of the skirt and then pulled her phone away from her ear. Had Eddie butt dialed her? "Hello, Eddie?"

"It's Eddie? He hasn't been around today," Grace stage-whispered.

As if Bianca didn't already know that. She waved Grace back to the rack as Eddie finally answered. "Hey, yeah. Sorry. The rain's coming down hard, and we're crammed in the dugout."

She put her hand to her chest. "There's a game tonight?"

"They finally rescheduled it last night from another previous rainout."

Which meant he could have told her about it but hadn't.

Eddie sighed. "But it just got rained out again. So then I made a quick decision and agreed to meet Mary for dinner."

Bianca's hand went up to her neck. He was meeting his mother? Maybe her mistake hadn't been that bad. "Th-that's . . ." Was it great or not? "Are you sure?"

A pause and then, "No, but Zack suggested maybe . . . Anyway, I thought one of the guys would go with me, but they're all busy last minute and all, and Zack also mentioned that maybe you should come. Two birds, one stone, so to speak. You could get your pictures of us out. I'd meet Mary and be finished. Maybe she wouldn't focus solely on me and . . . I would have backup. That's probably more like four birds."

Bianca covered her mouth. He wanted her as his backup. Even after what she'd done.

Grace tiptoed forward. "What's going on?" Her whisper echoed more like the next round of thunder.

Bianca plugged her other ear. "Of course. I'll go with you to see Mary."

Grace's eyes widened as Riley typed on her phone.

"Can you be ready in twenty minutes?" Eddie asked.

"Can I be ready in twenty minutes?" Bianca parroted.

Grace raised up both of her thumbs.

Bianca paced a straight shot toward the curtain. "Okay, yes. Where do you want to meet?"

"I'll bring an umbrella to your trailer and pick you up."

Raindrops hammered against the roof above. "How about the wardrobe building?"

"The gray building next to the makeup trailer?"

Grace threw out her arms as if to ask what was happening as Bianca responded, "Yes. That's it."

"I'll be there as soon as I get all my kids home."

After Bianca hung up, Grace raised her brows. "So?"

Bianca pressed her phone to her chest. "Um, Eddie asked me to have dinner with his mom."

Grace clapped. "Perfect. I'll call Ed. He's still in town and can get the best photos and—"

Bianca shook her head. "Tonight is not about me. No photographers." It was the least she could do for Eddie.

Grace lowered back onto her heels. "Okay . . . we'll hope and pray that someone in the restaurant spots you, then. I guess it will be more organic that way."

Yes, pray. Bianca needed to do more of that. Out of the corner of her eye, Bianca noticed Riley heading toward the door, and that's when Riley's unanswered question popped into Bianca's head. "Riley, hey, sorry. I never answered your question. Were you wanting to hang out tonight?"

Riley glanced over her shoulder. "Don't worry about me. Like Grace said, this sounds like a perfect plan. I need to meet with my brother anyway."

Bianca watched something that looked like hurt cross Riley's eyes. "If you're sure. We can do something maybe tomorrow."

Riley met Bianca's eyes. "I'm sure we'll meet up soon enough."

Grace grabbed a silver dress with lace sleeves off a rack. "Hope things work out for your brother soon."

Riley waved. "They will. Trust me."

Bianca accepted the dress from Grace and held it up to her shoulders. She turned and glanced in the mirror. If the plan for tonight was so perfect, then why had she been Eddie's last choice?

EIGHTEEN

THE SMELL OF GARLIC HIT EDDIE ALMOST AS strongly as the regret of agreeing to meet Mary. He held the door to Rachael's Italian Eatery and placed his hand on Bianca's back as the rain continued to spit outside.

Apparently, her sandals had no problems crossing the threshold. Then again, she wasn't preparing to battle her past.

Bianca paused by a potted plant whose leaves appeared to reach out for her shoulders. "You, okay?"

The door swung closed and whacked Eddie where his road rash had mostly healed. He slipped his hands into his athletic shorts pockets and managed a nod.

Whether the entry hallway wall had purposely been painted to match uncooked noodles or not, it served as a backdrop for Bianca's silver dress that floated around her knees as she both eyed him and walked to the hostess stand. Behind the welcome podium lined with ivy, either real or fake, a tall man dressed in all black gave them a welcoming grin, despite Eddie's simple coaching attire.

Eddie's tennis shoes stopped on the gold-swirled tiled. "I should have gone home first and changed. I was only thinking about how late I was going to be."

Ten years was far too late.

Bianca hooked her hand around his elbow. "Are you trying to tell me that you want me to drive you home to get your flip-flops?" Her fingers flexed on his skin, and the hairs on Eddie's arm seemed to lean into her touch.

Bianca dipped her chin closer to his ear. "I mean, do you want me to make an excuse to get us out of here?"

Did he?

"Good afternoon, Ms. Pearl and Mr. Rice," the still-smiling host said. "Your party has already been seated. If you're ready, I'll lead you to them."

Bianca gave Eddie her full attention. "I'll follow you, whatever you decide."

Lord, what is he supposed to do?

Had this been His doing, orchestrating everything? Or had Eddie been the one trying to unlock wrong doors?

Eddie's next breath sank low to his churning gut. "Let's get this over with."

The host kept his grin as if any future tips depended on it. "Right this way."

As they rounded a table of five, one customer pushed out their chair, and Bianca rocked backward in order not to ram into the elderly man, who reached for his cane.

Eddie's hands landed on her hips and steadied her.

A gasp came, not from Bianca, but from one of the young women sitting beside the old man. "Is that ..."

Bianca kept her head down as they passed three more full tables and then whispered to Eddie, "Thanks."

"Anytime," he murmured.

A bricked archway revealed another room, and the host stopped at the table under a painting of a water fountain with a group of children splashing each other. Mary, dressed in a flamingo-pink shirt with about five strands of lime chunky-beaded necklaces, sat facing the host's direction. A man with dyed black hair had his arm resting on the back of her chair as he whispered something into her ear.

Party of four. Not three. Eddie zeroed in on his mother's left hand but couldn't tell if she wore a ring by the way she held a piece of bread. Had she gotten married?

Whatever the man said, Mary tilted her head and released a laugh louder than the classical cello music being played overhead. The man noticed the host and turned his face.

Joel Gillian.

Eddie reached and gripped the nearest chair. He couldn't do this.

Bianca had frozen beside him. All except her gaze and her deepening brows.

Mary's voice boomed over his thoughts and the music once again. "Eddington, you came!"

Joel stood and extended his hand toward Eddie. "Good to finally meet you, son. I'm Joel Gillian."

Son? Somehow Bianca's fingers were now laced through Eddie's.

Eddie glared at Joel. "I know who you are. I just don't know why you're here."

Mary fluttered her ringless hand to her chest, then to her necklaces, and finally planted her palms on her lap. "I'll explain everything. Come, sit. This tiny place has delicious bread."

One chance. She had one more chance.

Eddie pulled out a chair three over from Joel. He gestured for Bianca to sit, and then he took the seat beside her.

Joel straightened his tie and then sat.

The host cleared his throat. "Can I start you two off with something to drink?"

Mary lifted her glass. "Their raspberry tea is lovely."

Eddie grabbed the cloth napkin. She used to hate tea. Said it was only dirty water. "I'll have water with lemon."

"And you, Ms. Pearl?"

"I told you it was Bia Pearl," came a stage whisper from the archway, where two women peeked from behind the wall.

Joel raised his bushy brow at the hostess. "I thought when I called, you guaranteed us privacy."

The host sent a scowl toward the women. "Everyone's privacy is our top concern. I will take care—"

"Do you mind if I take a quick selfie with them?" Bianca asked Eddie. "I'm sure they'll leave afterward."

Joel huffed. "One photo will lead to fifty. You're only causing more trouble by encouraging them to be here."

Eddie scooted his chair back. "I'll go with you."

Bianca smiled at the host and tucked her hand in Eddie's elbow. "I'll have lemonade, please."

Before they reached the archway, Bianca tilted her head closer, and her breath tickled his neck. "I won't blame you if you're plotting our getaway."

"Don't tempt me," Eddie muttered.

"This will be the only fan photo I take tonight. I was trying to fix the tension, but . . . how can I help you get through this night besides praying?"

He needed all the prayers he could get. She was already doing more than enough by giving him someone else to focus on. "Trust me, you're helping."

The two women peeked around the archway, and their eyes widened when they spotted Eddie and Bia.

The blonde seemed to use all her teeth to smile. "Oh, Ms. Pearl, can we get a picture?"

The brunette beside her held out a phone as if Bianca had never seen one before.

Bianca stepped away from Eddie. "I have time for one photo tonight."

Eddie extended his hand. "I'll take it with your phone."

The brunette hesitated, looking between Eddie and Bianca as if that wasn't exactly what she'd hoped for. Finally, the blonde handed over her phone from out of her pocket.

Eddie snapped three photos. "Here you go."

The brunette's gaze flicked back toward the table. "Could we get one with you and Joel Gillian together? I can't believe he's your life coach. I mean, his books are so great. It totally makes sense for him to agree to coach you—"

"He's *not* her life coach." Eddie took in a deep breath.

It didn't help.

Bianca pressed her shoulder against his. "We've got to go, ladies. Thanks so much for the pictures."

After he turned, she put her hand on Eddie's back. "Eddie?"

One word, and he knew what she'd asked. Just as she'd known how to anchor him with her touch.

Eddie's back muscles coiled. "Mary read one of Joel's books in jail. That *wise* life coach advised people to get rid of the things that held them back. When she was released, she relinquished her rights to parent me so she could find her happiness. Apparently, I was holding her back."

Bianca sucked in a breath. "How could she have brought him here tonight? Let's go. Milkshakes and fries sound way better than lasagna. Mary shouldn't have tried to manipulate this meeting."

Eddie placed his hand on top of Bianca's. "She gets tonight to explain."

Then that was it.

They reached the table at the same time as a server placed down Eddie's water and Bianca's lemonade. She set another lemonade next to Joel's empty glass before turning and walking away.

As Bianca and Eddie sat, Joel motioned toward his and Bianca's glasses and then toward the archway. "We're similar in more than one way. Except I've found that the more you cater to people in public, the more they expect for you to give up your own happiness for theirs."

Eddie almost spat his gulp of water out. "You're nothing like Bianca. Now, why are you here?"

Mary reached for Eddie across the table as if she could touch him over the candles and flower vase. "Eddington, dear, Joel's not only my favorite author, or my favorite wise man, he's my copartner in life. I thought it best for my two favorite men to meet."

Eddie tugged on his ear. Was he going deaf? Surely he hadn't heard what he thought she'd said. "You married Joel? The man who told you to get rid of me."

And he'd thought anyone would be an improvement over his father.

"You misheard." Joel took a drink from his lemonade and wrinkled his nose. "She's my copartner. We don't believe in needing a piece of paper for joint happiness. Like emotions, marriage only complicates things."

Eddie squeezed the stem of his glass until his knuckles paled.

Bianca straightened the fork beside her plate. "Marriage is a blessing."

Joel removed his locked gaze from Eddie and smirked at Bianca. "Strange coming from the woman who had been co-partnering with a con artist."

Eddie stood. "Don't belittle Bianca. And Mary, last chance. Why am I here? Time to talk or we're out of here."

Mary opened her mouth, but Joel paused with his lemonade halfway to his mouth. "She's here because you've caused a break in her happiness that needs to be fixed."

Eddie aimed his thumb at his chest. "I've caused?"

Joel clanked his cup down, and lemonade sloshed onto the white tablecloth. "Picking up the phone once could have saved me a trip out here."

Mary set her bread down. "I'm not sure that alone would have helped. I saw you on the news with Bia Pearl, and it brought back old memories. I hadn't had a stronger pull to come and hug you before. With some other things about to happen in our lives, I knew it was time."

Eddie lowered to his chair. "I believe that's called guilt, and it's there for a reason."

Tears filled Mary's eyes. "This is a long time coming, but I'm proud of you, Eddington. Proud of us both. Look where we are. When I saw you in that first heroic article online, everything had finally lined up." She wiped away a fallen tear. "I hadn't been the best mother to you. Drugs and addictions controlled me. In and out of jail. I didn't know where you were even when I was home." She reached for Joel's hand. "Then I found Joel's book, and it changed my life. But I needed more help. I knew Joel's words spoke to me. Turns out we needed each other to find our complete happiness."

Eddie shook his head. All this time, and she was still just as lost. "It's not about finding happiness."

Joel aimed his buttered knife at Eddie. "Son, I hear your tone, and it'll get no one at this table closure."

Eddie scooted to the edge of his chair. "It's not a tone problem. Mary . . . Mother, you need to look for answers from the Bible. It explains where our joy comes from, which is far better than temporary happiness. How our past can be forgiven."

How to find strength to forgive his mother.

Bianca put her hand on Eddie's thigh, and he rested his on top of hers.

Mary twisted the longest of her necklaces. "I can't be wishing my past away, because it's healed both of us."

Eddie didn't blink. She wasn't sorry for what she'd done. "I suppose I can't wish all the past away either. Without your decision to leave me, I wouldn't have ever stepped foot inside a church and heard the actual truth. If you hadn't dumped me—"

"She didn't *dump* you." Joel took in a quick inhale and rubbed his chest. Sweat shined on his forehead. "She was on her path to healing and self-worth."

Eddie's hand laced around Bianca's under the table. "A path toward your co-partnering and selfishness masked behind what you claim as happiness."

Joel grabbed his glass of lemonade and took a gulp. "Why is this so sour?" He set the glass down. "You really need to read my books. It'll explain everything. Without my books, you're still blocked."

Eddie tilted his chin up. "Mary's partly right. Without her road to so-called happiness, I wouldn't have been dropped into foster care. Wouldn't have been taken to church by Grand-ma'am and heard where my worth actually comes from. It isn't found in anything you've written about."

Joel dabbed his napkin against his sweaty brow and grunted. But it wasn't because of anything Eddie had said. The man stiffened and grabbed at his collar. Another strangled gasp came from Joel's mouth. His body jerked, and he fell to the ground.

Bianca's hand squeezed his. "Eddie?"

Eddie sprang from his seat and rushed over to a white-faced Joel. "Call 911!"

Mary released a shriek. "He's allergic to … to … cherries and … and soy!" Her hands flew to her cheeks. "Help him, Eddie." Then she threw her purse across the table, knocking over Joel's lemonade. "His epinephrine autoinjector is inside. You must save my Joely. I can't live without him."

Eddie put his two fingers against Joel's neck.

No, but she could live without her son.

Which had probably saved Eddie's life.

No pulse.

Bianca grabbed her phone and dialed for help as Eddie dropped to his knees beside the man he'd grown to hate. "He doesn't need epinephrine. He's having a heart attack."

NINETEEN

HOSPITAL WAITING ROOMS REALLY SHOULD BE warmer. Bianca shifted on the loveseat that felt more plastic than the leather look someone had probably been aiming for. A poster announcing the visiting hours had peeled away from the striped wallpaper and now flapped under the air-conditioning vent.

Beside her, Mary grabbed Bianca's hand and squeezed her fingers. "Tonight was supposed to have led to more happiness."

Eddie paced behind the chair he'd only rested in for about two seconds before he'd practically tossed a tissue box from the table to his sobbing mother.

Mary swiped a tissue from the box nestled on her lap. "Joel has to make it. We're so close to total happiness. So close to our adoption placement."

Bianca's free hand went to her chest. *Adoption?*

Eddie stopped and pivoted toward Mary. "What did you say?"

Mary released Bianca's hand and cradled the tissue box. She adjusted one of the beads on her necklace. "On one of Joel's last book tours, I held a woman's baby while she spoke to Joel about finding her own happiness. The babe grabbed hold of my finger and smiled at me. That's when my heart knew I was ready for my next step in happiness. Joel agreed that we'd be an ideal environment for child and would feel content helping another person out."

Eddie fisted his hands. "You're adopting a child?" With the raised pitch at the end of his sentence, it was both a statement and a question.

One of many Bianca had as well.

Mary's smile never wavered. "A boy. I wanted to tell you that you're going to be a big brother. Tonight was supposed to bring so much clarity."

The soda machine in the corner blinked out of order, and that's exactly how Bianca's brain processed the moment. She had no real-life experience or previous scripts to draw from for any kind of guidance on the scene that was playing out before her.

Eddie's chest heaved. "It brought clarity all right."

Mary sniffed and nodded. "I knew it. Now Joel just has to get better so we can bring a sweet babe home who needs us. A nanny's already lined up who's willing to travel with us. Joel's editing his next book, and it's centered around happy parenting. It's perfect timing. Which leaves zero time for a heart attack."

Eddie lifted his chin. "No one ever has time for a heart attack. But you can't adopt a child to help with Joel's book promotion."

Bianca rose and walked over to Eddie.

Mary fisted her wad of tissues. "Joel said you wouldn't understand. We can offer so much to a child. He will want for nothing, and we'll prove to you and everyone else that I'm a good and happy mother now because of Joel's books."

Eddie gripped the back of the chair in front of him. "You can't fake life so people can see that Joel's next book does what he proclaims. That's not how parenting is supposed to work. I still see your selfish heart. The one that promised me monster-truck tickets and vacations and new shoes if I'd steal a box of cigarettes or stay overnight at my friend's house while you partied or go to school when I didn't feel well. You haven't changed. You're still planning to manipulate things to make yourself happy."

Bianca placed her hand on top of Eddie's. He tensed but didn't move his arm.

A tear rolled down Mary's cheek. "I'm not the same woman you used to know."

"I hope that's true." Eddie shook his head. "But God knows our hearts. We can't hide anything from Him."

A nurse came through the door, and Mary jumped up to greet her. "Is Joel okay?"

The nurse nodded. "He'll be up to his room in a moment if you'd like to come with me."

Mary followed the nurse while Eddie laced his fingers through Bianca's and led her out of the waiting room. Bianca followed his lead to the elevator and then out to his truck in the parking lot. Without a single word, he released her and hopped into his truck.

Lord, please be with Eddie's heart.

Once he started the vehicle, Bianca locked her fingers around her seat belt to keep from reaching for Eddie's hands, which gripped the steering wheel as if it were his life support. She was supposed to be his support system tonight. But what words would make any of this okay?

God had canceled the ball game with rain. Given Eddie the brief desire to call Mary, and at a time when Mary had been available. So what had been the point of tonight's meeting? To have Eddie be told his mother was starting over again with another son? One she wanted instead of Eddie?

Bianca's chest ached, and she rested her hand on Eddie's thigh. "I'm sorry you didn't get closure."

Lord, how long would it take for restoration?

For Eddie. For her own family.

There had been no answers uncovered. Zero mending. No healing.

The only good had been that Eddie's CPR compressions had provided time for the ambulance to arrive and get Joel off for emergency surgery.

Maybe it had been to simply save Joel's life.

Eddie's words from the night of the fire hit her. *You're far more priceless than any material stuff. If only more people realized their true worth.*

What if Joel's heart needed changing? Wouldn't tonight's pain be worth it?

God knows our hearts.

Eddie was right. God knew Mary's . . . and Bianca's.

No wonder Eddie didn't want to have anything fake. He'd already lived through too much pretending from his own mother.

Bianca slipped her hand off Eddie's thigh, but his calloused palm caught hers, and their fingers seemed to intertwine on their own. "I never should have brought you into that mess. But . . . thanks."

"Anytime." And she meant it. "I'm not pretending to care. I don't want you to ever have to wonder anymore if you're not worth being there for. You don't need her approval. You only need God's."

The exact thing Frances had reminded Bianca of countless times. The very thing Bianca still wrestled with.

Eddie returned his grip to the steering wheel. Over the radio, a song about a broken heart echoed inside the cab until Eddie changed the station.

How many times had she wished someone would have been beside her when the world felt like it was collapsing? God had sent her Frances. She wanted to be that person for Eddie.

But would he let her?

She glanced up at the sky through the windshield, and a shooting star burst through the darkness. Just like on the night she'd had her first audition. "I know parenting must be hard, but . . ."

Eddie released a heavy breath. "Does tonight make you not want to have kids?"

Nathan had said he never wanted any kids, and she'd been too focused on her career. "With the right man, I want to have a family. But I hope my kids get to skip some of the emotions I had growing up."

Eddie pushed the turn signal, and the clicking noise harmonized with the squeal of the brakes. After he finished the turn, Eddie whispered, "I want my kids to know that they are loved and not a burden. Never a means to an end."

This man's heart had taken such a beating. How had he become so kind?

Only because of God. "You're not a burden, Eddie." He'd told her that very thing not too many days ago.

She pressed her lips together to keep her tongue from speaking anything about the L-word. Because Eddie would be all too easy to love, but this was supposed to be a business deal. No feelings. No crossing lines. That's what Frances had said about not mixing a relationship with her business partnership with Ace.

But Eddie would be worth the cost.

Bianca curled a few strands of her hair around her finger. "I never want my kids to feel like they're an embarrassment. But I guess that's what propelled me into acting. So I should be thankful."

Eddie turned toward her. Concern and something else she couldn't see in the shadows crossed his eyes before he faced the road. "Why would someone be embarrassed by you?"

Bianca scooted closer to the passenger-side door. "You don't need to hear about my woe-is-me moments. What you've had to endure tonight alone is much worse."

"Bianca." He switched off the radio. "Sadness isn't a competition. If you feel comfortable telling me, I could use a distraction."

He only needed a distraction. She was starting to wish she could be more than that. "I remember my parents getting frustrated that I'd only play by myself at the park, or that I wouldn't speak to their friends. I overheard them say how embarrassed they were that I was nothing like anyone else in my family. One day, my extroverted sister had a friend coming over. My mom made a big deal about getting a tea party ready for them, so I lied that I had two friends coming over as well. I went in my room and held pretend conversations at different pitches and created stories. I thought I'd locked my door, but my mom later came with some cookies and tea for my friends and me. She looked around and must have realized I had been doing the voices. She said that I sounded really creative, just like her, and never once mentioned my lie."

Bianca pressed her palm over her chest. "I loved that she'd said I was like her. So I started practicing mimicking the kids on commercials and television shows. One day, my mom asked me to do one of my voices for her friends. I felt far more comfortable pretending to be someone other than my shy self, so I did, and everyone loved it. That summer, I started dressing up in different outfits and clothes to help me *feel* the different voices that everyone loved. I begged my mom to drive me four hours to my first audition, but I froze onstage. The only thing she said to me on the entire ride home was how I probably didn't need to try any more acting because I wasn't like those other kids auditioning. That night I wished on a falling star. Wished that I could change—be better, more outgoing, and become an actress."

Eddie moved his hand to the seat between them. His pinky reached out and touched Bianca's. "Sorry you felt you had to change to please your mom."

She'd been changing to please people ever since—and not even for the right One, the Lord. Until recently. "My dad was not happy with my career choice, but once I made my first movie deal, my entire family seemed excited. Then my dad promised the college he had worked for that I'd do a meet and greet around Thanksgiving.

Except I'd never told him I would actually make it home for the holiday. I didn't have phone service where we had been filming. Apparently, he'd organized this huge event, but when filming got delayed, I couldn't make it. I not only embarrassed him, but he got fired too. My sister Madeline was the one who told me. She said that she heard Dad tell Mom that he hoped I'd just miss Christmas that year too."

Eddie hooked his pinkie around Bianca's. "Did you go home?"

Bianca shook her head. "I'd gotten a commercial deal that required me to travel over the holidays. I thought I'd figured out how to fix the problem, so I sent money to the college. They hired Dad back, except he refused their offer. He took a job with this family-owned building company who prioritized high family morals as part of their advertisement. Which was about the time the tabloids started feeding rumors about how I'd supposedly slept my way to my next not-very-family-friendly starring role, which wasn't true. But my dad was passed for a promotion because of it. Each time I messed up in real life—or "real" based on the paparazzi and tabloids—my family paid the cost. I promised my parents I'd help with their house payments. They've gotten behind recently. However, when Nathan was arrested, my accounts were frozen. I told my parents that I didn't have the money yet, but they said don't bother. That they couldn't trust my apologies or my word, and that I'd only embarrass them more with my lies."

But she was still determined to prove to them that she'd changed and would keep her word. To them and now also to Eddie.

Eddie turned onto the film set road and waved at Thad in the security box, who lifted the gate. "Your parents should have handled things differently."

Just like his mother should have too.

Bianca dipped her chin. "They were already upset that I hadn't married Nathan yet and was only living with him. They were right. I shouldn't have been living like I was. Shouldn't have done some of the movies I had. But after I did change and follow the Lord . . . I think they wanted more proof than my word."

Eddie pulled into a parking spot instead of next to the sidewalk and turned off the truck.

Bianca unclicked her seat belt. "That's why I needed this contract. To prove to them that I've changed for the better by doing a more family-oriented film and that I'd keep my word about helping them with their house. I'd hoped it'd be enough that it wouldn't be too embarrassing to let me attend my sister's wedding."

"You're not an embarrassment, Bianca."

She grabbed the passenger-door handle. "That's because you haven't been around me long enough."

Eddie let out a low growl, unbuckled, and reached his hand over, landing it on top of hers. The door was only cracked open wide enough for the soft glow of the dome light to highlight his heated glare. "They're wrong, B. It didn't take long for you to prove that you're reliable in chaos. The fire. The baseball game. Even tonight. You held Mary's hand in the waiting area when I could barely stand to be in the same room with her. That's the opposite of being an embarrassment."

Bianca shook her head. "I brought Mary to you. Tonight was partly my fault to begin with."

He leaned closer and gently tugged her hand away from the door, resting it on her thigh. "Something you've already sought forgiveness for, which I've granted, and now it's my job to keep no record of that wrong. Especially since you didn't even know who you had brought to me because she hid that fact. You're not responsible for someone else's lies and actions."

Bianca closed her eyes. But he still didn't understand all that came with just being around her. "There were people recording us at the restaurant. The media will spin their own view of tonight, and then you'll have to deal with the lies they spread."

He ran his thumb over the top of her hand and lowered his voice. "I'm not afraid of them."

It'd be too easy to lean her head forward, rest it against his. Draw in the strength he so willingly seemed to offer. How did he make it seem so easy not to care what the world thought?

"Though . . ." Another swipe of Eddie's thumb on her skin sent a current up her arm. "The truth is that sometimes . . . I'm a little afraid of you."

She popped open her eyes. *Her?* "You're afraid of me?"

When she pulled her hand away, he let her go but didn't slide over. "I'm not an actor. It's hard for me to remember that when you're showing compassion, it's out of duty, not because, you know . . ."

She pressed her back against the seat. "You think I'm faking being kind?" The one person she'd hoped was starting to understand the real her believed she faked kindness.

Bianca pushed the door all the way open. "Thanks for bringing me back. I'll keep your mom and Joel in my prayers. And I'm not faking that. I actually *will* pray for them." She shut the door harder than necessary.

As her feet pounded the pavement, her eyes burned with unshed tears. She sought the parking lot lights and blinked up at them. Crying wasn't an option. Someone could be recording her from somewhere.

God, You see my heart. Why doesn't that seem like enough?

The slam of the truck door echoed behind her, and Eddie's footsteps hit the ground. "Bianca, wait."

She sent a wave over her shoulder. "You don't need to walk me to the trailer. I know the way."

His stubborn footsteps kept coming until she stopped and turned around. She opened her mouth, but Eddie spoke first.

"I forget that you have to spend time with me." He stepped closer and slid his hands into his pockets. "I forget that your smile isn't only for me. I know your kindness is real. I know that when you say to trust you, you mean it. You're so much more than you show the world, but I'm afraid of you because I forget that we're just a deal. Nothing more."

His sigh made her want to erase the space between them. "Sometimes I forget that this relationship is actually fake, and that's a little frightening. My heart doesn't have much left."

And tonight had only shown a portion of what he'd survived.

"You're not only a deal to me." She moved toward him until their shoes touched, and she wrapped her arms around his neck. "I haven't pretended with you since the green dress. For better or worse, you've gotten the real Bianca."

His smirk appeared. "I feared you might break an ankle in those shoes."

She pressed her lips together. "I'm not that breakable."

She couldn't let the world see her weaknesses.

His gaze dropped to her mouth. "I preferred the you who returned to practice."

Bianca swallowed. He preferred the regular girl versus the actress. "What if I have to be both?"

His palms cupped her cheeks. "Would Bia be on-screen and Bianca be with . . . me?"

Bianca met his searching eyes. "You get the real me."

Eddie lowered his chin. "Sounds like the perfect deal."

She rose on her toes and closed the distance between them. His lips hit hers, and she allowed herself to lean into the hero that kept accepting the real her.

Eddie slowed down the kiss and then pressed his lips to her forehead. "It's getting late. You have an early call tomorrow. Don't you?"

She hooked her arm around his and rested her shoulder against him as they followed the path of the sidewalk. "It just means I get to see you sooner rather than later."

Eddie sent her his dimpled smile. As they neared the section of trees that housed the smoking section with its grouping of picnic tables, the sound of something being struck was followed by a male voice.

"Payment is your only redeemer from the Duke," a man growled from somewhere behind the picnic table inside the darkened area of the trees.

The Duke. She remembered that name.

A groan and then a familiar male voice. "I'll pay up. Tell him my word's honorable."

Bianca stopped before the curve in the sidewalk. "That sounds like Carter."

Eddie narrowed his gaze at the trees. "Are they filming?"

Bianca squeezed her fingers on his arm. "Those aren't lines from our script."

She pulled out her phone and peeked into the trees. A soft glow from one of the parking lot's dusk-to-dawn lampposts provided enough light to view Carter being held on the ground by a clean-shaven man. Blood coated Carter's face and white shirt. The other man was dressed in black pants and a gray shirt with a flat cap pulled low over his forehead. "Eddie, Carter's in trouble."

Eddie stepped in front of her. "Get back inside the truck and lock the doors."

She dialed security, but Eddie headed in the opposite direction than he'd told her to go. She grabbed Eddie by his back pocket. "You can't go over there without a weapon."

The hidden man rumbled out a laugh that sounded the opposite of funny. "Money's the only thing that speaks in this business. Doesn't matter who you are in the hierarchy."

"Hello," came a voice from Bianca's phone.

She released Eddie as he yelled, "Carter!"

Bianca pressed her phone to her ear. "Thad, help! I think Carter's being attacked. He's by the front trees in the parking lot where the construction worker was found."

"On my way." Thad's breaths came out staccato, as if he'd leaped from his security booth. "Get somewhere safe, Bia."

If only Eddie would listen to that command himself. But he'd already sprinted through the trees. A shadow slinked back into the darkness and disappeared in between two set buildings.

Bianca poked her head around a tree. "Eddie?" she whispered.

Another groan sent her rushing forward.

Please, Lord, don't let Eddie get hurt too.

Leaves scraped along her arms as she batted branches out of her way. Wood chips slipped into her sandals and poked into her feet. Finally, the trees parted, and two men were on the ground—Eddie squatting and Carter lying on his back.

Eddie moved his flashlight up to Carter's bloodied face. "Anything broken? Your nose is bleeding. Let's get you sitting if possible. Breathe through your mouth. Can you pinch your nose, or do you need me to do it?"

Carter sat and sucked in a breath as he gripped his side. "I don't need help pinching my own nose."

Another flashlight waved toward them, followed by heavy footsteps. "Carter!"

"We're over here, Thad." Bianca knelt beside Carter and pulled out a lone tissue from her purse.

Carter took the tissue and put it in his nostril. "I'm going to need about twelve hundred more of these."

Bianca winced. "What happened?"

Carter glanced at Eddie. "I tripped."

"Tripped?" Bianca stood to her feet. "It's not a good night to make jokes, Carter. Who was that? We heard . . . how much do you owe?"

Carter narrowed his gaze at the flashlight coming at them

through the tree branches. "Leave it alone, Bia. Trust me, you don't want it to become your business."

Eddie moved in front of her and sent a glare to Carter. "You could've been killed."

Carter spat out some blood that landed close to Bianca's sandals. "They wouldn't have killed me. Can't get money from a dead guy, can you?"

Why was it always about money? Bianca put her shaking hand on her hip. "How much trouble are you in with them?"

Carter sucked in a breath as he grabbed his side. "Don't worry, it's not as much as your ex took."

Her stomach tightened. Nathan had been talking about money over the phone the week before he was arrested. "This has to do with Nathan?"

Carter avoided her eyes.

Bianca stepped around Eddie. "How? Wait . . . is this somehow a debt to him? He did this to you? Is this why he keeps trying to contact me?"

Eddie rose to his feet. "He's still bothering you?"

Carter stuck his hand out to Eddie. "Since you always seem to be around, help me up?" Then to Bianca, "You really are as naive as they say you are, aren't you? Here I thought it was an act."

Eddie straightened without grabbing hold of Carter's hand. "You should probably stay resting there until an ambulance arrives."

Thad squeezed between two trees. He wiped his sleeve on his sweaty forehead. His eyes blinked wide, and he hooked his thumb over his shoulder. "Ambulance is three minutes out. Police, one."

"Great. More police." Carter sent a glare to Bianca. "Be ready to film tomorrow. Like the man said, money takes care of everything. And we both really need this movie to get done."

Eddie pressed his shoulder against hers. "Thad, do you mind

waiting with Carter? I'm going to make sure Bianca gets safely back with that man on the loose."

Thad nodded, and Eddie held a branch out of her way. There was no way she wanted to even pretend to be in a relationship with Carter. He was nothing like Eddie. Nothing like the man God would want her to be with.

Eddie pulled out his phone. "I'm letting the police chief know that we're going to wait in my truck until they need our statements. I figure that'll be safer until we know the set is clear."

Bianca kicked a rock along the sidewalk. "I'm tired of giving statements."

Eddie turned and looked at her. Something must have been written on her face, because he simply opened his arms, and Bianca fell against his chest.

He traced one of his hands up her back. "It's been a long day."

Bianca pulled back. Eddie's face was right before her—a place she wouldn't mind him staying. "Eddie, I—"

"Rice!" Office Ramble had his gun out and pointed at the ground. "Follow me to my car while the rest of my squad makes sure the set is secure."

Eddie wrapped his arms around Bianca, and she shivered against him.

Bianca watched Office Ramble check the hidden points around them. The trashcan at the third row of parking spaces. Eddie's truck parked in the front. "Officer, we heard parts of Carter and the attacker's conversation. It's something to do with the Duke."

Officer Ramble nodded without taking his gaze off the path behind them and then opened the back of his car. "A name I've learned to dislike hearing."

Bianca put her hand on the car door. "I know the jury didn't believe my testimony about Nathan, but I'm sure he has a criminal connection. I've heard him mention the Duke before. And Nathan's been trying to contact me."

Both Eddie and Officer Ramble locked their attention on her, but it was Officer Ramble who said, "Then you might be the exact person we need to wear a wire."

TWENTY

EDDIE SET THE PAN OF PERFECTLY COOKED brownies on the hot pad in the firehouse kitchen. He'd managed to get the dessert into the oven on their lunch break before the start of the last session. Apparently, the mayor's request for Eddie to be on the film set could be trumped by a safety webinar.

He grabbed his cup of coffee and downed the bottom of his fourth cup. He had three minutes to get back to the webinar and only two more training hours. Then he could go pick up Bianca—for a real date.

Eddie covered a yawn and grabbed a stack of plates. Unless he'd dreamed up his and Bianca's conversation last night.

Eddie had stared out the back window of Officer Ramble's squad car. "I'm not sure it's wise for you to get involved any more with Nathan."

For her own safety, not because he was jealous.

Bianca had spun to face him as they waited for the set's all-clear. "I'd only be seeing if he'd let something slip on the phone about the Duke or his involvement with Carter's attack. Or even my missing money. If this is my chance to clear my name, prove that I didn't lie, shouldn't I take it? Plus, the police need my help."

Eddie fisted his hand. "What if he figures out what you're doing? If Nathan is behind what happened to Carter, you could be the one . . ."

The one hurt.

Bianca's fingers rested on top of his. "What if you were beside me when I called him?"

She licked her lips, and Eddie's eyes traced the movement.

He scooted away from her. "I'll be there if you want me to be. You were there for me with Mary, and it's only fair—"

"Eddie." Her soft tone made him lock his attention on her eyes.

Hope and fear swam together. "What if you . . . were beside me not because of a deal but because you . . . What if we had a real date? No more deals."

"What do you mean, no more deals?"

"Your youth center donation is still safe, but you know in the movies, when the star and the hometown hero fake a relationship but then it becomes real . . ."

Had it become real? For her too?

Eddie swallowed. "I'm not sure the Bia Pearl would want to date small-town Eddie Rice."

Bianca shook her head. "I want to date the compassionate man who makes me laugh, worries about my safety, and points me to the truth. That's the man I'm falling for."

Eddie's heart boomed almost as loud as his mind. She was falling for him?

Wasn't he also falling for her? "What would a date like that look like?"

Bianca leaned forward. "Milkshakes, flip-flops, and . . ."

Eddie leaned closer. "A movie?"

Bianca stopped a breath from his lips. "I'm starting to think I like real life better than a pretend happily ever after."

He knew he did. Eddie had closed the gap between them at the exact moment Officer Ramble had opened the door.

But now, instead of Officer's Ramble's voice giving them the all-clear, it was Zack's.

"What's taking so long?" Zack marched straight into the kitchen and pulled out a spoon.

Izan jogged in next. "Don't let Zack take all the middle. Chief gave us a four-minute-longer break to help you with the brownies. I think the chief's craving chocolate."

Eddie shielded the top of the pan with his oven mitts. Maybe real life wasn't always better than the movies. "Chill. You gotta wait until I cut them so each slice has the highest ratio of crust to chewy center." Just how his grand-ma'am had taught him.

Izan shared a look with Zack. Then Izan said, "We can't let the brownies get cold. Stephens, hold Rice down while I grab the pan and run. We'll split the best part fifty-fifty. The chief can have the rest."

"Tempting." Zack pointed the end of his spoon at Eddie. "Our friendship could handle at least one rumble. Especially because we all know how delicious your brownies are."

Eddie pulled the brownies closer to him. "Can't hardly mess them up. They're from a box." Except his grand-ma'am had shared how to make them special—peanut butter chips.

Izan wrinkled his nose. "So was that tuna meal you made last week, and that was . . . interesting."

"Speaking of interesting . . . how did things go with Mary last night? Sorry I couldn't make it."

"Four minutes won't cover that update." Eddie tugged off his oven mitts. "Fine. One hot spoonful each."

Zack inched his spoon closer to the brownies. "Did you go by yourself to meet Mary?"

"Do I smell—" Ridge strolled into the kitchen but stopped halfway to the counter and gave Eddie a confused look. "Wait, I didn't know you still worked here."

Eddie rolled the pizza cutter through the brownies. Man, he

shouldn't have caved so early. The heat made the cut marks mash together. "Sounds like funny guy doesn't want any brownies to help him through the webinar."

Ridge grabbed a plate. "Nah, man. Just giving you a hard time about being with your girl while we've been at the day job all week."

"I've done my job and—"

Zack cleared his throat. "Speaking of *your* girl, did Bianca go with you last night?"

Eddie kept his focus, lifting out the squared brownie slice, but at the last second, the edge crumbled back into the pan. "She went. Joel Gillian was there with Mary. It went worse than I thought. Joel had a heart attack. Then when I took Bianca home, Carter had been attacked. I guess the only good thing from last night is that I'm going on a real date with Bianca tonight." He scooped out a piece of brownie. "Who wants this one?"

Izan and Zack stared at him.

Ridge shoved half his brownie in his mouth. "Should I schedule the class about how to have a long-distance relationship with your movie-star girlfriend before or after the one about how Mary still hasn't figured out how she hurt you?"

Zack shook his head.

Izan stole the rest of Ridge's brownie.

"Hey." Ridge's mouth popped open. "I said what you two were thinking. Fine, I'll say the other thing too. You can't—"

The fire alarm blared from its intercom on the wall, and Eddie shut off the water.

"Rescue needed at a wreck. Multiple vehicles involved at the corner of First and Wilson."

Eddie sprinted behind Ridge. The crew raced to the bay and pulled on their turnout gear. Bryce hopped into the passenger seat as Zack slammed his door shut.

"First and Wilson will bring us only a couple of blocks from downtown." Ridge sounded the horn as he crossed an intersection with a red light.

Finally, another set of red and blue lights flashed up again. An ambulance that wasn't Ambulance 21 was parked in front of a semitruck that had rammed into a restaurant front. Glass and patio chair pieces were scattered along the sidewalk. The awning rested on top of the semi's hood, and screams echoed through the broken door.

Two EMTs picked up a stretcher off the ground. It held an unconscious woman. The medic at the foot of the board hollered over his shoulder. "Glad you're here. It's a madhouse. Two semis, a car, and a truck."

"We're going to need backup." Bryce grabbed his walkie. "I'll call it in."

The semitruck's door popped open, causing the awning to wobble, and a man—mid-fifties, with more belly than hair—stumbled at the top of his steps. Bright red blood ran down his face, a stark contrast to the blue sky above him.

"Got him." Ridge raced toward the man.

"I'll check inside the restaurant." Bryce motioned Zack and Eddie forward. "Rice and Stephens, get me a report on the rest."

Eddie beat Zack around the far end of the semi, where they were met by at least twenty people, some drifting off the sidewalk and onto the roadway. All but a couple wore the same shirts. Definitely not a tourist group, with the words "Say no to stars, keep Last Chance County safe."

The smell of gasoline hit Eddie. He turned. The sun beamed off the silver-painted truck. Sometimes his helmet could use a sun visor.

The front end of a red pickup truck was smashed against the passenger side of the first semi, whose cab had crashed into the restaurant. The second semitruck's cab was practically up on top of the back bed of the pickup truck.

"That's him! Bia Pearl's hero."

No, there was no time for any fans. Eddie dashed for the pickup driver's door. An older man sat with both hands shaking on the wheel. The front and back of his truck were smashed, but the passenger section hadn't been touched.

The thin, white-headed man simply blinked out his front window. No blood. No signs of physical trauma.

Eddie opened his door. "Sir, are you—"

"I-I tried to stop. I did. But the light . . . the truck . . . I didn't see . . . Please, don't take my keys." Tears rolled down his checks. "Sarah's going to take my keys, isn't she?"

A pounding came from the pickup bed where the semi's cab rested.

Eddie stepped back. The thumps came again. Weaker. Except it wasn't from either truck.

What was left of a tiny gray car was wedged behind the pickup and half smashed under the semi's tilted cab. How had he missed it?

"Sir, wait right here for a second." Eddie dashed to the car. The car engine was somehow still running, and a teenage girl beat the driver's side window over and over.

Eddie swung his arms. "I'm coming!"

She rammed her shoulder into the door. Despite the caved-in roof, the door opened slightly. Eddie tugged on the door and wedged it enough to see that the car's ceiling had smashed down into the back seat.

Please, Lord, let no one have been in there.

The teenage girl tried to squeeze between the pried door and the twisted metal frame.

"Easy, let me help you out." He needed to assess and make sure her escape didn't hurt her further.

But the girl wedged through the gap in the door, holding

her arm against her stomach. As soon as her second foot hit the ground, she screamed in pain.

Eddie scooped her up and was halfway to the sidewalk when he heard a faint cry—from the smashed car.

Oh no. He tightened his hold on the girl. "Was there anyone else in your car?"

Please, Lord, let me have heard the cry from the sidewalk. That car is too smashed.

The girl burst into tears. "My sister was supposed to babysit our neighbor, but she paid me to do it, but I was running late. You've got to save Lacy."

He set the teen down and grabbed his walkie. "Lieutenant, I've got a trapped child in the car."

Trace and Kianna rounded the back of the semi and knelt before the girl.

"What do we got?" asked Trace.

"Her arm and foot, for sure." Eddie transferred the teen into their care, but the teen driver grabbed hold of Eddie's jacket.

Her lips quivered. "Please save Lacy."

Two men jogged over from the sidewalk with their phones. "Eddie, look here. Eddie Rice. Over here."

The taller man, wearing a Hawaiian button-down shirt, blocked Eddie's view of the car. "Right here, hero."

Eddie stepped around the man. "Return to the sidewalk."

The man kept his phone near Eddie's face until Zack yelled from the end of the other semi, but Eddie couldn't hear over the shouts of the photographers on the sidewalk.

Zack pointed to the rear of the semitruck as his voice came over the radio. "We've got a gas tanker spill."

No wonder he smelled gas.

That's when Eddie spotted the flammable sign on the back of the second trailer. That wasn't a pool of water the back end of the semi sat in.

Bryce's voice called over the walkie, "Stephens, get the crowd back. Rice, update me on the child."

Eddie grabbed his walkie and inspected the mangled car. "We're going to need cutters."

Behind him, Zack spoke to the onlookers. "Everyone back! The trailer contains flammable materials."

Eddie reached the car, and through the cracked window, in the backseat of the car, he spotted a full-back booster seat that he'd thought was part of the crumbled roof. The seat had tilted forward, and the ceiling had smashed down on top of it.

But where was the child?

Eddie squeezed in through the front door. "Lacy, I'm firefighter Eddie. Can you hear me?"

A whimper floated to him.

She was alive.

Thanks, Lord.

Now how to get her out?

Eddie pushed against the door. The metal groaned but wedged open enough for Eddie to get his chest inside. There, huddled in the shadows on the rear passenger floor mat, was a girl—from the size of her, around three.

Eddie shifted and grabbed his flashlight. "Lacy, can you see me?"

She didn't move out of her curled position. There was no way Eddie could fit back there with the roof smashed and the doors bent.

Eddie pushed his radio button. "Found the girl. Going to need those cutters."

"Roger, en route," came Bryce's reply.

"The trailer has caught fire!" Zack's panic was clear in his volume.

Eddie gripped his flashlight. Fire and gas were not the happily ever after he'd pictured. Cutters or not, Eddie had to get Lacy out—now.

He slid out of the car and yanked on the back door. But it didn't move. He could break the window, but he might injure the girl. He couldn't get to the passenger side with the car compressed against the building.

The roof was smashed completely over the passenger seat. She'd have to climb over the center console and to him. There hopefully was enough room for her to fit.

Eddie squirmed back inside the driver's seat and shined his light on Lacy. Sweat dripped down his neck. Hopefully from the stress and not from flames somewhere behind him.

"Hey, Lacy." He kept his voice gentle. "Can you do me a huge favor, girl? You like the playground, right? I need you to climb between the front seats so I can get you out."

Lacy lifted her head out of her curled position. Her blue eyes popped against his flashlight. Tears stained her cheeks. "I-I want my mommy."

"I know you do, sweetheart." Eddie reached and pushed the car seat enough for him to slide into the car a bit more. "Can you come to me? Then I'll get you to your mommy, okay?"

The girl sniffed and then climbed between the seat, squeezing her head and chest through first.

"That's a big girl. Look at you climbing."

She blinked up at the smashed roof that had pressed against her car seat and now threatened to scrape against her back. Her face puckered.

"I know. It looks scary. But you can slide the rest of the way out between the seat and console to get right to me."

Please let her fit.

She wiped a tear off her cheek and then eased her hips through the small space and into the front seat.

Eddie pulled her against his chest and backpedaled out of the car.

Right behind him, Bryce skidded to a stop with the cutters in his arms. "Anyone else?"

Eddie shook his head.

Bryce waved Eddie on while inspecting the smoke and flames that covered the tail of the semi. "Get her out of here before this thing blows."

Eddie shielded the girl against his chest.

Truck 14 must have arrived, because Izan and Amelia had firehoses aimed at the flames.

Would it be enough?

Bryce split off from Eddie and ran toward the sidewalk. "Get back!"

No one moved. At least ten phones and cameras were focused not on the wreck or the fire but on Eddie.

He nestled Lacy's face against his jacket. She didn't need this exposure. Eddie's gaze landed on both of the paparazzi who had stepped in his way earlier. What if they'd blocked him for a second or two longer? Would he still have gotten Lacy out?

An EMT Eddie hadn't met before jogged over as he reached the back of the first semi. "I heard the call. That's my neighbor's car. Where's Lacy?"

Lacy peeked at the medic. "Momma!" The girl nearly leaped from Eddie's arms at the EMT.

The medic squeezed her daughter to her chest. "Thank you."

"She was brave and had to climb to me."

The mother kissed Lacy's forehead and hiccuped before turning and running down the street to another ambulance parked behind their rescue truck and a police car.

His radio buzzed and Bryce said, "We need every hose out!"

Eddie sucked in the smoke-filled air and grabbed his walkie. "Heading there now."

"No, Rice, you get these paparazzi out of here before someone dies. Maybe they'll listen to you."

Eddie pivoted. His chest squeezed as if he were the spreader being shoved between two metal pieces. The Hawaiian-button-down guy stood with one leg over the hose Ridge had aimed at the flames devouring the front of the trailer.

Most of the crowd hovered against the brick building, whose corner blocked them from the heat of the fire. It was a start to safety. Now to get that last paparazzo out of the way.

Eddie waved his hands over his head at the Hawaiian-shirt guy. "Hey," he shouted. "It's not safe. You need to get back before the flames reach the gas tanks—"

An explosion boomed, and Eddie bent his knees until the ground steadied. Angry flames rocketed toward the cloudless sky. Black smoke hit Eddie's shielded face, but it didn't block his view of the Hawaiian-shirt man now on his back, motionless.

TWENTY-ONE

A BEAM OF SUNSHINE POPPED OUT FROM BEHIND the clouds as Grace handed Bianca her water bottle.

Grace scrolled on her phone. "Looks like you have an early makeup time tomorrow but nothing else tonight."

Bianca's eyes landed on Eddie over Grace's shoulder, standing in the shade to the right of the cameras. "Perfect. Thanks Grace."

Finally, a break from filming. Maybe she and Eddie could have their postponed date from last night.

Grace held up her finger. "Except we have a tiny problem." She turned her phone around.

On the screen was one of Carter's social-media pages and a picture of a gigantic sapphire ring. "I thought we weren't supposed to talk about the plot of the film yet."

Grace clicked her tongue. "Read the caption."

Bianca took the phone from Grace and read the words Carter had written. "Guess who said yes! Hint: I've been spending a bunch of time with her lately." Her mouth popped opened. "Please tell me people don't think it's me."

"Okay, I won't tell you." Grace yanked her phone away from

Bianca before she could read more than two comments that confirmed her fear.

"How can we fix this? I don't want to fake date Carter." She dropped her voice. "I don't even want to fake date Eddie. Grace, we were going to try the real thing. Me and Eddie. I don't want this scaring him away."

Grace glanced over at Eddie, who had his shoulder pressed up against the tree as he stared at the sky. "If you're sure, I'll try to set a meeting up with Leo and the producers to figure out a way to get you and Carter *coupling* off the agenda."

Bianca pressed her hands together. "Yes, please. I'll even do a hundred more interviews."

Grace pulled up an email. "Okay, I'll take care of the meeting. You better go let Eddie know before he sees this online."

"You're a lifesaver, Grace. Thanks."

Bianca jogged over to Eddie. With the dark shadows under his eyes, he looked as tired as she felt. How many callouts had he been on since they had sat in Officer Ramble's car?

Last night, when he hadn't shown up for their date, she'd called. No answer. Waited. Texted. When she hadn't received a word, she'd found out online that he hadn't stood her up but was doing the job he loved—saving lives.

"Hey." She smiled and opened her water bottle. "I believe the news clip I saw mentioned that you needed a badge of honor for saving that little girl. I can't do that, but I can reward you with a slice of pizza or three. If you're as hungry as me—"

"I don't need any special treatment for rescuing people. Those videos should never have been recorded in the first place."

Back to hangry Eddie. Noted. "I know, but they were a little helpful because they let me know you were safe." He was a perfect firefighter. Always had the needs of others in his mind. She wanted to erase some of the stress that lined his eyes.

She pulled the end of her ponytail around in front of her and ran her fingers around the curl. "I was thinking about having pizza delivered to my trailer. It's not exactly fancy, but it's all the date I need, if you're up for rescheduling for tonight?"

His attention snagged everywhere except on her.

He dragged his hands through his hair. "Unfortunately, pizza isn't going to fix yesterday."

No, but it could fix his hangry situation. Or was there more going on? She cradled her water bottle to her chest. "Did anyone die...yesterday?" Was she allowed to ask that? "Or did something else happen to Mary or Joel?"

Eddie paced under the tree. "People could have died. Accidents usually attract a crowd, but last night, they wouldn't listen. Too busy trying to gain my attention. A three-year-old could have been killed because paparazzi were trying to take my picture on a call-out. One photographer was lucky he only sustained a concussion from the explosion."

Bianca flinched. She hadn't seen the explosion part. "I'm sorry, Eddie. People get so caught up in—"

"You." Eddie watched her long enough for Bianca to drop her gaze to her shoes, which were scuffed from the stunt he'd helped her get through. Shoes that were a part of her job, not who she was as a person. Because right now, she really could go for the comfort of her flip-flops.

Bianca pushed the sleeves on her character's jacket. "You're right. People do get too caught up in not only me but most of the things centered around acting. If you don't want to eat with me tonight and need to be with your crew, I understand. I can have a pizza sent to your apartment or the firehouse. I'm sure the guys wouldn't mind some free dinner."

He slipped his hands into his pockets. "I don't think I can do *this* anymore, Bianca." His words were soft, but their meaning hit like another stunt gone wrong.

Bianca blinked. "This what? The pizza? The deal . . . or the real part of us?"

Please, not the last part.

A storm of emotions crossed Eddie's brown eyes. "My job is very important, not only to me but for the safety of this town. I can't work with the paparazzi interfering. If that child had died because of—"

"She didn't." Bianca crossed her arms over her chest. "We shouldn't worry about things that didn't happen. Didn't you say that once? Not to borrow trouble?"

"This"—he motioned between them—"can't really work in real life. Not with you being who you are and me having to worry about people stopping me from doing my job."

"Me being who I am?" She'd thought he'd seen the real her. "If this is because of what Carter put on social media, it isn't true. Grace is going to try to set up a meeting so I don't have to keep pretending. I'm ready to be real, Eddie. With you. We can figure the rest out together."

He dipped his chin. "I don't want to take your money either, Bianca. You have your own money battles to worry about besides my burden too. You were right the other night. We don't need any more deals. I'll figure something else out about the youth center."

Bianca squeezed her eyes shut. This was beginning to sound too much like the last time she'd talked to her father. "My money's not tainted, Eddie. You keep thinking my kind gestures are something they're not. We had a deal, and I'm going to keep my end of the bargain. Relationship or not."

By the shocked expression on his face, Eddie had gotten better at his acting skills. "I never said your money was tainted."

No, she didn't need his pity. "Are you going to take my donation or not?"

Eddie shook his head. "I can't, Bianca. I'm sorry. It wouldn't feel right."

She blinked away tears. Backed up. One step. Two. Maybe her family had been right all along. She only ever caused head- and heartaches. "Thanks, Eddie, for everything . . . The people of Last Chance County are lucky to have you watching over them. You're a great man."

He opened his mouth, but she'd seen the mask he'd placed over his heart with his simple nod. "I'll explain things to the team, and I'll have Zack help with the tourney."

She wasn't only leaving Eddie but the team too.

When he'd left, Bianca slipped between one of the nearby storage barns and the side of a parked trailer. She closed her eyes.

Alone. Again.

God, why can't those I care about see the real me and stay?

"Uh, Ms. Pearl?"

Bianca opened her eyes and blinked away the tears.

Thad, the security guard, stared at her. His brows pulled even lower. "You all right?"

Bianca sniffed and painted on her Bia smile.

His mouth formed a circle. "Oh, I see. You were only practicing emotions. Wow, you're such a talented actress. Those looked like real-life tears."

One of those very real tears slipped down her cheek. "You're a great security guard, Thad. Thanks for checking up on me."

Why couldn't she just admit to him the truth? That she was having a horrible day. But people too often only wanted to go surface level. Not get in the mud and help shoulder the heartache.

The man beamed back at her. "Wait until I tell my granddaughter about how one of her grandma's favorite actresses paid this old man a compliment."

Bianca tilted her head. "What's your granddaughter's name? I can sign an autograph for her and your wife. That is, if you'd think they'd like one. I can leave them at the security office for you."

The man chuckled. "They'd like it all right, but"—he held up his hand—"I'm not supposed to ask for—"

"You didn't ask. I offered." Bianca pulled out her phone. "What if you gave me their mailing address? That way *if* she so happened to get an autograph sent to her house, then you wouldn't get in trouble with your job."

"Bella would be tickled pink." Thad rattled off the address, and Bianca made a memo in her phone.

His radio buzzed on his hip, and someone asked if he'd completed his rounds. He answered and gave Bianca a salute. "Thank, Ms. Pearl. You've mightily proved that I can't believe everything I read online about you."

Her smile slipped. What had the reporters come up with this time? Did it have to do with Carter, Eddie's mother, or something else?

The shoes on her feet still pinched her toes, but she'd rather escape to her trailer for a quiet moment than get any questioning looks about her possibly runny mascara. She sent off a text to Grace.

Bianca

Want to share a pizza tonight?

Grace sent back a text.

Grace

I wish! I'm talking to Leo about your meeting. Plus, got a couple hiccups in the upcoming scene location.

Bianca dialed Frances and held the phone to her ear as she walked up the steps to her trailer. Frances's voice came over the speaker, but it was only her voicemail. Bianca ended the call and sank onto her couch.

Lord, now what am I supposed to do?

She kicked out of her shoes, and her stomach chose that moment to growl. Except pizza no longer sounded good.

Her phone vibrated in her hand. The ID that flashed onto the screen hadn't called her in months.

Home.

Her fingers shook as she swiped to answer. "Hello?"

Please, let them not have called by mistake.

"Hey, Bee."

Bianca fell back against the couch cushion. Her sister was calling from her parents' house. "Hey, Madeline."

Madeline cleared her throat. "How are you doing?"

Bianca stared up at the ceiling of her trailer. "I'm . . . okay. How's . . . everyone?" Her heart thumped. Once. Twice. Still no answer. "Maddy?"

A sniff snuck over the phone's speaker.

Bianca sprang up off the couch. "What's wrong? Is it Grandma? Mom? Dad?"

Please, Lord, don't take them from me before we get things fixed.

She ran to her purse and threw it over her shoulder. What else would she need to head home? "I'm leaving now. I'll be there in . . ." How long would it take her to drive home? Fly? Not quick enough.

Finally, her sister said, "No, Bianca. It's nothing like that. It's . . ."

Another sniff.

Bianca leaned against the trailer's tiny island. "Talk to me, Madeline. You're scaring me."

"We had a big fight." Her sister's words echoed over the phone.

Bianca slinked back over to the couch and sat down on the edge. "You and Zeke?" Had one of them called off their wedding?

A ragged breath, and then her sister's voice whispered, "Me and Dad. He said . . . I didn't need the Old Vineyard for my wedding. He's right. I don't. I love Zeke no matter where we get married. But we chose our wedding date specifically for when the Old Vineyard had an availability. We waited extra months for it. You know that place was my dream. Always. Mom promised they'd pay for it. They paid the first deposit, but that was before the house . . . and now the second deposit is due. Dad said they weren't going to pay. Zeke and I used all our savings to buy the sweetest little house. Do you remember Mrs. Keeper's old house? The one with the heart shutters?" A hiccup proceeded to a groan. "I'd marry Zeke in rags at the courthouse, but . . . you know what it's like to follow your dreams. I just wanted someone in our family to actually keep their promises."

Bianca rubbed her knuckles along her forehead. "I do know what it's like to follow your dreams." The dreams that she wasn't sure were worth it anymore.

She wanted a better happily ever after for her sister. "What if I cover the vineyard?"

It wasn't like she had to give any of her movie money to Eddie anymore. She massaged her temples. "I'll have to put the deposit on my credit card." But it would work. It had to work.

"Oh, Bee, you're the best. I promise Zeke and I will pay you back. I told Mom you'd help, but Dad overheard, and that's when the fight escalated. He said not to call and bother you."

Bianca fisted her hands. "You're not bothering me. But if I pay . . . I want to come to the wedding."

She pressed her lips together. Why had she made the money an ultimatum? She needed to stop making deals.

Bianca's heart thumped for far too many heartbeats before her sister whispered, "I've always wanted you there, but . . . even if you aren't letting us borrow—"

"Not borrow." Bianca traced the stitching on the arm of her couch. "It'll be your wedding gift."

"Do you have to film that day? It's almost nine months away. Wouldn't you need to hire more security?"

Bianca inhaled through her nose and out through her mouth. "I'll try to stay in the back so as not to cause an issue with anyone."

One more sniff. "It wasn't fair for Dad to blame you for his other job loss."

Bianca sat up straighter. "Other? I thought he only supposedly lost his promotion."

Madeline sighed. "Last month, he was laid off."

Eddie had been right to step away from Bianca now. Her dream had cost those she loved far too much.

TWENTY-TWO

EDDIE PULLED DOWN A BOX OF DOUBLE CHOC-olate brownie mix from the grocery store's shelf. He never did have any of his brownies the other day. Frozen pizza and brownies. A perfect breakup dinner. For both real and fake.

He tossed the box in his empty cart and then eyed the peanut butter swirl brownie option. Tomorrow already felt like it would need a double portion of a pick-me-up. He would start researching more fundraiser ideas for the youth center.

My money's not tainted, Eddie. You keep thinking my kind gestures are something they're not. We had a deal, and I'm going to keep my end of the bargain. Relationship or not.

But if there was no future between him and Bianca, he couldn't take her money.

I did the right thing, right, Lord?

"Boo!" a young girl shouted from behind him.

Eddie spun around and knocked another brownie box onto the ground.

The pony-tailed girl, who turned out to be Scarlette, darted to the dropped box while she smiled up at Eddie. "Since I got you, Coach, I think you should have to make these brownies for me."

Eddie took the box from her outstretched hand and placed it into his cart. "Why don't I make brownies for the whole team?" He frowned at the empty baking aisle. "Where's your mom, or grandma?"

Scarlette tilted her head, pointing one of her ears upward.

That's when Eddie noticed a measured squeaking sound.

Scarlette gestured to the end of the aisle. "Grandma was on the phone. She should be coming in three, two . . ."

A half-full cart rounded the end of the aisle, but Naomi's normal smiley greeting was missing. "Scarlette Joy, this is no time to run off. We've got to leave right now . . ." Naomi's attention flashed over to Eddie. "Well, aren't you a Godsend, Coach."

"Momma?" Jade's voice floated to them from another aisle over. "What's the plan?"

Naomi lifted her hand. "In the baking aisle. Found Scarlette."

Jade and Scout arrived, and Naomi grabbed her purse off the top of the cart. "Slight change of plans. Scarlette, why don't you push my cart behind your momma, and I'll give you money for my stuff. That is, if I can get Coach to give me a ride? He's going to take me to pick up Will. That way, Jade, you can take the kids and food home."

Eddie frowned. "What happened to Will?"

Naomi only gave him a look he couldn't read.

Jade tightened her grip on her cart. "I can get your stuff, Momma, and Eddie's too, if he'll take you."

Eddie placed the boxes of brownies back on the shelf. "My stuff can wait. Where am I taking you, Naomi?"

Naomi pulled out some folded bills.

Jade waved her off and pushed her cart back down the aisle.

Naomi put the money in Scarlette's hand and gave her a squeeze, whispering something in her ear.

Then Scarlette dashed after her mother and brother. "See you later, Coach. Raincheck on the team's brownies."

Naomi took Eddie's now empty cart and turned in the opposite direction.

Eddie waved to Scout, who strangely didn't wave back. "What's wrong with Will? Did he get hurt?"

Naomi shifted behind the cart as she pushed. "It's worse."

Eddie's feet stopped. His rubber soles squeaked against the polished tile.

Naomi gaped at him and then seemed to realize how her words had sounded. "No, honey, no. Sorry. He's alive. He's in trouble down at the police station. We all were going to leave our shopping buggies and hurry down there, but thank goodness you're here. I'd prefer not to let Scout and Scarlette witness the mess Will's gotten into. Scout already overheard more than I wanted him to."

Eddie's hand grabbed hold of the cart. "Will called you?"

Not *him*.

"I doubt he could have gotten ahold of that mother of his. Not that she deserves to be called such. But you know about mothers like that."

He did. That's why Will's father had asked Eddie to watch out for his son. Now Will was in trouble, and Eddie had failed.

He fished out his phone from his pocket. His chest felt as empty as his screen's display. No notifications. "He didn't call me."

Naomi pushed the cart again and placed Eddie's cart back at the exit. "Before you start thinking things that aren't true, we're going to go gather all the details. God has brought us both together at this moment for this specific purpose and this child. Let's go find the answers. Together. Unless you'd rather stay here and sulk?"

Was that what he was doing?

Eddie caught up, and Naomi hooked her hand on his elbow, just like Bianca used to. "Where's that truck of yours?"

He pointed at it, and they hopped inside.

Naomi hummed the hymn "I Surrender All" over his radio music.

Eddie turned the volume down on his speakers, and Naomi shifted toward him. "I went and saw Mary."

He rolled his shoulders back. Not that he'd had time, but he hadn't done more than send a text to Mary. "How's Joel?"

Naomi kept still for too long and then finally said, "There's a chance he'll get out of the ICU this week. Mary seemed optimistic."

Eddie kept his gaze locked on the green light ahead of him. "I'm happy for her. And Joel. She said that she couldn't live without him."

Unlike Eddie.

Naomi rested her palm on his arm. "I know she hurt you, son. But you can't let that continue to damage your own heart."

His own heart was fine. Or it would be. "I never should have met with her. All this could have been avoided."

"Avoided, maybe. But not mended." Naomi shifted her purse in her lap. "I gave her your letter."

Eddie pulled his sun visor down, but the sun sat low and beamed into his vision. "What letter?"

"You know that before your grand-ma'am passed, she reached out to Mary."

"Wished she hadn't done that either. She gave Mary my number." Which had led to the disaster dinner.

"After your grand-ma'am passed, I inherited her Bible. Inside of it were several papers and envelopes, including a letter you'd written after you realized who the Lord was."

Oh, that letter. "I remember."

He'd written to his mother to tell her he'd forgiven her for leaving him because he'd been placed with a woman who showered him with love and brownies, and how his next-door neighbor was a cool firefighter. "Grand-ma'am mailed it on Mary's birthday that year."

"It was in a return-to-sender stamped envelope."

Eddie pushed in the brakes at a stop sign. "I thought she was too happy to send a reply."

Naomi shook her head. "I don't know why it was sent back. But what I've learned at this old age is that I can't fix the broken. Only God can. He fixed me. He fixed you. Doesn't mean we don't need mending along the way, but one of the hardest lessons I learned was that I can tell people all about the true Hope, but only He can turn them to His truth and actually change their hearts."

She released a sigh that hovered in the silence of the truck like a whispered hug. "Last week at the women's shelter, I counseled the sweetest girl. People who come there are seeking help … and hope. Sometimes I get to share the truth that God loves them no matter the past. But for some, they only really want their circumstance to be changed. Not the hard work that might come along with it. Most don't want to have to alter their own habits … their own heart. Unfortunately, some relationships don't end in a happily ever after. It's hard to watch others reject God's salvation."

She drummed her fingers against her purse. "So, Eddie, I'm going to ask you what I asked that sweet girl who left, still laying blame to everyone but herself for her situation. If nothing else changes, can you still stand upon God's promises? Trust that His justice will one day be served. His mercy is a glorious gift, and His promises endure through all generations. Is there something inside your own heart that needs repairing?"

Eddie leaned into the turn into the police station's parking lot. He'd thought he'd long buried the stuff with Mary, but he'd only masked his dealings with their past.

Had buried his bitterness instead of surrendering it all.

Inside the police station, they were brought to Will, who sat hunched in a chair in a back office.

Officer Ramble explained the situation and rose from a desk in the corner. "I'll give you guys a minute." He closed the door behind him.

Will shrugged. "Don't know why everyone's making this into a big deal. The gang said no one has lived there for months."

Eddie flinched. "Like a real gang, or the group of boys Bianca saw you with on the bikes? The ones that call you Jimmy. Did you pick a lock to get inside that house?"

Will crossed his arms and faced the clock on the wall. "It wasn't a big deal. I learned it from my dad."

"Not a big deal? Your dad's in jail because of his bad habits." Eddie threw his arms up. "You damaged someone's property."

Naomi leaned against Eddie's side. "How about you find us both a coffee?" She winked at Eddie. "While I do some open-heart surgery in here."

Will stole a peek at Naomi before bringing his knees to his chest, making him look even younger.

Eddie understood how cold that metal chair beneath Will felt. Like sorrow and fear. All the while trying to mask it all and pretend the world around him wasn't crumbling. That was when Grandma'am had shown up and introduced a volunteer firefighter to hang out with Eddie. It had changed his life.

With a clenched jaw, Eddie left and met Conroy, who'd been leaning against the wall in the hall. "Hey, sir."

Conroy motioned his chin toward a door down the hallway. "Let's catch up in my office."

"Sure, Chief."

Once Conroy closed his door, Eddie took a seat in one of the open chairs in front of the chief's desk. "I've got to get that youth center built, or this is going to keep happening."

Conroy frowned. "A new fancy gym isn't going to fix any child long-term. But—"

"It's got to be the starting point." Eddie raked his fingers through his hair. "How else are we going to keep these kids safe? I promised Will's father I'd keep his son out of trouble."

"Rice, this isn't your fault." Conroy leaned his elbows on an open folder on his desk. "Will made the decision to hang out with those kids. With his mother picked up for drugs this morning, and his father in jail . . ."

Eddie stood. "Will's being put into the foster system?"

Conroy gave him a fatherly look. "There're good homes in the system. You know that."

He did. But what if Will didn't get a good foster parent? "I'll take him." The words flew out of his mouth before he could even process what that would mean. "I don't like my studio apartment anyway. I'll get a bigger one."

Conroy made his chair rock back and forth. "I'm assuming you aren't currently certified as a foster parent, but a temporary guardianship might work if both parents sign off on it. Though, not sure how your job would work with your shift times."

Naomi's words came back to him. *God has brought us both together at this very moment for this specific purpose and this child.*

"Will's already friends with Naomi's grandkids. They're on the same team. We'll get this figured out. I don't want Will to feel alone."

Conroy stood along with Eddie. "This sounds like a promising plan, but remember that Will still has to decide to live as he should. God is the only One who can truly save him. Not a youth center. Not even you."

Eddie nodded. "I can't change his heart, but I can hopefully be a good example to follow." Which meant examining his own heart.

Had Naomi been right? Did his own heart need mending?

Eddie's gaze landed on the picture on Conroy's desk. He tilted his head. "May I?"

Conroy handed him the photo. "Recognize anyone?"

The picture was of Roger Pointe with two other men. The shorter one had his back turned. The taller one with suspenders and a dimpled jaw popped into Eddie's memory. "That's the guy from the masquerade fundraiser."

"The arsonist?"

"Yes, this one paid off the security guard and lit the dress on fire. That's him."

Conroy stared at the picture. "You sure? This photo was picked up outside of Roger's office days before the fire."

Eddie picked up another picture on Conroy's desk of a different angle of the three men. The shorter man remained in the shadows, but this photo had a fourth man walking up to the group. Even with a pair of sunglasses on, he looked like Bianca's ex. "Have you shown this to Bianca? See if she can confirm an eyewitness testimony, but I'm pretty sure it's the arsonist. This fourth guy here resembles Nathan Kensington."

"Yes. Nathan and Roger have been easy to identify. It's the others." Conroy took the photos. "It's on today's to-do list to speak with Bianca. Speaking of Bia Pearl, thanks for helping out at the set. The smashed keys you found helped us make an arrest for the collapsed set building—an angry construction worker who'd been fired the day before. We're thinking he might have even messed with the car scene too."

"So, not an accident." Eddie blew out a breath. Finally. Some closure there. "What about the Jane Doe?"

"Has been identified as Tiffany Landson. She was in town with the movie crew. Her family finally filed a missing person's report."

Eddie flinched. He'd heard that name on set. "Tiff was the beloved makeup artist who had a family emergency. She either lied about wanting some time off to hike, or maybe it was foul play?"

"Her death hasn't been ruled suspicious . . . yet."

Yet still a possibility.

Eddie pulled out his phone and checked the time. "I bet you and your officers are ready for the movie production to pack up and for Last Chance County to get quiet again."

Conroy set the photos back on his desk. "Not sure that's Gregory's plan. Though, there's something else you might be able to help us with."

Eddie scooted to the end of his chair. "As long as it's no more fake dating."

Conroy raised a brow. "What about a fake interest in supporting Roger Pointe? That's the other thing I wanted to tell you earlier. When the mayor called this morning for an update, he mentioned that he overheard you and Roger talking at the ball game. He claimed Roger was trying to manipulate you. I brought up the precious failed grant as your possible motivator for speaking with Roger." Conroy placed both elbows on his desk. "Turns out the mayor claims he never denied your original grant request."

Eddie yanked out his phone. "I have an email that says otherwise."

Conroy rolled his chair closer to his desk. "Did it come from his assistant?"

At the mention of Janice, Eddie grimaced. "Yes."

Conroy opened another folder on his desk. "Evidence is starting to point in a certain direction. Would you be interested in wearing a mic and visiting Roger at his office?"

Sounded just like Officer Ramble's request for Bianca's help. Had she talked to Nathan yet? Except that information was no longer any of his business. He'd let her go.

Eddie squeezed his eyes shut. He'd given up, been too focused on what he thought everyone needed instead of fighting for her. He'd let her go because he'd been scared that her lifestyle would somehow prevent him from doing his job. She hadn't been the problem. She'd even found out Will was heading down the wrong path before he had.

He leaned over the chief's desk. Eddie needed to call Bianca.

Eddie had supposedly been doing his job, and he'd still allowed Will to get in trouble. And he'd hurt Bianca in the process by not trusting God that He'd take care of their future.

Conroy cleared his throat. "Not to rush you, but—"

"What would I visit Roger about? I can't come out and ask him if he's having Gregory's assistant play double agent between them. Or at least I think that's where you're going with the information."

Conroy grabbed his vibrating phone off his desk. "You could pretend you're interested in giving him your support like he mentioned at the ball game. See where it leads."

Bianca's face popped into Eddie's head, and he told Conroy the truth. "I haven't had the best of luck in pretending."

Or if he was honest, being real either.

TWENTY-THREE

NUMB.

That wasn't how a designer dress should make anyone feel.

Bianca stared at her reflection in the makeup trailer. The rose-colored silk moved like melted butter along her curves, and the sparkling overlay shimmered when she moved.

Grace had worked her magic and gotten Bianca her meeting with Leo and one of the new financial producers of the movie to go over her and Carter's contracts. But now it felt too little, too late.

"Perfection." Grace brought her fingers to her lips and made a kissing sound. "Riley, you wowed it with those curls. Tiff's level of greatness, to be sure. Messy yet classy. Love. It. All. Bianca, the producer will for sure realize that you're a gem—pun intended because of this movie about lost jewels." She added a giggle and then nodded. "You are and will be focused on keeping yourself happy. No more fake dating is in your contract's future. I can feel it."

Riley faced her pile of makeup. Hopefully, she would focus on Grace's compliment and not the comparison to the former makeup artist.

Bianca repositioned one of the curls tangling against its neighbor. Her hair looked more suitable for a night out for pizza than a formal dinner. One she wished she could have had with Eddie last night before he'd left with her heart.

Riley had arrived late but succeeded in spite of the tight deadline. "Thanks, Riley."

Riley turned and gave her a saucy look in the mirror as she pulled out her phone. "What else would I be good for?"

Grace held out two pairs of shoes—rhinestone boots and heels that made Bianca's back hurt just by looking at them. "I'm thinking boots."

"The heels." Riley typed on her phone screen.

Bianca turned to the side and pulled the hem down behind her. "How about my flip-flops or tennis shoes? Business up top, comfy on bottom. Plus, no one else is going to see my shoes when I'm sitting down."

Grace shook her head. "Never those flip-flops of yours. No tennis shoes. Those will look like Eddie's changed you too much."

Eddie *had* changed her, just not in the way her friend assumed.

Grace wrinkled her nose. "Riley's right. Put on the heels and thank us both later."

Bianca slipped on her tennis shoes and took the heels. "I'll put them on in the car."

"Fine." Grace gasped. "We almost forgot!" She hustled over to Riley's makeup area. "Where's the diamond heart pendant?"

Riley turned toward Grace. "Didn't you want the teardrop necklace?"

Grace's eyes bugged out. "Absolutely no tears. She's supposed to be thrilled to be working on this movie." She placed her phone down and shimmed toward one of the wardrobe areas.

Riley set her phone down beside Grace's on the counter and picked up an eyeshadow palette and a brush. "I'm going to go a shade darker. What do you think?"

"I think I'm overworking you, and you've already made me feel beautiful. Thanks for jumping into this position. It's like it was created for you."

Some emotion crossed Riley's eyes as she set the makeup down, and one of the phones buzzed on the counter.

Riley glance at the screen and her eyebrows shot up. "Looks like there's been a change of plans. You're riding in the limo. Right now. Dinner time has been pushed up for security reasons at the restaurant."

Bianca gripped the heels in her hands. "Like right now? But I'm supposed to drive myself. Justin was supposed to be off tonight."

"You know how things change around here. Grace's phone just got a text. Guess she's rearranged a few things. Says Justin's not officially off until he drops you at the restaurant to meet Carter, Leo, and the producer for dinner in less than thirty minutes."

Poor Justin. She didn't want to go out tonight either, but she needed to see if the producer would agree to the change in her contract so she wouldn't have to fake a relationship with Carter. Leo had said he held no sway over the newest producer. Bianca grabbed her gold clutch off the counter, and something dropped onto the floor.

Riley bent down and scooped the necklace off the floor. "Apparently, the heart pendant has been here the entire time. You better hurry."

Bianca grabbed the gold chain and her heels. "Tell Grace thanks. I'll put everything on on the way. I don't want to make them wait."

She really needed to stay on the men's good side. She hadn't met the new producer, but Carter had told Grace that he'd take care of getting him there so long as Bianca came and sat by Carter at the dinner to create some hype for his social sites tonight.

One last night of almost pretending.

It was a good thing she'd worn her tennis shoes. Bianca jogged out toward the parking lot. The limo engine was running, and the vehicle wasn't parked up against the curb like normal; instead, it was parked facing the gate.

Bianca opened the door and slid into the middle of the seat. "Thanks, Justin. You didn't have to take me on your day off . . ."

The window between the backseat and the driver wasn't rolled down. Nathan sat in the seat facing her.

She reached for the door handle, but Nathan moved to the seat in front of the door, blocking her exit.

He rested his ankle on the top of his knee. "Always drama with you."

"Standing up against illegal activity isn't drama." Bianca swallowed. "What are you doing here, Nathan?"

He smirked. "Didn't Carter tell you that I'd be at dinner too?"

The limo jerked forward, but Bianca didn't take her gaze off Nathan.

She scooted over. "Carter seems to have had a lot on his mind—or should I say, his ribs have been on his mind because one was broken. Do you know anything about that?"

Why couldn't she have a police wire on her now?

She positioned her heels so the spike faced outward.

Nathan tracked her movements. "Easy, Lady B. You've always been the levelheaded one between us. Let's not go on ignoring some of your good qualities." His eyes then wandered to her legs. "Though you do have so many. I've missed those."

Bianca pulled her dress down with her other hand. "You have two seconds to tell me why you're actually here, or I'm telling Justin to pull over."

Nathan chuckled. "So feisty. Tell me again why you settled on fake dating that firefighter."

"I was a fool." She should have dated him for real, but she'd lost her chance.

Nathan hummed. "Then there's still hope for us yet."

"Justin!" Bianca leaned forward and knocked on the glass behind Nathan. "Pull over. I think I'm going to be sick."

Nathan yanked her beside him. "It's past time for you to shut that pretty mouth of yours. No need for theatrics—though you are a gifted actress, which will prove useful. I just have a favor. One you should have given the night my lawyer asked you to testify for me. Not against."

Bianca scooted away. "You mean the lawyer who took a bribe to get your charges dropped? I saw that too. No, thank you."

Nathan shook his head. "Is it really a good idea not to help out the man who backed your movie when it would have shut down without his help?"

Bianca blinked once. Twice. "You're the newest producer? How? Why?"

Nathan pulled a golden case with a logo of a crown on it from his suit jacket and tugged out a cigar. "Money always talks, sweetheart. We've come full circle again. I need a small favor in exchange for the production money. It's only fair since I landed you this job in the first place." He lit the end of his cigar, and the puffs of smoke made Bianca wrinkle her nose.

He drew a long inhale from the cigar and blew an oval-shaped smoke ring up toward the light in the center of the limo. "You're going to be my alibi."

"I didn't lie for you before. Why would you think I'd do it now?"

"Because you need me this time." He shrugged and put out his cigar on an ashtray she hadn't even known existed in the corner. "Or at least my money."

She may not be wearing the police wire, but she could at least record their conversation. She slid the phone out of her purse. Kept it pressed against her leg. She unlocked the screen. Only needed to pull up the video button.

Except Nathan grabbed her phone.

She reached for it. "Give it back."

Something flashed in his eyes. Something she'd never seen before. Hate. Fear. Or both.

Had she ever really known this man?

He pointed the phone at her. "You will do this. Without me, this movie gets shuts down. Carter won't be happy. Once again, your name will be smeared in the press. You're still trying to buy back your mommy and daddy's love and—"

"Stop. You don't know what you're talking about."

Nathan shrugged. "Guess your parents really don't need you to save their house from foreclosure. What about your sister's wedding—"

"How did—"

"Then there's the youth center and your little firefighter."

The evil man. Why hadn't she seen it at the very beginning? Because she'd been looking for love in the wrong things.

Lord, I can't fix this.

Nathan leaned toward her. "Like I said, I do my homework. One lie and you get everything you want. Even me."

"You're a monster."

"But a rich one."

She shifted her gaze off Nathan's gleeful expression to catch a familiar building as it flashed by the window. Then a giant rooster yard sign by the road.

That couldn't be right.

She looked out the back glass. A blue gas station with a diner attached to it. The same place where she'd stopped for directions and to change before the mayor's fundraiser. The place with the best peach turnovers.

"Aren't we going downtown to eat? Or are we not going to a restaurant at all?"

"Changing the subject is never going to work. Make the deal with me so we can have a nice fake dinner with Leo and Carter.

Isn't your costar supposed to be your newest beau, based on your contract? I can let him have a few months with you if he pays up what he owes."

Her eyes snapped to her ex while her pulse hammered in her temple. She narrowed her eyes. "Carter said he owed the Duke . . . You're the Duke? You had Carter attacked?"

"Sweetheart, if you're struggling with one lie, you don't want me to tell you the truth about the Duke or what happened to Carter. You'll find yourself in an entire ocean of lies you can't get back to shore from."

So he *wasn't* the boss? "Is that what happened to you? You met the Duke, and now you're in too deep?"

He popped a mint in his mouth from another smaller golden metal container. "Life isn't a movie, Lady B."

"How many times must I tell people that I know that?"

His gaze flicked to the window. "This doesn't look like any downtown. Not that this city is anything close to the class it needs to be for the resort. But in time, it could work."

Her mind started to click off the details. "The Duke is trying to get that upscale resort here too. But why here?"

The smug expression dropped from Nathan's face before he lifted her phone and looked at the time. He thumped his knuckles on the glass. "You need to check your GPS. If we're late, your pay will be docked."

Bianca snagged her phone from him. "Be nice to Justin. He was supposed to be off duty."

The limo took a sharp turn. She bumped over into Nathan.

He snaked his arm around her. "If you missed me that much, all you had to do was say so."

She slapped his hand and pressed her hip against the opposite side of the seat.

The tires bounced all the way into the woods along a dirt path sprinkled with gravel.

Nathan banged on the window between them and Justin again. "You couldn't have found a more suitable place to turn around?"

Bianca picked up the phone that connected to Justin's Bluetooth. But there was no dial tone.

She held the handset toward Nathan. "Something's not right."

"What?" Nathan barked.

Her hand shook. "There's no connection."

He crawled over to her original seat and pulled on the door's handle. "It's locked."

She put her hand against her chest. Her lungs squeezed as if her dress were two sizes too small.

Locked inside. It was the fire room all over again.

Nathan rammed his shoulder against the door.

Except she didn't have the right man beside her.

She licked her lips. "Maybe the limo's phone is broken, and Justin's only having a bad direction day. No need to panic." But the pit in her stomach said otherwise. She banged on the glass separating them from driver. "Justin? You okay?"

Nathan held his phone and frowned. "I don't have any cell service, LB."

With trembling fingers, Bianca lifted her phone. Nathan was right. No service.

Lord, what's happening?

Finally, the woods cleared, and the limo stopped by a pile of dirt.

Not a single building in sight. No people. Only trees and some kind of construction vehicles.

She'd signed up for a family-friendly movie when she'd arrived in Last Chance County, not a horror film. And definitely not in real life either.

The driver's-side door opened. The limo rocked as a man got out of the car.

Shorter and sturdier than Nathan, he stomped down the length of the limo.

He wore a mask, just like the ones from the mayor's auction. But it was the gun in his grip that made her gasp.

"I don't want to die," Nathan whispered.

Neither did she.

Bianca grabbed her heels that had dropped onto the floor. She put one in her palm and handed the other to Nathan. "Let me do the talking."

Lord, give me the right words.

She needed to give her best performance yet.

TWENTY-FOUR

I T WAS HIS TIME TO PRETEND.

Maybe this moment wouldn't end in disaster. And then after he'd spoken with Roger, Eddie would apologize to Bianca in person. Really, he didn't blame her for not answering his earlier call.

Eddie fisted his fingers to keep from readjusting the wires Conroy had taped to his chest and followed a girl who looked barely out of high school to an office painted a dull matte brown. "Mr. Pointe will be right with you."

She closed the door, and a painting of a flower vase fell off its nail on the wall.

Eddie picked it up as the office door opened again.

"Ah." Roger raised his brows at Eddie. "You've already discovered this place hasn't hired a proper decorator. I barely refrained from allowing my decorator to clean up this space, but no need to spend money on a borrowed office. My true office will be ready before we know it."

Eddie hung the painting back up, but the frame tilted to the right. "Your confidence that you'll win the mayoral race is infectious."

Deep breath in. And out. He wiped his palms on his jeans.

Pretending with Bianca had been so much easier. Then again, he'd stopped pretending far sooner than he'd realized.

Roger pointed to the worn chair in front of his desk. "Sit. Tell me what I can do for you."

Eddie eased into the chair. The wire taped on his chest pulled against his skin. "You mentioned at the ball game . . . about being on the same team."

Roger paused before he sat down. "I assume you're here because Bia somehow wiggled out of whatever contract you should have signed between the two of you."

Eddie's back went rigid. "Excuse me?"

Roger held up his palms. "Easy. I won't go to the press about your arrangement to be seen together. It really made sense until she got what she wanted, but you failed to have her sign anything that would hold up her end of paying you."

Eddie cracked his knuckles. "How did you—"

Roger pulled out a cigar from his drawer. "You don't get where I am without connections. Want one?"

Eddie shook his head.

"Now, time is money, and I have more of one than the other, so let's get to it. You're here for your youth center?"

Eddie swallowed. Well, that was the cover story. "Yes."

"In exchange for getting your youth center built, I'd like your full support for my campaign and a year minimum afterward."

Eddie held the man's locked gaze. "What does my full support entail? Because like you said before, nothing's ever free."

A wicked grin erased Roger's stern expression. "Son, I think you're the exact man I need on the team I'm reshaping. In fact, a new position will be opening in a few hours."

A phone rang, and Roger pulled his phone off a clip on his belt. "Yes? What do you mean you're already there? I told you not before nine." With a deep inhale, Roger glanced at Eddie. "Fine. Don't mess it up before I get there."

Roger ended the call and stood. "Like I said, I'm reshaping my team. Shall I walk you out?"

Eddie released his grip on the chair's armrest. He hadn't gotten him to admit to anything yet. This was not as easy as the police television shows made it look.

He wiped at his forehead. "Is there another time we can talk about the youth center?"

Roger paused with his hand on the door to the waiting room. "Focused and persistent. I'm going to appreciate those qualities about you. Yes, shall we say Friday?"

Eddie tried not to frown. That was days away. "I'm free tomorrow."

He fisted his clammy palms. No wonder Officer Ramble had asked Bianca to contact Nathan. She already had tons of acting skills. But he hoped to be beside her when she had to go through this stress. If she'd let him redeem himself.

Roger pushed open the doorway. "No, I believe tomorrow will be quite full for us both. But do call me in between if you have any need to talk. I always make myself available for those on my side." He held the outside door open for Eddie too.

Eddie focused on the broken sidewalk ahead of his feet. He couldn't stare at the brown police van parked beyond Roger's car—the one Roger just unlocked himself.

Odd. "No driver today?"

Roger jangled his keys for one breath. Then two. "He's on a more important task at the moment." He clenched his jaw. "However, I'm afraid he's proved that he indeed isn't ready for his promised promotion."

Was his driver the one who'd just called? Would the police follow Roger now?

Eddie nodded. "Must be hard to find qualified workers."

"You have no idea."

Roger sped off, and Eddie unlocked his truck. He pulled out his phone. What was he supposed to do now?

Two missed calls. And twelve new messages.

His phone vibrated. Zack was calling.

Eddie swiped the screen and pressed the phone to his ear. "Sorry, Zack, can I call you—"

"Grace is here. She's hysterical and not making any sense. How fast can you get here? Maybe you can talk to her?"

Eddie started his truck. "Don't you think Bianca would be better to talk to—"

"Rice . . . Bianca might be missing."

TWENTY-FIVE

BIANCA HAD BEEN TIED UP AND BLINDFOLDED for a movie once. It hadn't prepared her for the very real-life knotted rope biting into her skin. Or the black stocking hat pulled down over her face.

Her heated breaths made an awkward rhythm against her unsteady steps; However her thoughts remained steady.

For the good and bad, God was with her.

She pressed her chapped lips together.

And she really wanted to live to see Eddie again. Tell him that he'd been wrong about them.

"Keep walking." Their kidnapper no longer sounded like he was right behind her and Nathan.

"That would be a lot easier if you released us," Nathan mumbled.

As they staggered forward, his shoulder bumped against hers—or at least she assumed it was his. The air smelled like mud and sweat and maybe a little gasoline mixed in. Gravel had been around the limo, but for the past thirty steps, her tennis shoes—thankfully not her heels—had almost sunk into what appeared to be soft dirt or sand. The rustling of the tree branches no longer seemed as loud.

But if they were heading deeper into the woods, that shouldn't be the case, should it?

Nathan huffed. "This isn't a game. Release me this second, or pay the price."

Great. Apparently, they had slipped into every-man-for-himself mode.

When the gunman had demanded they exit the limo, he'd been wearing a black masquerade mask, but it couldn't hide his short stature and muddy boots and carpenter pants.

His stocky steps thumped over in Nathan's direction. "You'll pay. Now, shut up before you make me go against the plan any more and shoot you."

He was definitely on the other side of Nathan now. Which meant he probably couldn't see her hands.

Please, God, let him not see me.

Bianca kept her pace as she wiggled her wrists. The rope burned against her skin. She gritted her teeth and inched her thumb up. If only she could get a little slack.

Nathan scoffed. "You stupid fool. Your *plan* will never work. You have no clue who you've taken."

"I know who you are, and you've become a liability." A thwack sounded, followed by a groan from Nathan.

Bianca froze from her feet all the way to the thumb she had squirmed in between the rope and her wrist.

"Go ahead. I dare you to speak to me again." The kidnapper's tone dropped an octave. "Then you'll never know the plan. Now get in."

Hands landed on Bianca's shoulders and shoved her down. Her head knocked against something hard, and the vibration echoed not only in her head but also in her ears. The space was cool to her exposed legs. Perhaps something metal?

Something collapsed on top of her stomach. She gasped at the same time the something—or rather someone, Nathan—groaned again.

An engine started, but not the limo. A deeper, more rattling noise. Smoke infested the air. The ground underneath them shook, and Nathan's head lifted off her. Had he fallen? Or . . . wait. They weren't going down, but forward . . . and also up.

What was happening? She needed the blindfold off.

She tugged against the ropes on her wrists. Crawled her thumb up. Still nothing. If she could only loosen them a bit, she could slip her arms down over her behind and pull her legs through. Then at least her arms would be in front of her.

Her ex shifted, and something wet landed on her arm.

"Nathan," she whispered as she pressed her back up against his. "Come here."

"Now you want me." He moaned. "It seems you'll have to wait your turn."

Bianca bit back her own growl and reached her fingers out. Metal. Then Nathan's suit. Finally, rope. She scooted closer to his tied hands. "Turn to the side so I can—"

The engine stopped. So did Nathan's and Bianca's movements toward each other.

She rested against the hard, cool metal, and the stocking hat serving as a blindfold seemed to lift a bit from the back of her head. She sank farther into the makeshift scoop of their confined space.

The stocking cap lifted higher. The ends rolled up until she could breathe in unfiltered air. Only a bit more and she could actually see where they were.

"What are you doing?" Nathan murmured.

She moved back toward him and rubbed her head against the curve of his shoulder. The stocking cap rolled all the way and uncovered one of her eyes.

The darkening sky stretched above them. Smooth metal formed

some kind of bucket around her and Nathan. "I think we're in some kind of construction bucket—"

"Where is he?" a familiar woman's voice yelled.

Bianca blinked at the stocking hat covering Nathan.

"You said he'd be here by now." The gunman spoke a little quieter.

Bianca leaned toward Nathan and bit the top of the stocking cap to pull it up with her teeth.

She spat out the coarse material, and a wide-eyed Nathan stared at her. The right side of his head had a gash, and blood had caked into his eyebrow.

Bianca wiggled her shoulders. "Now turn around so we can untie each other and figure out how to get out—"

"No, if he's late, he doesn't get half of the ransom money."

Nathan's brows lowered. "All this for a ransom?"

Bianca rotated and put her back against Nathan. "I don't have any money to get me out of this because you stole it."

"I didn't exactly steal it. Just put it in a safe place. You'll thank me later." Nathan shoved his rope against Bianca's fingers. "Here. Untie me."

"You liar. You said you didn't know what happened to my money." Bianca fumbled a bit, but Nathan's ropes weren't as tight as her own. She sank her thumbnail into one of the knots, then pulled with her fingers. Nathan shimmied his wrists, and unlike her own try, the movement loosened the ropes more, and Bianca found the last knotted loop.

"I think that's it."

"We're so not done talking about this, Nathan."

Nathan brought his hands in front of him. Instead of reaching over to untie Bianca's ropes, he stood up in the metal construction bucket.

He grabbed the side of the bucket. "Whoa. You're going to hate them even more, LB. We're not exactly on the ground." He pulled out his wallet from inside his suit jacket. "Hey! I've got your ransom money right here. You don't know who you're messing with. Now let me down."

Me. Not both of them.

"Nathan, what are you doing?" Bianca rubbed the rope back against the metal. Maybe the knot would snag on a rusted section.

He held his wallet over the side of the bucket. "If you had allowed me to make a deal, you wouldn't have had to call anyone and wait. Time is money."

"You were offered a deal," the familiar woman's voice said. "Are you going to do what the Duke asked you to do or not?"

Nathan swallowed. "I already took the fall once. It's not my turn."

"I don't like it when people don't follow the rules," the woman gritted out.

A gun popped. Nathan grunted and stumbled.

Bianca sucked in a breath.

Blood seeped into the white shirt under Nathan's open suit jacket.

"Nathan!" No, this wasn't happening.

"I . . ." His wallet dropped out of his grip and fell outside the bucket.

A gurgling noise escaped his bloodied lips. Nathan's eyes rolled back, and he collapsed, his head thumping against the side of the bucket on the way down.

A hoarse wheeze flew from Bianca's mouth. She pressed her lips closed, and tears burned in her eyes. She backed up until she was curled into the corner of the bucket.

Nathan didn't move next to her. No breath vibrated his chest. Dead.

And she would be next.

Help, Lord. Please.

Her lungs pulled tight. Black spots floated in her vision.

"You're late." The gunman's voice rose above the pulse in her ears. "And you're not getting half of my money."

A new man's voice chuckled. "Remember *your* place. You moved ahead of schedule, and you and your sister agreed to share a third. Don't get greedy. You see how that ends."

"That was before your woman shot someone!"

"I did what I had to do." Wait. She'd heard that voice before. Smooth yet brash.

I don't like it when people don't follow the rules.

It sounded like the angry lady from the auction, the mayor's assistant, Janice. Was the mayor the other man?

Bianca blinked. Focused on the shadowed clouds and not Nathan's body at her feet.

"You shouldn't have shot Nathan. He would have agreed to take my fall again eventually," the newer man's voice said.

"He gave an excellent point about his money," the kidnapper said. "Now we don't need to call in the ransom. Like he said, we have his credit cards right here. I'm sure it will be all the money we need."

Bianca still had no clue who the kidnapper was.

The newer male voice echoed in the still air. "You really are an idiot. It wasn't actually a ransom. You can't get money from a dead body."

Carter had mentioned something similar. Did this have to do with the Duke?

But why was she here in this mess? Because of Nathan?

The familiar voice sounded staccato. "You were supposed to keep things under control. Where's the girl?"

Bianca squeezed her eyes shut.

"Up there with the dead body. She banged her head on the corner when I shoved her into the front-end loader's bucket."

As if given a cue, pain flashed down her neck from her injured head.

"Fine. Dump and bury them. She's served her purpose. Your sister will have to get over the logistics of Bia's death—"

"I can't bury them here."

Nathan's blood pooled closer to her tennis shoes, but she didn't dare move.

Bianca couldn't see anything except the sky above, the metal around her, and Nathan's body. She pictured the newest arrival turning slowly toward the kidnapper.

"What do you mean not here?"

"It might get linked back to *my* company if they're found."

"It's *my* company now. Remember. I'm about to own this entire town. Don't forget your place like Nathan did. Or I'll make sure the bodies are found and you get tagged for them."

Bianca's heartbeat rattled three beats.

Roger Pointe.

That's who the newest male voice was.

So Janice and Roger, but who was the other construction guy?

"I suggest," Roger's whisper rose, "you bury them deep enough that only the worms can find them."

Bianca squeezed her fingers into a fist, and the rope tightened around her wrists.

She wasn't going to be buried alive. Not that being shot was any better.

She pushed herself up and peeked over the opposite side of the bucket, and one of her knees buckled. The bucket reached a little higher than the blow-up slide. A pile of dirt sat next to the bucket, while the front-end loader butted up against a parked bulldozer—more than likely waiting for its turn to shove the extra dirt into the pit.

The limo was parked back at the curve of the drive that went farther ahead. What was likely Roger's car had stopped before the front-end loader's original tracks.

She turned, and on the other side of the bucket lay a shadowed forest surrounding a giant pit.

No wonder the front-end loader had stopped.

She didn't need to squint in the dimming light to know that the hole below was far deeper than any stunt she'd survived before.

Her fingers trembled. Stupid heights.

The memory of Eddie lacing his hand in hers on the blow-up slide played through her mind. Then his focus on her as she sat in the car.

You don't have to do this.

If only he were here now. A hot tear dropped onto her shoulder.

No, it was better that he wasn't. Her life would have only brought him down.

And he couldn't always help her. God provided everything she truly needed. Not a man. Not fame. Not money.

The slam of the front-end loader's door had Bianca peeking over the other side of the bucket. The kidnapper had gotten back in the driver's seat.

Lord, I surrender everything to You.

The engine rumbled but never turned over. Then a second time.

"What's the problem?" Janice asked.

The kidnapper hopped down and walked away from the front-end loader toward Roger, who stood in a suit by a tree at the curve in the woods. "I've got to get some tools from my dozer."

"You mean *my* dozer." Roger laughed.

It was now or never. She would have to jump. But she couldn't aim for the open pit. She probably couldn't climb out without anyone seeing her. The loose dirt in front of the dozer might soften her landing. She'd been trained on how to do stunts. How to fall without injury. She'd never been so thankful for doing her own stunts before now.

Except she'd never had to climb without a harness. Or with her arms still tied around her back.

She got onto her knees. Lifted her gaze above the bucket. No one else was in sight.

She exhaled. She could do this. Had to.

One. Two . . .

Before three, she pushed onto her shaking legs, thrust her right tennis shoe onto the edge of the bucket, and leaped for the dirt. Her legs ran through the air. She gritted her teeth, bent her knees, and prayed that nothing would break.

Her feet hit the loose dirt, and she managed to tuck into a side roll that might have made her old stunt double jealous. She slid down the rest of the pile while the dirt clawed at her exposed legs. She may never want to wear a designer dress again.

Her scraped legs moved like jelly when she got up to run. She had to get to the nearest tree line.

On her fourth step, she stumbled, yet she managed to keep herself standing until she reached the brush before the trees.

She dove and rolled again. A stick dug into her back, and a pile of cockleburs stuck to her dress, stabbing her thigh. She sucked in air. Too loudly.

She closed her mouth, focused on breathing through her nose, and allowed her fingers to locate the knots on the rope. Her thumb slid back up into the extra space between the rope and her wrist as the front-end loader's engine roared to life behind her.

She needed a better hiding spot. She rose onto her knees and managed enough space where her thumb had moved into the rope to twist it around. The knot now rested in the palm of her right hand. Her fingers pulled and yanked as if they'd solved this puzzle before. The rope loosened enough for her left hand to slip free.

She crawled on her hands and feet until the rope dangling behind her snagged on a sticker bush, making the branches pull toward her. She retreated enough to wind the rope around her right shoulder. She had to keep anything that she might be able to use as a weapon.

Just as long as it wasn't used on her.

A tree stood ahead with a row of bushes lining the path. She could make it if she army crawled. Leaves and grime clung to her dress. Dirt caked her nails. The bush branches reached for her curls.

A bunny hopped out of her way as she reached the bark of the tree roots. She crawled around the base of the tree until she sat with her back pressed against the far side, then pulled her knees up to her chest.

"Hey!"

Bianca held her breath.

"Turn that thing off," demanded Roger.

The engine stopped. "What now? I barely got the thing going."

"Only one body fell out when you dumped it," Janice said.

Bianca peeked over her shoulder and around the robust tree. The trio walked around to the front of the front-end loader where the bucket had tilted over the pit. Soon they'd figure out that she hadn't fallen into the pit with Nathan.

She focused on the trees to the right of her. She could make it to one of those. Then one farther away. One step at a time.

Her gaze caught on something beyond the fifth tree in her planned route—a light.

A light could be a house. A house could mean a person. And a person meant help.

She shoved herself up and ducked, making it to the second tree. Then the third.

"Where's Bia? She's not down there," Roger roared.

She was really starting to hate her old nickname turned stage name.

Bianca rose to her full height and sprinted toward the fifth tree, skipping the fourth. She couldn't afford any more slow and steady.

She swung her arms faster, heading straight for the light that glowed through the trees at the end of the woods and what looked to be a cabin window. Finally, a way out.

Until a bullet whizzed by her head and struck the last tree in front of her.

TWENTY-SIX

EDDIE PACED IN FRONT OF MACON'S DESK AS Carter, of all people, sat in his chief's chair.

Officer Olivia Tazwell stared down at Carter, who'd arrived at the firehouse before Eddie after Bianca hadn't shown up to their dinner with Leo.

Carter pressed his head back against Macon's chair. "Leo said that Grace needed to schedule a meeting between him and the new producer. I set things up with Nathan."

Eddie pivoted. "You're telling me Bianca's with her ex—the one who might have had someone attack you?"

Macon had filled in Eddie's spot on the crew's recent callout, but maybe that hadn't been a good idea. Because right now, all Eddie wanted to do was find Bianca and punch Carter out of Macon's chair.

Olivia gave Eddie a raised brow, as if she knew his thoughts. "What else can you tell us?"

Carter hung his head. "That Nathan's a better actor than me." He met Eddie's eyes. "Except with him, there's no camera. There's only his poker face."

Olivia crossed her arms. "I think you'd better unpack that metaphor."

"He pretends to be your friend." Carter plunged his fingers through his usually sculpted hair. "Gets you into the top clubs. He even got me my first headliner contract. Except then you *owe* him. But really, you owe the Duke."

Olivia leaned forward. "Nathan Kensington is the Duke?"

Carter looked away. "No, he works for him. Sort of. By the time I realized that, I was in too deep. Owed too much. That's when he brought me into the gambling ring. At first, I was only there to help catch the bigger money. But then . . . the game got to me. To Nathan's credit, he did warn me not to start playing him."

Eddie stood and gripped Carter's shirt. "Nathan took Bianca because *you* owe money?"

Carter shook his head. "Bianca has nothing to do with that. We were all supposed to meet and talk over our movie contract. Nathan always has a plan. But he won't hurt her. Not if he needs her for something else . . ."

Olivia put her hand on Eddie, and Eddie released Carter. "What did Nathan need from Bianca?"

Carter's gaze darted around the room. "She's stubborn. She'll probably say no again."

Eddie grunted.

Stubborn. Beautiful. Kind.

And he'd let her go.

Carter rubbed his hands. "Not sure what Nathan will do if she refuses his plans."

Olivia tilted her head at the yellowing bruise on Carter's face. "Is that who hurt you?"

Eddie jumped to his feet. No way would he allow Bianca to get hurt.

He turned for the door.

Olivia held her palm out to Eddie and then asked Carter, "What plan would she refuse?"

Eddie crossed his arms. Too much talking. Not enough finding the woman he never should've pushed away.

Carter swirled the chair he didn't belong in to the side. "He needs her alibi. Nathan can't get caught with his hands dirty again. The first time cost him too much to get out of. Pretty sure that's why he owes the Duke."

Olivia's eyes wrinkled around their edges. "But he's already been tried."

"It's for another supposed crime. However the DA still needs more proof, which it looks like they're about to find."

"Just like you have no proof that Nathan took Bianca."

"I never said he took her." It was Carter's turn to hold up his palms. "Look. I'm not the one who should be getting an interrogation right now. I called Grace when they didn't show, because I figured Bia would've texted her with any delays. All I know is Nathan was supposed to meet me and Bia at the restaurant with Leo. He needed to speak to her and knew she wouldn't if she realized he was going to be there. I helped make that happen. That's all."

Eddie narrowed his eyes. "And you're helping out of the goodness of your heart?"

Carter pushed to his feet. "Neither one of them showed up. I care about my costar. It's not like the movie can go on without her. I need her to keep her end of the contract."

There it was. The movie. He didn't care about Bianca.

Eddie's chest still tightened. He took a step back. "Perhaps the reason Bianca's not answering her texts is because she turned her phone off and went to bed."

Olivia's radio buzzed, and she turned it down. "Why don't you two go to the movie set and look for her there, and I'll make my way to the restaurant in case Nathan and Bianca arrived late. Officer Ramble is finishing up a call, and he'll meet you at the set.

We'll put a BOLO out on the limo. There's not that many limos in Last Chance County. We'll find her."

Soon. They had to.

Eddie made it out the door first and nearly ran into Kianna, who had her arm around a sniffling Grace.

Grace stepped forward and hiccuped a cry. "You found her?"

Carter brushed past Eddie. "We're going to check her trailer again. The police think she could have just fallen asleep after long hours of filming."

Eddie clenched his jaw. That wasn't exactly what Olivia had said.

Grace kept pace with Carter. "I already checked before I came here, but I've got her extra trailer key. It's better than just sitting here."

Kianna jogged up behind Eddie. "Grace probably doesn't need to be driving. She's still really shaken up."

Eddie fisted his own shaky fingers. "I'll take care of it." He picked up his pace and darted around Carter and Grace. He held open the exit. "Grace, why don't you ride with me?"

Her eyes were glossy in the dusk-to-dawn lights posted by the entry. "I can't leave my car here. I need it in the morning."

Eddie opened and closed his mouth. How to handle this? "Want me to drive your car? That way you can be free to keep calling Bianca."

Another tear rolled down her cheek. "Yeah. Okay. That makes sense. Here."

He took her outstretched keys and hit the unlock button.

Headlights on a red car parked over the parking lines flashed.

He'd have to get Zack or someone to pick him up after they found Bianca.

Please, Lord, let this all be a misunderstanding.

Eddie started Grace's car and took off before Carter had even gotten into his truck.

Grace dialed Bianca's number. Once. Twice. Probably twenty times before he parked at the set.

Before they reached the path toward the makeup trailer, Leo stood. "I need details."

Eddie ran past Grace and Leo. At the moment, details weren't important. Only finding Bianca. He didn't know exactly what he'd say when he opened the door and hopefully found Bianca there.

That he was glad she was safe? He missed her? He'd been wrong? Sorry? That he really felt things for her that scared him. How she was worth surviving the hard things for.

He needed to tell her the truth. Wasn't that what he'd said he stood for?

When he rounded the corner, Bianca's trailer door opened.

This was it. And no matter how it went, she was okay. Nathan hadn't actually taken her.

Eddie jogged closer. Only it wasn't Bianca standing on the steps. It was Riley.

Eddie pointed to the door. "Please tell me Bianca's in there."

She stared at Eddie. "Bianca . . . Why? Wh-what's wrong?"

"Carter said that she and Nathan were supposed to meet, but they never showed. No one can get hold of her. She rode in the limo instead of her car."

Riley twisted a ring around her thumb. "Oh my goodness." She shook her head. "No, she's fine. Yes, she and Nathan had a disagreement, but she's gotten away from him."

She held up her phone. "I'm actually on my way to go pick her up. Her phone quit working, but she found a way to call. She told me to hurry."

She'd called Riley? Not him?

Will hadn't called him either.

Because Eddie hadn't been the person they'd needed.

Riley took off walking.

He marched beside her. "I'll follow you."

Except he didn't have his truck.

Riley sent him a side-eye. "Not sure that's a good idea."

"Listen, Riley. I really need to make sure she's okay. Please, can I ride over with you? I don't have my truck here."

Riley inspected his face. "Y-you actually fell for her?"

Eddie didn't hesitate. "Yes." He picked up his pace to match Riley's increased speed. "And I've already wasted too much time not telling her."

Riley darted through the taped-off construction zone. "You're right. You probably have lots to talk about. I've parked right over here."

Riley didn't go to the main parking lot but hopped into a white construction truck parked by a pile of lumber.

Riley started the vehicle, and the radio blared. The tires spat up dirt as she peeled out. After they exited the set gate and turned left, she finally spoke over the country song blaring on the radio.

"I'm actually a little surprised Bianca got her hooks into you. Carter, sure. But you . . ."

Eddie crossed his arms. It didn't matter who believed what about their relationship. He only needed to know how Bianca felt. To tell her that he had been wrong. The real her was worth the mess of the paparazzi. "I don't think Bianca's and my relationship is anyone's business but ours."

Riley adjusted the visor above her head. "I think you've forgotten who *the* Bia Pearl is."

The song about broken hearts ended, and he hoped the lyrics weren't foreshadowing what was ahead.

The mayor's voice came over the radio. "Last Chance County needs you . . ."

Riley pushed the number two button, and a classic rock song erased the rest of Gregory's vote-for-me commercial.

"I'm not a fan of political commercials either. They only tell part of the story."

Riley tightened her grip on the steering wheel. "People like him will never tell the whole story. He's wasting everyone's money. He's going to lose the reelection. Then things will finally turn around."

Eddie turned toward her. "Wish the locals cared as much about the direction of Last Chance County as you do."

Riley pressed her lips together. "I don't have to be from here to understand that some people never get the punishment they deserve. Roger needs to become mayor."

Roger? "You know Roger Pointe?"

"Something like that." She veered down a rocky drive with no trees lining the path. Eddie spotted another gravel road toward the right, but she kept going straight. The truck bumped along the drive until a cabin with a lone light on the porch welcomed them.

Riley shut off the truck.

"Did Bianca say how she ended up here?"

Riley narrowed her eyes on the cabin and then pushed open the truck door. "I was just told I needed to get out here right away."

Eddie exited the truck as a man walked onto the porch. So Nathan was still here too? At least the police would have more witnesses to whatever came out of his mouth.

"This isn't the reinforcement I was expecting."

Not Nathan.

Roger Pointe's chuckle didn't make Eddie smile. "It's even better."

Another woman came out of the cabin. Her stern expression looked the same as the last time Eddie had seen her. Only her outfit had changed. Conroy had been right. The mayor's assistant, Janice, stood next to Roger Pointe.

Riley stomped toward the porch. "Where is she?"

Roger stepped forward, and the porch light hit his face. "I guess tonight would be an excellent time to talk about your youth center after all."

He held Eddie's gaze before resting back on Riley. But he didn't get a chance to speak before a stocky man barreled out of the open cabin door and struck Roger on the back of the head with a shovel.

Janice screamed.

Beside Eddie, Riley didn't gasp. Instead, she raced forward. "Finally."

Finally?

Something cool slipped into his hand. Eddie spun to find Bianca's hand in his. All Eddie's firefighter training that would usually urge him to step toward Roger, who now lay motionless on the porch, vanished.

She pressed the rest of her body into the shadows of the truck as she tried to pull him toward her.

Her face was pale. Eyes wide. Blood stained her dress, and she mouthed one word.

Run.

TWENTY-SEVEN

BIANCA TIGHTENED HER HOLD ON EDDIE'S HAND and tugged harder. He shouldn't have come. But she had a better chance of survival with him. Only now, Eddie's life was in danger too.

The gunshot plus the shouting from Janice, the gunman, and Roger had changed her course to head back toward the gravel road. Otherwise, she wouldn't have seen Eddie arrive.

When she'd spotted the headlights coming up the drive, Bianca had tucked behind a tree, waiting to see if the newest arrival would be more trouble or not.

Now, as they ran, Eddie didn't resist her hold. "Bianca, what's going on?" His whisper still made her tense.

Had they heard?

She tucked them behind a tree.

The moonlight sprinkled down through the trees. Branches scratched at her arms, but they couldn't stop. Except her arm jerked backward, and the next thing she knew, she was being hugged up against Eddie's heaving chest.

He had his back pressed up against a tree. As much as she wanted to fall against him, she couldn't. "We've got to stay hidden and find a way out of here," she whispered and leaned out of his arms. "They killed Nathan."

"Killed? 'They' who? Carter thought—"

"That guy who hit Roger kidnapped me and Nathan. Then I think Janice shot Nathan. But it could have been Roger who actually pulled the trigger. I don't know where Janice ran off to after she screamed." She squeezed her eyes shut, but it didn't help the memory of Nathan being shot.

Eddie wrapped her up. "It's going to be okay. We're going to have to figure out how to get Riley out too. I'm so glad I was by Riley right after you called her for help."

Bianca froze. "I never called Riley. We couldn't get a signal in the limo, and then we were tied up."

Eddie frowned. "You think she'd be in on this?"

Bianca managed a shrug. "None of this has made sense. They wanted it to look like a ransom. But it wasn't, actually. I don't know. I'm not sure who's really in charge or why."

Eddie drew her tighter against himself. He was solid and dependable and everything the Lord knew she needed. But what if he got hurt? This wasn't a movie scene.

A shudder ran up her back. He needed to get out of here. "I'll distract them. I can't have you ending up like Nathan." She pulled away enough to see his eyes. "Eddie, I—"

"Eddie!" Riley's voice sounded too close. "Do you see Bianca? I think she might be hurt."

Bianca fisted Eddie's shirt. "I don't trust her."

Eddie kissed Bianca's forehead. "You keep running, I'll go back—"

"I can't lose you." Bianca shook her head. The movement caused stars to fly in her vision.

Eddie placed his mouth beside her ear. "I need you safe. I don't know what's going on, but you're going—"

Bianca reached for Eddie's hand and then laced her fingers with his. "Then we'll go together. Because I need you safe too." She took off running, and thankfully, Eddie followed.

"I think one went that way," the kidnapper hollered as a light flickered in the darkness from somewhere to their back left.

"Kelson, get a better light." Riley's reply held more anger. "I'm going to stop them before they reach the other cabins. Keep them away from the roads."

This time, it was Eddie's turn to pull Bianca behind a tree.

Bianca peeked around the scratchy bark in time for the moon to reflect off something in Riley's hand—a gun. Bianca grabbed on to Eddie's shirt. "Riley's got a gun too."

A stick snapped behind them.

Eddie put his finger to his mouth and motioned down. He flicked his fingers for them to move. He crouched low and waited for her to follow his lead.

"Bia!" Kelson spat as a flashlight inspected a bush nearby. "If you come out, I'll let the firefighter live."

Bianca stopped her crawling, and Eddie covered her mouth. He shook his head.

"You know you deserve to be punished for what you did." Riley's voice rang like a storm siren in the night. "Don't bring him down with you. You've got the poor guy blinded by your fakeness. He actually believes you might love him. No one deserves to be lied to! The world knows who you truly are."

Bianca's eyes watered. "What is even happening?" she breathed.

"You have any idea what she's talking about?" Eddie's whispered words were hot against her neck.

"No." She blinked, and through the trees, it looked like another cabin up ahead. This one was possibly smaller than the one Roger lay dead on.

Riley's position separated them from any escape to the next cabin, and Kelson was more than likely behind.

Surrounded.

"Don't move." A gun clicked over Bianca's shoulder. "They're to your six o'clock!" Kelson shouted.

"Keep their location. Try not to mess this up too." Riley's voice was laced with the same heated tone as the day she'd been caught crying, supposedly in anger.

But I'm forever fixing his messes.

Riley's story about her brother and his work and money problems came flashing into her head. Could the kidnapper who'd chased and shot at Bianca be Riley's brother? But what was the point?

Bianca squinted in the darkness. She couldn't see Kelson. "Maybe he's bluffing."

A bullet hit the tree beyond her. "Don't make me come over there."

Bianca lifted to stand, but Eddie tackled her. "No, you run. I'll stand."

She put her hands on the side of his cheeks. She pressed her lips to his, and he stilled. As much as she wanted to keep kissing him, she had to save at least one of their lives. "You go get help."

"Bianca . . ."

She pushed away from him and stood.

Please, God, keep Eddie from standing too.

"Stop!" Kelson shouted.

A flashlight blinded her until she blocked the light with her hand. Darkness may have fallen, but the moon reflected off the gun pointed at Bianca.

Kelson remained beside a grouping of three saplings no less than ten paces off to the left. Close enough to not have to aim too hard and still hit her. "Where's the other one?"

Bianca swallowed. "I tripped and fell. He kept going."

Kelson grunted. "Serves you right to be left with nothing. It's not a great feeling, is it? Start walking toward me, slowly, or I'm going to shoot you in the leg and chase down the other one before I finish you off."

Riley's footsteps circled back toward them as her flashlight bounced over the brush.

Please don't see Eddie crawling away.

Riley zeroed her light in on Bianca's back, creating a monster-sized shadow of Bianca in the treetops. If only she stood as huge as her silhouette. Then she could beat the enemies around her and Eddie.

Then again, God would be better to trust than Bianca's own power. No matter how weak or strong she remained.

Riley stomped around Bianca. Her face shadowed but her mood clear. She pointed her gun at Bianca's chest. "I get to kill her. You didn't have to listen to her whine every morning."

Bianca shifted her feet. "Why are you doing this, Riley? Why did Janice murder Nathan? What's going on?"

"Nathan ruined everything. He's a cheater, and you helped him. To those the Duke awards favors to, much is required. Nathan finally gambled his last."

"About time," Kelson grumbled.

"You played poker against Nathan?" Bianca's calf whacked against a stump, and she grunted. "That's why you wanted his money?"

Kelson shook his gun at Bianca. "He cheated. No one's that good all the time."

"It wasn't Nathan's money." Riley huffed. "He stole it. I don't care what the media says, you're not dumb. You can't pretend that stealing people's money isn't a crime. So keep up."

Bianca inched back another step. "You think I stole your money too?"

The light shined from Riley's direction into Bianca's face. Her body stiffened.

"No." Riley walked toward Bianca, gun in one hand and the

light in her other aimed in Bianca's eyes. "I don't *think* you did. I *know* you did it. Nathan isn't the only one who should've been convicted for his involvement in the gambling ring."

Bianca licked her lips. "Honestly, Riley. I didn't know what Nathan was involved with. I knew he played poker with his friends but—"

"Not friends. Naive victims who got invited into a club only to be scammed. You can't take our inheritance and not pay. Nathan invited my fiancé to his little game night. And guess what? His money's all gone too. But then Nathan was indicted. Finally. Some kind of justice. Except Nathan was let off the hook, and you were never tried."

Apparently, Bianca hadn't been the only one hoodwinked by Nathan. "I testified against him. I didn't know—"

"Yes, you did!" Riley screamed. "You knew how Nathan kept his expensive lifestyle. How he afforded your apartment. I saw you flaunting online the purses and shoes he bought you. If we can't get our money, we'll take justice. It's only fair. Because not only did we lose our inheritance, but when my fiancé got hooked into Nathan's poker ring and lost everything, he had to marry an heiress to recover financially. I lost the man I loved." Riley shrugged. "It's only fair that Nathan does too."

Bianca swallowed. "Nathan's dead."

"And you should've been dead already too, except my idiot brother can't seem to kill you. Third time will apparently be the charm."

Third time? "It was you all along." Bianca stumbled.

Kelson growled. "It was Nathan's fault that Roger stole my business. That wasn't supposed to be part of the deal."

"Until you gambled and lost the rest of our money." Riley trudged closer to her brother.

My brother's work company's in money troubles.

"Your brother owes the Duke too?" Bianca whispered.

The light on Bianca drifted to the ground as Riley turned toward her brother. "You might have finally done something right." A half smile took over her scowl. "By killing Roger, you just made me the new Duke."

Kelson tilted his head back toward the cabin. "Well, Duchess, only after you kill the old hag I tied up in the cabin."

Bianca probably should care what Riley was talking about, but nothing really mattered except getting herself and Eddie out of here alive. She rocked another step away. If she could reach the tree behind her, she could duck, and then what? Grab a stick for a weapon?

"Don't move." Riley's voice whipped over the crickets. The light refocused in on Bianca's face. "You better take ten steps—only—in my direction and not move any other way, or I'm shooting you and then making you crawl out. If you obey, I'll make it quick."

Bianca squeezed her fingers together. Whatever happened gave Eddie more time to get away. She lifted her chin. One step, then the next one. Her shoe crunched on a leaf.

"Keep coming. You think you're smart, but trust me, I'm smarter. It's taken me months to get you where no one can connect the dots to me."

"To us," Kelson mumbled.

Bianca forced her feet forward. "I thought we were friends."

"Friends don't steal my money."

Kelson raised his arm with the gun again. "I'll just shoot her."

"No. You're done planning. We're tying her up with Roger and his girlfriend. Then we'll burn down the cabin."

Kelson grabbed hold of Bianca. "Except you brought the firefighter."

Riley motioned with her gun for her brother to go ahead. "Don't worry. He'll come out soon enough."

"Leave him alone." Bianca jerked her arm, but Kelson thumped his gun against her head, and her knees buckled, making her lean against Kelson's hold.

"Let her go!" Eddie's yell echoed from what sounded like the direction of the other cabin.

Bianca tried to shake her head, but it throbbed too much.

"The police are on their way." If he'd reached the cabin, he should have kept going. Not returned. "Better to be arrested for attempted murder than *actual* murder."

Riley shined her light into the woods, sweeping east to west. "Good try. But there's no cell phone signal up here. A hero's luck runs out eventually, and yours is long overdue."

"My firefighter radio doesn't need the cell phone tower. Help is one minute out," Eddie's voice rang out.

Was he only pretending?

Please run, Eddie.

But all she could see were trees and bushes in the shadows.

Riley turned to the left as if she knew exactly where Eddie was. "Change of plans. I'm going to kill him first. Tie Bia up. Make sure you finish the job this time."

Kelson grabbed Bianca's shoulder and murmured, "I got rid of that makeup artist for her to get closer to you, but does she remember that? No. I make a couple of gambling mistakes and I'm the screwup. Nathan was a cheater. It wasn't my fault."

No wonder Grace hadn't heard how Tiff's family was doing. Riley had faked Tiff's family's illness to get the makeup artist away. All so Riley could get closer to Bianca.

What about Grace? Was she safe somewhere?

Bianca pushed against Kelson. "Run, Eddie . . . please." A tear fell from her cheek. She wasn't worth his life for hers.

But God was enough. Always.

She balled up her fist and spun, sending her knee into Kelson's groin.

Kelson moaned and released his grip enough for Bianca to wiggle free. She stomped on his foot. He grunted and bent over. His gun was in his other hand as it hung against his side.

She grabbed the gun and sprinted toward Riley.

He coughed. "She's got my gun."

Riley spun around. "Idiot."

Bianca aimed the gun at Riley's chest. "Drop your weapon, or I'm going to shoot."

Riley only laughed as Bianca's arm shook. "You really are an awful planner."

The moonlight reflected off Riley's gun. It was pointed right at Eddie, who was hiding behind a stump.

Apparently he'd tried to sneak back to save Bianca.

Riley smiled. "You *try* to shoot me, and I'll shoot him. Which is more important? Your life, or his? No room for your pretending now."

That was an easy answer. Bianca lowered her weapon.

"No!" Eddie yelled.

Flashes of red and blue lights seared through the canopy of branches.

The police were actually here. Everything would be all right.

Until Riley readjusted her position, and a pop came from her gun.

Pain burned Bianca's shoulder. She cried out and crumpled to the ground.

TWENTY-EIGHT

IT COULDN'T END LIKE THIS.

Eddie sprinted for Bianca. Riley and Kelson dashed off in the opposite direction.

He fell to the ground beside her. A stick jabbed into his hip, but his hands went to Bianca's face.

Her breathing was harsh and quick. She was alive, but for how much longer?

Why weren't the police moving in?

"I'm here." He pulled out his phone with unsteady fingers and switched on his flashlight app. Blood seeped from Bianca's shoulder.

He tugged off his polo, leaving on his undershirt, and pushed it against the blood.

Bianca whimpered.

"I know, honey. But I've got to get the bleeding stopped."

Her fingers reached up and grazed his cheek. He wanted to nestle against her touch, but he forced his strength to remain on her wound.

Her hand brushed against his shoulder and dropped against his thigh.

Her eyes closed.

"No. No. No. Stay with me." He kept his left hand on her wound and reached for her pulse with his right fingers. It was faint. "Come on, Bianca. You got to stay with me."

Footsteps crunched nearby. Was it the police, or Riley or Kelson coming back to finish them? Either way, he wasn't leaving Bianca. Not this time.

A bouncing light landed on his chest. "Rice's been shot." Ridge's hushed voice echoed over Eddie's own heartbeat.

His crew was somehow there, not the police.

Eddie glanced down at the light on his chest. Blood stained his white undershirt, but it must have come from Bianca.

"I'm not shot. Bianca is."

The light landed on Bianca—her pale face, her eyes still closed. Blood-stained neck. She needed a miracle.

Ridge slid to a stop right beside him, and Zack dropped on the opposite side.

Bryce set a stretcher next to Bianca. "On three, we lift and slide. Then we're racing out of here. One. Two. Three," Bryce commanded.

Eddie kept pressure on her wound until his team lifted the board.

Bryce shifted to the opposite end of the backboard. "Fast yet steady is going to win the race today."

They sprinted along the gravel as more and more red and blue lights appeared in the sky. "How did you even know to come for me?"

"Someone at dispatch messaged me. They knew it was you and knew we were the closest," Zack said from his hold of the stretcher, down by Bianca's feet.

Flashlights headed toward them. A dog barked in the distance. Someone raced right at them.

The headlights gave Macon a silhouette appearance. "Where's . . ."

"He's here, Chief," Bryce answered. "Bianca's been hit."

Macon slid in across from Eddie, and the weight lifted out of Eddie's hands. "Ambo's not here yet, but we'll load her up in the truck. Get her to the hospital."

A police car pulled around the corner, and gravel slid behind tires as the car stopped. Olivia hopped out, gun in her palms. "What have we got?"

Macon put his hand over the top of Eddie's on Bianca's wound. "I'll get her loaded. You give the police what they need."

As much as he hated it, his chief was right.

Eddie swallowed. He had to let her go. But for the right reasons this time.

She's in Your hands, Lord.

She always had been.

He released his hold on Bianca, and Macon took over.

Eddie jogged to Olivia. "Riley, the makeup artist from the film set, and her brother Kelson fled, probably to the main cabin up the curve. Both armed. Riley shot Bianca. I think Kelson may have killed Roger Pointe. Last I saw, his body was on the porch. Roger's girlfriend, Janice, the mayor's assistant, might be tied up in the cabin. Or dead too. I don't know. She might have killed Nathan Kensington. There are smaller cabins in various building stages. That's how I managed a callout. I got a signal by one. Riley has at least a truck on location."

Another cop car pulled in, and Olivia nodded. "We'll find them." She pulled her radio to her mouth and issued a series of commands, but all Eddie heard was the truck's siren as they drove away.

Eddie chased after the truck. He needed to be next to her. What if . . . what if she didn't make it? He'd never get to tell her how much she meant to him.

A horn blared from behind him. The captain's truck.

Macon rolled down the passenger window. "Get in."

Eddie didn't have to be told twice. His heartbeat and the truck's siren were the only noises filling the ride to the hospital. When Macon slowed down enough in front of the hospital door, Eddie jumped ship and ran inside.

Ridge and Zack met him before he could tackle the lady behind the welcome desk for information.

But it was Zack who grabbed Eddie by the shoulders. "Bianca's in surgery."

He didn't like the look in his friend's eyes.

Eddie gripped Zack's shoulders right back. "Tell me, what did the doctor say?"

Zack winced as Ridge clenched his jaw next to Eddie. "She's lost a lot of blood."

"Look!" A girl he hadn't noticed stood on top of a chair and pointed to the television hanging in the corner of the entryway. "It's live."

A helicopter was circling treetops on the television screen, a spotlight set on what looked like Kelson as he ran toward a half-constructed cabin.

"One down."

Macon, who had come up beside Zack, put his hand on Eddie's shoulder. "Why don't you guys both find Eddie a drink?" Macon steered Eddie away from Ridge and Zack in the opposite direction of the television.

Eddie waited for Macon to sit across from him. His captain's gaze met his, and Eddie dropped his to the shined floor. "I'm not ready to let her go yet."

"Good. Because I'm not here to make you." Macon cleared his throat. "But I'll be here for you if she's—"

"Where is she?" A woman dressed in a wrap cheetah dress and

heels raced in from the hallway and roared at the lady behind the welcome desk.

He remembered that tone. "Mom?"

Mary looked like she'd aged since the last time he'd seen her, with extra-deep circles under her eyes. She rushed to him, her necklace banging against her chest. "I saw on the television. Did someone really shoot her? Bia can't be . . ."

Macon moved beside Eddie. "Mary, why don't I help you find a glass of water?"

His stubborn mother shoved past his boss. "Who shot her? I pray it wasn't one of those creeps who stalked Joel. Joel was the one who pointed at the television when it came on upstairs. Come on, Eddington, we have to go check on her. You shouldn't have to sit by your loved one's side alone."

Her words sucker punched him.

He'd left her alone at this hospital when she'd been afraid of losing the one she loved.

Because he'd been angry. At what had been said at dinner, and from what had happened so many years ago. It was past time to surrender it all to God. "Mom, I forgive you. I don't understand why you had to give me away, but it doesn't help anyone for me to hang on to my anger. I don't always understand God's plan, but His plans are for His glory, even when I can't see it. He offered forgiveness, so I need to as well."

His mother pulled him into a hug. "You're going to be the best big brother."

Eddie closed his eyes. He couldn't stop her from adopting a child, but he could be around at least a little to make sure the child was loved.

With a sniff, his mother released him. "Let's go get your girl."

At the check-in desk, the lady picked up a paper map and unfolded it. "Are you lost?"

Thankfully, no longer. Eddie gripped the counter. "I need to see Bianca . . . I mean, Bia Pearl. What room will she be in?"

The woman pushed up her glasses and frowned. "She already has a waiting visitor. I doubt she'd want to wake up to her ex and her fiancé fighting over her."

His mother lifted her chin. "My son isn't Bia Pearl's ex, he's her—"

"She doesn't have a fiancé." He shook his head. Even if she had gotten back with Nathan—Nathan was dead. "Her visitor . . . what did the man look like?"

The woman pushed her glasses higher on her nose. "Umm . . ." Her cheeks reddened. "He's tall and dark-headed and . . . kind of looks a little like you, actually."

"Like me?" He remembered Bianca's comment about Carter's post hinting at something between them. "Carter? He must be after another publicity stunt."

"Yes, that's right. Carter Cane. I knew he looked familiar with that grin." The woman smiled but stopped when Eddie leaned forward.

He didn't know why Carter was pretending to be Bianca's fiancé, but he'd never trusted that man.

Eddie grabbed the hospital map off the counter. "Ma'am, I really need you to show me where the woman I love is."

TWENTY-NINE

BIANCA WENT TO MOVE HER HAND TO SHIELD from the flashlight, except something held her hand down. "Eddie!"

She had to get to him before Riley hurt him. But something was on top of her legs too. "Ah!" Pain flamed from her shoulder. She shifted her arm, but her left hand was pinned down by . . . wires? Wait. Why were her eyes closed?

She blinked them open. Only to squint at a ceiling light above her. Beeping monitors to her right gave the first clue to her new location. Not in the woods anymore. That's right. A nurse had wheeled her upstairs after surgery.

A hospital, which meant the hand holding hers had to be Eddie's.

She squeezed his fingers and slowly moved her head. Harder to do without shifting her shoulder too.

But it wasn't the smile she sought.

It was Carter, not Eddie, who looked down at her. "Morning, sleepyhead."

She curled her fingers away from him. "Carter."

Her throat burned. But that was probably normal after recovery. Hadn't the nurse mentioned a drink was on her table? But where was the table? Things blurred out of focus. She closed her eyes again. "Carter, could you hand me my drink? My mouth feels like I've eaten chalk."

What she could really go for was a marshmallow milkshake and Eddie, here with her, holding her hand. Her eyes sprang open. "Eddie. Forget the water. Where is he? Did Riley hurt Eddie? Please take me to him."

Carter's expression shifted into what she knew as his fake grin. "You're not going anywhere."

She leaned to see over the side of the bed, but pain shot along her head and shoulder. "This thing has wheels, right? I need to know he's okay. If a nurse stops us, we'll just offer an autograph."

Desperate times required her to pull out all the stops.

Instead of helping, Carter ran his tongue over his teeth. "I heard something interesting when Leo and I were waiting for you and Nathan to show. Leo mentioned that you didn't want to finish the movie at all."

Bianca pushed her good elbow against the bed and eased forward. "The movie is the least of my concerns right now." She grabbed on to Carter's shirt. Another flash of pain zipped through her bandaged shoulder. She clenched her teeth. "Is Eddie alive?"

Please, Lord.

Carter squeezed his fingers around her wrist and pulled her hand away. "You never should've made that deal with that firefighter. You said we don't give up."

She yanked back her arm. "Ow, Carter, you're scaring me. Why aren't you telling me if he's okay?"

No, he had to be alive. She remembered him telling her to stay with him.

Always.

She'd stay always if she had her way.

Carter sat on the bed and bumped into her hip, jarring her shoulder.

Bianca hissed.

Carter crossed his arms. "Is he going to be a problem while we're supposed to be dating?"

Bianca brought her good hand up to her forehead. Her skin was lined with sweat. "Carter, I'm not going to do it."

He narrowed his eyes. "Do what?"

"I don't want to fulfill all of the contract. I don't want to play this game anymore. I can't. No more faking relationships. I don't want to hurt the man I love. I don't want to pretend anymore. I want to actually be Bianca when I'm not Bia in front of the cameras. No matter what the world thinks of me."

Carter's Adam's apple bobbed slowly. "A deal is a deal, Bia. You have to finish to get paid. I have to get paid. You have to be seen with me. You can't ruin my online presence any more than you already have. My fans are expecting you and me. Together."

She shook her head. "You can't please everyone. I've been chasing after fame, then money, and still people pleasing. All of that isn't the most important thing."

She needed to remember it was less about getting money to fix all her problems and making people around her happy, and more about following Jesus.

Carter's hands shook as he moved them through his hair. "If you don't finish the contract, I can't finish mine. You know I have debts to pay."

Bianca arched her back, but it didn't help the pounding rolling down her arm. "That's just it. I'm not sure that you do. I think the Duke is . . ."

Before she could say dead, Carter ripped the pillow out from under her head.

Agony shot through her bandaged shoulder. "Ow! What are you doing? This isn't a pretend hospital. Not a scene. I really got shot."

He clenched the pillow in both of his hands. "If you're going back on your word, you're at least going to help me with my media. The hits I got off the ring post alone is a start. But I've figured out how you'll get me some of the money you owe me."

Bianca pushed to sit up. Her right hand reached for the call button. It had to be there somewhere. "Carter, I don't owe you money, and I'm really tired of telling people that."

Carter stepped closer. "Your contract says otherwise, and I'm not going to let you ruin all I've worked for. You know what will be trending soon? My sorrowful face. When the world learns of your passing and how we had been secretly engaged. And how we used the firefighter as a decoy for our eternal love. I'll play the part of a grieving near-widower perfectly."

Something hard brushed against Bianca's fingers. She grabbed the remote and hit the nurse's call button. Then used it to block Carter.

Carter lowered the pillow. Right for her face.

Bianca shoved with her movable arm. "No, Carter. Stop!"

He pressed the pillow over her mouth and nose.

Why had she survived Riley trying to kill her only for Carter to succeed?

She raked her fingernails down Carter's arm. He only secured the pillow more fully. Her nose smashed against the rough fabric. She gasped but couldn't draw in any air.

She pulled up her legs inside the tight blankets and kicked, but the lack of air made her lungs squeeze.

It was like being trapped in the car all over again. Except this time, Eddie wasn't coming to save her. She should have fought harder for the one person who challenged her to be the real Bianca.

A muffled shout rang in the distance. Her lungs burned. She was back under the water. Her nails loosened their hold on Carter. She wanted to move her hands, but she no longer had control.

The pillow vanished, and Bianca panted. Her vision blurred. Her lungs gulped in air as an oxygen mask slipped over her face.

"It's okay. You're okay." Fingers once again held hers. Calloused ones. Warm ones. Ones she never wanted to let go of again.

"Eddie." Her throat stung, and she winced.

He kissed the back of her hand. "I'm right here. I—"

"I'm sorry." Tears pricked her eyes.

Eddie frowned. "Tonight wasn't your fault."

"Carter? He . . ." Her hand flew to her neck.

Eddie helped her lie back against the pillow. "He's on his way to jail. He spilled the entire story about what he owed the Duke, but it turns out Roger was the Duke. He wanted to be mayor to protect his growing criminal activities and to make sure his business, the resort, got approved."

Bianca sank back into the pillow. "So the resort isn't coming to Last Chance County either?"

"That's the hope. And Riley, Kelson, and Janice were all arrested too."

She licked her dry lips. "I should be sorry for dragging you into my life. But, Eddie, I'm not. I'm sorry I ever agreed that there couldn't be a future with you. Could we try it again? This time for real?"

Eddie cradled her palm in both of his hands. She only vaguely registered the beeping of her monitors in the silence. "Some things have changed."

Bianca closed her eyes. She was too late.

He squeezed her fingers. "As much as I love hearing your offer, you need to know the truth." His eyes found hers. "I-I want to become Will's temporary guardian. I don't know if I can make a difference in the boy's life, but I don't want to give up."

She blinked. Was that it? "I wouldn't ask you to give up. That's one of the many things I admire about you. Your compassion for those kids."

He wiped his thumb along her cheek. "And your desire to see relationships heal."

She shook her head. "I've tried so hard to gain the world's approval. But I've been doing it wrong. No more trying to control the situation. Only God can restore relationships."

Eddie traced her thumb. "Mary was the one who helped me find you in the hospital."

Bianca placed her hand on his arms. "Do you want her in your life?"

Eddie shrugged. "Maybe. If it'll help point her to the Lord."

Bianca cupped Eddie's cheek. "You're a brave man, Eddie Rice."

"It's Eddington Darrall Rice. Darrall's after my father. The man I never want to be like."

Bianca rested her forehead against his. "I don't think I want to ever finish that movie, even if it is possible. But if I don't, there's no money."

She pushed herself to sit.

"Easy. I thought you might be worried about that." He lowered his face until his mouth whispered near her ear. "Instead of a youth center, my team's only going to need a full-time assistant coach."

Bianca raised her brows. "Are you offering me another deal?"

Eddie sent her a flirty smirk she rather enjoyed. "The last one turned out pretty well, didn't it? Minus the fire, death threats, and hospital visits."

She removed her oxygen mask. "Don't forget about crazy fans and family drama."

While he leaned closer, his face sobered. "You'd be worth going through it all again."

Her breathing hitched. Yes, her true worth rested in the Lord, but it didn't exactly hurt that the man she'd faced a gun for cared about her too.

He reached to pull her oxygen mask back on. "We'll talk later. You need rest."

She stopped his hand and tucked her fingers inside of his. "Wait, our new deal should be sealed with a kiss."

He brought the back of her hand to his mouth and pressed a kiss to her skin.

She tried to cross her arms, but the tightening in her shoulder around her bandage made her settle for wrinkling her nose. "You didn't want a real kiss?"

He closed the space between them. "With you . . ." His smile revealed the two dimples she'd noticed on that first night they'd met by accident. "Always."

His lips met hers—sweetly—with a promise of a tomorrow. One that held no more pretending. Or at least when it came to their future. The no-faking, happily-ever-after, real-life kind of forever.

EPILOGUE

AVING LIVES MATTERED. WHICH MEANT SOME-times, as a rescue firefighter, other things in Eddie's life got benched for an extra inning. Even important baseball tournaments.

He leaned forward in the fire truck and tapped Ridge's shoulder. "Just let me out here."

Ridge furrowed his brow and held his attention on the road ahead. Far more vehicles lined each side of the street than normal. "You want to run the last mile to the field, be my guest. But we'll beat you there."

Eddie glared at one of the minivans that had its rear parked too far into the roadway. But even with Ridge's slower driving speed, Eddie wouldn't trade his team's winning the draw to host the tourney. Plus, all the food trucks that Bianca had gotten were going to donate twenty percent of their night's earnings toward the youth center's fund. More money than he could have even imagined had entered their nonprofit banking account.

Beside him, Zack chuckled. "Give the coach a break. His team's playing for the championship."

Eddie drummed his fingers along his turnout pants. That and he hadn't seen Bianca in two days due to their schedules.

As if hearing his thoughts, Bryce sent him a smirk over his shoulder. "I'm sure that's the only reason he's eager to get to the ball game."

Eddie checked his phone. No new update since the game had been tied in the second inning. Thankfully, their last fire run had been in the ballpark's neighborhood, and it had been a false alarm. "Maybe flip on the siren you love so much."

Bryce shook his head as Ridge slowed the truck for a car that pulled out in front of them. "Speaking of love . . ."

Eddie's neck no longer heated when the guys teased him about Bianca. "Yes, I'm anxious to get to the game. Yes, I'm nervous to see how the team's doing. And yes, I want to see Bianca. But also, she's worked extra-long hours on set so she could help coach tonight, and I want to be there for her."

"How much longer on the jewel movie?" asked Zack.

"Not sure. However, they've already reshot the scenes that Carter was in." Eddie leaned his head back.

Leo had been able to find another producer—one who'd signed Bianca to a new contract that allowed her to help out her family. Even if they still hadn't thanked Bianca yet. But one couldn't change another person's heart. That was God's department.

Ridge turned the fire truck into the ball field's parking lot and stopped. "Get out of here, lover boy. Go win us a game."

Eddie jumped out of the cab and sprinted for the home-side dugout while his turnout pants rubbed together. With the visitors in the field, that meant his team was up to bat.

The scoreboard announced the sixth inning. Still tied, one to one, which was the last score update text Bianca had sent. The bleachers held fans shoulder to shoulder with the fencerow tight with lawn chairs and canopies.

Bianca stood next to third base, her ponytail tugged through the back of her hat, a smile on her face, facing home plate. Her uniform shirt was paired with black shorts and tennis shoes—one of his favorite looks on her. Only her beloved flip-flops would make it better.

He swung open the gate and stepped into the dugout. All of his team stood at the fence, staring toward the batter's box. "Hey—"

"Shh!" A feminine voice that didn't belong to Scarlette hushed him. When a uniform-wearing Grace glanced over her shoulder, her eyes widened. She grimaced and jogged toward Eddie with a clipboard in her hand. "Sorry, Coach," she whispered. "I only wanted to make sure Scarlette got the sign."

Eddie glanced at Bianca. "They wouldn't need to talk or hear to understand..." Over the boys' heads, he spotted Scarlette with Gregory Harrelson near the batter's box. And just over the mayor's shoulder, propped on tripods behind the backstop's fence, were not one but two news station cameras focused on Gregory.

Eddie locked his jaw. "I can't believe the mayor found his way into coaching. I thought Eli was helping."

Bianca glanced over her shoulder, spotted Eddie, and waved for him to come onto the field.

Eddie held up a finger. He didn't want to disrupt Scarlette's focus.

Tank, the closest boy to Eddie, turned. "Greg's kind of been cool."

Will grabbed a helmet off the bench. "Yeah, he actually knows about baseball. He argued with the umpire when the pitcher tried to throw the ball to first when he'd already started pitching. He knew that he'd balked before the umpire corrected the call."

Grace flipped a piece of paper over on her clipboard. "He apparently played college ball. Trust me, he was better than me out there. Eli had an emergency with one of his youth group kids. Will, don't forget you're next in line to bat after Scout."

Will rolled his eyes. "It's called being on deck. It's what happens after being in the hole."

Grace wrote a note on her paper. "Right. Deck and hole. Got it."

Will smirked and then opened his mouth. Eddie had seen that look too many times and shot Will a glare. Instead of Will's more-than-likely-sarcastic reply, a mumble came from someone farther down the dugout.

"Batter's up," Lincoln muttered around his bite of beef jerky.

Grace stepped closer to Eddie. "Scarlette got hit by a pitch the first inning and keeps backing out of the batter's box."

Poor girl. Wait. "Did you say Scout was on deck?"

Grace flipped over another piece of paper. "The doctor released him to play right before game time, or I'm sure they would have let you know."

Eddie moved closer to the fence. "They were probably just happy and focused on getting him to the game."

The pitcher threw the ball, and Scarlette placed the perfect bunt.

As the ball rolled along the third base line, Eddie yelled, "Run!"

The third baseman scooped up the ball and threw it right over the first baseman's head.

Gregory waved Scarlette on to second. Eddie tightened his hold on the fence as Scarlette slid into second, beating the ball by seconds. When the umpire motioned her safe, the dugout erupted in cheers.

Bianca cupped her hands around her mouth. "Eddie." Then she waved Scout over too.

When Eddie jogged over to the pair, Bianca lifted the front of her hat as if to hand it to him.

Eddie took her free hand and pumped his fingers around hers. "You got this, Coach."

Scout did a practice swing. "What do you want me to do, Coach? Bunt and get Scarlette to third? The game's time limit's up. If we score, we win."

Bianca glanced at Eddie.

Eddie met Scout's gaze. "Let's go out swinging. Watch it, though.

This ump likes to call them low. If you get two strikes, don't be shouldering any burdens. Go have fun on your first game back."

Scout nodded and jogged to home plate.

"Coach?" Gregory pointed at his spot by first base.

Eddie shook his head and ran back to the dugout. If the mayor was helping the team, that's what really mattered. Not worrying whether Gregory's help was self-seeking or not.

Scout watched the first pitch, and sure enough, the umpire called the low ball a strike. The pitcher threw the next ball, and Scout swung. The ball cracked against the bat and soared through the air. The hit skirted over the yellow fence top, giving Scout his first out-of-the-park home run and the team's victory.

To cheers from the crowd, Bianca reached the backside of home plate to high-five Scarlette first, the rest of the team right behind. Scout crossed home, and the boys surrounded him, locking Scarlette and Bianca inside their group hug.

Eddie took out his phone and snapped a picture.

Gregory came up beside Eddie and cleared his throat. "Congrats, Coach."

Eddie stuck out his hand to the mayor. "Thanks for helping tonight."

Gregory shook Eddie's hand. "It was fun. You've got some good kids. Kids who need a place for the winter. Sorry I wasn't able to give you your grant."

Eddie nodded. "The women's shelter needed that money as much as I thought we needed it. Some area churches have planned some events for the kids this winter until we can get something more permanent. If you ever want to share your wisdom on getting Scarlette to place that perfect bunt again, just stop on by the field."

Gregory chuckled. "I'm going to hold you to that. These kids have been eye-opening in a fantastic way."

Eddie turned to his team. "Everyone line up. Make sure to tell the other team *good game.* Then team meeting at the dugout before the awards."

But before Eddie could line up behind his team, Bianca stood before him and smiled. "You won."

"We won." Eddie wrapped his arms around her and kissed her.

Bianca smiled against his lips. "Not that I'm complaining"—she pressed her lips against his again—"but there are not only news cameras but paparazzi probably filming and creating stories about us."

He tightened his hold on her waist. "Yeah, well, got to give your followers a reminder of us every now and then."

Something tugged on the back of his turnout pants.

Scarlette sent him a sheepish expression as she played with the end of her ponytail. "I know that we already had the huge slide once, but do you think Coach B could get us another one to celebrate?"

Eddie erased his smile. "No."

Scarlette's shoulders drooped. "You don't want us to get spoiled."

Eddie bumped Bianca's healed shoulder. "Do you want to tell her?"

Scarlette's eyes widened. "Tell me what? You know I can keep a secret."

Bianca grinned. "Team cookout, water slide, and movie night at the fire station with marshmallow milkshakes."

Eddie shrugged. "Plus a ride on the fire truck."

Scarlette pumped her fist and sprinted for the dugout. "We get to ride with Eddie's friends on the fire truck."

Bianca slipped her fingers around his. "So, who do I need to talk with to officially snag the assistant coaching spot again next year?"

Eddie brought the back of her hand up to his lips and pressed a kiss to her skin. "That someone would be me."

She winked. "Always."

Because the two of them were more than a deal—they were a team. The kind where two hearts would someday become one.

BONUS EPILOGUE

Thank you for reading *Rescued Heart*. We hope you loved this story. Find out what happens next for Eddie and Bianca with a **Bonus Epilogue**, a special gift, available only to our newsletter subscribers.

This Bonus Epilogue will not be released on any retailer platform, so get your free gift by scanning the QR code below. By scanning, you acknowledge you are becoming a subscriber to the newsletters of Megan, Lisa, and Sunrise Publishing. Unsubscribe at any time.

LAST CHANCE
FIRE AND RESCUE
RESCUED DREAMS
USA TODAY BESTSELLING AUTHOR
LISA PHILLIPS

ONE

WHOEVER SAID THE TRUTH WAS LIKE A FLAME got it wrong.

Lies were the real fire. One moment there was a tiny flicker. Then it grew and spread, destroying everything until there was nothing left but ash.

From that destruction, Amelia Patterson had rebuilt her life. Come hurricane or high water, she would do whatever it took to keep it.

No one was going to take from her ever again.

"Single file. Keep it steady." Amelia stood on the landing between two floors, ushering residents of this fourplex down to the ground floor.

An older man stumbled. His shoe slipped off a step and he started to fall.

She braced her weight in a squat and caught him, bringing him up to standing height. "You good?"

"Thank you." His face flushed, a little embarrassed.

"It's my job." She led him to the next set of stairs, where he grabbed the rail. "Everyone keep it steady."

A young mother and her little son came down, moving fast. The woman had a stuffed-full tote bag over one shoulder, even though they'd instructed everyone to leave their belongings. Even the kid had a tiny suitcase behind him, decorated with a children's cartoon about puppies. Amelia said nothing.

At the top of the stairs, one of her firefighters emerged from the apartment to the right. Four doors, two on each side that faced each other. Della Nixon said, "Lieutenant, apartment 2-A is clear."

The other female on the team, Zoe Lewis, came on the open radio channel. "1-B is clear. Working on the others now."

Amelia's radio hung between the open sides of her turnout coat, clipped to a strap that went from one shoulder to the opposite hip. "Copy that." She pointed across the upper floor, and Della nodded before heading there to clear the apartment and make sure no one had stayed behind. "Collins, status."

Izan, the only guy now on Truck 14 after years of Amelia having mostly guys or all guys, was clearing the area where the fire had originated. A hot pan of frying oil had caught alight, burning the resident trying to cook their chicken.

The ambulance at the curb had the injured victim inside already, the EMTs of Ambulance 21, Trace and Kianna, treating their patient.

They wouldn't be here long unless something else happened.

"Collins!" she called out, shoving at the front door of the apartment. It bounced back toward her, and a man emerged, moving at speed. Had he jammed the door shut? She caught sight of dark facial hair and a thick hood in the split second before he shoved her and she went down onto her backside.

Amelia cried out. "Hey!"

She could only watch him race away, the wind knocked out of her. What had that guy been doing inside the apartment that was on fire? And where was Izan?

Amelia clambered to her feet and headed for the door again. She stepped into the hallway of apartment 1-C. Black smoke had filled the air, rolling up to the ceiling and down the hall in billows. She turned and ran back to the truck, tore off her helmet, and got her air tank and face mask on. Radio situated.

She replaced her helmet as she went back to the apartment. "Izan! Dixon, Lewis, on me. The fire is spreading! Get me foam extinguishers." A grease fire wasn't going to be put out by water, and this one had kicked things up a notch. She shoved through another door to the kitchen. "Collins!"

Izan had come in here armed with a fire extinguisher to subdue the small fire less than ten minutes ago. Now the thing was close to being out of control. Where had he...

She spotted a boot and the hem of a turnout coat leg. "Izan!"

The fire raged to her left on the stove, now spreading across the floor, melting the linoleum where the grease had splashed. Flames licked up to the ceiling, scorching whatever popcorn texture had been sprayed up there buy the construction workers. Now it was dripping onto the floor.

She ran an assessing eye across the room as Dixon and Lewis ran in. "Get the fire smothered. I'll get Izan out. The gas should be off, but I'll check it."

"Yes, Lieutenant." Della aimed the hose of the fire extinguisher on the base of the flames.

Amelia went to Izan, unconscious and lying on the floor beside the breakfast bar counter. His fire extinguisher had rolled under the dining table.

She ducked her head, lifted his upper body, and stood with him over her shoulder. Amelia gritted her teeth and headed for the door. She walked through the entryway and out to the grass in front of the apartment building, where she deposited Izan on the soft, muddy earth. She ripped off her helmet and air tank. "Medic!" She shouted as loud as she could. Trace stopped what he was doing and ran to her. Amelia sat back on the grass, breathing hard. "We need another bus."

Trace stuck a stethoscope in his ears so he could listen to Izan's breathing. "Give yourself a second."

This was supposed to have been a routine callout, but fire was never routine. Things could go wrong a million different ways. One moment a fire extinguisher was all it took, and evacuating residents was only routine. The next, she'd have to call for the hose.

Behind her, the fire boomed, blowing out the windows of apartment 1-C. Everyone in the vicinity ducked, covering their heads. Someone screamed. An older woman tripped trying to walk faster, and a young man moved to help her up.

Amelia switched her radio to the dispatch channel. "This is Truck 14." She gave the address. "We need back up."

She listened to the dispatcher's response in her earpiece while she replaced her mask and helmet. "Copy that." She ran back to the apartment. The natural gas line had to have caught the flame somehow and gone up. It should've been off. What on earth had happened here?

She shut off the analysis she could save for her report, wondering how the hyperawareness that meant she saw the worst coming was even supposed to be helpful. It wasn't like she could've stopped it in time.

Useless.

How many times had she been called that? As many as it took for that word to sink into her bones. For it to become a part of her.

The Christians at the firehouse kept telling everyone to pray, but God had never shown up to save her before. Why would He start now?

Amelia shouldered the door to the apartment open.

The manager ran over between the buildings. "Hey! What's going on?"

She yelled from behind her face mask. "Keep everyone back."

Amelia ducked inside the apartment. She spotted one of her firefighters in the hallway on the floor. She grabbed Zoe Lewis under the arms and dragged her out the door, across the concrete to the grass.

Rescue squad pulled up, but they weren't close enough. She left Zoe on the grass near Izan, who was now stirring as he woke up. Trace moved over to assess the downed female firefighter.

Amelia ran back to the apartment.

Inside, she could barely see her hand in front of her face. She clicked on the light on the side of her helmet and pressed on into the dark. Searching for her friend.

"Nixon, call out!" She found the base of the fire, but the main blaze of the oil pan had been extinguished. Amelia found flames in the living room, coming from the gas fireplace and an open line. The buildup had caused the explosion, but now the running gas was coming out—keeping the fire going. The front of the unit had blown off, and the blaze swept up the wall and across the ceiling now. Moving fast, toward the hall. Seeking out fuel. Destroying everything in its wake.

"Nixon!"

She went back to the kitchen, trying to figure out where—

A heavy hand dragged her shoulder back. "We've got this."

Bryce Crawford. Twin to Logan. Ladies' man turned one-woman good guy. Penny was a blessed lady. Bryce was a good lieutenant.

Amelia considered him the brother she'd have preferred over the one she actually had. But his family, the Crawfords, were all overachievers, and she had to fight for every inch just to measure up, so belonging to the Crawford clan would never have worked.

Besides, there was only one guy at the firehouse she would even consider dating. The rest of them...She knew too much personal stuff about them. And their locker room smelled like a high-school gym.

"Get clear." Eddie Rice tromped in after Bryce, followed by

Zack Stephens—whose wife was pregnant. He spent every spare moment at the firehouse reading baby books.

"We'll find Della," Zack said.

Then Ridge was there in front of her. "You good?"

Every word they said would be heard by everyone on the comms channel. All the firefighters on scene, and the EMTs as well, if they switched over to hear what was happening.

He stared down at her, close enough their face masks were nearly touching. She saw his eyes scan her face. Checking if she was all right. His dark gaze held hers, those brooding eyes that always seemed to see far too much.

Until he got too close and she had to tell him to back off. Give her some space.

Amelia squeezed his elbow. "Find her," she said into the comms channel. "I'm going outside to check on the others."

She tromped out, partially irritated that rescue squad had to swoop in and save their bacon—even if she'd been the one to call for backup. She and her Truck 14 crew wouldn't hear the end of that one for a while.

Amelia saw Izan had sat up. Zoe pushed away Trace's hand and did the same.

They spotted Amelia coming, depositing her helmet, mask, and air tank on the grass. She sat and leaned against them. Fists tight on her knees.

Cops had arrived, easing people back from the scene.

"Another bus?" she asked Trace, sweat rolling down the sides of her face.

"Almost here."

"How is the patient?" She tipped her head to his ambulance, asking about the resident caught in the initial blaze.

"She needs to get going." Trace's expression held a shadow.

"So go. We're good."

Zoe said, "Go."

Izan nodded. "Get the patient to the hospital."

Trace grabbed up his gear. "The other ambulance will be here in a minute. No one gets up until they're cleared. Got it?"

Amelia lifted her hand and gave him a salute.

Trace ran for his ambulance.

Zoe said, "Did you see Della?"

Amelia shook her head. "Looked like the gas fireplace exploded."

"No way." Izan shook his head. "I turned the gas off from outside before I went in."

Amelia shrugged. "It blew."

"That makes no sense."

Zoe turned to watch the apartment. She had a smudge line of ash on the shoulder of her turnout coat and sweat on her hairline at the back. The dark-haired state women's hockey champ two years running had two brothers who were Marines, and she'd married a US Army soldier—much to their dismay. Her husband had been deployed for eight months and wasn't due back for at least another year. Her mother pitched in watching their two kids, aged four and seven, while she worked long shifts.

Izan hadn't had a girlfriend in a while. Amelia got the feeling he had a thing for Olivia Tazwell, but since she had her own un-requited thing going on, she wasn't going to get into it.

Eddie was first out the door, Zack on the other side of him with Della between them. They held her upright, walking at a rapid pace.

Amelia stood, shielded her eyes with her hands, and waited for them to get close enough. "Where was she?"

"Behind the dining table. She's awake, just dazed." They set her down on the grass, laying her back. The EMTs who had just arrived ran over.

Amelia wanted to sink back onto the grass.

"Takes two of you to bring out one of us?" Izan grinned. "Amelia dragged me out on her own, then went back for Zoe. She got us both out." Izan brushed imaginary lint from his shoulder. "But that's Truck versus Rescue for you, I guess."

Amelia bit the inside of her lip so she didn't smile. She lifted her brows.

Zoe twisted around. "You really did that? Never mind, of course you did."

"We go back for each other," Amelia said. "No matter what."

Zoe nodded. "No matter what."

Izan reached over and squeezed her shoulder. Amelia watched the EMT assess Della like it was just another day on the job. But when someone could die at any minute, when a routine callout could go wrong in a thousand different ways and an innocent could get a call that their world would never be the same…

Amelia couldn't let go of her focus for even one second.

She'd been right to tell Ridge that she couldn't get into a relationship. Not when being a lieutenant meant everything to her and, with one tiny flick of the hand from Whoever was in control up there…

She could lose it all.

No, it just wasn't worth the risk. Not when any day now, her carefully constructed life would come crashing down.

She didn't have the strength to rebuild it all again.

THANK YOU!

Thank you so much for reading *Rescued Heart*. We hope you enjoyed the story. If you did, would you be willing to do us a favor and leave a review? It doesn't have to be long—just a few words to help other readers know what they're getting. (But no spoilers! We don't want to wreck the fun!) Thank you again for reading!

We'd love to hear from you- not only about this story, but about any characters or stories you'd like to read in the future. Contact us at www.sunrisepublishing.com/contact.

NOTE TO READER

Dear Reader,

Oh, how I wish we could share a cup of tea or coffee and discuss this story together. I don't try to put hard themes in my stories, they just tend to happen. Probably because life is often difficult, and unfortunately for my hero Eddie, he had a rough fictional childhood. My real-life son and daughter have their own unique adoption stories that—thankfully—are nothing close to my hero's. But whether our parents are by blood or love or neither, like Eddie and Bianca, we tend to process some of the same kinds of life questions: Who am I? And am I loved?

I don't know your past, but I know people. And we let each other down, don't we? Sometimes relationships never find healing, yet no matter what the world or even our hearts tell us, we are seen and loved and can be forgiven by a holy, awesome God. Our identity, hope, and joy are found in Him. He alone is our rescuer. Turn to Him, dear one. He is trustworthy with the little and big things. For he sees our hearts and loves us anyway.

With love and prayers,

Megan Besing

ACKNOWLEDGMENTS

To my Lord and Savior. You are so great. Thank You for Your love and truth. Thanks for not only allowing me to finish another story, but again, using it to mold my life too. May these words always point to You.

To my husband. Thanks, my love, for encouraging me to be… me. When this book releases, we'll have been married for twenty years. 20! Man, we're getting old, and it's still wonderful with you. Thanks especially for enduring deadline writer mode.

Sis and Bub, thanks for reading my previous book, even if I had to pay you five dollars to do it. You still made your mother's day. And you know what also would make me happy…a hug from you. (Hint. Hint.) Hug or not, I love you! I'm so honored to be your mother. Thanks for putting up with my crazy author ways.

Mom and Dad. Thanks for raising me in a loving home that talked about Jesus. Thanks for all the book talks and dinners. Also, thanks to all my family and my all my in-laws. Everyone of you is a blessing. Thanks for reading my stories and for letting my kids play with yours so I can edit.

Abbie Wilson—you rock. It still amazes me how God brought us together in this writing career, and I'm so thankful. For your

Marco Polos, listening to my book plots, and doing life with me. #iheartyou #wemesh #istillwantyoutomovecloser

Laura Conaway. This series has us going from strangers to a friendship that I'm so blessed by. Thank you for your prayers and encouragement and words of wisdom. You are a treasure.

Erin Smithers, yes, I'm putting you in here again. Because once more, you've helped me be a better writer. Thank you for praying for me, for your Godly counsel, and your friendship.

Thank you, Sunrise. The entire team. But especially, Lisa Phillips. Thanks for reading the roughest draft of this story. Sorry! But I think it got better, so that's good. Thanks for understanding that I needed more time with these characters. You're a fabulous author, mentor, and friend, and I'm still ever thankful that the Lord matched us together. Thank you for letting me write in your series.

And Susie, thank you for all that you do. Honestly, I was scared to receive my very first edits from you, but now, after three, I'm like yes! Bring them on. Because I know the book will be better. And I truly appreciate you sharing your time and knowledge.

My agent, Rachel Kent with Books and Such, thanks for representing me. I appreciate you greatly!

To my fellow teachers, thanks for morning devotionals and praying over my writing journey.

And to my readers, THANK YOU. I keep getting to do this journey because of exceptional readers like you. Thank you for not only reading my books but also sharing about them.

Despite adoring happily-ever-afters, **Megan Besing** didn't unlock a love for reading until her mid-twenties, which quickly expanded into writing. Her stories have won many awards, but her most cherished achievements are being a wife and mother. She lives in a pocket-size Indiana town, centered around extended family. She's always planning a road trip with a view, yet her favorite place may just be on her front porch drinking tea.

Connect with Megan at meganbesing.com.

Lisa Phillips is a USA Today and top ten Publishers Weekly bestselling author of over 80 books that span Harlequin's Love Inspired Suspense line, independently published series romantic suspense, and thriller novels. She's discovered a penchant for high-stakes stories of mayhem and disaster where you can find made-for-each-other love that always ends in happily ever after.

Lisa is a British ex-pat who grew up an hour outside of London and attended Calvary Chapel Bible College, where she met her husband. He's from California, but nobody's perfect. It wasn't until her Bible College graduation that she figured out she was a writer (someone told her). As a worship leader for Calvary Chapel churches in her local area, Lisa has discovered a love for mentoring new ministry members and youth worship musicians.

Find out more at www.authorlisaphillips.com.

LAST CHANCE
FIRE AND RESCUE

USA Today Bestselling Author

LISA PHILLIPS

with **LAURA CONAWAY, MEGAN BESING** and **MICHELLE SASS ALECKSON**

The men and women of the Last Chance County Fire Department struggle to put a legacy of corruption behind them. They face danger every day on the job as first responders, but the fight to become a family will be their biggest battle yet. When hearts are on the line it's up to each one to trust their skill and lean on their faith to protect the ones they love. Before it all goes down in flames.

We solve the problem of what we read next.

Available on Amazon

WE THINK YOU'LL ALSO LOVE...

Fire Department liaison Allen Frees may have put his life back together, but getting the truck crew and engine squad to succeed might be his toughest job yet. When a child is nearly kidnapped, Allen steps in to help Pepper Miller keep her niece safe. The one thing he couldn't fix was the love he lost, but he isn't going to let Pepper walk away this time.

Expired Return by Lisa Phillips

Stunt double Vienna Foxcroft's stunt team are the only ones she trusts. Then in walks Sergeant Crew Gatlin and his tough-as-nails military dog, Havoc. When an attack on a film set sends them fleeing into the streets of Turkey, Vienna must face the demons of her past or be devoured by them. And Crew and Havoc will be tested like never before.

Havoc by Ronie Kendig

When an attempt is made on Grey Parker's life and dead bodies begin piling up, suddenly bodyguard Christina Sherman is tasked with keeping both a soldier and his dog safe... and with them, the secrets that could stop a terrorist attack.

***Driving Force by Lynette Eason
and Kate Angelo***

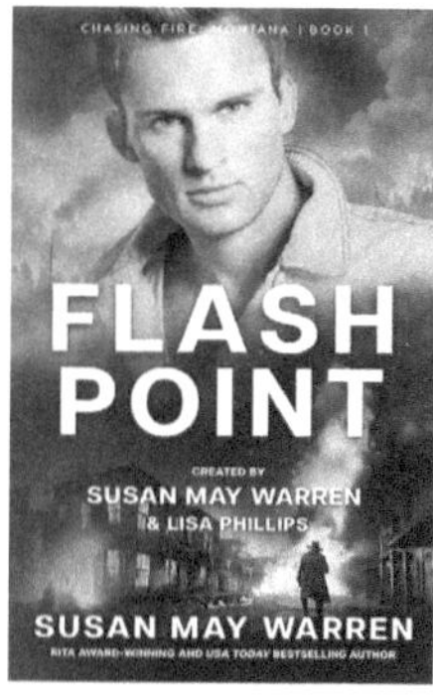

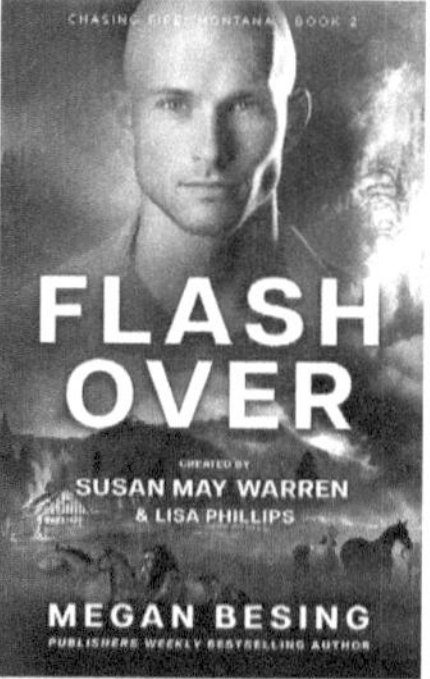

CHASING FIRE:
MONTANA

Dive into an epic series created by

SUSAN MAY WARREN
and LISA PHILLIPS

We solve the problem of what we read next.

Available on Amazon

**WHERE EVERY STORY IS A FRIEND,
AND EVERY CHAPTER IS A NEW JOURNEY...**

Subscribe to our newsletter for a free book, the latest news, weekly giveaways, exclusive author interviews, and more!

follow us on social media!

@sunrisemediagroup

@sunrisepublish

@sunrisepublishing

Shop paperbacks, ebooks, audiobooks, and more at
SUNRISEPUBLISHING.MYSHOPIFY.COM

www.ingramcontent.com/pod-product-compliance
Lightning Source LLC
Chambersburg PA
CBHW061111310726
48974CB00002B/491